A TWIST
OF FATE,
THE MAGE'S
AWAKENING

Book 1 of The Mage's Fate Series

A.G Fava

*To my mother, for igniting my passion, this is
the book you never got to write. As well as to
my father, whose love for fantasy spread like a
wildfire in my heart and mind. Without them
both, my creativity woul dhave lain dormant
and none of this would have ever been possible.*

PROLOGUE

The year is 872, or it would be if we counted years as we once did. They are no longer marked by the birth of our world but instead by the time since the Great Breach. This opening in the fabric of our world acted as a gateway or doorway to another universe. One in which life existed much as it does in ours, this we know as some of it came to our side. The portal opened on the 13th day of summer month upon the outskirts of the town of Silverveil. From it emerged humanoid figures, yet one would never confuse them for a man or even one of the mystical elves. These people have come to be known as the Raital.

The Raital are the height of a tall man with skin of blue or green, like a river or the sea. Their eyes are pure black as if shards of obsidian or a starless night sky. Their hands are similar to that of a man's, but they are webbed to the first set of knuckles. Otherwise, they appear much as any other human does, and yet they move in such a way that makes you think of waves washing gently upon a shore. Their appearance is similar enough to feel familiar but different enough to be alien to the mind. Like a tree made of stone rather than wood, different but possessing an understandable form.

Thousands of them poured from the rift that linked our worlds all plainly fleeing something within their own. All manner of them came through men and woman, children and elder, the strong and the weak. This was a mass exodus from their world to ours with no one wishing to stay behind. It was only until later we learned they were fleeing something, some force we do not know, and they cannot even begin to explain as it was more alien to them than they are to us. These poor souls, new to our world, were not greeted by diplomats or kings, nor any priests or generals. No, the first faces they saw were those of a town garrison, faces showing nothing but confusion and fear. This "mass migration" happened for only a few moments ending when several figures turned to the portal, all dressed in robes as blue as the sky or white as snow. These people began to chant in a language alien to our ears and with not but a few gestures towards the rift closed it with a flash of energy and light. Those people who made it through fell to their knees and upon the ground of their new world they wept. The tears they shed were of relief, terror and above all grief for the tens of thousands they had left behind.

Those few minutes, mere moments in the history of our world, were a catalyst that changed Eoch forever. With these people came knowledge that in some way we were not alone, as well as giving us our first taste of what we now call magic. This force now permeates our entire world and defines our very existence. Whether brought through or awakened by the rift, magic is now an ever-present part of all our lives.

It has been a hundred years since that day and the dawn of magic upon Eoch, the Raital now reside upon the island continent of Talinsana with the avian Winsentti people. In our world where dragons fly ever present in our skies and magic now flows in the very veins of the earth and its inhabitants, they are now nothing more than another oddity in this newly awakened land. They have become a fixture like any other in our world, taken in by their new guardians the Blue dragons as the Browns protect the Deep Folk and the Platinum dragons the Humans and Elves.

The Raital may have fled their world in search of peace and sanctuary...but instead found only more war. They have stumbled into a world filled with hostility in the form of Orks, Goblins and their Red Dragon masters, these creatures bringing the Coalition of Men, Elves, Avian and Deep Folk to their very breaking point. Even as we fight, we now know that Eoch itself is threatened not by just these creatures, but also by an unknown threat that will surely follow the Raital. A darkness now hangs over this world, one that has been upon it for more than one hundred years, its dark dealings have come to fruition, and it may soon be too late to stop its plans. Now there is only one question that remains, only one question to answer. Has Eoch found a new beginning or is this the beginning of our end?

- Master Cameral Darkweave the 20th of winter month year 100 of the Breach

CHAPTER ONE

Thirteen years, for thirteen long years this war has raged on, with no end in sight. To think I have been a part of it since it began anew, when those Ork monsters crossed the ocean to land upon the Coalition's land once more. It is strange to me that I have known nothing but war for thirteen of my forty-four years on this earth. It is stranger still to know that there are those born to this world, in a time such as this, a time in which they have never known peace. Until then I will continue to fight and lead you, my brave soldiers, not just soldiers but warriors. I swear to lead you brave warriors the best that I can as I have for the last thirteen years. Let us see the end of this war, but let it end not seen in a glorious last stand, instead let us see its end greeted by shouts of victory!

—First General Agastion De'vil

Captain Thalen Melodyr finished reading the letter sent to his command, taking exaggerated care to fold and place it into his breast pocket, he looked out upon the soldiers under him. The faces he saw before him were less the mighty warriors described and more so those of men and woman overworked but pushing through, nonetheless. These fine soldiers were tired and ragged with hard days and sleepless nights, their faces accompanied by bodies that no longer knew what a soft bed felt like. As haggard as they all looked, these were the finest men and woman in all the First Infantry Corps, having been assigned the number two, two, nine upon deployment from their home, the Kingdom of Isari. Through their ferocity and daring they quickly made a name for themselves, in only a few years becoming one of the premier companies within the Coalition's forces. As he looked upon his gathered followers, his mind wandered back to simpler times before this war, before all the horrors witnessed and committed, these acts which felt like grime and filth which stained his very soul.

Born to a smith and basket weaver within the seventieth year since the breach, Thalen was brought up in a simple but good life in the town of Farfield. His early years were filled with hard work in the forge, and he came to love it and his home as he thought very little of the world beyond the wooden palisade guarding it. He was a shy child with a good heart, mind, and sense of humor. He was not popular but did not wish to be as he kept close company with two other children, Artus and Sarah. From an early age the three became inseparable and if you could find one, unless there was work to be done, you would find the other two. As he grew to the age of eleven, he became more involved with his father's work, hardening his muscles and giving him strength that could test even most men in town.

Finally, upon his seventeenth year he came to full size and his features became fully set. He looked much like his father with sandy brown hair cropped short with beard to match, his skin was of a rosy-white complexion, which he learned at a young age was much more likely to burn than tan. He stood tall and strong at two and six feet, with shoulders broad enough to take up an entire door frame, accompanied by arms that would pass for some men's thighs. He was never handsome, at least not to his mind, but he was well featured, a square jaw, high cheekbones but with his large nose and thunderous brow no one would call him perfect. Yet, his most arresting feature were his eyes of deep emerald green, being the one trait he had received from his mother.

Life was good but it did not last, as life can always change in the blink of an eye. His family, his home, his life as he knew it was torn from him by those Red Wyrm bastards. With little effort or desire the memories returned to him unbidden. On the 10th day of spring month 87th year of the Breach, three dots appeared on the horizon at midday and descended upon his sleepy coastal town. Red Dragons appeared, burning and destroying everything, the evil bastards took mere seconds to tear apart Thalen's home, his family, and his friends. Accompanying the Reds were ten Orks, each of the brutes armed and prepared for the slaughter. His father fought with the desperation of man protecting his family, wielding a two-handed sledge he struck powerfully, his weapon rising and falling to slam down upon the creatures until a spear stabbed him through the back. Thalen himself managed to kill two before being slashed across the face and left for dead. To this day he could still feel the scar when smiling or closing his eyes, a scar that reached jaggedly from brow to chin, from right to left. His old life long gone, he joined the Corps two years later, leaving behind the ashes and corpses of his burnt home, though he could not leave the screams or all-consuming flame, behind.

He shook himself from those memories as he looked out upon his men as his mind flashed to more recent and better time. He found himself thinking of the time he and his company had spent in this war, of the story they had forged and the merits they had won.

Since the moment they landed upon the continent of Talinsana, home of the Winsentti and Raital, his command became known as the most versatile and successful of the Corps. Thanks to this every moment on the isle was filled with anything the command staff required, from fighting hard on the front line to intercepting enemy orders, hell they even spent over three months behind enemy lines burning and disrupting their foes supply. Yet, where they truly exceeded was in their quick strike raids. Even the Talons of the Winsentti people, known for their quick attack tactics and overwhelming speed were impressed by this mixed group of humans and elves. Thus, they became known as Talon company to those serving beside them.

Thalen let the memories of times past slip and looked back out upon the eighty-one soldiers making up his command, "That was quite an inspiring letter from high command now, wasn't it?" Thalen began, pausing as a few gruff chuckles emanated from those gathered; "I will not lie to any of you as I have never in the past, we are hard pressed in this war with those filthy Orks. They are many and their overgrown Wyrms litter the skies, although our friends in the air have kept their numbers from reaching our positions. Since they are doing their jobs, it feels only fair that we do ours and kill every pig faced bastard that comes our way." Those gathered around let out a yell of approval, each voice tired but filled with eagerness and more than a touch of malice. When the yelling died down Thalen continued his voice strong and filled with command. "We are to hold this line here, with Sparrow and Lion companies holding our flanks. We will have no support from the dragons as they are busy keeping the red ones from coming up behind our position. We are on our own, but we aren't the best because our missions have been easy! We are the best because we only know how to do one thing... And that is to win." With another cheer roaring from the throat of his men his next words were swallowed by the sound, forcing him to pause as he allowed it to die down.

As the noise began to quiet, Thalen continued, "This battle will be difficult, it being far beyond almost any challenge we have faced before, but I know that with you all standing with me victory is assured. Now then Sergeant Callaway, I want rotating watches of five, have the rest of the men remain around the fires, we may be coming out of winter but let's not allow the cold to surprise us." Thalen began to turn and as an afterthought continued, "Also come to my tent and bring along Jennings and Donte as we have some planning left before this day is done." Not waiting to know if his orders were followed, he turned with a flourish striding away, he trusted his men and Callaway to do as asked. *"After all they are the best."* he thought to himself with a chuckle *"Maybe not clean or innocent, but without a doubt the best in battle and in slaughter."*

Letting his musing slip from his mind Thalen looked out upon the landscape surrounding his position, upon the hill one could see for hundreds of meters in all directions before the forest blocked the view. Taking it in, he took note of the dips in the surrounding area, yet they were nearly impossible to see with the snow that decorated the ground. Allowing his eyes to wander towards the camp he examined rows of tents all in neat formation along with several large fires where he knew his soldiers could be found. Thalen hid himself deeper in the folds of his cloak in a vain attempt to fight off the cold. Though it was nearly spring there was still a bite to the air, it suggesting a few more weeks of winter. *"In a few weeks more we should be back at headquarters with the chance at a warm bed and hot meal."* he thought *"Yet it is far more likely we will be sent straight out to the next assignment"* with a sigh he walked towards his command pavilion, dreams of warmth slipping further away as the grim thoughts of the battle ahead returned to his mind.

As the sun began to fall past the horizon, he moved through the last few rows of tents and weary faces that separated him from the marginal warmth of his abode. Entering into the spartan like space, its cloth walls housed little more than a cot and small desk with chair. A small stand with wash basin atop sat along the far wall accompanied by a silvered mirror that hung gently above it, this being the only true comforts in site. Near the center pole sat a table arrayed with arms and armor, save for the sword slung upon his hip. Thalen made his way to the basin, pouring cool clear water from the jug seated within it before setting it aside to wash his face and hands. He took the time to wash away the dirt, dust and other filth that caked him from the hard day in the field. Looking up he saw himself in the mirror, the same face that it had always been, even the scar that danced across it from eye to jaw. The more he looked the less he liked what he saw, a tired man with far too much darkness beneath the eyes. Looking deeply into those piercing orbs he shivered knowing these were the eyes of a man that had helped kill hundreds in battle. He tore his eyes from the mirror and turned towards the entrance, eyes locking with the figure standing just inside the tents flap.

"Enjoying your own reflection, Thalen? I never took you to be so vain." the figure quipped, their tone filled with playful sarcasm "Perhaps when we return home you could commission a statue of yourself, yes that sounds nice a statue of the conquering hero." Thalen let out a low chuckle "Well Callaway how could I not want to look upon this handsome face every opportunity I get. After all, how many more chances will I really have?" he mused, before turning to his desk. Callaway moved forward, coming into the tent properly and taking a seat in the extra chair near the desk. "Come now Thalen, none of the men are around us now, you know I prefer you to call me Sarah when it is just us. After all I have known you forever." she said with an easy smile.

Thalen closed his eyes as memories flooded back to him from a time before the war before his life changed forever. Believing all were dead after the attack on his home he had left the ruins of his burned village with haste, not staying to search through the charred corpse of Farfield and of everyone he once knew. Yet, unbeknownst to him he was not the only one to survive that day. Sarah had recounted the story to him twice, as the fighting began and the fires started to rage, she was helping to move the younger children to the town hall. The quickly forged plan was to hold there to keep them safe, yet it was a complete failure. As it was the first building to burn, fortunately Sarah and some of the youngest ones were hiding in the basement as the hall burned above them. If not for that old cellar, they all would have died the same as so many others, nothing but a pile of ash or if lucky a charred corpse. She joined the military soon after that, as she had nowhere else to go and through sheer chance was assigned to Thalen's forces. Over the years together they built a strong reputation for success and dependability side by side. *"Without her strength and determination Talon company would not be even a shadow of what it is today."* thought Thalen, eyes snapping open and to attention, as he once more met her gaze. "Thinking of anything in particular?" Sarah asked, seeming to know the answer before the words passed her lips. "Not but wondering how we got here." came his sad reply. After a moment of quiet, in less than a whisper he went on "Thinking of home." Giving him a pained look filled with understanding and sympathy she nodded.

Wanting to break the tension Thalen spoke "Sad times, far too many people have seen the same things and have similar stories to our own. Enough of the past, let us look to the present. Where are the others? Donte and Jennings?" Just as Sarah began to reply. Thalen looked to the entrance of the tent; his hearing sharpened as he focused upon the approaching footsteps. "Ah, here they are…" he said without thought.

Not but a moment after Donte, followed soon behind by Jennings, entered the tent before coming to attention in front of Thalen. Taking a moment to look them up and down, they could only be described as typical military men, sword at side, shield on back with chainmail sitting upon their square shoulders. "You asked for us sir?" Donte said snapping a quick salute, returning the gesture Thalen responded "Yes, I did. I want an update, is our trap set and ready for tomorrow's battle?"

"Yes sir, the pits are dug out and covered with rough grass and snow making them nearly impossible to see. We've also set a watch on the South side of our position to warn of any incursions into the area." Jennings replied. After a moment of thought Thalen spoke "Very good, before you go off to enjoy the evening, I need you two to set some of the men to carving out stakes and place them in bunches outside of the camp. I want them to form choke points to force the Orks to attack narrow gaps." He paused for a moment ensuring he was understood before continuing "We expect the bastards to attack sometime in the morning so be sure the men are up and prepared soon after sunrise. You're dismissed." The pair snapped another quick salute before exiting the tent. After a moment of quiet passed Thalen looked over at his dear friend. For just a moment, his eyes caught hers and with a laugh Sarah stood and smiled at him. "Get some sleep Thalen, morning will be here far too soon." as if on impulse she jumped over to him and planted a kiss on his cheek. Thalen reached up putting a hand to the spot in shock, but before he could say anything, Sarah gave him a quick smile and salute. "I'll see you tomorrow." she said as she left his tent leaving him with nothing more but his thoughts and dreams.

Thalen leaned further back in his chair and sighed *"How things could have been different if there had been no war."* He thought to himself before shaking his head and standing to remove his sword belt, placing it beside his cot. He sat upon the edge of it scanning the room one final time, eyes stopping to rest upon his armor. *"You shall be worn tomorrow for yet another battle. I hope it will soon be for a final time."* He let the thought slip away before laying down to think of Sarah and what could have been before falling into a deep and dreamless sleep.

CHAPTER TWO

"Thalen! Thalen! Wake up!" a voice, seeming from so far away yelled. "Thalen!". Something accompanied the voice, a banging sound like a hammer striking a pot or bell. "Wake up damn you!" suddenly the world came rushing back to him, opening his eyes, he sat up with a jerk finding himself staring directly at Sarah. "About time, something is wrong, there is smoke coming from Sparrow's position, far too much to just be from campfires. Come quickly!" she said as she ran to the tent's entrance. Thalen surged to his feet pulling on his chain shirt and cloak, grabbing his sword belt and strapping it in place, before following quickly behind. Entering the early morning light, he shivered briefly at the cold, eyes scanning the horizon towards the East. Plumes of black smoke rose into the sky from Sparrow's position, he sniffed the air which told him all he needed to know. It smelling of pitch, wood, burlap and worst of all flesh, yet beneath it all an acrid smell played at his nose, it being completely unrecognizable, this concerned him far more than the rest.

"Callaway send scouts towards the Eastern

camp and a messenger to Lion's position prepare the men and do it quickly! Orks have already arrived and when they come for us, we must push them back." Hearing a quick yes sir in reply he looked around his own position ensuring everything was in place as thoughts raced through his head. *"What happened? How were they caught so unaware; Captain Xavier is one of the finest I have ever served beside? He would have never allowed his lookouts to miss an Orkish force, especially not one that could take out an entire position without warning."*

Turning back to scan the East, a pressure suddenly began to push against his head. He spent a moment shaking it to try and clear the odd feeling before he turned toward the center of the camp. As he turned the pressure moved from the side towards the front of his head as he looked at the area surrounding his command tent. Suddenly the pressure dissipated as a silent thunderclap rocked him, with a shimmer, a group of orks appeared yelling war cries as they rushed to attack the unsuspecting soldiers. With a gasp of surprise and horror Thalen yelled out "To arms, orks are in the camp!" the nearest soldiers turned just as the bestial creatures smashed into them. The creatures struck their ranks hacking and crushing man and elf alike as both blood and screams were ripped from the defender's bodies. As the last nearby defenders fell a yell of defiance ripped out from between the tents as Thalen's soldiers filtered into the area meeting the pig faced creatures head on as the battle started in full. With his head finally cleared Thalen prepared to charge into the press but stopped as voices called out to him. "Thalen are you alright?" Callaway yelled as she rushed to his side flanked by several soldiers.

"I'm fine but we have to move quickly!" Thalen commanded before turning back to resume his charge. With a quick nod Callaway and the rest of the soldiers surged forward towards the hulking orks. For a moment time seemed too slow for Thalen as he took in the monstrous enemy before him, these hulking creatures all standing more than six foot tall with horrid green tinged skin. Large tusks protruded from their mouths, their taut muscles rippling as they scythed through his men like a farmer does wheat. With a snarl his small company smashed into the enemy, Thalen narrowly ducking a slash meant to take his head from his shoulders. Adrenaline rushing, he delivered a quick heavy slash across one beast's chest cutting through its thick hide and felling it with a single blow to the heart. Looking for his next target, he saw Callaway come up alongside him and, with a nod, they moved throughout the area hacking through the orkish ranks aiding their soldiers wherever hard pressed.

As the area stabilized and the orks were pushed back to one large pocket in the center of the camp, Thalen took a moment and stepped back to survey the area. His sharp eyes searching for any orkish leaders and after a few moments one of the monsters stood out to him, its garb giving it away. Where every ork he had fought up to this point was bare chested, this one was dressed head to toe in brown boar skin with a bone staff gripped in its meaty palm. Sensing his eyes, the ork's head snapped towards Thalen its own narrowing to slits as it began a chant of power, a red fiery light coalescing within its palm. His eyes going wide Thalen yelled out as he dove aside barely managing to avoid a ball of flame the size of a small boulder as it shot from the creature's hand. The ball exploded as it hit the ground with a consuming heat that turned five men and a pair of orks in the area to ash. Thalen looked back at the charred corpses jumping to his feet with the hope of avoiding any further magical attack.

With a gasp of suddenly hot air Thalen yelled "Callaway, they have a magic user! We must kill it, or its magic will consume us all!" with a yell of assent and a strike to the neck of her orkish opponent she followed after him. Running past pockets of men and orks covering the distance between themselves and their foe as fast as their legs could carry. When they were only a few meters from their quarry a sudden roar of deep voices rose from their left and right as several orks charged into them.

Turning back-to-back, the pair just managing to defend themselves from the heavy blows of the hulking creatures. With great skill they narrowly dodged and redirected the creatures' heavy strikes as the great strength of even the most average ork would crumple even the heartiest of men. Looking for any possible opening, it was Callaway who managed to strike first, avoiding a wild swing and following up with a blow across an ork's chest. Before it could recover from the strike, she delivered several quicker cuts to its arms keeping it off balance before delivering the finishing blow stabbing it through the neck.

As the creature slumped to the ground, Thalen found himself hard pressed by his two opponents. The two beasts hacking at him with their weapons as he used every ounce of his skill to avoid complete disaster. Avoiding a swing with a quick sidestep he realized too late that his back was to his other orkish foe. Diving forward he yelled in pain as he took a vicious cut across the back, the strike rending his chainmail as if it was cutting through cloth. Managing to angle his body he rolled clear of a wild club swing, and using his momentum he surged past the club wielder coming up behind it. Using the moment of surprise, he slashed the back of the creature's legs hamstringing it, as it fell to the ground Thalen reversed the grip on his sword stabbing down through the base of creature's neck silencing its roar of pain. Looking to his other enemy he dove aside releasing his swords as a swing from a giant axe cleaved where he once stood. The creature, in a rage, swung wildly at Thalen who was able to easily sidestep the blow and roll out of the way in an attempt to stay ahead of the creature's massive swings. With a growl of frustration, the ork shoulder charged Thalen its unexpected move sending him sprawling to the ground landing heavily on his back. The ugly creature howled with glee, its victory appearing at hand, it raised its axe in the air preparing for a mighty swing meant to cleave him in two.

Shielding his face Thalen looked away waiting for the inevitable blow to fall, yet it never came. Looking up he saw a sword point sprouting from the monster's chest, before it slumped to the ground revealing Sarah behind it. With a smirk Sarah grabbed Thalen's arm, pulling him to his feet and handing him his lost sword. The pair turned as one their eyes scanning for their quarry once more, with the moment of calm Thalen once more felt the strange pressure pushing upon his mind. Turning in its direction the magic wielder came into view, it's concentration tight as it drew energy for another spell of death and destruction. Thalen dashed towards the creature in a mad hope of reaching it in time before it could unleash its spell, yet even as he took his first few steps its palm rose firing a beam of molten energy from it far faster than Thalen could hope to react. Closing his eyes he accepted his fate, yet instead of feeling fire upon his chest he instead felt an impact on his side causing him to hit the ground with a heavy thud. Gasping, he lifted his head and saw a body laying atop him; his savior's side was burned away showing nothing but bone and charred flesh. With a flash of recognition, he pulled the body off of him cradling it in his arms, tears flowing freely from his eyes.

"No no no, Sarah please no." he pleaded as he scrambled to his knees, pulling her close to him he bent kissing her on the forehead. "Please stay with me, don't go. Please, don't leave me alone." He lifted his head hearing her shallow breathing, his eyes meeting hers. He saw life still in those eyes and a small smile upon her lips, one she had given him so many times before. After a moment she let out a wheeze wet with blood as her eyes focused upon him, a look that almost seemed regretful crossed her face, as though seeing an opportunity lost. With the red shine of blood upon dry lips she forced words from her failing body "It's okay Thalen, it's okay. I will always be here for you. I love you and I always have." as the last word left her crimson colored mouth the whisper of one final breath escaped her body and the light left her eyes forever. With a cry of anguish Thalen clutched her to his chest, the last of her blood washing over him. As he lifted his head from the world he would never know, to the one around him he took in the battle playing out before him. His men dying overwhelmed by the ferocity of their enemy and the cunning of their tactics, their blood soaking the ground and snow a crimson red. As he stared at the untold death before him the light of the early morning sun was suddenly blocked casting him in shadow, looking up his eyes met those of the shaman, the black beady eyes of Sarah's killer.

A sudden surge of power and rage filled him as a now familiar pressure filled his mind, yet unlike before it was not focused on a point but instead felt as though it filled his entire being. With a yell of animalistic rage, the pressure released, ripping through his body as he felt energy, more than he had ever felt before, burst forth from him in all directions. Suddenly the word turned cold, as cold as the harshest of winter's days as a thunderclap went off within his mind. With that rush of energy, ice shards that were the size of arrows flew from him in all directions skewering both the shaman and every green bastard near him.

As his eyes began to blur and darken, he took in the carnage. Shards of ice stuck from the corpses of his nearby foes and where the shaman once stood nothing remained, nothing but a pierced and broken body. His last bit of energy gone darkness blurred the edge of his vision and he slumped to the ground. The last thing he felt was blood, Sarah's blood, warm and wet upon him. The last thing he saw was Sarah's face for one final time before darkness. No more sight, nor sound, as his mind succumbed to unconsciousness.

CHAPTER THREE

Slowly Thalen's senses returned to him as the deep blackness of unconsciousness released him, his first sensation being the softness of the bed now beneath him. Raising his head from a pillow he looked about the room taking in the scene now before him. He found not a battlefield filled with broken bodies and the remains of his camp but instead a room filled with many beds with not a soul to be seen. As the fog cleared from his mind, he realized he was in an infirmary, *"How did I get here?"* he asked himself as memories slowly begin to return to him, the battle, the ice shards, Sarah. Tears welled in his eyes as the unwanted and unwelcome memories returned to him, *"Dammit Callaway, why did you have to go and be a hero...Why did I have to lose you..."*. After a few moments, his sadness changed to confusion, *"How am I still alive... those shards of ice shot out of my body. Didn't they?"* Looking at his arms and hands he saw nothing except for the cuts and bruises of battle, something he had seen many times before, no holes or ice to be found, no evidence of the ordeal his body must have went through.

With a mental shrug, he tried to stand and yet his body did not follow his commands, his muscles felt drained and tired beyond description. *"Why am I so tired, what happened? I need answers, yet I cannot...cannot seem to..."* Thought unfinished, his head fell to the pillow sleep overcoming him, deep yet filled with dreams of the battle and the loss of the last piece of home.

As Thalen's head hit the pillow, a figure unseen and silent turned from the infirmary door and walked down the cold stone hallway, lit by little else than the bleary orange glow of torchlight. After a few moments it walked through an iron banded door entering into an office being greeted by the sight of an old soldier sitting behind a desk. The man looked up from the papers scattered across the large oaken surface his eyes searching for who would disturb his solitude. Two eyes, one milky white, yet the other attentive and seeking, looked upon the seemingly open air before him. Slowly the figure blurred into view leaving invisibility, the weary man ran a calloused and scarred hand through his long salt and pepper hair before letting it come back to rest upon his goateed face.

"How is our man?" Agastion De'vil asked of the figure now before him, his eyes trying in vain to pierce the darkness of the cowl hiding the intruder's face with little succes. After a silent moment, the figure pulled the cowl back with a flourish saying, "He awoke a moment ago, but is still too weak to be up for more than a few minutes at a time. Yet, I am impressed, most that expend so much magical energy for the first time would not have awoken for at least another two days." After another pause, De'vil responded, "So, he can make use of the power, from the report I received it sounds to be a large amount of it. He is old though, is he not, for this ability to only just manifest now?" the figure paused allowing themselves a moment to consider before responding "Yes, what you say about his age is true, yet, with the power he has displayed we have no choice but to take him. We must bring him to Moon Shade Keep as soon as he is able, we must begin training him in the magic arts for I fear if we do not, he will inevitably kill himself or others around him."

Agastion looked at them concern plain on his weathered face "Is this truly our only option? His unit is one of the best that we have, the loss of him as a Captain would be a devastating blow to their effectiveness. Especially after the complete destruction of Sparrow and the high number of casualties to Lion, even his own company barely survived that disastrous ambush.

The figure looked to First General Agastion

De'vil, highest ranking officer in all of the Coalition military, as though he was a child making a foolish statement. "He must go, otherwise he will do more harm than good. His powers are unlocked now, it cannot be bottled up or hidden away. It came out once and it certainly will come out again, possibly with far more destructive results. No there can be no argument, it would be better for him, and us, if he had more control, as with this training he would become a stronger weapon for the cause." Taking a long weary breath, the First General let his eyes wander to the ceiling "I know the words you say are true, yet it is just a shame to lose him at this time. We are losing this war and losing him now is just another blow to our forces." The figure nodded in understanding and turned, leaving the First General to his thoughts.

Thalen opened his eyes squinting them against the light that poured through the arched windows and bounced off the whitewashed walls. Blinking away the sensitivity, his eyes slowly focused upon a figure in dark robes leaning against the infirmary door. Their cowl was raised keeping their features indistinguishable from the depths of the garbs hood. They were not opposing in size or appearance, not more than of a middling in height and weight, as they hardly stood more than five- and one-half foot accompanied by a slight build that indicated no real power or physical strength. After what felt like an eternity Thalen's patience ran its course and he broke the silence. "Hello, who are you friend? Why were you watching me earlier from hiding?" he paused awaiting a reply. Yet the figure continued to stand in silence, as they seemed oblivious to his words as they appeared to stare into his soul. "Why do you not speak, are you a friend or an enemy? I have buried many of both and would prefer not to add another to the former's count." Waiting for a reply Thalen looked for any sign of threat within the figure's stance, any hint of an intention or a plan, yet nothing, as they remained still, unmoved by the veiled threat within his words. *"Perhaps it is best to ignore this person until they deem it a worthy time to speak. In my current state I would be hard pressed to fight off this person either way if they hold me ill will"* With a sigh, Thalen settled back into the folds of the bedding relaxing as much as possible while under such unusual observation.

Thalen awoke with a start finding the room no longer lit by sunlight, but instead the flickering light of torches and hearth. Cursing himself for falling asleep so easily, he scanned the room in search of the silent watcher, his eyes locked upon the figure who had remained at their post still standing there in silent sentry, as they had been earlier that day. What seemed even stranger about this individual was they appeared to have not moved at all, though certainly hours must have passed during his slumber. With confusion over this person's complete lack of response or movement, Thalen slowly pulled himself up to a sitting position before carefully swinging his legs over the side of the bed. Wincing in pain from the injuries littering his body he took a moment to catch his lost breath keeping watch over his mysterious warden out of the corner of his eye.

The figure neither spoke nor moved as Thalen pulled himself to his feet, slowly stepping into the aisle as he approached this ominous figure. As he closed in on them, wary of this mysterious individual, he was so focused on his approach that Thalen nearly jumped as the head turned towards him revealing nothing but the impenetrable darkness of the hood. Silently scolding himself for his reaction, he looked upon the figure once more, noting that not an inch of the body, aside from its head, had moved. With a deep breath, Thalen squared his shoulders and continued to move toward his unexplained guard, his stride measured and careful. As he moved his way towards the figure the unseen face continued to follow his every step, staring as he came to within a meter away. Taking a hard look at them Thalen saw no movement nor any hint of their intentions; with a growl of anger Thalen spoke his annoyance plain with every word "I do not enjoy being watched by some stranger. I ask you once more friend, who are you and why have you been watching me?" Upon finishing Thalen set his arms across his chest awaiting a reply. He had no wish to strike first, especially at a potential friend and ally, yet as the silence drew out longer, he began to have difficulty controlling his anger and frustration. Just as he reached his boiling point and prepared to lash out, a sudden lilting chuckle came from his left. Snapping his head towards the sound, he found himself nearly face to face with another figure, one that looked a near copy of the one standing before him, their face still hidden from sight by the darkness of the hood. Quickly looking back at the figure in front of him, he found that to his astonishment, it was gone leaving nothing but empty space and the doorframe it had been leaning upon.

The chuckling from his left soon turned into a roar of laughter as the newest intruder could no longer contain their mirth. Thalen wheeled on the source of his anger, fuming as his voice rising to a yell as he spoke "What is the meaning of this? What is this trickery and by the Gods who are you? Explain yourself damn you or I have no choice but to force the answers from you" Thalen found himself shaking, barely able to keep his anger from overwhelming what little good sense he had left.

With barely suppressed mirth the "trickster" spoke his voice light and musical "Come now Thalen, why so serious? Why not enjoy the levity in the situation? Although, I understand that this has been very disorientating for you so please allow me to answer at least one of your questions with speed. I am Cameral Darkweave, first mage of The Order of Eoch's Embrace. I am also the reason why you are here and not slowly thawing out in some cold field hospital." he finished with a flourish removing his hood to reveal pointed ears and eyes of a rich blue, those eyes had a slight upward slant almost as if someone turned two almonds into these orbs of white and blue. The elf's face was as cleanly shaved as a young boys with hair of a golden white flowing down to his shoulders. A thin-lipped smile decorated his face with a youth showing no true signs of age. Finishing his inspection Thalen returned to the mage's gaze, his earlier anger melting away to pure confusion.

Smirking, Cameral continued, "To state the obvious, I am an elf and to answer the obvious question, yes I am much older than I appear." After a momentary pause his tone changed from relaxed and joking to one of complete business "Before you begin asking the many questions that I am sure you have, please allow me to explain some things. If we are fortunate most of your questions will be answered. Agreed?" He waited for a moment, allowing only a nod from Thalen before continuing. "Very good, so for a start I will be blunt, you possess magical power whether you knew it or not. You have also cast your very first spell only a few days ago to great effect. Though impressive it was sheer luck that you did not kill yourself or every single man and woman of your command." He paused, allowing the information to sink in before continuing "Now due to this you are immediately being reassigned to The Order of Eoch's Embrace to be trained in the arts before returning to the front line. You are not being stripped of your rank nor is it a punishment, some in fact would even see this as an honor, although you are not able to lead until we have deemed you are a boon and not a hazard."

Thalen felt his legs go weak, quickly finding a nearby chair, his mind raced as he tried to sift through all the thoughts and emotions threatening to overwhelm him. In the blink of an eye the entire world he knew disappeared, everything taken from him in one fell swoop. The loss of Sarah and now his Company, the last piece of her he had left, emotion threatened to overwhelm him completely, though he only just managed to keep it under control. After a few minutes he managed to get his emotions back in check, his stoic practicality fighting back the despair that still threatened to breach that last bastion. Looking at Cameral, he said "This is much to take in all at once and I do have some questions for you. The first being, how is it possible that I have these powers? I was tested just as all youths are and nothing was detected.

How could it be only now these abilities have surface?" Thalen thought his voice sounded as tired as his body felt, as his voice held little of its typical strength.

Cameral spent a few moments in silent contemplation, his chin resting in the crook of his hand giving his angular features the look of a statue. "We are not sure, but we have a theory. Though, in truth it is not much better than a guess. We believe that the ability was within you but was buried deep to the point of being completely dormant and inactive. The battle, or something during the battle, had a triggering effect upon your will allowing you to tap into the magical energies within the world. I would also guess that perhaps you have been using a small degree of your powers, and that part is why you have, more often than not, been victorious in battle and even in defeat have never suffered a major route. Perhaps this power residing deep with you had guided you in some way, maybe through a sixth sense while you were under heavy stress or in danger."

Soaking this new in information, Thelen felt a new surge of emotion and thoughts filled his mind to bursting. Yet, one thought rose above the roar of the rest coming to the forefront of his mind. *"If only I could have tapped into this power sooner, this disaster, the death of my soldiers...Sarah's death could have been prevented. I could have saved them all..."*. Barely mastering his overflowing emotions, the logical part of him took back control *"No don't think that way, that is the path of self-destruction"* though he told himself such, he couldn't help but feel responsible for the disaster and the deaths of those closest to him.

As if reading his mind Cameral spoke his voice filled sympathy and understanding. "It was not your fault, whether you believe me or not. You did everything you could and there was no way for you to know you could unlock these powers. Likely if you had even known or had these powers in full you may not have even been in the position you were to begin with. Though many lives were lost you, saved many as well." Thalen lifted his head looking into the elf's eyes, he could not bring himself to speak yet he knew that the caster's words had a ring of truth to them. Though they did not remove the sense of responsibility for what happened, he no longer felt the overwhelming sorrow. Though the loss of Sarah sat deep within his chest he felt that for at least the moment he could keep moving forward, as he sat straighter looking into the mage's eyes as he spoke. "What is the plan Wizard? What is it that I am to do now?"

Noticing the change in Thalen's demeanor Cameral spoke "You will come with me to Moon Shade Keep and train in the arts. You will continue moving forward to the best of your ability as you always have and upon completion of your education we will see where you can best be used." With that said Thalen came to grips with his reality, giving a grim nod he spoke "Very well Cameral, I will do this." With those words, Thalen slumped down into a nearby chair as exhaustion washed over him. That act seeming to take all of his remaining strength. "Good, we leave in a week. You should be healed of the worst by then. For now, I will bid you a good evening and shall see you in a week's time Thalen." The elf turned with a flourish of their cloak, the dark colored garment flying out behind him as Cameral left the infirmary. Thalen gently stood and stumbled over to his bed, falling down into it he felt the last vestige of energy leave his battered body as sleep overcame him.

CHAPTER FOUR

The next week sped past with most of Thalen's time being spent in a bed, yet no matter how fast the days went by the week was grueling. Waves of sadness washed over him at random as the memory of his loss was still fresh in his mind. As the week of inaction mercifully came to an end and the journey drew near, the sadness he felt waned, giving way to an aura of indifference that hung over him, muting every other emotion he felt. No true feeling of excitement passed through Thalen, though a small amount of interest in the future was present, after all a new journey is never easy to overlook.

As the seventh day of the week came, preparation for the journey finished, Thalen's wounds had healed, and his exhaustion had nearly passed. His pack prepared for the journey, he donned both it and his sword belt, taking a moment to look into the mirror beside his bed. He examined his reflection intent on seeing himself as others did, strong, determined and dangerous, and yet he felt the yawning emptiness within him, an emptiness that he knew not how to fill. With a sigh of resignation, he prepared to take his first steps upon the new path laid before him. *"If nothing else, I must make the best of this moment and perhaps those that come after it."* His mind made up, he turned, letting out a sigh as he walked from the room and eventually into the courtyard outside.

Looking around the space he examined the open area, noting the distinctive feel of stone beneath his booted feet. Scanning the grounds he saw the few trees and brush, still bare of their leaves, set within patches of grassy dirt that littered the area. Suppressing a shiver, he could not help but notice the cold bite in the air and the snow still lightly blanketing the world suggesting winter still maintained its hold. The world was silent and peaceful in such stark contrast to the battles he had been fighting without pause over the previous months.

As his eyes drifted towards the gateway Thalen watched the passing and movements of men and horses, he viewed them with the studied eye of a commander as they checked their packs and saddlebags. Each ensuring the contents and provisions held within were as they expected determined both themselves and their steeds were ready for the journey. From the press of bodies Cameral emerged moving towards him before giving a wave. "It is good to see you are up, we leave in ten minutes. Are you prepared for the journey?" Thalen paused for a moment considering the pack slung over his shoulder and the equipment he had, fortunately, most of his equipment had come with him to this place and was in good order. *Well except for the chain, those ice spikes ripped through it as though it were parchment.*" he thought to himself before speaking., "As prepared as I could be, where do we travel too exactly? I know you have given me a name, yet it means very little to me as I have never heard nor been to this Moon Shade Keep before." As he turned to take in the day Cameral responded "Ah yes of course, not many people have reason to go to Moon Shade Keep, beyond if you are brought there by the order. It is a small castle located within town of Talisar, upon Lake Vorinth here upon the continent of Talinsana. It would take far too long to travel back to Isari, as the journey to our home would take many months." Pausing, Cameral beckoned Thalen over to a pair of horses near the center of the group and continued as they walked. "The Council of The Order of Eoch's Embrace made the decision to establish training locations upon the continents of our allies. They were established soon after the war began to provide both a home to the members of the order and a location for the continued training of our casters on the front lines. After all, and this is something you will learn, there is always more to know, learn and understand in the world of magic. This will be especially true for you!" He finished with a chuckle and a shrug of his shoulders, with a wave of his hand Cameral indicated for Thalen to check the equipment on the chestnut next to the bay he himself was examining.

"It will take about a month of travel to get to the Keep. Fortunately, we will be moving away from the lines and should not have any issue with those cursed orkish brutes. Nonetheless you have seen firsthand their shaman's powers so we must be wary until we reach Talisar. As once we are in site of its walls the protection offered by the local defenders should be enough to ensure our safety." with that final sentence, he mounted leaving Thalen to finish his check and mount up himself. Tearing his eyes from the odd mage, Thalen scanned the rest of the group, with a start of realization he saw that they were all mounting up, the time for travel finally arriving. Putting a foot in the stirrup, he pulled himself up into the saddle wincing slightly at the pull he felt from his still bruised muscles and fresh scars. Awaiting the signal to move, he closed his eyes, taking a moment to ponder the journey and the effect it would have on his still healing body, if not his still healing mind.

After a few minutes, the sound of crunching chain reached his ears as the soldiers sat straight for, what Thalen assumed, was the commanding officer of this expedition. Opening his eyes, he was greeted by the site of a man the size of a mountain. This giant of a man, his face weathered and scarred, possessed a presence suggesting he had seen plenty of combat in his life. His face was bearded and eyes piercing as he examined his charges and the escort group. After a momentary glance he looked at Cameral and Thalen and walked towards them with a grace not seemingly suited for his size.

"Greetings, I am Sergeant Gerard, and I will be leading your escort." He began snapping a quick salute, his voice was deep and rough "These fine soldiers and I will do our best to get you to the Keep as quickly as possible with as few issues as can be managed." With a smile, Cameral responded, "It is good to meet you Sergeant, I am sure that we will have a rather uneventful journey, none the less we appreciate your protection and assistance." with a pause the mage looked over the group before continuing "Let us be on our way with all haste the sooner started the sooner ended after all, on your order Sergeant." With a nod, Gerard turned towards the men voice booming, "Alright form up standard order, I want two scouts sent ahead at all times once we make it past the gate. I do not expect too much trouble, but caution keeps us alive. Questions? No? Then let us get moving."

Moving over to his own horse Gerard pulled himself up into the saddle, waiting as the first six men passed by before coming up beside Cameral and Thalen with the last four of the group following close behind. As the column made its way out, Thalen withdrew into himself considering those around him and his unusual traveling companion. Looking at the group of soldiers escorting them, he noticed immediately that many of the faces were quite young, many not seeing more than 25 winters. Yet, though obviously young, they each carried themselves as a veteran, these soldiers being yet another example of this cursed war taking many young men and woman from their homes and turning them into warriors whether they wished to be or not. Each member of the escort was dressed in the same style chainmail donned over leather jerkins, all equipped with a sword or axe at one side and their shield hanging to the other. Glancing at the rear guards he noted each holding a crossbow their stocks set upon the pommel of each horse's saddle, a bolt knocked and prepared, their eyes scanned the woods they were passing, keeping alert for any threat as they traveled further from safe and gated walls.

Although these soldiers were greener than the ones that had served under him, he felt confident they would give pause to any number of bandits or most other potential threats to be found on the road. *"Not to mention the caster that sits in our midst, I wouldn't want to attack a group of soldiers with a caster so readily available. Not to mention the Sergeant, he looks as though he could take most any group of bandits by himself."* he thought with a silent chuckle. With his companions in his thoughts, he could not help but glance over towards the mountainous Gerard. Taking in the hulking mass that was the Sergeant, it was immediately obvious to Thalen that this man had seen many fights and survived them all noticing quite a few silver strands within his brown beard.

The sergeant was a veritable arsenal, with an arming sword decorating his left hip and a short sword upon his right. A shield was strapped to his mounts saddle with a long-handled axe matching it on the right, unlike the rest of the men his armor was full plate, leaving only his head and hands exposed, seeming to have forgone these for the moment. Even without them he was an imposing armored behemoth that was armed to the teeth. The display would look comical on nearly any other man but between his large frame and the way he carried himself, he was a terror to behold. Taking a moment to adjust his seat, Thalen glimpsed a large crossbow, though some might say a small ballista, rested upon the pommel of Gerard's saddle, loaded and ready to use at a moment's notice.

Feeling a small shiver Thalen pulled his cloak closer around him shifting his gaze to Cameral, a man, though smaller, that was arguably more dangerous than his armored counterpart. By all appearances, the mage was completely at ease in the saddle and hardly looked out of place amongst the armed escort even with his slight build. Though certainly smaller than himself in weight and height, the caster carried himself with an air of confidence as though nothing in this world or the next could threaten him. *"He is hardly threatening on a physical level, but his demeanor gives me great pause. His supreme confidence and surety as if he had nothing to fear. He seems a decent enough comrade, though his sense of humor is questionable at best."* Thalen thought to himself with a chuckle. *"I suppose that for now the elf will simply have to remain a mystery it is not as though I could pierce his shroud of secrecy simply by staring at him. None the less this is going to be a long trip, so I just might get my chance to wean something from his enigmatic character..."* with that final thought he allowed the comfortable numbness of travel to wash over his mind leaving behind all thought and feeling in favor for the gentle rocking of the saddle.

The small company took it slow alternating between a walk and trot to conserve the horses' strength. Although there was another reason for this as they were still close to the front and occasionally a group of Orks would slip past the defensive line or be carried over by one of the red dragons. Absentmindedly, Thalen noticed Gerard taking a quick look around before yelling out to his soldiers "All right lads, let us be as careful as possible until we make it to the Torith River. We've lost three patrols in the past month to ork incursions, and I do not want that same fate for us." The soldiers let out a chorus of "yes sirs" and began scanning the area more carefully as they continued down the snowy path. Thalen could certainly appreciate the sentiment, though he doubted any trouble would present itself, it was a stressful time traveling through the wilderness in the best of times, which these were not. However, with a caster of First Mage Cameral's caliber he doubted there was much the troop would not be able to handle. After all, one does not become a First Mage by being poor at magic and though the patrols would have certainly had a mage in their midst, he seriously doubted that they held a candle to the one beside him.

As the morning's light strengthened and noon approached, Gerard called for a stop at a small stream near the road. The company moved the horses off to the side of it and into a natural break in the trees, it being just large enough to house the thirteen men and their respective mounts with only little room to spare. Once they had all dismounted Gerard addressed the group "Alright, you have twenty minutes to eat and rest, then we mount up and don't stop again till dark." With a wave of dismissal, he walked off to take his own meal; once the soldiers had finished tending their mounts, they pulled out trail rations, each eating the hard biscuits and jerky with acceptance if not enjoyment. Finding a fallen log Thalen sat upon it taking out his own meal from his bag, slowly he chewed his food, taking a swig from his water skin after nearly every dry mouthful.

Thalen felt like the rest was over before he knew it, as suddenly Gerard's voice broke his reverie, commanding the company to mount up and move out. Rising to his feet Thalen quickly made his way to his horse swinging into the saddle, his mind elsewhere as he considered the future and to some degree the past. *"I have to come to understand these powers that I now possess, not that I have much of a choice in the matter. Though I never imagined I would ever come to this point...yet I have this power now and it will give me the opportunity to avenge Sarah. Perhaps it will also help me keep others from experiencing the heartbreak I have."* Shaking off that final thought he guided his horse to its place just as the company began to move out at a light walk.

As the afternoon slowly turned to evening, the light and warmth of the sun began to wane bringing with it both the darkness and cold of night's embrace. Once night began to take full hold, Gerard called the column to a stop, when Thalen's own mount came to a halt, he looked about the surrounding area. As his eyes scanned, he found a section not fully clear of trees, yet they had thinned considerably with little underbrush hiding the thick trunks. A stream flowed lazily through the area with the hard-packed earth clear of most debris, providing a fairly open space for what he assumed was to be their evening's rest.

Dismounting Thalen looked up and down the line of soldiers, puffs of white smoke coming from both man and animal as the temperature slowly dropped and the cold night approached. Gerard's voice broke the silence "Alright you lot, set up camp, I want a fire in the center with enough wood to keep through the night. We do not want anyone getting frostbite tonight, we may be close to spring but frostbite is still a major danger for us! Private Benjamin and Carter go collect wood and be quick about it lads this is no time for lollygagging. The rest of you, I want a rotating watch set by the time they return." Orders given, Gerard stepped away letting his soldiers go about setting up camp, which they got to with often drilled efficiency. Finding a spot near where the fire would be set, Thalen made himself as comfortable as he could on the hard-unyielding ground. Settling in, he took a moment to scan the area again focusing on the quickly darkening forest for any sign of unfriendly eyes. "Good evening, Thalen!" a voice said causing him to jump before turning his head to find Cameral sitting next to him, the mage having approached silently without alerting Thalen's honed senses, "You seemed unhappy during our ride so I thought I would check in on you. How is our newest member?"

the mage asked, eyes gleaming. Heaving a frustrated sigh Thalen gave Cameral an annoyed look, eyes narrowing to slits. With a wry smile playing at his lips, it being the only suggestion he recognized Thalen's mood, Cameral spoke "Come now my friend, no need to be so down. You are on an exciting new journey to an unknown place and unknown things. What more could you want?" he finished his arms sweeping out wide with a showman's flourish.

Eyes rolling Thalen made no effort to mask the sarcasm lacing his voice as he replied "There are many things I could want and, by far, none of them include traipsing along to an unknown fate. Some things I want include a decent meal, a decent bed, by the Gods I would even take some willing woman in that bed. I can say with certainty this is not on that short list, at least not when I last looked." The elf gave him an amused look saying, "I don't believe that is what you really want, I believe what you really want is far gone. That aside I do realize you desire answers and most of them will have to wait but the least I can do is give you a few of them. Assuming you can keep your patience long enough to listen." As he finished Cameral's features took on a more businesslike demeanor as he asked, "Is that agreeable to you?" Thalen, taking a deep breath, calmed his emotions before he gave the mage a nod, turning to face him full on.

"Very good, let us begin." Cameral said as

he stood and with a wave of his hand, created a pair of stools which suddenly materialized from thin air. Sitting upon one he indicated for Thalen to take the other, whom after a moment to ensure that it was indeed real sat opposite the grand mage. "As I said I can only tell you some, for not even I know exactly what is to happen with you or the lessons you will be taught. Nonetheless I will answer any question you have that are within my power." Finishing, Cameral placed his elbows upon knees and leaned forward into a more comfortable position. Thalen took a moment to adjust his seat upon the small stool, clearing his throat, he went to speak but paused as a realization struck him. He had no clue what he wanted to know or ask; the changes had occurred so suddenly he had not bothered to really consider the circumstances he was getting into. "*I should not have allowed my temper to get the better of me. Now I look the fool…*" he thought, looking across from him, Thalen noticed that Cameral appeared very much the master preparing to teach the student, a look of complete patience and neutrality upon his angular features. After a few more awkward moments passed questions finally managed to form within Thalen's mind and with a sigh of relief he began "You have told me where we are going and to a degree why, you have also told me of your order but, I know very little of The Order of Eoch's Embrace. They are often not spoken of on the front lines, at least not in more than the occasional deployment orders for the various mages." Cameral leaned back briefly and looked at sky seeming to consider his answer before turning back to Thalen.

"The first thing I wish to say is keep in mind that The Order of Eoch's Embrace is now your order as well, seeing as how you are now on your way to learn to wield magical power" he reminded with a gentle smile before continuing "Where to truly start when speaking of our order is difficult, though it has existed for only a short time, we have accomplished much since its founding. Before I can answer your question, I must first ask one, what do you know of the Breach event one hundred years back? After all it is more than just something we chose to count our years by." Thalen answered as he recounted the events one hundred years past, they came to him easily as it was taught to every child in their early years of school. He spoke of the coming of the Raital and the sudden opening and closing of the great portal that lasted for hardly more than fifteen minutes. Cameral, head nodding as Thalen finished, began to speak again "Yes you know it mostly, yet one key element is missing from your tale. It is an extraordinarily little known or remembered piece of information, given how much it has changed our world, as one hundred and one years ago magic itself did not exist."

CHAPTER FIVE

Cameral paused as though for dramatic effect, seeming to allow this revelation to sink into, which it did as Thalen found himself hanging upon the mage's every word to the point where he could feel himself leaning forward in anticipation. After what Thalen deemed to be far too long, Cameral broke the silence, "Magic itself did not exist in our world until one hundred years ago when the breach formed. Now we do not know much about magic but something we do understand is even though magic may not have existed on this plane, it does on others that we had, and have, no way of reaching." Cameral stood up as the fire the soldiers had been making grew larger, it quickly crackling to life behind him. Cameral moved to stand directly between Thalen and the fire and as the world darkened it seemed as though the flames behind him painted his face in a mystical and shadowy light. "Back to your original question, The Order of Eoch's Embrace was formed several years after the awakening of magic on our world. It was decreed by the human King Alaverdi that a college of sorts would be created to aid in the teaching and honing of magical skills that manifested in many of those within our shared land. When emissaries of your King were sent to King Del'tairin of the Elves, both he and the council deemed it a wise path and agreed" he took a moment to reseat himself before continuing.

"Thus, The Order of Eoch's Embrace was first created with schools located in the capitals of the two lands, your city of Misanthril and the Elvish city of Tal'Aquarn." He paused a moment, taking a swig from his water skin. Wiping his mouth, he continued, "Over time the two colleges grew as those who could harness magic did, eventually the Council of Magi determined we would need other places to teach of the power including what is now the headquarters of the order Sunvale Keep located on land declared to be neutral between our two kingdoms. The process was slow at first, securing land to create new places of learning take both large amounts of money and the political candor. However, soon after the war started, it was deemed the order needed to be strengthened to help in the fighting. This has proven to be a wise decision on the part of the Kings as a good mage is worth either twenty soldiers or ten doctors depending on what they specialize in. With the agreement of all the goodly races and their own respective Orders, we established colleges on every continent of our Coalition. As I had mentioned these places are used to both house, and further the training of, our members and those that show the potential to join the order. Though there is a deep respect for the other magical orders it is with great pride that I can say ours is both the strongest and most advanced in our world. This is yet another thing we can thank our Kings for as they gave great importance to the advancement of magical studies…"

After another moment where he seemed to be deep in thought he finished with a question, just a touch of his previous humor returning to his voice. "Was that a satisfactory answer?" The tale complete and lain bare before him Thalen looked up to the stars, the pinpoints of light just peeking through the canopy above, his mind swirled as it tried to process what he had been told while also thinking of what to ask next. After a few moments he picked a question that seemed an appropriate follow up "You said you were a First Mage, what exactly does that mean? I will admit when I acted as a Captain, I never would have considered the differences in a mages title, outside of knowing if they could handle the tasks given or protect my soldiers from the enemies spells." He looked squarely at his impromptu teacher and forced himself to patiently wait for the answer. Though given the mage's penchant for the dramatic, he hoped he would not be overly tested.

After a moment of pause, Cameral cleared his throat showing no discomfort with the question posed before him but seeming unsure how to answer, "The question you have asked is far more complex in answer than I believe you realize. I can only promise to answer it as simply as possible to give you the best understanding that I can. My being a First Mage does entail that I have great power, both in spell and in a political sense. The Order of Eoch's Embrace is broken into circles, as a First Mage I am of the First Circle. There are three other circles and though I am sure you can guess their names they are the Second, Third and Fourth Circles. Now, mages of all circles have power but the circle a mage is in represents the amount of power and skill they possess, however, this can mean that a mage in the Second Circle could in fact have less raw power than one in the Third Circle, but have greater skill and control over it. We value finesse with magic and skill in its application over simply pure power, this helps us ensure that even those with the most raw power will have a desire to increase their finesse and their ability to apply their power to greater effect. So, to answer the unspoken question once more, yes that does make me a very powerful mage. However, it comes with a catch as the First Circle is composed of only ten, as we are also the Council of Magi. I am sixth in rank as there are those both more experienced and skilled than I, however, through practice one may gain more power and knowledge. Through this practice one can hope to gain a higher rank and this helps create a growing and competitive environment as one can be surpassed at any time, within reason, so even those at the top will continue to improve." He stopped for a moment appearing to gather his thoughts before continuing on "There are two levels below the Fourth Circle, one being official while the other is not, they are *initiate* and *hopeful* respectively. An initiate is one that is a member of the order but in only an apprentice capacity as they are not yet full mages. The hopeful is how many describe those who have yet to be accepted by the Order, as they need to display their abilities to show the fact they would belong. Again, this is not an official rank but has become a common reference of these individuals."

Before the mage could even draw breath to continue, Thalen put forth another question. "Would I be one of these hopefuls?!" he asked the concern evident in his voice. The First Mage sighed, in what seemed more thought on than frustration at the question, after another moment he spoke "No, you would not be as you have already displayed your power, and with it, proved your worth to the Order. Even more so, your age would not allow you to fall under the initiate category. As a member of the Council, I have already made the decision that upon your arrival you will be given entrance to the Fourth Circle. This will both be a boon and a detriment, as you will not have the opportunity to learn spell theory, but it will give you more freedom of movement and allow you to retain your rank. As for spell theory you will be tutored to ensure that you understand the cost of magic and the spells we cast." He finished his tone going a bit dry as if he was becoming bored with the subject. Thalen was honestly surprised that the seemingly flighty mage had managed to maintain his composure as long as he had. Having heard an answer, he deemed acceptable Thalen relaxed letting out a relieved breath, one he had not noticed he had been holding before chuckling slightly to himself. "If that was a short answer, I would hate to hear the long one." He thought, making a mental note to be prepared for, what were likely, many longer answers in the future.

The sun having long ago fallen below the horizon, its presence only being felt in the pink and orange hues playing across the sky, reminded Thalen that darkness would soon be upon them, barely stifling a yawn he spoke. "Thank you for the answers Cameral, you have provided me with enough to think on at the moment and I will bid you a good night." As if noticing the coming darkness for the first time Cameral looked about with a start exclaiming "Yes you are right, it is getting late, and we have long to travel still! Good Evening to you Thalen, may Katri the Moon Goddess protect you this night." With a slight nod of his head he moved around fully-grown fire, leaving Thalen to his awaiting thoughts and dreams. With the smell of a stew cooking above the fire, Thalen gave pause considering whether to wait for the evening's meal, yet even as he considered it, he could feel pure exhaustion wash over him and instead took to his bedroll to fall quickly and deeply asleep.

Fire, houses burning, the tall spires of the cities of the Raital and Winsentti. People fleeing, being slaughtered, as pig faced Orks pour through the streets. The world a red hue as wood and thatch roofs fall to ash, as great red wyrms fly over the city spraying down deadly flame from their agape jaws. A keep falling with pieces of mortar and stone flying from explosions. Blood, warm and red sliding through his fingers as he covers his side. A spear rising and falling, magic thrown followed by screams of fear and cries of anguish, pain. Pools of blood surrounding bodies as they are hacked to pieces with cruel weapons. He looks up, an axe falls, darkness.

With a start, Thalen awoke sweating, hand to his chest searching for the killing blow that was delivered. His breath quick and heart pounding he looked around only to find sleeping bodies and the embers of the fire. *"Just a dream."* He thought to himself *"A nightmare for sure but nothing more."* With a sigh of relief, the tension fell away from his body, laying his head down once more he fell into a dreamless sleep.

CHAPTER SIX

As dawn broke the men and woman of the small troop woke finding a light chill upon the air. Once camp was packed, they went to their horses intent on returning to the journey once more eating a breakfast of biscuits and smoked sausage from the saddle allowing them to continue on towards their destination. Quiet conversation rippled throughout the party, speaking of home, the war and many other things. Thalen spoke little as he chose to keep mostly to himself, as the relative silence and plodding pace allowed him to doze in the saddle, a benefit of being the protected and not the protector. Enjoying the opportunity to not be the one on high alert, he was more than happy to leave all of the worrying to the Sergeant. *"I have enough to worry about already, no reason to include the journey."* He thought to himself with a chuckle.

As though a portent or jinx of what was to come, a yell of pain came from the front of the group. His eyes snapping open, Thalen immediately began scanning the woods searching for danger, within moments his well-trained eyes caught the movement of a large hulking form. "To our right, to arms! We have been caught in an ambush!" he yelled as he slid from his saddle, Gerard's bellows following soon behind directing his men "Down right side, form a line quickly!" hearing the order soldiers scrambled to form up as the monstrous creatures rushed towards them barreling through the trees. The creatures ran headlong for the defenders breaking low hanging branches and tearing up the soil as their tusked mouths bellowed war cries in their guttural language seemingly spurring them to greater speeds.

Just as the soldiers formed, the first Ork hit their line swinging its weapon wildly hewing through the chain of two soldiers in the blink of an eye. With a bellow it swung towards another sending the man sprawling to the ground, uninjured but dazed by the power behind its strike. With a cry of anger another soldier struck at the ork, his sword biting deep into its side causing greenish, black blood to ooze from the wound. Before they could get out of reach the monster gave a bellow of rage and swung one massive arm at its attacker, hitting the soldier with a glancing blow which knocked them back several feet. Thalen tore his eyes away from the scene, barely in time to avoid a powerful charge by another of the creatures. Managing to dodge a wild swing of a crude axe, he felt wind from it not but a hair's breadth away from his head.

Taking the opportunity, he turned fully upon it, dealing a quick deathblow stabbing up into the armpit of the ork, his sword hitting home within the creature's lungs. Thalen pulled his weapon from the creature's flesh turning away as it fell to the ground with a thud, it's wet breathing coming to an end. His opponent dispatched he searched for any companion hard pressed by their foes, and once seeing one of their green-skinned enemies making towards a woman reloading a crossbow he prepared to sprint. Yet, before he could even take a step, he saw a blur of movement hit the creature as the giant Gerard shoulder charged the ork head on with enough force to knock most men flat to the earth. Unlike a man, however, the creature only stumbled before turning enraged, its weapon rising to strike the Sergeant. Yet, it was far too slow as, like a viper, Gerard's short sword cut deep into its gut, disemboweling it before it could even bring its weapon to bare.

With a grim chuckle, Thalen turned about searching for a spot where he could be of aid, only then realizing the depth of their situation. Though the creatures were less skilled, poorly armed and the party was striking them down in droves, there were simply too many of them. Of the original thirteen soldiers, only nine remained as four of them had fallen in the initial shock, two of them having been the forward scouts. These nine were arrayed against another fifteen Orks and if not for the staggered way in which they had attacked, they would have been overwhelmed almost immediately. Gritting his teeth in frustration Thalen moved forward intending to take a few of these beasts with him before going down himself. Charging in, he flew into the press aiding a pair of soldiers being attacked by several Orks, coming in on their flank he brought his blade to bear with great efficiency. As the Ork stuck at the target in front of him, Thalen forced his blade through the back of the larger creature, the point thrusting out from its muscled chest. With a twist and sickly crunch, the creature fell, turning the tide of the fight briefly for the defenders.

Pressing the advantage, Thalen engaged a second Ork avoiding the wide, unskilled swipes of its giant club. The creature growled, whether in anger, frustration or both Thalen could not tell, it's rage seeming to push it forward blindly as it redoubled its efforts. Narrowly avoiding several swings Thalen took his opportunity darting in on the tail of a backswing and stabbed deep into the creature's side, its dark blood poured from the wound as the blade retracted. With a wild swing faster than Thalen expected the creature clipped him on the shoulder its great strength sending him sprawling to the forest floor. Before he could return to his feet the ork was upon him, its club high above it as it prepared to strike. Thalen's eyes widened as he barely managed to throw himself to the side just moments before the club thudded into the ground. Taking the initiative he turned, looked up at the creature, and with great effort surged forward stabbing upwards deep into the creature's gut. Using the momentum, he surged to his feet and in the same movement, slid the now dead ork from his sword allowing it to fall to the forest floor.

Turning about Thalen searched for another creature when suddenly he felt the meaty impact of a large fist across his jaw. Stunned, he tumbled to the ground breath exploding from him as it came up to meet him. His breath being further driven from him by a large hide boot that grinded down into his chest, looking up he found himself in shadow as a green skinned figure dressed in tattered hide armor came to view above him. Its toothy maw set in an evil grin it spoke in thick and garbled King's tongue "You die now human." With an evil barking laugh it raised its weapon to deliver the deathblow. Thalen, helpless before the creature, closed his eyes awaiting the crude axe to fall...one...two... three seconds passed before Thalen opened his eyes finding the creature still above him but with a large bloodied shared of ice peeking through its massive chest. Thalen barely avoided the creature's mass as it fell to the ground, moving to a sitting position he looked about confused at the sudden turn of events.

"I suppose I must get involved now." A relaxed voice said from where the creature once stood. Thalen looking up from the fallen creature saw none other than Cameral the First Mage seeming to glow with power, giving a small nod to him Cameral turned to unleash his magical fury upon their foes. Finding no shortage of enemies, Cameral made a few quick gestures sending a deluge of green tinged arcane bolts from his palms, each bolt unerringly striking home into every orkish foe, all receiving multiple strikes to their large bodies. Each dart left scorch marks upon their target as they struck with great force and power, launching the creatures as though they were ragdolls, across the forest floor as they fell before the magical barrage of the slender elf. Within mere moments the forest came to silence except for the harsh breathing of the remaining defenders, a field of bodies felled by both blade and magic alike stretching out before them.

As the adrenaline left Thalen, he took a moment to slow his breathing and still his fast-beating heart. *"By the gods if not for the Mage we would be but corpses in the snow."* He thought to himself, having regained his composure he set himself into motion trying to keep his muscles from succumbing to battle fatigue. Gerard, after giving the tired defenders a moment to recover, roused the party into action once more. Giving a few quick commands he set them to searching for the bodies of their fallen comrades amongst the carnage before them. *So much death in only a few minutes, I have spent too long in large battles. This seemed as though a snap of the fingers compared to what I have become accustomed to*" Thalen thought to himself. Seeing Gerard and Cameral in conference, Thalen moved towards the pair stepping over the crumpled bodies of their enemies still freshly struck down by Cameral's magic. Coming up next to the pair Thalen took in Gerard's now haggard appearance, the large man looking worse for wear, as the helmet he had donned for upon leaving the fortress was missing from his shaved head, a reddened bandage taking its place. Beckoning Thalen closer the sergeant spoke quietly for just the three to hear "That was hard fought, if not for the First Mage we would have been annihilated and that I am grateful for, yet this concerns me. There has never been a force this large behind the lines, let alone with how far from the front we are." Gerard paused, checking the soldiers' progress before looking back at the pair.

"How far are we from the front?" Thalen asked, "I admit I am not sure due to my unconscious travel after my powers awakened." With a grunt of understanding Gerard replied "I am not surprised from what I heard you were dead to the world for the entire journey. We are 4 or 5 days from the front to my best reckoning, and unless they broke through the lines themselves these orks must have been dropped in by those red wyrms." With a sigh he looked across the body-strewn battlefield. "If not for your magic, we never would have managed to fight them off. They were far too numerous and too strong, I do not have to tell either of you that our few advantages over these creatures are that there are normally more of us and we are better at tactics" Gerard went silent giving Thalen the opportunity to voice a nagging thought as he considered the power the caster had displayed. "I must ask Cameral, why did it take so long for you to act? Without a doubt if you had acted earlier more lives would have been saved. I daresay you could have handled them with no aid from us in the first place."

The First Mage gave a slightly cool look to the pair before speaking "You are correct I could have dealt with them to great effect with no aid. However, I fear I could not afford to reveal myself too soon in this conflict. If there had been one of their magic users, known to us as Shamans, within their ranks revealing myself may have spelt disaster for all of us and not just those unfortunate souls that have fallen" Pausing he cast a weary and sad look over the bodies of their fallen comrades. After a moment longer he continued "Though I wish I could have acted sooner, I did not wish to risk us all by acting with too much haste. Though be assured our losses weigh heavily on my mind." Thalen took in the elf's words, the regret in his voice plain to any who would look for it, even so, he could not stop himself from voicing the question within his mind. "Cameral, why would you be fearful of any spellcaster, having seen the might that you wield I cannot fathom any foe besting you. What concern could you have had that would stop you from taking action to prevent this?" Cameral sighed, a weary sound suggesting fatigue as opposed to any annoyance at Thalen's question. Looking at both him and Gerard he spoke his voice even and patient as he explained. "I will not deny that I could defeat many spellcasters, whether they be singular or striking at me all at once. However, much like a soldier, no matter how strong I may be I can be felled if taken unaware for I cannot guard against an unexpected attack. If I had acted too quickly without the knowledge of if a spellcaster would appear then it is likely that after my first spell I could have been injured or, if they were quite powerful, struck down entirely. This would have left the entire troop to the mercy of a superior force with magical aid, without a doubt this would have spelled doom for all of us." As he finished, he looked up to the heavens as though in an effort to forget the death around them even if only for a moment.

Thalen stood in silence contemplating the words of the caster, he would admit that the words rang true to his mind, it being a logical conclusion to draw let alone be told outright. A soldier approached the trio pulling Thalen and the others from their internal thoughts. "How many did we lose Corporal?" Gerard asked, his voice filled with fatigue from the battle. In a voice that was hoarse from yelling, she replied, "We lost six before the mage was able to put an end to the battle, three dead with three wounded, all others got away with only minor scrapes and bruises. I have the names of the fallen and will have letters drafted for the families once we arrive at the Keep. What shall we do with the bodies?" the words were spoken without emotion, yet her face was filled with both fatigue and some sadness at the loss of those she likely had known well.

Letting out a long steadying breath Gerard spoke "The ground is still too hard to bury them, and we cannot bring them with us." The sergeant paused thinking for a moment before replying, "We will have to build a pyre for our fallen. Leave the Orks to the crows; it's the best they deserve. Set a few men to collect good wood, long branches and any scrubs you can find." He dismissed the corporal before turning to the mage "Would it be possible for you to speed up the burning? We are short on time as you know, and I wish for as little smoke as we can manage as well as little evidence of our passing. We know not if there are more watching and waiting." The First Mage gave a nod of consent "I can and shall as it is the least I can do for their sacrifice, once the pyres have been built I will make them burn with speed. They should burn hot with little smoke as whether the wood is frozen or wet my fires will burn true." With a grunt of acknowledgment and appreciation, Gerard turned to oversee the building of the pyres, leaving Thalen and Cameral in silence neither of them possessing the energy to speak.

Within the hour a pyre was set and prepared to burn, upon it lay the brave soldiers that had fallen to the weapons of their enemies. Cameral took a step forward once all was prepared, his hands moved in quick, yet complex gestures accompanied by whispered words. Perceptible only to Thalen, a sudden wash of power emanated from the First Mage's hands and with a flash the pyre lit and a fire seemingly hotter than those made by normal means consumed the branches and bodies alike. After a few moments of prayer and remembrance the remaining soldiers mounted up and with a signal from Gerard moved out quickly away from the battleground and the bodies of their enemies left to rot upon it.

CHAPTER SEVEN

The party traveled onwards, the miles and weeks melting away like the last scattered snow drifts as the weather turned towards spring. The remainder of the journey passed quickly to Thalen's reckoning as he found himself at ease with the soldiers, especially Gerard, forming a fast friendship with the large man. The pair swapped stories of past battles and heroics, finding a mutual respect and recognition of the other's skills in battle, being not just skill of arms but in the ability to command. Thalen also found himself talking far more often with the mage, yet unlike Gerard he did not feel the same sort of kinship. No, it was more of a teacher speaking with a pupil, their conversations often centering about magic and some of the more basic principles of it. Though he did not always wish to listen, he did find these lectures passed the time just as quickly as any conversation with the giant sergeant. At times he even found himself listening intently to the words that passed the elf's thin set lips.

With the final days of the journey passing Thalen found himself almost reluctant to see the end of it as everything beyond was both unfamiliar and unknown. Yet, time passed, and the days stretched on until one evening when the column came to a stop for one of its final times. Gerard, having surveyed their potential campsite nodded before speaking loudly for all to hear "Let us camp here tonight, we are only two days at most from the town if our luck and the weather holds, we should find the last two days uneventful. Set up camp and get settled in, get to it." Orders received the soldiers dismounted and with practiced precision began setting camp and collecting every dry piece of wood in site.

Taking a moment to scan the area himself Thalen dismounted, he went about tending his mount, removing it's saddle before rubbing it down and ensuring that it was well cared for, even as he slowly stretched his cramped and tired limbs. Once his task was finished, he took another look around, finding the camp was quickly forming before his eyes, with a fire built and the small tents being pitched. He looked about until he found what he searched for, the First Mage who was walking towards him with purpose. *"I had best preempt whatever he is going to say, I've learned better than to let him control the conversation otherwise he will speak long into next morning."* With a soft sigh, he shook his head, the motion acting as if to dislodge a proper greeting from his fatigued mind. "Hello Cameral, how are you this evening?" he asked as he waved his hand in greeting.

The First Mage stopped his approach and cocked his head to the side and seemed almost as though he was trying to read Thalen's mind, yet after a few moments more he chuckled before walking to stand before him. "I am well and greet you in kind Thalen, do you have some time to spare for me?" Cameral asked with a small smile that played at the corners of his lips accompanied, as always, by a mischievous light in his almond eyes. *"I will never know what this cursed elf is thinking; even when he seems to offer choice it is just an illusion. I cannot imagine telling him no as we sit here in the middle of the woods."* Shrugging to himself, he said the only thing he could "Yes Cameral of course, how may I be of service?" He tried to put more interest in his voice than he was truly feeling although he was not sure if it had the desired effect. With a chuckle, Cameral replied as though a teacher to an unruly student "Well, there is little service you can do for me, this is more of a question of what I can do for you. Yet, if you have little desire to learn something more of your power, at least more than we have had time to speak of thus far, then perhaps I shall leave you to your evening." The elf's once hidden smile broke into a full grin as the wizard turned away from Thalen, making as though to leave.

"Hold Cameral!" the words bursting from his lips before he realized. Heeding the call the First

Mage turned, his eyes quizzical, being given the chance Thalen continued an undercurrent of embarrassment in his voice. "I apologize, I spoke with too much haste...I am the fool. I would appreciate your knowledge and instruction. Though it may not seem so, I do realize I am at a disadvantage and should take every scrap of knowledge I can from you." His piece said he awaited the mage's response. Cameral flashed a near evil grin before turning fully to face him. "Well, when it is put so perfectly how could I refuse? Yes, I will certainly teach that which I can in a single night. Now if only you decided this weeks ago! Perhaps then you would be going in with as much knowledge as your peers will have, but we cannot go back in time now can we." Finishing with a mocking tone he moved in front of Thalen magicking a comfortable stool before sitting with inhuman grace.

Though his face remained passive, at least to the best he could tell, Thalen's mind was filled with thought *"By the Gods, I can't tell if this is how most mages are, how most Elves are, or if he is simply, completely insane."* He shook his head attempting to get his own wandering mind back on track though not before unconsciously mumbling under his breath "I think I will have to assume the last one." Cameral, having obviously heard him, looked at him questioningly "Assume the last what?"

Thalen started with surprise as he

responded quickly trying to cover his blunder "Nothing, nothing, please begin the teaching, after all the sooner started the sooner learned and known." He took a moment to silently admonish himself for his stupidity and hoped the change in topic would distract the elf from what he had said. "Well said, very well said my young friend, to start let us begin with the very basis of magic as we understand it." The mage began a sparkle in his blue almond eyes. "As we spoke of in the past magic in our world is a rather new thing. It did not exist as we know it until after the Breach opened those one hundred years ago. Before that, rather obviously, no magic could be cast within our world, there are questions about this, specifically in consideration of if magic was an existing energy our world contained before the event or if it came to it through the rift itself. Although interesting, this is a rather unimportant question to consider, as it does not affect how we create and craft spells." He paused, taking a breath, appearing to take a moment to consider his next words. "When we cast spells, a mage draws upon the latent energy that is dispersed throughout the world. It is called many different things—stamina, mana, energy, power, these are all words to describe the same thing and different casters can absorb and use different amounts of power. Now as I said the power is distributed throughout our world, but it is not equal in all areas." Upon hearing this Thalen interrupted "What do you mean it is not equal? I have seen mages cast spells all over this world, so how could there be areas with less of this energy? Would it not affect the casting?"

The Elf looked at him for a moment as if considering the worth of what Thalen had asked. "That is actually an exceptionally good question, the answer is that it is not that there is less energy, it is more so the type of energy in the area. Imagine that all powers are broken up following the elements these being water, fire, earth, air and so on. Though there are things such as light, life, dark and many more, this unto itself makes this example imperfect yet what I am trying to say is that different areas are stronger in certain "elements" while weaker in others. An example is that upon this continent, Talinsana, the latent energy tends to flow strong in the elements of water, ice, and air." As the last word left his mouth the elf's face scrunched in distaste, seeming to take a moment to consider what he had said. "Even this is not fully correct, as we also have the abstract concepts that I had mentioned such as life, light and dark. These are not elements, but the magical energies are still very real, as an example you would use the life-based magic to heal an injured ally." Pausing Cameral took a quick swig from his water skin wetting his mouth before he continued.

"I digress, magical energies flow everywhere

and even if the energy is weak in an area, one could still call upon it. However, it would require more will from the caster, and a more powerful caster at that, to draw upon the energy with any real effect. Though this may be the case there is more than just the location and individual that affects the energy that a caster can use. It oddly enough also seems to align along with the different races in our world as well." Curiosity bursting from him Thalen interrupted Cameral before he could leave that particular topic "What do you mean exactly by the energy is divided along race line? Are you saying that certain races such as the Dwarves are unable to use certain magic?" Even as the last world left his mouth, he saw the First Mage shaking his head "No Thalen, although I understand how you could come to that conclusion, that is not what I am saying exactly. The fact is that every single one of the races are able to use all types of magic, however there is a caveat. All races, except for humans and elves, are more attuned to certain types of magical elements. Every race is able to use the different abstract energies but have different attunements to the elemental based energies. Using the dwarves as an example, or rather all the Deep Folk, they are more attuned to earth-based magic. However, that does not mean that they are unable to use the other elements, it just means that more will, and strength is required to call upon them. This implying that a strong caster of the Deep Folk may produce weaker results using water magic than an average human caster, with of course the reverse being true when considering earth magic."

Thalen interrupted once again "So, if my understanding is correct, a more powerful caster of the Deep is able to call upon the other elements with greater ease than one that is weaker. While at the same time they would be stronger in earth magic than an equally strong user of a different race. Correct?" Cameral nodded a smile on his face "Yes, yes you are starting to get it. Maybe you aren't as slow as I thought." He said with a chuckle, upon hearing this Thalen shot him an annoyed look, his voice laced with sarcasm as he spoke "Your praise and faith in me is inspiring. You said that our races are able to use all elements with ease, is there some known reason for this?" The caster let out a long breath before replying "That we unfortunately do not know, as much as we have discovered about magic it is still so very new to us. We still have far too much to learn about it, that very question being one of those many thing. We theorize that it has to do with your ability to live and survive in all climates and lands. What is the word?" the mage paused his head cocked to the side obviously in thought as he searched for the right words "Ah yes, your adaptability that is the word I was searching for we believe it is that which allows your race to easily use all magic. Simply put we believe your bodies adapt to it just as easily as you would any environmental factor. When it comes to the elves, it becomes a bit more obscure. We can only assume it has to do with our attunement to the world; we as a race have always been very close to the land and the earth. Though, there are other factors that come into play which are deep seated in our history. Those that are not worth exploring for now." With a shake of his head, he looked to the canopy above before saying "However, these are, for the moment, just theories, in all truth we simply do not know."

Exhaling, Thalen considered what he had just heard, looking away from the mage and towards the roaring fire in the center of the small glade as he tried to collect his thoughts. He closed his eyes and let his other senses extend from him, he felt the soft breeze fighting its way through the trees, heard the talk of the soldiers, and smelled the scent of stew cooking for the evening's fair. Opening his eyes once more he looked at First Mage Cameral Darkweave, taking in the elf before speaking. "Thank you Cameral, for the time being I would like to eat and think about what you have said. It has given me many things to consider." As Thalen finished the mage got to his feet the stool dissipating into thin air as he dipped into an elegant yet mocking bow. "It is my pleasure Thalen, though I did not teach you much of importance." A crooked smile upon his face Cameral bid a farewell before walking off into the darkness of the night, leaving Thalen with nothing but his thoughts.

CHAPTER EIGHT

The final two days of the journey passed with both speed and ease. Those two days allowing Thalen to think about his talk with Cameral as well as consider the path lying before him. Examining his feelings about his situation, he found a stark change from those he felt when the journey had just begun. Reflecting upon his talks with the First Mage and the journey itself, he was struck by a realization that although the situation was not as he wished, he could not deny the spark of excitement that had grown. That spark had been slowly building into a roaring fire as the miles had passed, journey progressed and finally flared to a full blaze as the majestic spire of Moon Shade Keep came into the battered troops' sight.

Having crested a hill, they paused allowing a sense of relief to wash over them as a true end of their harrowing pilgrimage came into site, releasing a breath of wonder Thalen took in the town and spires before him. His new home was one to behold, the sprawling courtyard protected by a curtain wall made of large stone blocks, the wall having an ornate feeling thanks to its many crenelations and designs. Dominating the center of the yard was the Keep itself a truly massive building, its tall stone spires rising high into the air, topped with shingles of an unexpectedly deep blue. Even at this distance he could easily make out the large windows that decorated the lower levels of the structure each containing a myriad of colors contained in each pane of glass, each piece easily the size of several men. This was without mention of the town in which it stood, the area and keep had been described to him as small, yet to his eyes it was far larger than most of the mot and baily style of encampments he had become accustomed to.

Outside of the Keeps' walls the town of Talisar lay, though called a town it appeared more as a small city, buildings more of stone than wood dominated the landscape with towers laced throughout as one traveled deeper in. A palisade of tall thick logs surrounded the town, with a causeway manned by soldiers, in the livery of the coalition, sat atop it. The wooden wall stretched to the shores of Lake Vorinth which provided protection to the East, many small craft sat upon the crystalline waters of the lake, this giving the scene a truly picturesque appearance. As the company moved down the hill and through the gateway set within the wall Thalen took a closer look at the structures that lined the city's streets, his eyes were drawn to the flowing lines of blue and white paint as if a river or the air itself decorated the gray stone walls.

As they passed through the busy streets Thalen switched his view from the surrounding buildings to their owners and inhabitants. He saw people of all coalition races, with the most plentiful being humans and Raital, yet he caught the occasional glimpse of one of the deep folk and even the lithe features of an elf. Regardless of race, their faces looked calm with little concern or worry, one would not even be able to tell that this was a place at war. Though the simple weapons, such as clubs and axes, each man carried along with the fine stiletto knives the woman had suggested this place had not escaped the conflicts notice. As they traveled deeper into the town Thalen experienced a moment of shock as he realized the structures he took for towers were in fact not towers at all. These tall twisting building of grey stone and dark wood had no entrance on their ground floor. Instead, their doors and windows sat high above tantalizingly out of reach as the Winsentti landed upon what could only be considered porches set before each of the doorways. Every building was decorated much as their sister structures, which housed those more accustomed to the ground, with the vibrant white and blue paint flowing up the buildings, branching out as if fingers, reaching out to the thatched roof far above.

As the shadow of the Moon Shade's gatehouse loomed before them, he took in the true size and might of the walls and gatehouse itself, the grey stone reaching nearly thirty feet above them easily dwarfing the surrounding palisade and buildings save those of the Winsentti. Gerard stopped the group before the open gateway as they were met by a group of soldiers each dressed in scale armor. Iron fish faced helms covered their faces and heads as they held tridents in their gauntleted hands, Thalen could not help but notice the jagged short swords they wore comfortably upon their hips. *"Wicked blades for wicked work. I would not want to be on the other end of their swords or their tridents."* Thalen thought to himself. "Hail and well met, please state your business." One of the soldiers said stepping away from the rest of their group.

As the man came to a full stop before them, Gerard spoke formally, authority lacing his voice as he addressed the man before him. "Greeting, I am Sergeant Gerard Dalyander, and we have come in the Company of First Mage Cameral Darkweave and Mage of the Fourth Circle Thalen Melodyr who is to take residence here for instruction in the arcane arts. With this I ask to discharge these fellows to the custody and protection of yourself and the greater forces of Moon Shade Keep." The guard nodded as he took in Gerard's words and after a moment signaled his understanding "Very well, come in and be welcome to the Keep." With a wave of his hand the path was clear, and the column passed through the monolithic portal. Looking about Thalen took his time passing through the gateway, allowing a chance to examine the guards more closely, he noted the blue tinge to their exposed skin and the mass of braided brown and black hair that spilled out from the opening in the back of each man's helm. He could not help but be impressed with both the readiness of these Raitalian soldiers as well as the good order with which they kept their weapons and their armor. *"Even their strange fish faced helmets are impressive"* He thought to himself *"...though I will never get over how life like they appear. I swear those eyes almost seem to have been taken right from a fish's face."* He shivered slightly at the thought before looking ahead to the courtyard beyond the gateway. As they passed the second set of portcullis and came properly into the courtyard Thalen's eyes drank in the site before them.

The large courtyard spanned before them silver-gray flagstones filled with people milling about, their robes flowing as they moved, yet as the party entered heads turned towards the group, those onlookers' eyes seemed to widen in surprise, before looking quickly away. *"I wonder if they are more shocked at seeing heavily armed strangers here...or perhaps it is Cameral that gives them pause. I wonder how many of them have ever seen a member of the First Circle in the flesh."* Thalen shrugged as the thought flitted through his mind, it was not as though it mattered, what mattered far more to him was the group of mages that were approaching them. These robed men and woman looking excited and expectant as they made their way towards the party. Sighing, Thalen took his last few moments of freedom to take in more of his surroundings. It took Thalen only a few moments to truly appreciate the massive size of the Keep, or rather the College itself as the milling of what were obviously students milled throughout the area. Bringing his attention back to the enormous building, it consumed a fair majority of the grounds beyond the wall and seemed to span higher than even the tallest tower within the city. What was once only the small outlines of stained-glass windows seemed more like giant murals that were painted upon the walls of the College itself as opposed to glass set within them with how great their detail was.

Each window was a work of art that spanned fifty or more feet above the heads of the men and women in the courtyard below, the depictions of shadowy mages in billowing robes casting spells of fire, ice and more. These monolithic pieces were duplicated five or six times up the walls of the massive structure. As he looked to the left and then right of the great fifteen-foot door that lay down the path before them, he found the walls of the College keep stretching thousands, if not tens of thousands, of feet. As he examined those walls more closely, he found his eyes slipping along painted lines that seemed to shimmer in the sun, these lines and swirls being the colors of the elemental magics present within the world. *"This place is strange; I don't believe I have seen a Keep this large outside of the Capital itself...and yet Cameral referred to it as small. Even so in this remote place not only do I find one so strong and protected but it has decoration and beauty beyond that of even the grandest of the Gods' temples. How were they able to create something so grand especially somewhere so remote?"* he thought in both disbelief and wonder before he thrust the thought from his mind as suddenly a shadow passed over him, his eyes instinctively looking for threats in the sky above.

Instead of a dragon or some other terror above him, he found himself taking in a site he had not seen in months. *"Ah of course, I should have expected this, especially given their homes throughout the town."* Seeming to float high above them were both men and woman of the Winsentti, these peoples would easily be mistaken for humans, if not for their large wings spanning out from their backs. These feathered appendages, each being nearly as long as a man was tall, could hold one of the Winsentti aloft for hours with little sign of overall fatigue. "Fascinating aren't they." A voice said from beside Thalen, taking his eyes from the sky above he found Cameral, the elf's own eyes looking to the sky as well, the same wonder Thalen had felt unapologetically held his almond orbs. "Their ability to fly is just truly astounding, our greatest minds have no true idea how they can do so. By all appearances they should be far too heavy for flight, yet there they are alighting above us without a care. In some ways I can't help but be jealous of them, the freedom they have from being able to look down from the sky above...I can't help but wonder if they take it for granted." Cameral paused and stared almost longingly up at the open sky above, after a few moments more he reluctantly tore them away returning Thalen's gaze, a wry smile on his face. "I am sorry, I get caught up in the wonder of our world sometimes. We have discovered so much and yet know so little at the same time. What most people do not truly realize is being a mage is far more than just throwing the elements, spells or conjurations at enemies. In many ways we are scholars and alchemists, we wish to know how our world works. This is for various reasons, some selfish and some altruistic, yet at the end of it all we all wish to know everything." He chuckled and blew out a long and steadying breath before finishing "This is something which will never happen though, even though I have lived longer than the lives of many men, and will likely live many more, I accept that I will never know all there is to our world. Yet, it is such good fun to try." His voice grew wistful as the final words left his lips.

Thalen found himself both surprised and moved by the elf's words and he had to admit to himself, he had started to see Cameral in a new way. Not only, was he something of a mischievous mentor or First Mage Cameral Darkweave, one of the most learned and powerful casters in the Coalition, he was also just a man like any other doing his best in a world likely different than what he had wished. Taking a moment to regain his composure Thalen responded "No need to apologize, you are right, they are truly a sight to behold. I have rarely seen so many of them in one single place, in fact I have only ever seen them as they fought alongside my forces on the battlefield. Even so, that was at a large distance as they were harassing our enemy's formations and disrupting their movements." Thalen paused, unconsciously looking to the sky before continuing "I must also admit the appearance of the Raital has also come at a surprise, I have never seen any but their soldiers and with their being covered in armor similar to those we passed. I have never seen much more than their black eyes and their blue tinged skin, yet beyond that they are far more like us in appearance than I ever imagined." Cameral let out a small chuckle, which begrudgingly drew a smile from Thalen before he responded "Yes thanks to those black eyes and their skin they would never truly be confused for a human or an elf. However, as you say they are very similar to us, in many ways in fact, both physically and culturally. I have known a few in my time and have always found conversations with them to always be enlightening. Did you know..." the First Mage was interrupted as voice rang out addressing them all.

"Greetings my friends and welcome to Moon Shade College. We are very excited and happy for your visit as unexpected as it is." Both Cameral and Thalen turned their heads taking in several people that stood in front of the entrance to the keep itself. The one addressing them was an older human male, his voice possessed a weathered quality, like one that had seen many winters and held the wisdom of the ages within it. "First Mage Darkweave, it has been long since I have seen you. Not since our days teaching together, I believe. How have you been?" Cameral, his mouth forming a wistful smile, dismounted his quick steps revealing his excitement as he approached his former classmate wrapping the figure in a friendly embrace. "Darvin, it is very good to see you, my friend! It has been too long since we last saw one another though it feels as though it was almost yesterday." He said as he released the elderly man from his grasp. With a sad smile, he continued, "I am sorry it has been so long since we last spoke. Sixty years is not but the blink of an eye to my kind, I sometimes forget the effect time has on humans. This is of no matter though as it is good to see you my friend and I hope it is not another sixty years before I think to visit you again!" The First Mage finished, his usual cheer returning to his voice before sweeping a hand towards his traveling companions. "I have some people to introduce you to Darvin, the mountain of a man to the left is Sergeant Gerard Dalyander of the King's Infantry, he has been so kind to as to escort my person as well as our newest ward safely through these dangerous lands. Speaking of wards, the man standing next to him is Captain Thalen Melodyr, he is a newly promoted Mage of the Fourth Circle." Cameral said, looking meaningfully at Darvin. The old mage nodded indicating he understood there was more to this than met the eye and spoke "I see, well it is good to meet you both, I hope the time that you spend here is restful and educational. As for me, my name is Darvin Pelorin Mage of the Second Circle, I also serve as the Headmaster of this particular college. To my left is Captain Kelari Ravenkind and to my right Captain Crixus Bardible, they are in charge of the town guard and keep's garrison respectively." The Headmaster's hands moved to indicate each in turn, the two soldiers inclining their heads in greeting.

Thalen took in the two captains, a welcome distraction from the thoughts beginning to run through his mind. Starting with Captain

Ravenkind, the Winsentti captain's most obvious feature was the two large wings sprouting from her back, the majestic black feathers framing her slender frame. Her hair was colored nearly as dark as those feathers, her features sharp and angular much as a bird's, her eyes of a fiery red darted over the group. A pair of gladiuses could be seen upon her hips, they were not ornate in appearance and seemed well used but equally well cared for. Thalen found her to be pretty but somewhat unsettling as her eyes seemed lifeless much as a bird, though they were of a human appearance. As though reading his thoughts her eyes darted to him arresting his gaze as though a fire preparing to ignite, feeling a small shiver go down his spine he tore his eyes from hers shifting them towards Captain Bardible. Though not natural to this world, the blue tinged Raital man seemed far more human compared to his counterpart. Although hIs eyes were black as onyx with a smile set on his square jawed face, he seemed far more welcoming than his bird-like counterpart. The Raital man was taller than Thalen by an inch or so, but it was his broad shoulders and steel corded arms that made him seem nearly as large as the mountainous Gerard. His powerful build looked completely unencumbered by the scale armor he wore and sword which sat upon his hip. The only hair on his entire head was a snow-white beard that forked out almost as though tines from the tridents the Raital were known for. *"What an unusual pair these two are, I have no idea why I keep finding these unusual people. First Cameral and now a bird person...thank the Gods that this man Crixus seem somewhat normal."* Thalen was so lost in his own thoughts that he nearly missed the headmaster addressing him.

"So, Thalen you are new to the Order that is quite the surprise, normally we would not see someone of an advanced age join our ranks so suddenly. How did that come to be?" asked the headmaster his shrewd eyes examining the newly minted mage. For a moment Thalen's mind ground to a halt as memories and visions of the battle and the death of Sarah overrode his senses. He found himself unable to speak, his mind blank as he stared back at the old man, fortunately it seemed as though Cameral noticed and understood his plight as he leaned in and spoke softly to the headmaster. "Darvin, let us talk of this matter in a more private setting. There is much to discuss as this is a unique situation." His tone of voice was filled with authority making it clear that this was less a suggestion and more a command. The headmaster picked up on this immediately and it shown in his response "Yes, very well let us go to my office on the main floor. We will be alone there and it will give an opportunity to catch up, come along. Captain Crixus, please find those poor soldiers somewhere to bed down. I imagine they will wish to remain here for the time being." He waited for a return nod before turning to the saluting Sergeant. As Gerard's hand came back down from his offered salute he replied "Thank you sir, it would be much appreciated. We shall remain for a day or two; until the first mage deems it time to leave once more. Until then we will happily take to some soft beds and hot food." With another snapped salute he turned on his heels and walked towards his men where he was met by the Raital officer who led them away. Once the soldiers were away Captain Ravenkind spoke, her voice like the chirping of a songbird, soft and musical. "If that is all you need of me Headmaster I must return to my duties in the town." Darvin nodded his permission and upon receiving it the Winsetti woman unfurled her wings and with a leap flapped her mighty wings and after seeming to hover for a moment sailed through the air, over the walls and out above the town itself. After a moment the Headmaster looked once more towards Thalen and Cameral "Let us be off to my office, it seems we have much to talk about." He said with a smile before making his way into the College Keep, Cameral and Thalen following closely behind.

As they passed through the massive doors a sense of wonder came over Thalen as the feeling of power and mystery filled the entire area beneath the high arched ceilings. Hanging from bronzed chains ornate chandeliers lit the room, yet the light itself did not come from candles as he was accustomed to. No, instead it was from hundreds of glowing orbs. People moved throughout the space entering and exiting beautiful oaken doors that opened and closed of their own accord, the doors springing silently open for those who wished to travel through them. As he looked about his eyes were drawn to the gray stone walls, tapestries hung uniformly covering them, each one perfectly placed a few meters apart. These works of threaded art depicted members of the Order, each displaying vastly different scenes, some showing them defeating enemies in battle, advising monarchs in peace time or helping build some great construction. The depictions of the strength, intellect, and abilities of the Order seemed to shimmer with a true to life quality. Whether this spoke of power imbued within them or the amazing skills of the crafter Thalen did not know. Yet, no matter which may be the case they were unquestionably magnificent. The trio passed by servants doing daily tasks or mages going about their business, each ensured they gave a slight bow to the Headmaster and his entourage. Before long the group found themselves stopping before a dark ebony door. The deep wood was inlaid with streaks of color that flowed into the pattern of a hand, its palm facing them, a depiction of Eoch, the world they were upon, held within it. The first finger and thumb of the hand touched while all others stood straight. Floating just below the hand were four stars, each a color used within the pattern itself being red, blue, green, and white. Thalen's wonder must have been painted upon his face as he felt the first mage lean in and whisper. "That is the symbol of The Order of Eoch's Embrace, the symbol of the order you now belong to. Remember this moment well for it is when your life as a mage truly begins. From this moment forward you are no longer just Captain Thalen Melodyr, do keep that in mind." With a gentle pat on his shoulder, Cameral stepped away giving the newly minted mage things to consider as they waited for the Headmaster to open the immense door. After a moment, Headmaster Pelorin shaped his hand in that of the order's symbol, he appeared to concentrate as after a moment Thalen felt a surge of power as the door slowly opened itself. When the portal was finally clear the Headmaster walked into the sparsely furnished office and with a wave, motioned for Thalen and Cameral to sit. The pair moved to the low backed armchairs sitting before a large ornate desk, they seated themselves just as Pelorin sat heavily into the high-backed chair facing them.

The pair settled comfortably into the plush leather chairs enjoying the comfort after the last long days in the saddle. As he himself relaxed Pelorin let out a sigh before speaking "I am truly glad to see you once more Cameral, though you seem to have barely aged while I sit here slowly withering away. Before I know it, I will become a soft minded fool as I suddenly find myself unable to remember even the most basic of cantrips!" Darvin lamented, even as the Headmaster finished Thalen saw a smile creep onto Cameral's thin lips, seeming amused at the obvious overacting of his friend. Darvin, seeing his ploy had failed, broke into a small chuckle before continuing. "Yes, well as you said before we came in here time for you is hardly the same as it is for me. I imagine it must truly seem to have been only a few years since we were both fresh faced instructors in these very halls, and now here we sit as two of the more powerful members of the Order." Cameral opened his mouth to speak, but before any word came the old man continued. "Though that is enough reminiscing for now, we have pressing business to discuss. After all you were always quick and to the point my friend." The Headmaster looked over at Thalen as he continued. "He always seemed to be onto something important when we were teachers. He never had time for lollygagging and would refuse even the mildest of entertainment or intrigue. I hope that eventually he will find himself time to truly relax and enjoy the smell of the roses. At least before I pass from this mortal realm." Seeming to shake his head in mock sadness the man chuckled. Unable to help himself Thalen looked at Pelorin as if he were insane, his mind jumping to the many times the First Mage's "sense of humor" was on full display. *"I take it back; all mages must be absolutely insane and disconnected from reality and not just Cameral. I hope this is not a side effect of becoming a mage and is just the personality of most of them"* He thought as he considered the fact that he was about to be joining this supposedly esteemed order. "So Cameral, tell me about our young friend here. It is good to have a new member of the order even if he does seem a little dense." Pelorin said prompting the first mage, as his tone become more businesslike.

Thalen's aggravation must have shown on his face as when he opened his mouth to speak Cameral kicked his leg hard drawing a sharp breath from him. Taking the initiative the First Mage spoke "Headmaster Pelorin, rest assured Thalen is an intelligent and highly competent individual who seems to have come into his magic very late in life. I have personally seen him in action on the battlefield as well as seen the aftermath of his magic being unleashed. Though I admit I did not see his actions during the event." The First Mage said, "With all of this in consideration, I have decided that, due to special circumstances, he is to be marked as a Fourth Circle Mage immediately." Cameral sunk back comfortably in the chair as he finished, his words leaving no room for interpretation, and looked expectantly at the man before him. Leaning forward on his elbows Pelorin formed his fingers into steeple coming to rest before his face as he seemed to contemplate the mage's words. "I see, it is most certainly within your right as a member of the Council to make such a decision. Yet, I cannot help but be curious as to what these special circumstances are. This man must be truly prodigious to both catch your eye and for you to make these decisions personally. Then again, that was always your style." Darvin said as yet another chuckle escaped him before he turned to Thalen. "So, tell me lad, what has brought you to these halls and through that into my care?" the Headmaster asked his brown eyes showing what felt like eons of patience and more than a little interest.

Thalen sat back in his chair, feeling as though he was preparing to go into battle as he took a deep breath to steady his nerves before recounting his tale. Starting not but since his powers had manifested but instead going all the way back, for as he had thought more about how his life had been, he noticed more and more times that the power may have played an influence. He had always had an unnatural ability to sense when someone was approaching, as well as on the battlefield, he seemingly always knew what the enemy intended to do before they acted. He told them about the pressure that had been playing across his mind that day and how he could sense its buildup and finally release when the stored power was used. Lastly, he spoke of those final painful moments before the journey itself, retelling of the battle and, with great difficulty, recounted Sarah's death at the hands of the shaman. At this point things were far fuzzier, as he could only speak of the feeling, he had experienced along with how the strong emotion seemed to unlock the power he now came to possess and how those final desperate moments came to an end. Wiping an unbidden tear from his eyes Thalen let out a long sigh, it had been weeks since he last thought of Sarah's death, yet the wound still felt fresh, almost as though no time had passed at all.

Once the recounting was finished Headmaster Pelorin sat back in his chair, sympathy showing in his eyes, as he settled deeper into the well-worn leather of the seat. After a moment he let out a breath, it seeming to restart his mind as he spoke to Thalen. "What a sad tale you tell young man, I am sorry you had to experience such a loss yet, it coupling with a sudden change to everything you ever knew… I can only imagine how this must feel to you." He was shaking his head, as though the mere thought of such a loss wounded his own soul. "Yet, I hope you come to understand and accept the powers you now possess. Though they may not seem it now these powers you now possess are a boon and, I hope, will give you something to focus on as the pain of loss dulls over time." He paused and ran one wrinkled hand through his thinning grey hair, during this pause Cameral spoke "I am sorry gentlemen, but I am afraid I must go attend to a few things as I leave in a few days. Thalen we will need to speak later as there is some things left for us to discuss before I go." He stood and nodded towards the Headmaster and after putting a hand on Thalen's shoulder the First Mage exited the office, his boots clicking on the stone floor. As the door closed once more Thalen took the opportunity to speak "Thank you Headmaster, I appreciate your words. Yet, instead of dwelling in the past I wish to move towards the future. Since my change of circumstance, it has felt as though every move I have made has been dictated by the man that just left this room. And now I find myself at my destination and a member of the order. Though now I find myself a ship without a rudder, what is my lot in life now, what am I to do? The Headmaster was nodding his head throughout Thalen's small speech "Of course, that is a fair question as a start, you will remain here in these halls as a student. This is to be the case until you have control over your powers, regardless of the rank you have obtained, you are raw with no training in the ways of magic. Those gaps in understanding will be filled here. While you are with us, you will attend classes to hone your skills and abilities with magic, yet I wish for you to understand that you will always be behind your peers. We will not be able to teach all you would have learned in the years of training you would have had if you were found to have power early in life."

Pelorin paused as he began muttering under his breath, just soft enough for the words to go unheard, within seconds Thalen felt a line of power connect from the mage to a construct, that had gone previously unnoticed, set behind him, set upon a perch. With sudden life a mechanical bronze sparrow hopped to life and without a moment's notice flew out of a gap that opened within the study door. As though a previously unmoving object did not suddenly dart past his head the Headmaster continued. "To help you in catching up with your peers a tutor will be assigned to you. They will help you come to understand the theories of magic and its application as well as aid you in understanding your lessons themselves. Do you have any questions?"

The question was left hanging in the air for a few seconds as Thalen took a moment to recover from the shock he had received. The spectacle of the once inanimate sparrow having only just hit home, he leaned further back into the chair before speaking "When will I be able to return to the war? I left my unit and though I understand the need for training it does not feel right sitting safely while others fight in my stead." Pelorin's brows crooked into something of an amused look before he replied "I understand the sentiment, the answer to that question depends entirely on you. During your time here you will be tested and as you pass the tests you will rise in rank within the Fourth Circle, this culminating in promotion to the Third Circle. Upon your ascension to the Third Circle, you will be a full-fledged mage. This may seem confusing as I am sure you thought with your ascension to a full member of the Order it implies you are a mage. Though the Fourth Circle may appear to be powerful mages to those outside of our order they are in fact little more than accepted apprentices with much to learn. However, I digress back to the original point, when we have confidence in your ability to use your powers safely and with ease, you will no longer be just an apprentice but instead a true mage. Before you ask the obvious question, this can take some years, however if you are diligent, you could be done in as little as a year and a half."

Thalen let out a long breath and nodded his understanding slouching a bit lower into the chair he turned over this new information in his mind. *"A year and a half...that is far too long... I will have to find an opportunity to shorten my time here as much as I can."* A sudden rapping knock echoed throughout the office; Thalen sat straighter as the Headmaster looked past him towards the door. "Good that must be your tutor now." He said to Thalen before bidding the person to enter, as the door opened Thalen turned towards his new tutor and had a moment of surprise. His tutor was not a human or elf as he had expected but rather a dwarf.

CHAPTER NINE

The dwarf standing before him was cut of a typical stocky and strong figure, his nose long sat above a grin, which was hidden by a thick bushy beard that dominated his features. The dwarf's hazel-colored eyes peered at him with his light brown hair, it's length decorated with clasps as it tumbled down to nearly the same lengths as the braids his beard was kept in. A robe of an earthy brown covered his barrel-like body while streaks of a fiery red played throughout the fabric. Emblazoned upon the right shoulder sat a crest much like the one upon the headmasters door, yet unlike the crest of The Order of Eoch's Embrace there was only one star beneath the palm and not four. The dwarfish man came into the room and stood before the Headmaster, upon his shoulder sat the bronze sparrow that was sent from the room. "Ye sent for me Headmaster?" the dwarf asked, his voice rough but friendly. With a warm smile the Headmaster addressed him "Indeed I did Dolgrath, this here is Thalen he is a brand-new member of the Fourth Circle, he has been brought to us under special circumstances and requires some extra tutoring. When considering who best to place him with I could think of none better than you, young man." though the Headmaster was old for a human it seemed likely to Thalen that the dwarf may have had some years on the man, even if this was the case Dolgrath showed deference to Pelorin bowing slightly before turning to Thalen hand out in greeting. "It's good to meet ye Thalen. As the headmaster said I be Dolgrath Boardolin Mage of the Fourth circle much as yourself. Now before ye start to worry I be preparin' for me ascension to Third, so I promise I know what I be talking about." As he shook the strong, rough hand Thalen could not help but feel a little more at ease thanks to the dwarf's friendly nature. He smiled broadly as he spoke "It is good to meet you Dolgrath I look forward to working with you. I will say now I appreciate the role you will play in my betterment as a magic user." As he finished, he released the dwarf's hand. The headmaster waited patiently until the greetings had been shared before speaking "Well now that you are friendly. I will leave you to your devices, Dolgrath will help you in all aspects from here out. I have arranged for your room to be next to his. Now, I have much to do so get out of my office." His voice was light with humor, but the wave of his hand dismissing them was unmistakable. Taking his queue, Thalen stood and bowed slightly towards the older mage before following the dwarf out, keeping pace only a few steps behind.

The new companions exited the office, the door closing behind them silently as if of its own accord. As they passed through the portal Dolgrath looked to Thalen beckoning him to follow with a small gesture of his hand. They made their way through the large wood and stone halls of the College; Thalen could not help but marvel at the construction and the beauty of the place. The intricate stonework played throughout every room, hall, and ceiling. "I see ye gawking at the stonework of the place." The dwarf said casually causing Thalen to jump from the sudden disturbance of the relative silence. He could not help think to himself that for somewhere so large with a fair number of people everything felt peaceful. Dolgrath chuckled, the sound gruff and deep before he continued "We Dwarves made this place you know, we be the finest builders in all the kingdoms, the finest workers of stone and metal upon the face of this world. Not a one can surpass our ability to work in any and all materials...well except wood. Those durned fairy Elves be better but in iron and steel none be surpasin us." As he finished his voice was filled with unapologetic pride. Thalen chuckled, though as he looked back at the walls, he could not help but agree with his tutors boastful words. Thalen could only think that it seemed as though the walls themselves were as much tapestries as those that sat upon them, the many intricate patterns decorated every surface being a truly amazing feet given the obvious strength and durability of the gray stone.

Looking over at his tutor Thalen could not help but think of how odd it was to see a dwarf in such a remote place "Tell me Dolgrath, how is it that you have come to be here? I do not mean offense, but I find it strange to find one of the deep folk in such a remote place, especially being so far from the front lines or the mountains and forests of your homeland." The dwarf sighed seeming annoyed, though Thalen was unsure if it was at his question or something else and spoke "Well lad ye bring a good question and a good point in kind. I was at the front but after taking a pair of arrows to me chest I was brought to an infirmary near the front. After a few days they felt it was best to bring me'self back here to be looked after. Not that I be needing care as though I be some sort of babe." He grumbled in annoyance. Thalen was somewhat confused by the dwarf's words, his expression showing it plainly as he spoke "I thought that only Mages of the Third circle are considered fit for battle. Are you not of the Fourth circle and therefore an apprentice and not a full mage?" Even as he was finishing the dwarf was chuckling and shaking his head. "Ye are a quick study aren't ye. Yes, ye be correct if I were a human or elf, however, I be far too short and good looking for that to be the case." He said with a toothy grin, before clearing his throat "We dwarves do things a little differently than ye do. There be far too few of us to be pickin and choosin who can 'nd can't fight. So those of us that be part of the Fourth circle are already accomplished warriors and fighters by the time our magical potential shows. Unlike ye humans who take only till ye be a few years of age, it won't appear in one of my kind until at least twoscore years have passed. I myself be forty-eight years past me birth 'nd only showed the ability at forty-four. So, though I be a member of the order I still fight alongside me kin as for every hunerd of ye there be merely ten o' we." He finished pounding his fist upon his robed chest.

Nodding Thalen lapsed into silence, as they made their way to the Western end of the keep. As the pair passed through archway after archway one couldn't help but notice the area becoming less ornate and more functional and all the while he found them passing more members the order, these members being of all races and circles. They stopped after passing the final archway, taking the chance to examine his surroundings, his eyes wandered to the keystone of the arch they had just passed through. Set within the stone was a glowing symbol of the Order and as they approached the next archway, he realized that each arch they passed had a symbol similar though not identical. The symbols were all the same save for the number of stars below the palm, going from three to two and finally to one as they reached the end of the long hall. "This be our section of the hall; it may not be the nicest, but it be home for now." Dolgrath said before pointing to two doors set next to each other as he continued. "The one on the left be yer room and that on the right be mine. I'll give ye a moment to settle in and change into your robes. I'll come a call at lunchtime, it be just a few hours from now, to bring ye down to the main hall. After that we'll begin teaching ye about magic." Nodding his farewell the dwarf went to one of the two doors and entered leaving Thalen to enter the other, the door closing with a soft click of the latch behind him.

Thalen took a breath to steady his nerves before making his way towards the entrance of his room, once he felt centered, he opened the heavy wooden door and stepped inside. As it slowly swung closed, its latch clicking behind him, he looked about the mid-sized room taking in what was to be his new home. It was a modestly furnished room its walls were much the same as those of the hall, intricate carvings giving texture to them as the patterns lead lazily to a peaked window set within the southern wall, it facing out into a corner of the large courtyard outside. A chair and small desk sat in the northern corner with a bookshelf beside it already filled with variously colored texts. A chest of drawers sat below the window. Atop it was several unlit candles waiting to be placed and lit as needed, stretching along the western wall of the room was a small bed, a pillow sat atop it accompanied by a neatly folded blanket. The room's configuration left a good amount of the wooden floor free of furniture or general clutter. Thalen found himself appreciating that, as it gave him enough space to continue his sword training in solitude. He doubted that there was much call for a martial practice area, though he resolved to check if the garrison had one.

Taking a moment to get acclimated to his new world, he approached his bed quickly setting up the blanket and pillow before laying down to think. *"So, this is how it all begins. Sitting in a room waiting for my tutor to come and get me for lunch, not exactly as fantastic as I had originally imagined it would be."* Chuckling to himself he stood and walked to the wardrobe, opening the top drawer he found a set of robes waiting for him. Taking them out he placed them on the bed inspecting them he found he appreciated their black steely color, it making the material seem almost shiny. After taking a moment to check the size against his body he felt satisfied with them and took off his travel worn clothes setting them aside before putting on a fresh linen shirt and hoes accompanied by his new robes over top. The robe hung rather loosely upon him unlike his various military garb causing him to instantly dislike them and their movement restricting properties, he decided he much preferred his more fitting military cloths and armor. Letting out a frustrated sigh he examined his discarded sword and belt which sat upon the bed. Making a decision he set it across his waist, cinching it to a point where it was comfortable, the addition of the belt relieved some of the looseness of the robes and the weight of his weapon reassured him of his place in the world.

Looking out the window towards the sun he gauged the time, figuring he had just over an hour to midday meal. That in mind he examined the spines that lay visible within the bookshelf, he brought the chair over to it and began reading the titles to himself. *The History of Magic, The Order of Eoch's Embrace: The Start of the Order* and many other such titles littered the shelves, he continued reading until one caught his eye *"Spells and How They Work, a bit on the nose but I suppose this might be useful."* He thought to himself, as he took the book from its spot. Moving the chair once more, he brought it over to the desk, setting the thick leather-bound tome upon it. Opening the red hued cover to the first page he began reading silently.

"The ways in which one works, and forms spells vary depending upon multiple factors. However, the important thing one must always remember is that any mage may cast any spell in any place and at any time. The power of any mage is simply equal to the mages ability to exercise their will upon the energy flow present within our world, though the ease of use can be affected by the magical affinity of the area itself. However, some mages are better at this than others, just as some mages are better suited for certain types of magic. First let us examine the races and the different types of magic…"

Thalen continued reading for a few minutes before stopping, only making it a few more pages as he found the words matching Cameral's lesson regarding magic. As he realized the effort Cameral had put into educating him during their journey, he found himself very grateful at the First Mage's efforts. He turned past the first few chapters before coming upon information the First mage had not covered in his lessons.

"There are two types of magic that play a part in our world. We have what one would call elemental and arcane, though both of these types of magic have vastly different effects their power is derived in the same fashion. Whether one is creating a chair or blasting their foes with fire, a wizard or mage must draw power into themselves before releasing it with the appropriate combination of words. A mage will also determine where the power is released from, though any part of the body may be used most mages prefer to use their hands. This is typically due to the hands being able to provide greater control and finesse when one directs their spell's abilities. Granted some mages will use certain objects to enhance and direct their power, however, this is more advanced magic and requires greater practice and natural ability."

Thalen stopped once more rubbing his eyes as the fatigue of travel, unexpected happenings and excitement set in. He could not help but think that though the information was interesting it was neither practical nor useful at the moment, at least not until he learned how he was to gather in the power around him. He closed the book as he stood to his feet, as if on cue there was suddenly a rapping knock that came from his door. Placing a hand to the sword at his hip he slowly opened the door relaxing as he recognized the figure before him. Dolgrath gave him a small nod saying "Good to see ye in yer robe, ye look mighty fancy. Come let us be going to lunch now and after we be starting your learnin quite proper." With wave of his meaty hand, he started walking back towards the main hall. Thalen grumbled with a little annoyance before shutting his door and walking quickly to catch up to his dwarfish tutor. Hearing his grumbling the Dwarf let out a goodhearted chuckle and with a large smile spoke "I take it ye are less than pleased with the situation. Well don' ye be worryin' I promise ye will find yer time interesting." The dwarf seemed to be oblivious that he was the source of Thalen's annoyance and continued to assure him "Don't ye fret, classes don't start till tomorrow so ye will have time to adjust yerself to the building. I'll give ye the grand tour before we be startin your learnin." He said clapping in excitement.

The pair continued on in silence for some time, passing far fewer people than they had earlier that day. As they drew closer to their destination Thalen picked up on a sound like a low roar that came from the main hall. It only growing as they came closer to its large double doors as they loomed before them as they entered into the room, they found a veritable sea of people within. To the best that Thalen could tell nearly 350 mages of all shapes, sizes, and ranks milled about the great hall, each person moving towards tables laden with food and drink of all types covering every inch of the long oaken surfaces. He looked towards Dolgrath opening his mouth to speak but was stopped by the dwarves' upraised hand. "Aye, there be many mages within these halls. Far more than ye can tell when we be all spread out; follow me and I'll get us to our designated tables. Before ye ask the tables be separated by the circle ye belong to. Our tables be the ones in the southeastern corner of the hall, follow me." He turned and started pushing his way through the throng with Thalen following in his wake.

The suddenly surly dwarf pushed his way past everyone creating a veritable fissure behind him allowing Thalen to follow easily behind until they reached a table with space for the pair. Dolgrath sat beckoning for Thalen to take a seat at the dark wooden table, which Thalen did gratefully though he found himself nearly overwhelmed with the fare before them. The table was filled with all forms of meats, cheeses, breads and more. A platter with knife and fork sat in front of him and without a second thought he followed his dwarvish companion's example piling the plate high with food and eating his fill. As he ate, he looked about the tables taking in his fellow diners, taking the time to take stock of their varying features. From the pointed ears of elves to the blue tinged skin of the Raital many different people were attending the college, though he could not help but think they likely took far more traditional paths compared to his own. No individual stood out amongst the throng, all speaking in various languages to friend and strangers both, all accepting, at least on the surface, those around them without question.

Thalen and his companion spoke little, enjoying their meal as they sat absorbed in their own thoughts, as once the spectacle had worn off Thalen felt little need to look about the room as he had before. That is save for passing glances around the room whenever quick movements occurred, as his unconscious habits took over. When they were both finished Dolgrath motioned again for Thalen to follow him and guided him out of the main hall once again. The pair had passed through the eastern door of the giant room before the dwarf finally spoke again "Sorry for not talking much, I don't much like it in there. Far too many people be in there at these times, makes it hard to hear one another. So ye know we be going to the practice rooms o'er here, this wing be housin' the classrooms, practice rooms and the library. Ye may be findin' some interestin' things in there, meself well I don't be goin' in there too often." Stopping in front of a room Dolgrath spoke again. "Ah, here be one. Ye know which they be by the glowing rune carved next to the doorway." He said pointing towards a fiery yellow symbol on the doorway's right. The symbol appeared as an explosion surrounding a palm. "The builders wished to use our dwarvish letters, but they realized the rest o' ye don't always read our language. So, they went with these runes instead, they be more like...what be that word...right they be like pictures." The dwarf said snapping his fingers in remembrance. Beckoning Thalen to enter the room, his short companion continued on "Come on, let's get ye started. The sooner ye be learnin' what I be teachin' the sooner we be drinkin' instead of thinkin'" Dolgrath finished with a hearty laugh as Thalen followed, eyes rolling ever so slightly towards the heavens.

CHAPTER TEN

As Thalen entered the room, it's appearance took him by surprise, as the room was in stark contrast to the rest of the College. It was neither intricately decorated nor beautifully furnished, in fact the room was bare, its stone walls completely empty of decoration with a plain wooden floor to match. Though the room itself seemed plain Thalen felt it thrum with power and was shocked by the sheer amount that seemed to be contained within this room. He felt himself involuntarily freeze mid-stride, barely free from the doorway leading in as the room threatened to overwhelm his every sense. Noticing Thalen's reaction Dolgrath spoke with poorly disguised amusement "Aye my friend I had the same experience meself when I first came into one of these rooms. Ye'll get used to it I promise ye that. Take a moment to adjust and when ye are feelin good we'll get started."

Thalen nodded, and took a few moments to center himself, slowly he felt his body adjust to the raw power surrounding and coursing throughout the room and by extension himself. As he felt his mind clear he shook his head in wonder, finding his voice once more "So much power in one room, I know I have little experience but that was truly overwhelming. How is this possible? How can one area hold so much power that it rendered me senseless..." he asked his tutor, his voice trailing off with wonder and just a little concern. The dwarf nodded his understanding as he spoke "Do not worry yerself this is not a normal thing. Ye see when me kin built this place, rooms like this were built upon pockets of strong natural magic. The magic was harnessed by runes set within the stone and wood o' the room. If ye look hard ye'll see them and ye'll see them glow as we start to draw upon the power." In time with his words, he began to create a glowing white light that lay delicately within his palm, as it came into being various runes lit up throughout the room, the sudden multitude of colors washing the room in an eerie, though enchanting, glow. Thalen was caught off guard as he found himself feeling the light's creation as well as its release, as Dolgrath released the power feeding the spell.

Upon the spells release the runes' light died out leaving nothing but the light coming from previously unnoticed skylights above, along with a few lights like the one the dwarf had just created. "Why do those lights not cause the ruins to glow?" Thalen asked, pointing towards one of the golden lights suspended near the ceiling. While he looked in the direction Thalen had pointed, he answered, his voice becoming of a teacher, as the dwarf fell fully into this role. "The ruins only glow so much when the power is being gathered during a spell's creation and when power be fed into the spell itself. Those lights were created a long time ago by immensely powerful mages and do not require a constant source of power like the one I created meself. Though they'll last about a month before they'll be needin more power channeled into them. I don't right understand how to do it meself but there seems to be a way to create something without needin' to constantly fill it with power." The dwarf's face scrunched in thought and curiosity, yet he soon shook himself from his thoughts and continued. "Alright Mr. Fancy Robe let's get ye started. First what I'll be teaching ye is how to draw upon the power o' the world at will. Now be sure to do what I tell ye, ye can start by movin over there." The dwarf said as he pointed a thick finger at a spot in the center of the room.

Quietly sighing to himself Thalen moved to the indicated location before turning back to his tutor. Once Thalen was in position the dwarf nodded and began teaching "Right now here is what ye need to do, follow me instructions closely and ye should manage. Now, I want ye to close your eyes and relax yer body, ye want to feel the power flowing through ye. Ye want the power to move through ye as though ye were nothing more than a channel it be moving through." Taking in the dwarf's words Thalen focused, closing his eyes and slowly allowing the power within the room to course through him. "Right, now lift yer hand and think about a globe o' light like the one I did meself. When ye have it in yer mind say the words, *Col'tith Dorint,* and when ye say them be sure ye have the globe set in yer mind." Dolgrath went silent allowing Thalen to concentrate upon his task.

Allowing himself to fall further inward Thalen began to picture his intent, slowly and carefully form small ball of blue light in his mind's eye. Taking his time, he shaped the ball and thought of its faint glow, surrounding the soft shape with his will and desire. Once the image was set in his mind he gathered the power, it surging through the room and gently pulling it into himself as he transferred it to a singular point in his hand. As he did this it felt almost as though he was not in control of his own body, it was as if instinct or the very power itself took control for a few moments. As he lost himself in the feeling, he did not notice as he lost the shape in his mind just as he spoke the words "Col'tith Dorint." The power released, yet instead of forming a soft glowing org a beam of pure light shot forth from Thalen's upturned palm striking the ceiling above. Yelling in surprise Thalen and even Dolgrath jumped back covering their eyes from the suddenly bright glow in the dimly lit room. After collecting themselves the pair looked up finding a dark black mark upon the ceiling's previously pristine stone. After composing himself Thalen turned to find a wide eyed Dolgrath staring his way, shaking his bearded head as he spoke "Well that was one hell of a try, just next time be sure ye keep the shape of a ball in yer mind. I cann'ie say I ever seen somethin' like that afore though, nearly singed me beard! Ye give it another go, I'll be takin' meself over here while ye do." The dwarf finished making a bit of a spectacle as he took large steps away from where Thalen stood.

Thalen shook himself of the shock from his previously failed attempt, once settled he again began drawing in the energy of the world around him. Closing his eyes, he once more slowly formed the orb of blue light in his mind's eye, while blocking out them soft, but distracting, glow of the runes as they flared to life around him. The vision set within his mind he focused, channeling the power into his palm once more all the while taking time to ensure his mind remained on the task and did not lose his all-important image. His confidence grew again, as he saw the power take form into his desired crafting, the gentle form of a lightly glowing green orb suddenly flickering to life in his hand. Opening his eyes he took in his work *"Not blue but this was a step in the right direction at least."* He thought to himself as he took a few more moments to admire his effort before dismissing the power with the close of his hand.

Thalen heard his tutor give a grunt of approval "Well done lad. Ye did it and ye didn't get us killed doin' it, ye be a quick learner that be without a doubt. Alright how bout we try one more thing and then well do some talkin'. Now I be wantin ye to create yourself a chair, nothin' fancy or special just so we can sit. Now, be watchin me as I do this." As the dwarf walked toward him Thalen felt the power begin to grow within his stout frame. Upon reaching Thalen, the dwarf mumbled some words causing white smoky tendrils to spill from his hand accumulating slowly into a high-backed chair. Thalen noticed a few beads of sweat trickling down the dwarf's brow as the end of his spell approached. With a final word Dolgrath cut the flow of energy and took a deep breath to steady himself as he sat in his new chair. "If ye can't tell magic that creates an object takes a bit out o' the caster, I'll be takin a moment as you craft your own spell. Much as when ye made the globe, picture what ye wish and when ye go to form the energy say *Talin Dorint*. There be one last thing ye need to be sayin when ye finish the spell. If ye don't remember to say it ye'll find yerself falling to the ground as ye go to sit. Ye must finish with *Alzalar* it will seal the magic and allow the object ye make to exist, as more than just an image, for a few hours afore the magic breaks apart." Settling deeper into the chair the dwarf let out a grateful sigh, leaning deeply into the cushioned chair he watched Thalen expectantly.

After a few failed attempts Thalen managed to create his chair and seal it correctly, he quickly found that keeping the magic from tearing itself apart was harder than Dolgrath had made it seem. He could not help but think of the several failed attempts and a bruised backside attesting to that sentiment, as at one point he sat in a chair for a minute before it broke apart. However, through trial and error he finally created a chair that had lasted, sitting upon it when it became apparent it would not leave him falling to the floor. Thalen sat back comfortably in his creation, a small feeling of pride washing over him only to be ruined by the sounds of snoring. Roving his eyes to his tutor, Thalen found him asleep as the dwarf leaned deeply into his cushioned chair. Thalen felt his temper well up yelling at the dwarf in a rage "Wake up or by the Gods I will set your damned beard on fire!" Thalen watched the dwarf jump awake, falling out of his chair and landing unceremoniously on the ground, his eyes wide and looking around in surprise. Seeming to finally remember where he was, he quickly jumped to his feet and took a threatening step towards Thalen face overwhelmed with anger and annoyance. "What do ye mean set me beard on fire? If ye even look wrong at me beard, I'll beat ye until ye won't even recognize yerself in a mirror" the dwarf's eyes were squinted a dangerous gleam in them. Thalen glared back at his tutor, yet slowly the anger broke, and he began to chuckle, his mind fresh with the dwarf's graceless fall to the ground only a few seconds before. As his chuckling grew slowly into laughter, he found the demeanor of Dolgrath cracking as the dwarf himself slowly began chuckling. This continued until the tension eased and laughter erupted from the pair, relaxing as the dwarf returned to his seat.

The dwarf ran a hand through his thick beard as he addressed his pupil once more "I like ye lad, ye've got stones, not every day that someone threatens a dwarf's beard and lives. Still, I don't think yer friend the First Mage would be happy if he came lookin' for ye tonight only to find yer body." The dwarf said as he slowly became more serious. "Alright, time for the fun stuff to be over, let us get to business after all we still have the room for a wee bit longer." Thalen came back to himself and nodded his assent to the dwarf. "Aye, I like you as well Dolgrath. You seem a good man and I look forward to lessons with you going further. I leave myself in your more than capable hands, please begin teaching." As he finished his mouth involuntarily upturned into a mischievous smirk, he could not help but imagine the many ways he would get back at his new companion for falling asleep during his lesson. Dolgrath looked at him suspiciously, as if trying to read his mind, before shrugging his broad shoulders in surrender.

"Alright now ye have a lil practice at drawin the power into ye, that be a good thing and ye did it pretty well for yer first time. Yet, yer only a beginner so don't be getting too full o' yerself. Ye've only scratched the surface of what ye might be able to do. Now we'll be talkin bout a few other uses o' yer magic might, not all thing we can be doin' with magic be as benign as what we've done in here. Ye be keepin' in mind any mage has the power to do this" he pointed at the chair Thalen was sitting upon and then continued "and other things like create balls o' fire or shards o' ice. The feelin the power gives ye as ye do these are different nearly every time. When ye create a ball o' light or even an arcane missile ye will always feel the neutral gatherin of the power, much like ye felt when ye created yer chair. Ye will feel what I can only describe as full o' the stuff, yet when we start talkin bout the elemental like magic well that be a different type o' iron." He started chuckling at some joke that Thalen did not quite understand. "What exactly do you mean, how exactly is it so different?" Thalen asked as the dwarf's laughter stilled. Dolgrath became more sober as he placed a hand beneath his chin as he thought, his face scrunched in concentration. While Thalen awaited his tutor's answer, he looked up through the skylight noticing for the first time the fading light, it became immediately obvious that the afternoon was near its end and night was fast approaching. *"I must have lost track of time. I did not think it had been so long, I must not forget that Cameral wishes to speak to me tonight. Though I don't know when, he never did mention that did he, though I suspect he will appear when I least expect... and likely when it is least convenient."* Thalen let out a soft sigh of resignation before allowing his mind to wander a bit as he waited for Dolgrath's response.

Suddenly Dolgrath yelled out in excitement as he turn to face Thalen "Ah ha! I got it, sorry it took me a minute to figure out the answer to yer question." Seeming to realize how loud he had been, his next words were quieter though a chuckle of embarrassment did escape his lips before continuing. "Sorry about that, so anyway each magic feels different. It be pretty easy to understand the ways they be feelin' different, ye see ye feel the element that yer using. So, if ye use fire ye feel the heat contained within ye as yer casting, if yer casting ice ye'd feel cold as ye gathered the power within ye..." though Dolgrath was still explaining Thalen for just moment heard nothing as his mind went back to the battle, the feeling of extreme cold he had felt returning fully to his senses. As his mind traveled back in time the shards of ice and the blood of friend and foe once more consumed his thoughts and senses. "Hey, ye durned fool are ye even listenin to me?!" Thalen snapped back to reality as the words of the thunderous and angry dwarf finally took hold. He shook himself from his stupor immediately apologizing "I am sorry, I was remembering the first time I used my powers, continue please." He accepted the dwarf's annoyed look with good grace as his tutor continued. "Anyways as I were sayin, before ye drifted off, ye experience the feeling o' the type o' magic ye are lookin to cast. Yer personal strength and will shields ye from the power otherwise ye may do real damage to yerself and others. If ye draw in more power than ye can handle, then it'll exit from ye unpleasantly. Doin anythin from killin ye to renderin ye unconscious for some time, that also depends on yer personal strength. That danger be why it is right important to practice and make yerself stronger through it."

Thalen was hardly aware the dwarf had finished speaking before his mind once more wandered to the day he discovered his ability. The dwarf's words echoing in his head as he realized how close he had come to his death, yet he was not quite sure if he was relieved or sad that he hadn't met it. As he pondered this, he looked to Dolgrath realizing he had missed yet another thing his tutor had said. "I am sorry Dolgrath, I drifted away again. What did you say?" the dwarf shook his head in annoyance before he answered "It's a good thing I said what

I did and not somthin important. I was sayin let's be done for the day, I know the First Mage is wantin to see ye afore the day comes to its end. So, feel free to head back to the main hall to eat and to yer room until he comes for ye. Meself, well I be stayin here for a time be wantin to get some practice in meself. Next time get yer head together, yer almost as bad as an elf, can't be keepin the topic in ye head." The dwarf waved for Thalen to go but not before flashing a reassuring grin as he talked to himself under his breath about something Thalen would never know. Thalen stood and turned fully towards the dwarf before giving a small bow and turning to move towards the practice room doors. Once out of the room he briefly considered eating but found that his hunger was muted by the rolling emotions that sat deep in his stomach, bypassing the main hall to continue his trek back to his room.

CHAPTER ELEVEN

As Thalen passed through the final archway leading to the Fourth Circle's section of the dormitories his mind began to wander, thinking of various things before he eventually settled yet again on Sarah and the opportunities he missed. His lesson with Dolgrath about the experience of power flowing through the body had struck a chord in him, triggering his memories of that day, it reminding him again of just how fragile he still was when thinking of her. As Thalen finally reached his room, he let out a sad sigh as he reached out and pushed his door open. Where he expected to find an empty room, he instead stood facing the First Mage Cameral Darkweave sitting calmly in a plush high-backed chair. "Ah, hello Thalen I was expecting you. Please take a seat." He finished indicating the chair across from him, one which matched his own. Thalen's first thought was of the fact that neither of the chairs were previously within the room and looked completely out of place in the typically modest abode. Rolling his eyes at the mage's antics Thalen crossed the room taking a seat as indicated, sinking into the soft fabric appreciatively. He had not realized how tired he was, feeling the last of his energy drain away, making him appreciate the comfortable chair even more. Between the long journey and his use of magic he felt stretched thin and wished for nothing, but his bed and the sleep promised within it. Cameral chuckled softly at Thalen's reaction "You appear a little on the tired side Thalen. I didn't realize that learning would take so much out of you, after only one day you seem ready to fall over." The First Mage said this with a smile, one which widened as Thalen returned his words with a dry look.

When it became, apparent Thalen would not rise to the bait more than he already had, the elf chuckled "Well Thalen, I did not come here to make fun of you. I suppose it is more correct to say I am not here to only do that; I have come to tell you that I must be off for a time. Having seen you safely here I am afraid that I must begin another journey as sadly a member of the highest circle has very little time to truly rest." He said with a rueful smile. As the elf spoke Thalen sat up straighter in his chair, the implications of what the First Mage was saying had fully dawned on him. Accompanying this realization was the cold hand of uncertainty that gripped his heart. Thalen was surprised to realize that he did not want the mage to leave, as he was the only real point of familiarity left. *"If he is leaving, so is Gerard. I am now to be left in this place by myself. Dolgrath seems good enough, yet I have spent but a short time with him. Apparently, these strangers are more than just that to me now, either that or I have no one else to consider friend."*

Thoughts whirled through his head as he truly understood just how much he had come to depend on the eccentric, if not steady, mage. Fully recognizing that he was about to be dumped into a very new and unknown world was a concerning one to say the least and must have shown in his expression. This being evident as the normally mischievous elf became somber and serious "You will be fine here Thalen; you are going to be a capable mage, and this place is safe and won't let you blow anyone up. Truthfully, I wish I could stay and ensure your transition was smooth, yet the war goes on even while I am away. Things have developed and I must be there to help guide their course, else things may go awry. Nonetheless I wish you the best, my friend, in this new adventure. I leave in the morning long before you will awaken and you have so many interesting classes tomorrow!" he said with greatly feigned excitement, resting upon his face.

"However, before I leave, I feel obliged to give you something, both a bit of knowledge and a small gift. That is if you would accept them." Cameral paused awaiting Thalen's answer expectantly, looking at the elf Thalen couldn't help but smile a little and let out a sigh before nodding his acceptance. Cameral chuckled at his display and grabbed a bag that had been unseen to this point from behind his chair. Thrusting the bag into Thalen's lap he spoke "I think you may find this useful during more than just your time here at the College. First, I will let you take a look at it, and then I will tell you a bit about it." Cameral fell silent which took Thalen by surprise, yet the elf made it clear he intended to say no more until Thalen opened the bag. Reaching in he found his hand touching a very familiar item, wrapping his hand around it he pulled from the velvet sack a sword and scabbard, the item familiar and yet unlike anything he had ever seen. Taking a moment to examine it Thalen took in the deep brown scabbard, bands of a silvery metal wrapped around it, each halo equally spaced from hilt to tip. Examining the hilt of the blade he found that its cross guard was relatively thin yet seemed sturdy, in place of more typical square ended quillons, two wings, as if those of a bird, stretched out from the hilt and blade, the tips of the wings bending slightly downward to cover the hands. The grip was wrapped in leather with enough space for a hand and a half, making it perfect for either a single or double grip as the situation called for. The pommel appeared to be the head of a robin, its appearance seemingly out of place on the weapon, yet he could not imagine a better fit in its place. Thalen came to his feet, checking for space before he reverently drew the blade, its silvery white metal gleamed in the low light as it came free from its scabbard. Scrawled upon the blade were elaborate ruins which ran their way up stopping at the area where the fuller met the central edge, yet even as the runes stopped intricately inlaid patterns played their way up the remainder of it before finally reaching the tip.

As Thalen marveled at the weapon the First Mage began to speak once more "The knowledge I wish to gift you has to do with this blade you have within your hand. I will not tell you much as I wish for you to learn of it yourself, however there are a few bits that I will share. One of the first things being the name of the blade you now own, in the common tongue it is named *Robin's Tail*, it's elvish name is far too difficult for you to pronounce let alone remember and so I will not tell it to you." He chuckled good naturedly, before he could continue Thalen interrupted, respect and awe clung to his voice. "Thank you Cameral, this is a Kingly gift and one I feel I do not deserve in the least." He moved to return the blade to the mage. "No." Cameral said holding his hands up as he motioned for Thalen to sit back down. When he had seated himself, the elf continued

"I wish for you to have this as you will find far more use for it than I ever would. You would also certainly have more use for it than the vault it has been sitting in for the last twenty years." The mage paused to take a swig from a wineskin Thalen had not noticed, wiping his mouth with his sleeve he continued "There were more things I had considered telling you about the blade but now that I have thought on it more that does not sound all that fun." Hearing this Thalen threw the mage an annoyed look, which only seemed to increase the elf's mirth, yet before Thalen could say anything Cameral continued. "I wish for you to discover things about the blade for yourself. It will give you something to think upon as you spend your time in these dusty halls beyond that of your studies or the wanderings of a mind from outside of these walls. There is a vast library here with much history perhaps you might find your answers there as you will find none from me." He stood dissipating the magic of his chair as he did. "I am sorry for the sudden end of our meeting, as sadly it is getting late, and I must go and prepare for my journey tomorrow. Have a good evening, Thalen."

With that the First Mage made for the door yet as he did Thalen stood quickly surprising the mage by grabbing his arm in a warrior's grip. "Thank you Cameral Darkweave, I wish you a safe journey and though it pains me to say... I look forward to any meeting of ours in the future." Thalen released the mage from the grip and took a step back. The First Mage regained his composure and smiled a little as he spoke "Thank you Thalen, I am sure our paths will cross again. Though sadly it will not be for some time. Please do try not to tear this place down while I am away, I do not wish to explain to the Council how someone I brought in tore a chunk from a spire." Laughing, Cameral waved his hand in farewell before disappearing, the door left untouched and unopened, yet Thalen knew he was alone, left with nothing but his thoughts and more questions that needed answers.

Thalen looked from the door towards his new sword, *Robin's Tail,* his eye again catching the sheen of the silvery white blade. *"How odd, this metal I have never seen before. It is a truly amazing blade, even as I held it, I felt as though it wished to reach out to me, no...that's not exactly right almost as though it wished to sing out in glory. Perhaps I will take Cameral's advice and learn more about this weapon."* He yawned as he felt his mind slow as the excitement of the day and the moment truly started to slipped away *"I don't think I will be answering any questions tonight. Tomorrow will come soon enough and having classes...that will be annoying. Well, I may as well sleep now and worry about the rest later."* His mind made up, Thalen placed the sword, once more in its scabbard, upon his desk and laid down in his bed. *"Well...I wished for a bed not too long ago. I suppose I got one."* Sighing in relaxation, Thalen closed his eyes dropping into a restless sleep.

Fire, death, and destruction rampant throughout the town. The College Keep damaged as the massive spires fall to the ground. Spells of fire, ice, and pure arcane shoot from atop the walls of the town as hundreds of arrows shot by the defenders fall from the sky. Looking out at the previously bare ground filled with bodies both dead and alive, a veritable sea of orkish forms moving towards the dwindling defenders. He fells another feeling, a form pressed against his back before turning to see Dolgrath as Orks surround them. Even against these odds they whip their weapons about striking at any opening desperately fending off their foes. A great club smashes into his chest knocking him to the ground and a weapon held within a meaty green hand descends towards him for the killing blow. His eyes lock upon elven ones, her golden hair framing a dirty and grimy face yet her natural beauty shining through the filth as she screams silently in his direction. Suddenly the world goes dark.

Thalen awoke with a shock, his eyes wide as he sat up bare chested in the darkness. Slowing his breathing he created a glowing light within his palm lighting up the room in a blue glow. Looking about he saw nothing, recognizing that he was completely alone, the other chair Cameral created having dissipated some time ago leaving the room as it was before. *"It was just a dream, just a nightmare. It felt so real, yet I am here, and it is still night so it could not have been"* He let out a long breath calming his nerves once more as he wiped the sweat from his brow. After a few moments he settled down completely, allowing his eyes to close and drift off once more, but this time into a deep sleep.

CHAPTER TWELVE

Thalen woke just as the sun began to color the sky in the East, finding himself instantly awake and alert, his years of practice and training kicking in. It took him a moment to recognize where he was and tried to relax as he slowly fell back into the warmth of the bed. Although the bed was soft, he found himself surprisingly uncomfortable after having spent so many nights sleeping on either a hard cot or the ground, as it seemed his body did not know what to do with true comfort. Grumbling with displeasure he threw off the covers and stood stretching to alleviate himself of the many cramps that developed overnight, the room was surprisingly warm, feeling nearly as warm as the bed, though it held little adornment that would normally keep that warmth from seeping into the cold stone. Though he could still see a small film of frost on the windowpane hidden behind the curtains, it still felt as though spring had finally overtaken the cold bite of winter. Walking towards the window he gave a quick yank pulling the curtains aside to view the world outside. The snow that once covered the ground was slowly melting away as splotches of green and brown grass fought through reaching out towards the rays of the still wintry sun. Smiling at the thought of winter's passing he turned from the window and moved towards the desk and the sword resting upon it. His mouth set in a grim line as he considered again the First Mage and his gift. *"I wonder if I have the time to go to the library before classes. Wait...when are my classes anyway. You fool, I should have asked Dolgrath before going to see Cam..."* a knock on the door interrupted his rumination. Without thinking he turned on his heel and strode toward the entry to his room, taking a moment to steady himself, he opened the door with a quick jerk of the handle. Beyond the open door he found Dolgrath a surprised look on his face, his arm still raised as he was prepared to knock once more. Within moments the dwarf regained his composure "Well lad ye didn' have to be so quick about commin' to the door fer meself. I wanted to be lettin' ye know yer first class be startin in about two turns o' the water clock. I thought ye might be wantin' to get a bite before we be goin' to them." Scratching his chin the dwarf added "I forgot to say it yesterday, but we be in the same classes as well the headmaster thought it be better if yer around meself as much as possible.

So ye will be movin' around with me for now." As the dwarf finished, he threw Thalen a toothy grin.

Thalen relaxed, throwing his dwarvish companion a grateful smile while he spoke "Good, here I was worried that I would never know when my studies began...let alone where in this building they were." After a few moments of thought he continued "Yes, I do think I would like to eat before the classes. Let us be off then." Thalen went to step out of the room, but Dolgrath stopped him with an upraised hand "Now me friend I am sure the lasses may find yer figure attractive, but I don't think ye want to be leavin' yer room showin' it to the whole world." The dwarf declared as he laughed a broad grin growing on his face. Confused Thalen, looked down at his outfit...or rather lack of one, his chest bare as he wore nothing but the pants from the day before. Chuckling with some embarrassment he stepped back into the room "Yes, you seem to be right, give me a moment I will be out shortly. Closing the door Thalen walked over to the chest of drawers, taking out and dressing in shirt, clean breeches, and soft soled boots. Once dressed and comfortable in his attire he pulled on his robe, taking a moment to adjust the cowl to stop it from bunching uncomfortably behind his neck. He took a breath moving towards the door before stopping, his hand inches away from the handle, before turning to look at the sword still sitting in the same place it was before. Taking a few moments to decide, he chose to take it with him, walking over to it and attaching the scabbard to his belt in place of his old weapon. He took a moment to adjust the blade, adapting to its unexpectedly light weight, before walking over to the door once more, opening it and stepping into the hallway beyond.

Looking around the area he spotted Dolgrath waiting for him by the exit of the fourth circle dormitory, as he approached his dwarvish friend, he saw his face screw up in some confusion before shrugging and returning to a more casual demeanor. The dwarf's reaction made Thalen a little uneasy as only one thing came to mind that would cause it, that thing sat upon his hip bumping his leg on every third stride. Yet, it gave him comfort as well as firmed his resolve as he strode with the confidence of a military man. Once Thalen reached the dwarf, his tutor falling in step with him as the pair walked out of the dormitory wing and unerringly towards the hall. "Nice weapon ye have there, it's not the one ye had when I saw ye last night if my memory be right. Where'd ye get it and why did ye bring it with ye if I may be askin?" the dwarf asked his tone revealed far more curiosity than his typical stony face had shown. Thalen's hand moved involuntarily to the weapon's hilt as he answered. "It was a gift from the First Mage and before you ask my friend, I don't know how it came to him. He would tell me very little, yet that is the way of Cameral Darkweave, he is enigmatic in the best of times. Though far easier to answer is the reason it lies upon my hip. It is a twofold answer one being partly of habit and the other the desire for preparation, even in the safest of places one never knows when one may need a sharp blade." Dolgrath gave a grunt of agreement as he lifted his robe slightly revealing an axe hidden in its folds. With that they quietly continued as they slowly approached the start of their grand adventure to slay breakfast.

Once they had finished their meal the pair made their way towards the practice rooms, yet passed them all by, instead walking until they reached the end of the hall. Thalen looked around, his confusion evident, as he tried to understand the purpose of their coming down this hallway if it was not for one of the practice rooms. When suddenly, Dolgrath quickly gestured saying "Doth." After a moment, to Thalen's wonder and concern, the floor began to rise, and the ceiling above seemed to disappear as they were lifted to the second floor of the keep. As they rose his eyes went wide with childish wonder as he looked over to his tutor, who returned his look throwing a knowing wink at him before motioning down the newly revealed hall. As they moved through the overcrowded hallway Thalen found it difficult to keep up with the stout figure, as the small sea of bodies moved slowly in differing directions. Streams of people added to the mass as they rose into the hall from the floor below, descended from the floors above and filtered out of the many doors lining the walls. Finally, seemingly at random, Dolgrath picked a door and approached it before stopping at the entrance. As they did Thalen noticed a sigil, its pattern like that of the practice chamber they had seen the previous day. Yet, the symbol differed, as chiseled within the wall was a shape lit up with a blue light, it depicted an opened book with the numeral 324 scrawled below it. After a momentary pause they entered into the classroom, though just as they made it through the door Dolgrath stopped holding his hand up as he turned to Thalen "This be our first class, it be about the Formin' o' Magic, ye'll be learnin' a great deal of new words so be sure to write them down." Motioning for Thalen to follow him, the dwarf went on into the room stopping before two open desks "If ye put yer hand upon the desk it'll produce what ye need, parchment and the like. When yer done just place yer palm upon the desk again an' say "I'm done thank ye." When ye do the items will sink into the desk. Ye can do it on any desk, even that one in yer room, I don't be knowin how it be knowin who be tryin to get their things, but it be best not to question it. Alright we best be getting to some seats." Sitting in his own seat he motioned for Thalen to do the same.

As Thalen got comfortable in his chair, he took some time to look around the room. The space itself was surprisingly large, in fact it was closer to an amphitheater, stairs lead down to a large platform that stood slightly raised before the sea of desks. Sitting upon the back wall was a chalkboard awaiting use by the proctor of the class. Lining the walkways down were chairs and desks much as the one he sat at, each of them set at a near identical space as they stretched down to just before the stage below. As Thalen shifted again, he decided that it was uncomfortable at best, these chairs, which were made of an unpadded dark wood, matched the color and material of the desks set before them. Finally accepting his discomfort and he questioned if the lack of padding was to keep students from falling asleep, Thalen waited patiently for the class to start absorbed in thoughts of no great importance or note. He slowly grew bored before unconsciously examining the other men and woman entering the room, taking stock of his classmates, or he supposed his future comrades, as they each found a place for themselves within the cavernous room. What he found odd was not the assortment of peoples, as they represented every race within the Coalition, but instead there seemed to be so few of them. The more he thought the more he realized that he had seen very few people within the College itself, given its size, of course the place was not deserted, yet there could not be much more than one thousand within a place that could easily fit more than twenty times that number. As the trickle of students slowly came to a stop, he found that the desolate feeling struck home even harder as the auditorium they were in could have easily held at least a hundred students, yet he found his class to be hardly more than twenty.

Looking at Dolgrath, Thalen put words to his thoughts "Dolgrath, why are there so few people here? I would have thought this citadel of learning would have held thousands, it certainly is big enough to, yet it seems to barely hold hundreds within its walls. What is the reason for this if any that you know of?" Dolgrath looked over at him before returning his eyes to the front as he answered "What ye say be correct. There be so few here for a simple reason, this be a pretty remote place. Most o' the newer members are brought to one o' the larger collages on the other continents and not a small place like this. Those o' us who are here, are here because we have to be near the front lines...err at least as near as we can be if ye get me meanin'. We be the ones who are either close to bein' completed with studies or have actual battle experience for one reason or another. There be few o' us that are close to rising to the next circle and fewer o' us who've done some real fightin'" as he spoke a wolfish grin grew on his face, the thought of a fight seeming to draw it out of him. Thalen took a moment to absorb this but before he could respond he was interrupted by Dolgrath's raised had, his other pointing towards the stage below. Thalen shot him an annoyed, which the dwarf ignored or at least didn't seem to notice, before looking forward, finding a previously unnoticed feminine figure had entered the room and stood upon the stage before them. As the room gradually came to silence Thalen took the time to examine the woman standing before them. She was unquestionably human with blue eyes set within her soft rounded face, she was of middling height and slender with whitish grey hair pulled to the back of her head in a bun. She did not appear an elder, as her hair suggested, but seemed close to her middle years, yet even so her face held some youth, not girlish but filled with life. Once the room was fully silent, she spoke in a rich and strong voice "Good Morning all, I am Mistress St. Royne, however while you are within this room you may call me Professor. I shall be your guide through the world of Advanced Magical Theory and perhaps if we are lucky some of you will leave with a better understanding of forming magic. Now I know that most of you know me, but this is for those of you that have joined us recently and are new to the College. I greet you and hope that I am able to ignite a passion and love for learning as well as magic itself."

Mistress St. Royne turned towards the board and apparated a piece of chalk into her hand, much to Thalen's surprise, before reaching a slender arm up to head height. She spoke a few quiet words and with a small surge of power took her hand away from the chalk, leaving it suspended in midair. She turned to address the group "I understand that many of you have taken the basic courses as well have had some practice in the art. So, let me ask who can tell me how to form a basic spell?" Before she had even completed her sentence several hands shot up into the air, whether to impress the teacher or not Thalen could not say. After taking a moment to look them over St. Royne picked one at random. "Yes, Miss Skylark." The professor pointed to a young woman with blonde hair which sat just below her shoulder.

The woman stood to address the professor and in a quiet and soft voice spoke "The way we craft and create spells are through the gathering of the magical energy around us and the use of a word to cause the power to be released, we also use some form of gesture to direct the power in a certain direction depending on the intention of the spell." As her confidence seemed to grow her voice reflected it, becoming stronger and more animated until she finished answering before sitting back down. St. Royne seemed pleased with the answer as she complemented the woman "Very good Elara you are correct, however, there is a bit more to it than that." She began to pace seeming to collect her thoughts, as Thalen followed her with his eyes something seemed out of place in the background. He looked at the board and found to his surprise that the young woman's answer was written upon the board and the chalk had moved from its original place. It floated above waiting patiently for more words to dictate. *"The chalk wrote without Mistress St. Royne even touching or seemingly commanding it. Wait, didn't Dolgrath say something about taking notes if I..."* the thought remained unfinished as he placed his palms upon the top of his desk and without any effort a leather-bound book and quill seemed to ooze out of the desktop, it coming into being upon its still unmarked surface. Thalen shuddered slightly at the way in which the items appeared before picking up the book and flipping to the first page, unsurprisingly it was completely empty of script. His mind turning to the quill, he picked it up and searched for an ink well, yet none had appeared from the desk to accompany it. As he grew bored with the novelty of the situation he sighed in frustration before unconsciously placing the tip of the quill upon the blank page. To his surprise a blotch of ink appeared exactly where the tip had landed, his hand shaking slightly he continued scribbling before turning to a fresh page. Placing the quill to paper once more he wrote out the words that sat upon the board, finding the quill never seemed to run dry or light though no ink seemed to be stored within the quill itself. Thalen shook his head in wonder before realizing that he had lost focus on his professor, who he only now realized was mid-sentence far deeper into the lesson. He admonished himself for his lack of attention, though he was fortunate as he had not missed much, quickly catching up with the lecture as he provided his full attention to the difficult task of being a competent student.

"...it is quite interesting what one can do with magic without using a large number of words, this meaning that you do not have to spell out exactly what you wish to accomplish. For example, think of an act as simple as summoning a ball of light, consider the many words you would need to describe. These not only what you want to exist and when you want it to exist but also its appearance. Imagine if you had to describe the exact shape, color, how many you want there to be, and the many other aspects of the item you could describe. With further practice visualizing and a deeper understanding of what you want to create, along with your growth in general power, you will find that the same outcome can be accomplished with fewer words. Of course, the example I use requires only a single set of words, however there is a reason for this. We as a society have reached the point where the nature of light is locked within our minds, orbs of light are everywhere around us and so through the viewing of them we easily form the image within our mind because our concept is more solid. You see we speak words when we cast to solidify our intention for the magic as it forces us to think about our desire and leaves little room for the magic to interpret our casting. However, as I said, those with greater power and practice can accomplish the same things one could with those words and with greater speed and accuracy. These magic users are able to impress their will and intention upon the magical form simply through their thoughts, similar to what we can do with a simple ball of light.

This sounds simple yet is far more difficult than one would imagine. Another example of this is the simple offensive spell we refer to as fire bolt, you would say the words "Col'Fir" for fire, "Tole" for bolt or projectile and "Dorint" for it to form. Those words are essentially communicating your intention for the magic and solidifying your will, yet that is not all that is shaping your spell. Within your mind you are also applying certain parameters to the magic such as you want it to be hot and to fly out from perhaps your raised hand and not simply drop to the ground or sit within your palm. Your mind is already exercising a portion of your will upon it, yet that may not be strong enough to fully resolve the spells creation to the desired effect. Very few mages are able to exercise their will with single words let alone only their mind and singular gestures, though there are some high in the second circle and the first circle which can accomplish this feat." Thalen found himself barely able to keep pace with the Mistresses lecture, yet he knew it was a losing battle as he slowly started falling behind her words. After phrasing her words the best, he could he looked back up towards the stage, just in time to see a practice dummy appear out of the very air itself. *"I suspect this is going to get...interesting, I should try to keep my head down for now. The last thing I want are for people to think me incompetent... especially since I am. This should give me a good chance to get a measurement of those within my Circle."* He thought feeling both a combination of excitement and dread.

Finished with her creation magic the Professor addressed them again, her voice and smile mischievous "Now let us have a live demonstration of the theory, I know this is not practice time nor is it an applied magics class, however, this should be useful...as well as a little fun." She motioned for the young woman that had answered her previous question to come down the stage. "Miss Skylark if you would be so kind as to be our first demonstrator. Come now don't be shy, this has a good purpose not just for the fun of it." Standing and bowing to the Professor the young woman approached the stage allowing Thalen to get a better look at her, she was on the shorter side and was rather pretty in his opinion though his junior by at least a handful of years. As the woman reached the bottom of the stairs, she stopped near the dummy awaiting instructions. Looking towards Elara the professor spoke "What I want you to do is demonstrate the fire bolt spell for us. Once you have cast the spell I will then demonstrate as well, this should give us a live example of the difference I was speaking of." The professor moved to the opposite side of the platform and once set signaled Miss Skylark to begin when ready. After a few moments Thalen could feel the woman gathering in power and without further warning she spoke a series of words "Col'Fir Tote Dorint" and within the same second a mid-sized bolt of golden fire released from her palm striking the dummy with a terrific force as flames licked up its sides. Her display complete the woman lowered her hand and upon the teachers signaled turned to bow to the professor and then the class in turn before returning to her seat. The classes polite clapping echoing throughout the large room.

Once the student had returned to her seat Mistress St. Royne raised her hands for silence. "Well done, Elara, a good example of the spell, now watch as I cast the same spell." With that the Professor crossed the stage coming face to face with the dummy, in less than a quarter of the time she collected her will and with a singular word "Col'Fir" released a larger and more powerful bolt of purple fire from her palm, that bolt slammed into her target it, turning it into ash. The display of comparatively overwhelming force left the class in shock, as St. Royne turned back to the class, she raised an eyebrow making it plain she was waiting for their reaction, that understanding slowly sunk into the class as they broke out into an enthused applause. Thalen thought she seemed to chuckle a little before half bowing and raising her hands for silence once more. "As you can already tell I both collected the power quicker and was able to use fewer words to accomplish the same goal. That may have appeared easy for me to accomplish, yet that would be misleading as it took an equal amount of effort to accomplish that spell. The difference was instead of forming and informing the desire of the spell with words I did so within my mind, picturing it with detail and clarity. Yet, if I had done so with words, it would have taken me less effort than it had Elara due to our difference in practice and power. You may be wondering why it would have been slower than if I had simply used words and this would be because your image has to be near perfect as any loss of it would render the spell either useless or something other than what you wished. It is admittedly one of the few spells I am able to do that with and I am of the second circle, so do not think this is something you could go out and try without a great deal of practice. If you leave this class with nothing else remember this one thing, practice will improve your power, your spellcasting ability, and the efficiency of your casting." It seemed as though she was about to say more, when suddenly her head cocked slightly as if listening to something, after a moment of this she addressed the class once more "I'm afraid our time is up, so all of you please have a wonderful day and I will see you all tomorrow." She waved her hand and disappeared signaling definitively that the class was at an end.

As the class came to its sudden conclusion, he watched his supplies sink back into the desk before him, shuddering a little yet again at the sight. "That was different, that was a lot to take in for my first real day." The dwarf grunted in agreement and beckoned Thalen to follow him from the room. As they moved through the hallway his companion spoke, "I understand what yer feeling me friend. It can be tough to adjust to this place it be very different from... well it be different from anywhere. Then when ye start realizin' ye are in advanced classes and ye only just started usin' magic a few weeks ago." He blew out an exasperated breath "But don't ye fret between yer studyin' and me teachin' ye'll be all caught up in no time at all." The dwarf flashed a grin as he started walking down the hall making it obvious, he wished for Thalen to follow, after a few seconds of walking they reached another elevator pad, taking it up several levels as they went to their final class of the day.

As they walked the last few meters to the door Dolgrath looked at Thalen "I want ye to know that we only be havin' these two classes seein as we should be graduatin soon. Yet fer ye, well ye've been accelerated in yer rank for a reason not known to meself. And I don't think I want to be knowin' either, yet that means ye are gonna be workin hard and practicin a lot to catch up on what ye be missin." The dwarf put extra emphasis into his last sentence, obviously intent on driving the point home. Thalen nodded his understanding, as he fully understood his disadvantage when compared to the other fourth circle mages. He knew very well how much work he had to do, he wanted to make a good showing of himself so he could rejoin the fight. He started thinking about his situation and with a sudden realization, stopped cold putting a hand on Dolgrath's arm "Hold a moment, Dolgrath, Headmaster Pelorin mentioned tests when I spoke to him in his office yesterday. I only now realize I have not the faintest idea of what they are of nor when they are…" Dolgrath took a moment pursing his lips in thought on how best to answer the question. "Well, ye be lucky I have that answer for ye. Every year those who be good and ready to advance to the next circle will be given a shot to do just that. Most o' the folks ye saw in the class are gonna be among them includin' yerself and meself. There be three tests ye have to do to advance yer circle, the first is a show o' yer strength and control o' yer power. Now before ye go askin' they change 'em every time so I don't know what they are exactly." He looked in the direction of their destination after a moment he pushed his way into one of the empty practice rooms.

Once the door closed the dwarf looked at Thalen "I forgot we won't be havin our other class for a while, the professor was called to the front, and he won't be back for a month or so. The class be Battle Magic based so I'll be takin the time to teach ye some stuff for it. Where was I..." he trailed off his face set in concentration. After a few minutes Thalen prompted him "You were telling me about the tests Dolgrath." After a moment realization dawned on Dolgrath's face as he continued with his explanation "O' course how could I have forgotten. So, I told ye about the first test but not the other two, the second test is a puzzle of some type, it's supposed to make ye think about what yer doin', supposed to show yer magical control. While the third is a test o' yer magical might in a fight, it be the only test that never changes, it's a tournament o' sorts where we be pitted against other mages o' the fourth. Whoever wins has a banner put up with their name on it and some other prize that only the winners know about." Dolgrath finished pausing, seeming to give Thalen a moment to digest what he was just told, which he very much so did, considering the implications of the tests and what success in them would mean for his future. *"This can't get better can it, not only do I have to figure out all of this magic stuff so I can get back to the war. I also have to worry about these silly tests to show that I deserve to go back to it. By the Gods this turn of fortune has been anything but fortunate hasn't it."* He let out a long sigh crossing his arms and rested his chin on an upraised hand when, yet another wrinkle came to mind. "When is the next test my friend?" He asked, the dwarf was silent for a few moments before answering "It be in six months."

Thalen felt his heart drop at those words, his mind racing "Six months, by the Gods man how am I to be ready in six months! Hardly more than one month ago I did not even possess this damned power let alone understand it! Yet now... gods be damned Pelorin..." he cut short dropping his head in frustration, after taking a moment to collect himself he continued "When is the test after that one?" The dwarf looked at him, his expression sympathetic "It be a year after the next one, that be usually how long it takes fer a new fourth mage to be ready. I don't think ye have a choice if ye want to get yerself out o' here soon yer gonna have to be ready for this one." Thalen nodded; his goal identified he set his shoulders in determination. "That is the only option I have my friend, no matter how difficult the task I must attend the test in six months." Dolgrath smiled fiercely at him, the dwarf's sudden fire helping fuel Thalen's own. "Alright laddie, ye want to be ready for this one comin'! Then we better be getting to work."

CHAPTER THIRTEEN

The next few weeks were eventfully uneventful as Thalen spent nearly every waking moment at study or in the practice room with Dolgrath. Though not as rigorous training as that when he was in the Corps nor nearly as sapping as when he was in the field every day, he still found himself dropping into his bed each night falling deeply into a restful sleep.

Over those weeks, he slowly became more proficient in the use of magic and through daily practice stronger in turn. It also felt as though setting his mind to his various studies had grew his hunger for knowledge as he suddenly found Mistress St. Royne's class to be less of a chore and more of a treat. He had always been an indifferent student at best, yet he quickly found that he could not resist the mysterious lure of study which had so suddenly become a major part of his life, if not his entire life. He had made few friends as he found his compulsive need to learn consuming most of his time, yet he slowly grew close with Dolgrath and through his various assignments befriended Elara Skylark, the young woman from his first day of class, as well as an elvish woman Keela Balhorn.

Keela was young for an elf, yet that still made here nearly four times Thalen's 31 years, she had golden eyes shaped much as Cameral's with a slender physique that possessed an unnatural strength about her, one that all elves seemed to have. She had long dark hair that traveled down to the small of her back, it was shockingly straight with an odd mystical sheen to it. If looked at in the right light it seemed almost as though it was made of the finest glass. The few times Thalen found himself unoccupied, he would find himself in the main hall eating or in the library with his newfound companions, speaking about theory or on rare occasions just plain gossip. In the years to come when he would look back at that time, he found that it was the happiest time of his life, at least since this had all began, as when he was with them he found he could almost forget about the war and past beyond the College's stone wall. He found he could almost forget the loss of his greatest friend and companion, he could almost forget the pain the still flared now and then in his heart...but sadly only almost.

Thalen woke with a start, taking a moment to look about his surroundings, he found himself sitting at his desk in his room a book set before him, *The Theory of Advanced Conjuring* a dusty tome that was at best boring and at its worst sleep inducing. As far as Thalen was concerned it was only sleep inducing, having spent the last several hours trying to get through the first few chapters only to find himself having obviously fallen victim to its lackluster prose. He shook his head in disgust as he pushed the chair away from him standing near immediately into a stretch before he began to pace from one end of the room to the other. His mind came alive thanks to his impromptu nap. *"That book is just so boring, how is it that someone could take something interesting, like the summoning of creatures and objects, and make it put me to sleep! It is almost as though those that write these books have never had an interesting or engaging thought or conversation in their entire life."* A sudden knock at his door interrupted his train of thought and taking a few short breaths to calm his mind he walked over and opened it. "Evenin' to ye Thalen, wanted to come in and check on ye to see how ye were doin'. Do ye mind if I come in?" Dolgrath asked waiting just beyond the doors threshold, Thalen gave his friend a small smile as he swept aside beckoning the dwarf to enter.

Looking to the center of the room Thalen pictured a small table and pair of plush armchairs in his mind's eye and with a wave of his hand cast his spell "Talin Dorint...Al Zalar." With a small surge of power, the furniture appeared into being coalescing from a fine mist into solid material before them. One of the chairs appeared directly before a surprised Dolgrath who nearly ran into the back of it, an uncharacteristic yelp of surprise coming from his lips. Shooting Thalen an annoyed look Dolgrath grumbled at him "Ye could o' warned me ye were gonna be doin' that." Though his annoyance that did not stop him from sitting in one of the chairs. Thalen sat across from his grumbling companion, a poorly hidden smirk decorated his face. Sighing with some appreciation Dolgrath spoke "Well at least yer chair is comfortable. Nice work, ye've been figurin' stuff out fast. Afore ye know it ye'll be as good as First Mage Darkweave hisself" Settling deeper into the chair Thalen grinned in response "I appreciate the praise, however, I can't imagine Cameral, let alone any orks, would find the working impressive...nor do I even truly understand how it will be of use when I am finally free of this place and back at the front." He said, allowing some humor into his voice.

Dolgrath chuckled before responding "Well maybe ye could just ask 'em to sit and talk about everythin'. Yer stubborn enough so ye may manage to get 'em to listen to ye." he barked a laugh as he settled further into the chair. "Well, me friend I came here fer more than just yer fine company, I wanted to let ye know the professor fer our other class came back this mornin'. So, startin' tomorrow we'll be havin' it at about two in the noontime. I figured I'd be askin' ye if ye wanted to get a lil practice in afore we went to the class. We'll be havin' a couple o' hours after our first class." Thalen took less than a moment to consider the offer before responding. " Yes, that would be a fine idea Dolgrath." He said resting his chin within his palm "It would certainly be good to practice spells meant for battle more intentionally, at least more so than what we normally do. Now that I think on it every attack spell, I have ever cast has been either fairly simple or completely by accident." He grew troubled at that realization and found himself asking once again what god had so disliked him as to throw him into his current mess. He shook his head to dislodge such a pointless thought before addressing the dwarf. "I wish it were not so late in the evening otherwise I would ask if we could begin now. Unfortunately, that is simply not an option as they closed the practice rooms over an hour ago, at least we should have the opportunity before class as you said. What is the name of our professor?" As the last word left his mouth, he summoned a small barrel of ale and a pair of goblets indicating Dolgrath to fill his with the dark amber liquor. The dwarf didn't need to be told twice as he filled the offered goblet, filling and draining it within a second. He smacked his lips in appreciation before more reservedly pouring himself another cup. "That be pretty decent stuff boyo, maybe a wee bit off in some ways but better than when I first made some, nearly took meself a year to make something half decent." He paused and took a long sip before settling back down once more into the soft confines of the chair.

Thalen took the barrel and poured some of the golden-brown liquid into his own cup, he appreciated the hints of fruit that permeated from the glass both in smell and taste before agreeing with Dolgrath that something wasn't exactly right with it. He took a longer pull from the cup before placing it on the low table. *"If the whole being a mage thing goes badly, I could always open a tavern."* He couldn't help but chuckle softly at the thought, yet as the levity faded, he felt a small tingle of sadness at his still too fresh loss, this relaxed moment being something he would often share with his departed friend. Though he had been enjoying the study and practice over the last few weeks he could not help but remember the world outside of the rather safe walls, as long as another mage didn't almost blow you up, of the college. He had known war and fighting for nearly half his life, for nearly fifteen years all he had known was the struggle against the Coalition's terrifying foes. In many ways he could not help but feel that he was letting down all of those he had lost, he felt he was betraying those still alive and fighting by sitting here away from danger drinking ale with his friend. "What's on yer mind me friend?" Dolgrath asked, making Thalen start in surprise, "Ye sigh when yer thinkin' o' somethin' that be botherin' yerself. So, go on tell me, what be the problem." Though he had drank nearly half the keg by himself, Dolgrath's eyes were still alert and his demeanor patient.

Thalen paused considering how much to tell his friend and caught himself mid sigh barely cutting it short in favor of a relaxing breath. Shaking his head at his foolishness and transparency he chuckled to himself, and after another moment more he began picking his words with care. "Have you ever found this all absurd, I mean look at us! We sit here safe behind the walls of this near impenetrable fortress while others are outside fighting and dying to allow us to do exactly that. I feel as though I am not doing my part in this war. Damnit man, I went from fighting for my life every day and conducting some of the most difficult missions in the entirety of the Coalition, and now I am being coddled. It is as though I have no value, and I do not like it one bit." Taking a moment to collect himself he felt a black ball of anger settle deep within his stomach. After a few moments more he slowly managed to ease the tightness, slumping down into the chair as he put a hand to his brow and looked at the ground. Having come back to his senses he continued "This lack of action is beginning to grate upon my nerves my friend, I do not enjoy feeling as if I was a child being led by the hand constantly." Grabbing up his cup, he emptied the vessel and slammed it down upon the table in frustration, Dolgrath unfazed by the outburst took another sip of his own before speaking. "I understand yer frustration, ye are not the only one who be having trouble keepin' out o' the action. I have felt it meself more times than I would admit, lad I have been fightin' far longer than ye have been alive. Now I be sitting here doin' nothin except drinkin, true I be havin chances to make my way out here and there but it don't be the same. I know it don't make ye feel better, but I understand, and it may not be the battle ye be looking for, but we'll be put into a real scrap tomorrow during class. Trust me." He grinned and finished his own cup, placing it down upon the table and standing, though somewhat unsteadily. "Well lad I be off to bed. I'll see ye bright and early tomorrow." He took a step, an involuntary groan escaping his lips. "May have drank a bit more than I meant." The dwarf said seemingly to himself before making his way to the door, throwing Thalen a final wave, he left the room, leaving Thalen with nothing but his thoughts.

Thalen took a moment to calm his mind, using it as an opportunity to dismiss the extra furniture and remainder of the keg with a wave of his hand. He looked to his desk and specifically at the book which lain atop it, feeling an involuntary shiver he decided to leave the boring text for another day. He yawned as he walked to his bed stripping off his robe and tunic before clambering under the covers, once comfortable he dismissed the orbs of light placed throughout the room. As darkness fully engulfed him, he felt his thoughts swirl, memories of his path and life to this point that moved sluggishly within his drowsy mind, until sleep came, forcing him to leave those thoughts for a different day.

He stood within the main hall as the screams and cries of pain, anguish and struggle filled the air. Yet he hardly noticed, his entire being focused upon the large ork shaman facing him. The sea of bodies fighting desperately seeming to have formed a circle allowing the pair to reach each other without interference. A cry ripped from the orks lips as he raised a large cruel looking axe, tendrils of darkness and fire playing upon its edges, into the air as it charged towards Thalen a vicious yell ripping from its tusked mouth. Thalen took up his sword...his sword? Finding within his hand Robin's Tail, Cameral's parting gift to him, yet it seemed somehow different as if it was attuned to his hand. Giving a war cry of his own, one that Robin's Tail seemed to match, he charged forward weapon meeting the ork's axe and as they did his sword gave a flash of light as if a golden fire surrounded the blade...The weapons met again and with another spark of fire and light Thalen's world went dark.

Thalen awoke, feeling unexpectedly calm given the dream he had been jolted from. Summoning a light he scanned his room, eyes resting upon the sword from his dream. He chuckled a little at his dreaming minds imagination before dismissing the light. As the room went dark, he laid his head back down, hoping to return to slumber before the sun's rays breached the horizon once more.

CHAPTER FOURTEEN

Thalen found that the first few hours of the following day flew by, from the bustle of the main hall during breakfast to the studious nature of his first class, it all swept past without registering to his preoccupied mind. He found he had grown used to the pattern established through his first few weeks and could already feel that this well-worn schedule would be broken. In fact, he had come to the realization that he had very little exposure to battle magic, it fully striking him as he spoke with his friends over breakfast. Though they had all seen his rapid improvement, it was still easy to tell that he was far behind where he would have been if his talents had developed earlier in his life. As the conversation continued Elara suggested getting in practice before the class started, which they all agreed to, deciding to meet in one of the many practice rooms later that day.

When the entire group was in the practice room Dolgrath shut the door turning to them he fell into his tutorial role immediately. "Alright me friends, it be time for us to start workin' on our fightin' ability. As I be the only one with any experience in this I hope ye all be acceptin' me tutelage of ye." He waited a moment for them to give their agreement, which they each gave within a few moments. With that out of the way his face lit up with excitement rubbing his meaty hands together, grinning wildly he began to teach "Perfect, so ye already know how to form things into a bolt so we are gonna be only usin' that type of spell for the moment. The other thing ye'll need to be knowing is how to make yerself a shield against those attacks. Now this shell o' defense, it'll only lasts for a bit o' time before breaking if yer under duress, this be a truth no matter how advanced ye be. It be true the stronger ye be the longer it be lastin' but it still be only a matter o' seconds if ye are being hammered by attacks. It also don't stop attacks from a good sword or hammer, it only be useful against enemy spells or any attack from ranged weapons. Ye got it?" Thalen and the others nodded in turn "Alright, now here be the words ye need to cast the spell, they be "Sin Tor Kalak" now this be one o' the easier spells to make happen just be using yer thought. O' course this be meanin' that ye need to be given it a few tries so ye can be sure ye have it strong in yer mind and ye won't be needin' to use words when it be matterin'. Now ye need to imagine ye have a bubble oh yer power around ye, be sure it is not too brittle, or it'll break quicker. Alright, best way for ye to learn it is to be doin' it so get to it and ask me any questions while ye do." He folded his arms across his barrel-like chest as he leaned against the wall waiting to see their efforts.

Thalen took some time to practice the words, ensuring the inflection and pronunciation seemed correct, once he felt confident, he began to trickle in the power he needed to make the spell come to life. He took his time as he formed the idea of a pliable but strong shield, layering the power in sheets on top of each other, much as that of a shield wall. After a several heartbeats he felt secure in his mental picture and spoke the words, the power feeling as though it escaped through every pour before forming like scales over his body as it became fully transparent. He smiled with pleasure and checked the progress of his companions, he felt the two women beside him release the energy forming their respective weaves, though something he could not help but notice was that opposed to his layering they created a singular sheet of power. Filing that away in his memory he was determined to ask Dolgrath about it later. Grunting in approval the dwarf examined their spells "Ye all did well, though I'm thinkin' a certain elfie person has done this afore." Casting Keela a suspicious eye, her thin lips smiling mischievously in return, as she spoke, her voice light with amusement "Yes

Master Dolgrath I am afraid I have certain experience in doing this. Before you protest, I wished not to disturb your lesson, you were doing such an admirable job." She flashed him a brilliant smile which was met with nothing more than a grumble, after a moment the dwarf returned the smile, though his seemed almost evil. "Well then m'lady perhaps ye would be so kind as to be my first targe...er...I of course mean participant in this practice." As he spoke, he plastered an innocent look on his face, seeming to try and cover for his stumble. Keela laughed, the sound musical like a song, as her mirth over the dwarf's poor acting overflowed "Of course, I would be most pleased to be paired with you for this exercise." She said smiling sweetly at him, who in turn raised an eyebrow before turning to Thalen and Elara. "Though I feel I may have gotten meself in trouble it seems ye two will be partnered. Just be using the fire bolts till ye get used to avoidin them, the magic o' yer shields should protect ye for the most part but keep yer attack spells as weak as ye can just in case ye break through. We don't want to be cooking each other alive." Turning back to Keela he said, "Alright girlie, let us go see just how bad this will be for meself." He motioned for the elf to follow him to the other side of the practice chamber leaving Thalen and Elara to their own designs.

"Are you ready Thalen?" he heard Elara ask, her voice bubbling with excitement. Looking over to her he was immediately struck by how attractive he found her while realizing in nearly the same moment that this was the first time it was only the two of them. Though the others were only about ten meters away, he would be speaking to her without the dwarf's and elf's constant presence, except for Dolgrath, he had only ever spoken to his companions in a group setting. The feelings of awkwardness took him by surprise, and he was forced to take a moment to force them away. To try and break those feeling he flashed her his most winning smile "Of course, let's get some space between us so we can start hurling balls of fire at one another." She nodded to him and the pair moved a further ten meters from their friends before splitting off each going to different sides of the room. Though he had tried to put it from his mind, he could not deny his attraction to this young woman and, if he was to admit it, the bit of guilt that seemed to accompany those thoughts. For an unknown reason he felt that he was betraying Sarah, though she had been gone some months now and there had never been anything intimate to their relationship. *"At least nothing intimate until the end."*

He shook his head to dislodge the foolish notion and focused instead on the task at hand. Breathing deeply, he removed the last distracting wisps of thought from his mind, instead giving his full attention to preparing his spells. Within moments he had formed the spells in his mind and began gathering power preparing for the duel. "I am ready when you are Thalen. Count it down so we can get started." Elara called from the other side of the room. Thalen raised his hand in acknowledgement and began counting down from 10, as he did, he took in the distance between himself and his combatant. *"About forty meters, alright that should give me enough time to maneuver...at least I hope."* Once he finished the countdown a ball of fire flew at a surprising speed towards him leaving him with only a sparse few seconds to dodge. *"Ok maybe I was wrong, these come in rather fast don't they."* His concentration broke as he couldn't help but flinch from the loud impact on the wall behind him. Admonishing himself for the lapse he prepared to move right as a second spell hit him in the chest, though he felt almost no impact as the scales of his shield rippled absorbing the force and displacing the impact throughout his magical defense. Though he had been struck the impact forced his lagging instincts and training to fully kick in as he reacted almost instantly. Focusing on his opponent he launched two golden bolts of pure flame at her. Each flew true, striking Elara squarely in the chest causing her to slide back and nearly lose her footing. Sensing his advantage, he pressed forward throwing flame into his opponent's crumbling defenses, as she scrambled in the vein hope of avoiding the barrage, as he threw one after another into her quickly falling shield. While he struck, he felt power flow through him drawing more and more into himself as he maintained his furious pace in the hopes of ending the fight as quickly as possible. Though his opponent managed to fire off a bolt or two it was a rare occurrence and typically went far wide as she spent more time avoiding his attacks than focusing upon her own.

Thalen's relentless offensive finally wore down his opponent's stamina and as she slowed more attacks landed until he finally caught her squarely, with that strike he knew the fight was all but over. Seeing an end to the fight he pounded four more bolts into her before she fell to her back. His opponent down he quickly moved in intent on finishing his downed enemy before they could recover. His strides quick, he prepared his killing blow before suddenly finding himself off his feet as he felt a battering ram's force throw him to the side. He struggled for a moment before the heat of combat wore off and his senses returned to him. As he took back control, he found that it was not in fact a battering ram that threw him to the ground but rather a dwarf in a robe that had taken him from his feet. As even now the dwarf was atop him pinning him to the floor, as the last of the haze cleared his mind, he finally heard the dwarf's words. "That's enough lad ye don't want to hurt her. Damnit Thalen, get it together ye durned fool."

It took several moments for Thalen to regain control of his breathing, which he found difficult with the dense dwarf currently above him, when he finally had the dwarf let him to stand back up lending a hand, which Thalen took greatly. As he looked across the room, he saw Keela tending to the still down Elara, seeing this he felt a rush of fear bubble up in him. His voice laced with emotion he spoke "Elara are you well, are you alright. I beg your forgiveness I did not mean to cause you any true harm." Her eyes open and lips set in a small grimace, she looked up at him. "It is alright Thalen; my shield took most of the punishment. Though I certainly felt every one of those shots!" she chuckled before the grimace returned "Thalen, you definitely made me work, I don't think I have seen any member of the Fourth Circle manage draw and use so much power so quickly. As painful as that was it was rather impressive." She finished flashing him a bright smile. Thalen released a breath he had not realized he had been holding, feeling himself relax as he smiled back at her. "Thank you, however I am just happy you are okay. I thought I had hurt you badly, that is something I have no real desire to do. Here let me help you up." He took her by the arm gently helping her to a sitting position and then to her feet.

Dolgrath, who had come over to ensure his

"students" were safe and mostly uninjured, blew out a breath as relief seemed to wash over him. "Alright, I think that be enough for today. Class starts in about two hours so we've the time to recover from this. Elara needs to be makin' her way to the infirmary and Thalen I be thinkin ye should be kind enough to accompany her after yer fine effort. Me and Keela will be seein' ye in class." With that he waved and signaled for Keela to follow him out, the elf gave a small shrug to the other two, before making her way out of the practice room behind the somewhat surly dwarf.

Accepting the semi-disguised reproach from the dwarf he turned to Eowyn "Do you require help walking or will you be able to manage it?" he asked her, honest concern was reflected in his tone. She took a few tender steps before shaking her head in frustration. "I'm afraid I will need a hand Thalen, I seemed to have rolled my ankle at some point, I also think I might have a few bruised ribs. No need for concern though, this is the danger of any practice bout, so remove that look from your face!" she said to him. Thalen smiled at the woman as he had not even realize his concern at her words so openly shown upon his face. Motioning his intent Thalen moved to her side and put her arm around his shoulders in support, yet after taking several steps he realized this method would not work as his six-foot plus frame was hardly a match to support the much smaller woman. After taking several more steps towards the door Thalen found a solution stopping them mid stride, Elara looked at him her confusion plain, but he held up his hand to forestall any questions. With the same hand he pointed out into the open space in front of them where what could only be described as a mobile chair slowly conjured into being. The chair's typically padded feet were instead replaced with four mid-sized wheels, the chair was relatively low but had two handles that extended upwards.

Once the chair was completed Thalen invited her to sit in it, and, after a moment of open skepticism, Elara agreed settling into the chair. Once she was seated, he took up a position behind it, grabbed the handles, and began pushing her out of the room and to one of the elevators that would lead to the hall's infirmary. *"I believe there is an infirmary in every hall isn't there...does that speak to the desire to keep the mages healthy...or more concerningly that there are that many accidents within these halls."* Feeling a small shiver go down his spine, he quickly disregarded his thought as the infirmary door soon came in sight. When they entered, the attendants asked questions regarding the injuries and how they had occurred, all of which Elara masterfully brushed off citing a training accident. The attendants had readily accepted her answer and gave her a quick check over. Once it was completed, they confirmed nothing was broken but that she would likely be in pain and bruised for the better part of two weeks. After giving her a potion to reduce the pain and swelling, as well as confirming she could participate in combat classes today, they sent them on their way.

Once out of the room Thalen let out a sigh of relief and looked over at the now walking Elara, the chair having been dismissed as they left the infirmary. "That was far easier than I thought it would be, I suspected a full inquiry regarding this...that was a much different experience than I am familiar with. Then again all of my experience is with the army's medical corps. I appreciate you not mentioning your injuries were my doing as I feel horrible that I was the cause of your pains." He hoped his voice truly reflected how sorry he was for the entire mess. As Elara waved him off, he felt that it had been understood "Please Thalen, don't worry about it really. As I said, injuries do happen in training matches, especially when you are tasting your power fully for the first time. You do not know your strength or your limitations yet, it is something you can only come to know with practice and time. Of course, I won't pretend it wasn't scary at the time, but I am happy I could be your first." Thalen found himself blushing at what she had said, for a few reasons, and to his surprise it must have shown plainly as Elara giggled slightly, it sounding girlish and somewhat embarrassed as her lightly tanned skin turned slightly rosy. "That is not how I meant it, and you know it." She said in mock outrage, and as she did Thalen found he could not help but laugh at her intentionally poor acting before responding with his own "No why of course not my lady, I do apologize greatly for my unclothe thoughts." He exaggerated his words further by bowing deeply to her, his mirth reflected in his tone. They both laughed at the spectacle before lapsing into a silence that lasted a few minutes before Elara spoke her tone taking on one of gravity "Come now Thalen, I have just noticed the time and we must get to our class. We wouldn't want to be late on the first day!" She grabbed his arm and pulled him forward, increasing the pace. The unexpected touch of her soft hands sent a jolt of electricity up his spine. A surprised smile found its way to his face before it was tempered by the unexplained guilt which wormed its way into that seed of happiness. *"Nothing is ever simple"* he thought to himself as they raced down the hallway to their class.

CHAPTER FIFTEEN

The pair made it to the classroom with barely moments to spare, quickly finding a place near Dolgrath and Keela as they seated themselves and summoned their supplies. Now that he had a moment to breath Thalen looked about the space, taking it all in and immediately noticing that this room was very different from every other he had seen, the room contained a single row of desks on a slightly elevated platform. This platform surrounded a large oval pit that was at least one hundred meters in length and another twenty-five in width. The pit or arena was set relatively deep within the floor, with it being about five meters into the ground, the desks, as he thought about it more, appeared to be more like stands as they sat near the top of the pit's walls and were angled slightly to allow an easy view of the space. As he examined the middle of the pit further a sudden flash of light causing the entire class to shade their eyes. As suddenly as it had appeared, the light dissipated and standing in its place was a man, his blue green skin and black eyes made him instantly recognizable as one of the Raital.

Unlike most of his brethren, the man was bald, yet much like his brethren a neatly trimmed black beard decorated his cheeks and chin. Allowing the class no time to recover from their shock he spoke out in a booming and harsh voice, it being more suited for the commanding of troops than for teaching of students. "Alright you lot, I am Master Dominus Keelas and while you are in this room I am your Master in the art of battle magic. You will not refer to me as Master Keelas, you will not call me Master, you will simply call me sir. Is that clear?" He paused, waiting for a reply, Thalen could immediately tell what was expected of the group and though he lent his voice only a smattering of the expected answer came in reply. The Master's brow creased in anger as he shouted at them in rage "I can't hear you! I asked you a question and I expect a proper answer, so let's try this again. Is that clear!?" Within seconds he was answered by a small roar as the class yelled out yes sir in response.

Master Keelas gave a single nod as he began looking about the arena at each of his thirty students in turn, seeming to weigh each of their worth in his mind before he continued on to the next. "That was much better, now let me make something clear to you all. I am not here to be your friend; I am not here to help you or coddle you. I am here for one reason and one reason only, that is to make sure you don't kill yourself or anyone else around you because of incompetence. You will do what I say when I say it and you will like it. Are we clear?" Fortunately, the class did not need to be told twice, as all thirty voices added to the chorus of yes sirs. "Ah so you lot can learn something, maybe there is hope for you yet. Before I can get to teaching, I first need to know what you know and what you can do. You each are going to be paired up with another and no you will not be choosing who you go into combat against. I will be pairing you with someone completely at random, you will then make your way into this arena and try and blow each other's head off. Do I have any volunteers to be first?" With the challenge raised a smattering of hands shot into the air, and to Thalen's surprise he found one of them being his own.

Fortunately, he was not picked, in truth he had no desire to be part of the first pair to go. He was not full of himself and realized his battle magic was at best below average, yet his military training had simply taken hold due to the master's bearing. Keelas had sparked in him the ingrained desire for action that he felt every soldier, no every warrior, had deep within them. "Alright, you and you come down into the pit you'll find stairs down at the four cardinal points of the pit. When you get in say your name and when I give you the signal you can get to it." A younger human man and Dolgrath had been singled out for this first bout, the pair entering the arena and said their names in turn.

While his dwarvish friend looked every part the dangerous mage, his opponent, a wiry man with a nervous fidget, left much to be desired. Once they seemed prepared the professor gave the signal to begin, immediately both combatants erected a shield, yet that seemed to be the only move they made in sync. As within the first few attacks Thalen could tell it was going to be a very one-sided duel. The duel ended suddenly, and in Thalen's opinion unsatisfyingly, as Dolgrath avoided with ease a bolt of red flame while simultaneously attacking with something Thalen had never seen before, as the dwarf suddenly punched out in front of himself. That motion caused a fist of stone to appear before the stocky figure, which, as though propelled by that same move, rushed forward striking the wiry man directly in the chest. Though his shield took most of the damage the man was flung back several meters onto his back, a groan escaping from his lips as he curled into a ball clutching what was likely several bruised ribs. As the young man continued to squirm on the ground in pain Master Dominus spoke "Huh, not bad. Well done Mr. Bardilon I see the service you have been doing with your kin at the front has honed your skills somewhat, your opponent however I can't say as much for." He paused as a groan from the floored man interrupted him, his face showed his annoyance as the professor looked at the source of the sound with an undisguised disgust "Stop whining and get the hell up. By the gods man you're groaning and moaning like some common street walker after their first job in the city. Get up and get the hell out of my ring." When the arena was finally clear, he went around the remainder of the room, pointing and pairing off various students as he pared the remaining group down further and further until it was only Thalen and an Elvish man remaining. During the previous duels both Elara and Keela defeated their opponents soundly though not as decidedly as his dwarf companion had and Thalen found himself boiling with excitement at the prospect of a fight against a mage outside of his cohort of companions.

As the previous pair exited the arena, Thalen took the opportunity to look over at his opponent. He noted immediately that the elf was very similar to, well, every other elf he had ever seen. Though not identical, features such as the telltale almond eyes which floated above a sharp angular nose remained much the same. They were not overly large, finding him to be smaller than Thalen by a few inches and more than likely a few score pounds, yet he carried himself with, what Thalen found to be, an annoying overconfidence or snideness. The elf seemed to look down on anyone that was not himself or at the very least not an elf. Thalen had noticed early in the matches the way he had reacted when a human would lose was one of smug satisfaction appearing on his face, while at the same time pure outrage seemed to consume him whenever one of the elder race lost. It took Thalen seconds to decide he did not like this pompous self-important bastard, and he knew that without question he wanted to beat them to a pulp. His internal rage was interrupted by the gravelly voice of Master Keelas "Last two up let's go! You're all that stands between us and the end of this class so get a move on!" Before the last word had even left his instructor's mouth, Thalen got to his feet and moved quickly down into the arena. Taking the final step onto the rough stone floor Thalen's gaze locked upon his opponent as the elvish man slowly sauntered to the stairs. A look of complete indifference was painted on his angular features enraging Thalen further as the elf acted as though the match was an annoying chore that would take moments to complete and was unworthy of the effort.

"That pompous ass, acting as if I am so far beneath him. Well, I'll make that elvish bastard regret taking me so lightly." Thalen thought, a snarl curling his lips involuntarily. Once the two contestants were set across from

one another Master Arius cleared his throat impatiently awaiting introductions from the two combatants. The elf took the initiative speaking in a musical voice that contained the discordant notes of superiority "I am Doryan Telmasar, and this is a waste of my time." Pointing at Thalen as though to indicate what was wasting it, this insult ripped a growl from Thalen as he felt the anger threaten to bubble over and to some degree did during his own introduction "I am Thalen Vorholt, and I'll grind you into the ground." Doryan laughed at Thalen's threat, his voice filled with scorn, as he replied "As if you could do such a thing, you are nothing and I will enjoy proving it. "Interrupting their jibes Master Dominus stepped between them "I like the fire but that's enough, settle this on the battlefield not with words like a couple of schoolboy whelps. Begin on my signal." Once he saw they were each prepared, Arius stepped back to the side and after a tense moment gave the signal for the contest to begin. Thalen sucked in power, preparing and setting his shield as he prepared to make good on his threat and grind the man across from him into dust.

Thalen first act was to call up the power intent on forming a ball of flame as he wanted nothing more than to scorch the pompous elf, yet his opponent was faster sending several bolts of yellow arcane energy in his direction. He dodged out of their way, yet his concentration was broken, and he found himself on the back foot, all the while the elf pressed the attack firing off spells in quick succession. The calm part of Thalen's brain, developed over years of commandership, noted that the elf most often made use of pure arcane blasts accompanied by the occasional bolt of flame. Although that recognition did not help Thalen, he gave his best efforts to dodge though he could not avoid them all as he felt the occasional impact upon his shield. Though his defenses seemed to hold strong under the assault he could feel them slowly weakening as it absorbed more and more force as time passed. As the minutes dragged on his opponent began to slow as longer pauses appeared between his opponents attacks, taking the opportunity Thalen shot fourth golden fire and white arcane energy at his opponent putting the elf on the defensive for the first time in the match. Within moments the tide had turned, Thalen going hard at his opponent, his offensive growing stronger with every spell thrown. All the while he barely recognized that instead of it becoming more difficult to pull in power it was far smoother as he easily absorbed more and more, tapping into the seemingly unlimited pool within the room. Suddenly, the elf shot his hands up towards the ceiling and uttered words far too quickly for Thalen to comprehend, within a moment a wall of pure stone appeared in front the elf protecting him from Thalen assault.

Surprised and confused Thalen paused as a grinding and crunching sound echoed throughout the chamber, adding to the confusion, after a moment it became apparent what the sound was as the wall of stone shot forward towards him, the projectile slamming into his body as though it was shot from a catapult. His defenses crumbled as the wall rammed into him, its mass carrying him backwards nearly twenty meters until he met the wall behind him. After a moment the wall holding him up crumbled and Thalen fell to his knees, his breathing ragged as his strength had been with that last attack. As he knelt amongst the rubble a shadow overtook the light above him and looking up, he found Doryan standing over him, a satisfied smirk upon his face. "Nice try fool, you have been tested and have been found wanting. Your kind has always reached too far, I found great pleasure in putting you in your place." Laughing, the elf turned his back on Thalen as he walked towards the stairs of the arena. His anger igniting, Thalen only saw red as he struggled to his feet, drawing power once more, yet he found he could not stand as a strong hand kept him on his knees. "That be enough lad, ye've done enough for today. Ye'll have yer chance at him later, that durned elf ain't worth ye gettin' in trouble over." Dolgrath's voice whispered into his ear. Looking at his friend, he was surprised to find the normally calm dwarf grinding his teeth, his eyes shooting daggers at the back of the retreating form. The last of his anger and remaining adrenaline drained from him, and within moments he found himself tired and worn, his body sluggish in response to commands. After a moment, he tried to rise to his feet, yet found he only could with Dolgrath aiding him in his effort, gratefully taking dwarf's shoulder he leaned on the stocky figure, the pair slowly making their way to the stairs.

As they crested the final step Thalen found Elara flinging herself into him, grabbing him into a tight hug before quickly releasing with an apology. The contact having reignited the pain, he groaned softly, but found himself comforted by her concern showing his appreciation the best he could with a small smile. "Thalen, thank the Gods you are alright we had feared for you when the wall had pinned you." Elara said, concern evident in her voice, Thalen took a moment reassuring her that he was in good health overall, even so she remained close at hand taking the place of the shorter dwarf in supporting him in his losing battle against gravity. "Well, I want you to know you did very well and you were very brave. We should get you to the infirmary to make sure nothing is broken." She said to him, her concern still present but seeming to have eased. He turned to look at her, grimacing as he felt the soreness of his muscles, after taking a moment to recompose himself he spoke. "No, no let's just get me to my room. I am sure nothing is broken. I'm just very sore my shield took most of the hit, though it could not disburse all of the force. Even so, that was still likely a few hundred pounds of rock that had slammed into me. Given that I cannot say I am surprised that I feel so awful." The teacher wrapped up the class, saying a few more words before calling it to an end, the following day being given to them so they could recuperate from their bouts. As the group exited the classroom Dolgrath looked at Thalen "Thalen, ye said yer shield disbursed the force, did ye mean it absorbed it?" Thalen, with the aid of Elara, turned to face the dwarf, his confusion evident on his face at the dwarf's seemingly random question. "No, my friend, it disbursed the force from the impact. Why do you ask?" the dwarf was silent for a moment before shaking his head "Never ye mind, we will be takin' o' that later, fer now we need to get ye restin." As the dwarf fell silent Thalen mentally shrugged before a thought of his own came to mind. "Keela, who was that bastard?" The last word fell like a stone from his mouth as he mentally kicked himself for his tactlessness. He went to apologize yet was forestalled seeing a flash of uncharacteristic anger painting her normally serene face.

Quickly composing herself she began to speak, yet her voice had a cold and detached quality "That bastard as you put it, and trust me you put it rightly, is Doryan Telmasar, son of Lord Seran Telmasar. He is pompous, mean spirited and if you could not tell a racist or supremacist. I can never remember which they call it, nonetheless he is a terror and deserves nothing but scorn." Her voice gained a steel hard edge as she spoke the final word, the unusual anger silenced the group as they continued on. Once she had seemed to relax, having taken a few deep breaths, she continued "Him and his family feel that we Elves are dragging ourselves down by associating with the other races of the Confederation. They view all non-elves as a lesser form of life, ones that are at best a nuisance and at worst a pest to be removed. Of course, they are not the major voice of the people, yet they have recently been gaining followers as the war rages forward." Keela let out a soft sigh, and stopped her stride looking to them. "Sadly, this war has not helped the opinions of most of my people, yes, we have always been relatively close to humans, yet our two kingdoms remain very separate from one another. We do not often cross the political boundaries our ancestors formed, when we chose to join the Confederation, we were already stretching our people's goodwill. Now that this war has dragged on and as so many perish, the question is being raised as to why we bothered to leave Isari at all." Keela seemed to grow tired or melancholy after what she had revealed and lapsed into silence as she began walking once more, the rest following behind, as her ominous words echoed like a death toll within Thalen's mind.

CHAPTER SIXTEEN

As the rest of the week passed by Thalen could not fully shake Keela's words from his mind, the ominous thought of the Elves breaking ties with his kind was one which caused some sleeplessness. For his entire life, and that of a few generations before, the elvish nation had always been a great friend and ally to them and with that the mere thought of them turning their backs on that alliance, let alone that of the entire Confederation, was nigh unthinkable. Yet, as the days continued to pass by, his mind turned from the wider world and back to his current circumstances, the most important one being how he was to pass the tests he was ill prepared for.

Thalen felt himself hit the ground for the fifth time in a row, his body screamed at him in pain as he pulled himself from the cold stone of the practice room, settling into a seated position. Since his defeat at the hands of Doryan Telmasar he had realized just how inadequate his battle preparation were, he recognized that his magical vocabulary as well as his imagination was severely lacking. Stretching his cramped muscles, he thought about what made a caster powerful, his defeat last week truly making him appreciate the fact that his magic was only limited by the vocabulary and imagination of the caster. Though power was certainly important he came to realize it meant nothing if the user could not wield it effectively and skillfully, these quickly showing themselves to be his biggest hurdle. This being demonstrated fully by his current seated position having been flung away yet again while a rather smug looking dwarf stood on the far side of the room. Dolgrath had once again trounced him in their practice bout, the crafty dwarf had hurled spells of all different kinds at him in quick succession each of them chipping away at his defenses as he was kept on the back foot for the entire match.

Drawing in a few deep ragged breaths he replayed the most recent fight in his head, trying to reexamine the decisions and strategies he had attempted, discarding those that were ineffective and filing away those that had seen some success. He also thought about how his opponent defeated him hoping to glean some knowledge from Dolgrath's movements, spells, and decisions. He knew that he could fight, he had for a fair part of his life, yet magical combat added an element he had so little experience with that he stumbled into obvious traps, ploys, and feints of his opponent. His recent bouts were a far cry from his first session when he defeated Elara and as he considered it more, he realized that his victory was mostly due to surprise and her inexperience in battle. Since then, he had exclusively been against Dolgrath and Keela, both were well versed in magic as well as each having at least some experience in battle over the years, this combination made it so he could not even lay a finger on either of them.

Once he finally regained control of his breath Thalen stood and approached his dwarvish friend all the while preparing himself for his tutor's inevitable critiques. As he approached, he saw that Dolgrath's demeanor had taken on a serious one dropping the previously smug expression as he began his instruction "Well lad, yer gettin' better I can tell ye that without a doubt in me mind. Ye may not be feelin' that be the case, yet ye nearly stuck caught me with some o' yer spells." He paused to take a swig of water "How do ye think ye did?" Thalen's first instinct was to say poorly, yet he knew that would not be good enough for this exercise as this was about honest reflection, only comparing this match to how he himself had done previously and not to those surrounding him. This exercise had become almost a ritual, it being done religiously when their practice matches ended, even though more often than not Thalen found himself on the floor. Yet, he knew the dwarf wanted him to see beyond that initial feeling even if he found it both helpful and frustrating in equal measure.

After taking a few beats to think it over he felt he had a decent answer "Well, I do not feel I performed exceptionally well, though I can see the improvement as you said. I feel slow, too slow in wording my spells and forming power to my will, though I can tell I have improved in harnessing the power, it does very little for me as I cannot seem to make effective use of it. I lack the vocabulary to be creative and lack the experience to adapt, I feel as though I cannot think fast enough." As he was speaking, he felt disgusted in himself, he had never felt so inept, not since he had tried out for the aerial force. Though that failure was more due to lacking a head for heights than inability, as he was honest being in the air with only the scales of a dragon beneath his boots held little appeal to him. Looking at Dolgrath, Thalen saw that he was silently nodding as he thought on Thalen's analysis "Well lad ye be right with most o' what ye be sayin, yer slow. Ye don't know enough of the words and yer thinkin' far more than ye need to be, it should be natural to ye, and it would be if ye had been practicin' yer entire life. But ye haven't been, ye've been doin' this for a few months and ye have been improvin' fast. Yet, ye don't know what ye don't know." Dolgrath's face split into a smile seeming pleased with his little saying, as he continued "What ye need to be doin is learnin more o' the words, 'nd practice formin spells, ye need ta be doin it till it be the same as swingin yer sword. Somethin' yeve been doin so much ye don't even need to be thinkin what yer doin and instead just know yer strike be true or block be right. Do ye get me meanin?" the dwarf fell silent seeming to be waiting for Thalen's confirmation. Thalen took a moment making sure he fully absorbed his friends words and as he did quickly recognized the truth they held and in some ways they were what he was already thinking himself. He took another long relaxing breath before conjuring both the dwarf and himself a chair and took a seat. He found that he recovered faster and faster after every match and though each match seemed to always end in defeat, he thought it was a sign of his progress.

Shaking his head, Thalen settled deeper into his chair, finding it difficult to accept his current skill level, as it in turn made it difficult to appreciate how far he had come in such a short amount of time. As he thought on it more he began to notice more often that even his positive thoughts were tinged with negativity, although he could not determine why. Even so, he could not help but feel inadequate as he compared himself to those around him. This by itself bothered him as it was flawed thinking, those same people were a blessing as they accelerated his growth by leaps and bounds. He easily recognized that without Keela, Elara and Dolgrath helping him he would likely not be even close to the level he was at currently.

Thalen's mind wandered for a few more minutes before he focused on Dolgrath's words and advice. He started picking out times where he had felt slow in action as he lacked any decisiveness during the fight, and without much effort thought of multiple instances of it. They hadn't cost him the fight themselves, but as they compounded it had made his position nearly untenable. He felt like he had followed a script, instead of read and reacted to the situation that was before him, and it came down to a singular fact, magic still did not feel natural to him. This upset him as he realized the only remedy was to improve and the only way to do that was with practice. It truly was as Dolgrath had said, it should feel the same as swinging a sword or breathing, yet instead it felt closer to climbing a tree, it required focus and mental effort. Thalen chuckled at his duality of fate, accepting once more the insanity that gaining his new powers had forced upon him, coupled with the sheer absurdity of having so little time to learn how to use them if he wanted to return to his previous life. Releasing his worries as much as he could, he looked at his dwarfish companion "Well Dolgrath, I have said it before, yet I will say it many times before we are done. I thank you for taking so much time tutoring me and striving to bring me to the point of fighting readiness. It truly is as you say I require more time learning the language and casting without pause, yet there is little time left in the grand scheme and I cannot help but worry that I will not reach my goal within it." Thalen could not help but wonder when he became so willing to voice his troubles, few had ever heard them, and though he spoke now to the dwarf, he did not remember when his tutor had become such an important confidant.

A smile appeared on the dwarfs bearded face as he looked at Thalen "I understand yer concern me friend, though as I be sayin ye been improvin quickly." As the seconds passed Dolgrath's face took on a shade of thought and then concern before suddenly jumping to his feet. "Damn, we be forgettin the time, we best be getting to class!" Hearing the dwarf's words Thalen's own sense of time returned as, like the dwarf, he jumped from his chair dismissing the furniture with a wave as the pair quickly exited the practice theater and made their way to their respective rooms to wash and prepare for the class ahead.

Thalen nearly jogged as he traversed the halls of the college, the time he had spent getting ready took longer than Dolgrath's and so he was not ready when the dwarf came to his door. Instead, instead decided to go to their classroom separately planning on meeting up just before class started to meet, though he wasn't sure if he would even make that deadline as the top of the hour approached. It had felt longer than usual to reach the room, though he knew it was not, and blew a sigh of relief as he saw the classroom door came into sight its door still open and allowing entrance. He slipped into the room just as the door began to close and made his way to his seat as Mistress St Royne began class in full. "Hello all, it is good you have all decided to join today as you will find our topic to be truly indispensable." She paused to ensure all attention was on her, that pause giving Thalen enough time to call his supplies out from the desk and open to a fresh page as she began. "As I am sure you all are aware we are coming up to the testing period to advance circle. It is approaching quickly but fortunately for you the guessing of what the tests themselves is over, they have been determined by the headmaster at long last. As the decision has finally been made by that old dotard, the faculty has been given approval to provide details of the tests today. This is today and today only; I hope you all understand they will not be spoken of again." She looked about the class her eyes piercing them as though trying to read their very souls. As she scanned past Thalen their eyes caught for a moment, and he thought he saw a mischievous sparkle held within them. He wasn't sure if it was his imagination or if the

Mistress was enjoying herself, though he felt it was likely the latter, as he had come to notice she did enjoy keeping her class uncomfortable. *"What is it she typically says... thinking when you are ill at ease is practice for when things go wrong... something like that"* Thalen rolled his eyes at the thought, though he could see the merit in it, though only barely. "As I now have all of your attention I will begin, but first can anyone tell me the gist of the tests? Though none of you have details you surely know by now, whether through talking to your peers or otherwise, what the exams are in general."

After a few moments, Dolgrath raised his hand and once acknowledged began "The tests be as follows—the first be a test o' strength n' control ensurin' the caster be showin' enough power in their castin. Yet even with power the caster must be controlin' the magic well, no one wants a mage that cannie cast without blowin themselves ta bits." St Royne raised a slender hand, the gesture causing the dwarf to pause as she filled the void. "Yes that is well put, with this in mind the first test will be simple but deceptively difficult. The object of the test will be to break ten panes of specially created and magically enforced glass. The objective will be to destroy the glass, which sounds easy enough, however, the glass will require varying amounts of force to break. Apply too much force and the glass will break in spectacular fashion breaking a following pane, yet too little force and the pane will not shatter as it should. The panes will all be set in an order you as the testee will determine. You have ten attempts to destroy ten panes, however, you will not fail if you do not break all ten panes as proctors assigned to you will score you based off of the strength and control categories. The average score will determine your pass or failure, though a penalty will be applied for each incorrectly broken or unbroken pane. Questions?" Upon asking a hand raised immediately and was acknowledged "What do you mean by incorrectly broken pane? Ones unbroken are obvious enough but how can you break the glass wrong?" Thalen actually felt himself groan somewhat as she had just explained it, yet the Mistress seemed to be enjoying herself as he thought he once more saw a twinkle of amusement within her gaze which coupled with the corners of her mouth curling into a somewhat evil smile. "Good question, though if you had been paying full attention you would know I already answered it." She admonished somewhat gently before continuing the explanation. "As I had said the glass will break in a spectacular fashion if too much force is applied to it and will shatter a later pane. Any pane that is shattered due to this will be marked as incorrectly broken, this meaning both the glass broken on purpose and the one broken accidently." As soon as the explanation was finished it seemed as though a collective groan came from the group, the fact that any misfire would cause the loss of two panes and not just one made it bad, but coupling that with the fact that if they were too worried about that and used too little power they would not manage to break the pane at all.

Hearing them the Mistress started chuckling as she continued "I see you all understand the implications of this yet fear not we are not so cruel as to make you guess at the force required to destroy the panes. They will each be marked with two numbers which will go in sequence from one to ten. As an example, two panes will be marked with a five and six. These numbers do not just tell the difficulty of breaking but also indicate the pane that will break if the other has too much force applied to it. Another benefit you will be given is the panes can be set in any order you choose as long as they are not in full descending or ascending order. And before you even ask! Separating the numbered panes a long distance won't matter the panes are magically paired as I said so even if the two panes were miles apart if too much power is used the other will break." she emphasized the last few words to ensure there was no confusion in them, as it was extremely clear that if you used too much power on one glass, the next numerically would break no matter what. The professor paused seeming to give them an opportunity to consider what they had been told, an opportunity which Thalen took greedily.

He started running through potential setups and situations as he tried to find a way to increase his already low chance of success. He couldn't decide if it would be best to group the harder panes together towards the back guaranteeing the most possible breaks or if he should lead with them. His biggest obstacle was not being able to fully trust his control as most strategies he came up with were based on having at least good consistent control, something he knew he lacked. He felt the frustration over his inability start to bubble, but with effort managed to suppress it as he knew it would not help him, as he took a few deep breaths to help steady his rising heartbeat. As his mind calmed a though occurred to him, if the test was monitored and scored by proctors there may be more than meets the eye to the test, or perhaps even more than what they were told. He wondered if breaking higher level targets would in fact be the better option, though he did not have the chance to continue down that line as his thoughts were interrupted by the professor's voice asking Dolgrath to begin describing the second test.

The dwarf seemed to be pulled from his own ruminations and once he had recollected himself he began his description "Let me be seein' if I be recallin correctly the second test be one o' yer creativity with yer magic. Thisin bein more o' a challenge to yer brain ye needin to be solvin some puzzle or riddle. Er...that be all I know Mistress." The dwarf finished lamely; Thalen could tell his friend felt the answer was inadequate even though it seemed to be the best he could do. "You are generally correct." Mistress St Royne replied "Though there is more depth to it than you indicate. Where the first test measures strength and control this second test does measure the creativity of the caster but also the problem solving they possess. These puzzles or riddles that are given exist to have the caster both at wits end but also will test the limits of their casting knowledge. As we all know magic has many different combinations and effects, let alone the styles that different casters have. I will not let too much slip but will say that the answers to these challenges are not set and could in fact be displayed in different ways. As an example, if the answer to the challenge is water, ice would work just as well as a drop of water yet there may be other ways to solve it without using water specifically. Though not the best example, it should give you all the gist of it. The particular challenges for this test will be determined at a later date, however, I can reveal the scoring and number of challenges that will be faced. There will be five challenges and scoring will be based off of time of completion as well as creativity of completion. The faster each challenge is completed the more points assigned, however, a longer time with a more creative answer may garner more points. Though keep in mind that a non-creative answer can instead deduct points, this is because the time completed will assign an overall point value out of sixty, then points will be added or deducted as according to creativity as determined by proctors." She paused a moment to allow the scribbling of quill on paper to subside, once all attention returned to her she asked for questions and when none were forthcoming motioned for Dolgrath to speak towards the final test. "The final test be a tournament o' sorts, we be fight..." yet before he could go into further detail he was cut off by Mistress St. Royne "That is enough dear, thank you we do not wish to spoil the surprise for those newer here." she said her smile sweet. "More information will be provided to you on the test day itself...oh it seems we are out of time for today. I will see you all tomorrow." as if to accentuate the point she disappeared. Having gotten used to their somewhat eccentric professor the class concluded without much surprise at her actions.

Thalen spent the rest of the day within his room studying books he had borrowed from his friends. The group had separated, all of them completely absorbed with their own preparations for the upcoming exams, deciding to keep their time together to only meals and the occasional bit of practical training. This freed

Thalen to search out the solitude that had been far more fitting for his mood as of late, with time passing by quickly and such a major event fast approaching, one that he barely convinced the Headmaster to allow him to participate in, he found himself slipping further into himself and his studies. As he studied, got beat in training, and attended class he began to truly feel inadequate, his abilities, much as he had been thinking for some time, lacked and though he had improved to the point where it was not completely debilitating he found it became more difficult to engage with his peers in a good-natured way. He knew his frustration would boil up into anger at random moments and he did not wish to subject them to his darker moments, especially as they had done nothing to deserve it. He knew he had made large improvements, but still felt he was, at best, as proficient as the most average of his peers. Though logically understood this was for no reason other than his inexperience and his coming to magic later in life, it still ate at him from the inside out. One evening as his room darkened, he stood from his desk leaving a half-finished book upon it as he made his way to bed for what he hoped would be a restful sleep.

Thalen felt the heat on his face as he narrowly avoided the gout of flame launched at him, he found himself trying in vain to keep his eye on the shaman to his left as he engaged an orkish warrior before him. Quickly taking in his surroundings, finding himself upon the immense walls surrounding the college grounds as the city burned below. He moved to engage the creature before him striking at his opponent and shearing clean through its crude weapon and deep into its collarbone killing it instantly. He turned just in time to see the orkish spellcaster throw another bolt of flame towards him, instinctively he swung his sword shearing the spell in half dissipating the magic before it struck. The previously unnoticed golden glow leaving a trail of light, which clearly showed the path his blade had taken. He brought his still glowing blade in tight, the blade's light illuminating his face as he wordlessly charged forward once more...

CHAPTER SEVENTEEN

Thalen woke with the remnants of his dream pushing through the sleep that still fogged his mind, he could not help but think of the other dreams he had over the past months that had shown scenes so similar. He shoved the distraction aside for now as he left the warm embrace of his bed, he lifted his arms stretching them into the air as he looked out of the windows into the courtyard beyond. Taking a deep breath, he basked in the warm sunlight that cascaded through the portal's clear glass. His mind clear, Thalen replayed the dream in his head, examining the details and turning over the events that transpired to examine all angles. Though it felt much the same as his other dreams one detail stuck out to him, the sword was glowing. He let his eyes drop down from the window to the desk that was only a few feet from where he stood, that gaze sliding inevitably down the length of the weapon that sat upon it, his eyes stopping to rest upon the silvery robin's head. He knew it was just a dream and though he swept the dream itself away something kept his mind stuck on the sword itself *"It was given to me by Cameral...I know there is more to the story...perhaps it is time to truly investigate it."* he thought his mind made up.

He sighed somewhat annoyed at his decision as spending the day looking into the origin of the sword itself hadn't been something he considered a priority, though luckily, he did not have much else to do as today as it was a day off from classes. As he dressed, he considered where best he could find the information he sought, he suspected the best place would likely be the library or study areas, yet the sword was shrouded in such mystery that it likely would not be in any normal text. Even more so, if there was any mention of the swords name it would likely be in a more literal sense, being about robin tails and not about the unusual weapon, yet he knew there would be no better place to begin the search. His course set before him, he finished pulling on his boots and marched from the room, strapping to his hip the sword he was determined to learn more about. Once he arrived at the library, Thalen took in the expansive room, shelves filled with tomes of all shapes, kinds, and sizes appeared to stretch for hundreds of meters in all directions. Looking above he found himself still amazed with the height of the ceiling and the three-tiered structure of the library, each floor filled with just as many shelves and just as many books as the one he was one now. Within the center if the library stood an open-air staircase that stretched up as though to the sky, it leading from the lowest floor to those high above. After a moment he felt his smile of wonder turn into a frown of concern as he realized what a monumental task stood before him.

The sheer amount of material he would have to pour through to ensure he did not miss any speck of information was likely in the hundreds. That number being after he mentally limited the search to only those books that would be related to weaponry, he sighed and longed for the answers as he felt the First Mage must have had but did not provide. Resigned to his fate, Thalen began walking the corridors of shelves each filled with volumes upon volumes of books, scrolls and more, at long last he arrived at the section he intended. Fortunately, the library was laid out in an easy grid with each section marked clearly in the language the works were written in. He took a moment to steel himself for the task before picking up the first volume that caught his eye, *Weapons of Wonder, and their Stories.*

"There have been many weapons imbued with great power by mages. These weapons have come in all sizes and deadliness..."

Thalen sighed and prepared himself for something he had started doing far more than he ever had before, researching, examining and reading longwinded and tedious books.

Thalen read book after dry book hoping for any mention of the sword or anything resembling it, yet he could find nothing. Nearly every work he read would speak of imbuing weapons with magic or of weapons that had been created in more recent years that contained magic for only short amounts of time. Some of the books spoke of exotic and rare weapons, yet none of them bore even a passing description of that which was upon the long table in front of him. Counting the number he had scoured already Thalen realized he had poured through at least ten books, each a few hundred pages each. Having lost track of time during the process he checked the giant water clock that stood suspended high above the floor and realized in horror that nearly ten hours had passed since he began his investigation. He took a moment to message his temples, the traces of a headache playing just behind his eyes from the strain of reading in nothing, but the dim light of the orbs strewn throughout the place. He felt, not for the first time, his frustration welling within him as so much time had passed and yet nothing, he could not find a single shred of information about the weapon whatsoever. *"How could something so ornate...something that the damned First Mage himself had in his possession seem to not exist in any records of man. This place has more books, tomes, scrolls and the like than I have ever seen in my entire life and likely the lives of my father and his father before him. Yet, nothing!"* Frustration getting the better of him he slammed shut the work before him, the sound an explosion within the silent room. He stood and strapped the object of his ire back onto his hip before he stormed from the room, intent on food, wine and something to break, in the hopes that a combination of the three would restore his frayed nerves and ease his rising temper.

Reaching the great hall Thalen sat heavily at an open table, setting his meal and drink before him he began ripping into a roast duck with abandon, as his hunger fully took over. Stripping the last piece of flesh from the carcass he took a sip of the cheap but satisfying wine in his flagon and sat back considering the issue before him, the lack of information on the sword was detrimental if not somewhat concerning to him. Even so, he could not believe that Cameral would have given him something and told him to search for answers with there being none to have. Although he had to admit to himself that he could not help but feel that given who his benefactor was it was always a possibility, even a small one. He wished more than anything in that moment that the elf had simply told him where to look, or better yet simply told him about the sword in the first place. Thalen huffed as he nested his chin between his hands and took a deep breath in an attempt to release some of his frustration, eventually letting it fade away into nothingness as he let the sounds of the hall wash over him momentarily.

Sitting in silent contemplation he caught himself listening to those around him, though not overly fond of eavesdropping it could hardly be helped in the crowded space. "...I need to get a book from the library later then I can joi..." a young man with a neatly trimmed beard was saying. "...Can you teach me that one spell you do...the one that makes use of earth to trap your enem..." said a small Raital woman. "...yeah I couldn't find information on that in any of the human text...yeah it surprised me too, turns out, human text doesn't have much about the Raital's culture, I had to look at books in their native tongue..." Thalen's eyes shot open, as he realized his own stupidity. *"That's it, I can't believe I ignored something so obvious! If I cannot find anything in the words of man, perhaps those of elves have that which I seek...of course I am not well versed in their tongue. Yet, it is worth the shot, I will have to spend another day or so checking a few more potential human sources, but if that fails I will have to move on."* he felt a surge of excitement at the new possibilities before him and with renewed vigor made his way to the library once more.

Even with the epiphany Thalen still found himself spending not only the remainder of that day, but in fact several days searching through material in both his native tongue and that of the elves. He had completed the works of man in relatively short order the task taking him not but another day and a half before he had exhausted all likely sources. However, his lack of familiarity with the language of the elves turned what was before a tolerable task into a true slog of parchment, translative references, and frustration.

Thalen ran a free hand through his hair in annoyance, the slickness of it, from the natural oils, sending a small shiver down his spine. *"I have to bathe soon...I have been too consumed with this search."* he thought to himself as he stretched his arms high above his head before having a hand fall to his neck probing an annoying kink. He could tell the days of sitting hunched over the dusty tomes was starting to take a toll on his body and was seriously considering giving up his search for now. Yet, he was determined to at least give the task until the end of the day picking up the book before him and snapping it closed. Walking over to the nearest shelf, he replaced the book in its spot before scanning the spines of its neighbors for his next conquest. Taking his time, he made sure to read clearly the titles laced along the spines of each book, he lamented his middling familiarity with the elvish language as he knew it was slowing his progress considerably. Suddenly his eyes stopped, his attention drawn, as they rested on one of the tomes, plucking it from the shelf he turned it over in his hands, he could not say for sure what had drawn him to this particular book. Unlike the others it was a very ordinary looking brown leather, held together by a very normal binding with the engraved lettering of the title being not much more than the outlines of the characters themselves with no fill of gold, silver or bronze, as was the case with many others. Perhaps, he thought to himself, it was in fact it's normalcy and simplicity that had caught his attention, it seeming out of place amongst the garish works beside it. Returning to his borrowed desk, he placed the book down and seated himself, before slowly reading the cover and translating the script in his mind. *"Dir'Nir Actith...what is that...That which was previous to the change...no that doesn't seem right, That which was before the change. That seems more correct. I have no idea what made me grab this one but since we are here."* He ran his hands along the spine once more before opening the plain tome, determining it would be best to translate as much of the text as possible before reading it for substance, much as he had done with the previous works. It was slow going, but after about three or four hours he had a rough translation of the three chapters that most likely seemed to have the answers he was chasing.

"...Long ago in an age far past, the world of Eoch was filled with power, the very veins of the

world overflowing with that which we call magic. "This power was a raw thing and only the most rudimentary understanding was had by the mortal creatures of this world; even the most long lived of the elves could claim no greater than a passing understanding forming spells of a rudimentary sort with little power and even less affect. This continued on for some time until they came, little is remembered of them or what they appeared as. Truthfully the only thing even the longest lived remember is the warmth that seemed to permeate the area around them, as though their very existence was kindness and comfort. These people came through a rift that seemed to exist in the very fabric of our world, coming through as though they were but friendly visitors interested in our world. With them they brought a greater understanding of the power that lay within the soil, though they should have been seen as threats they instead seemed to integrate themselves with those native to not just this world but this dimension..."

Thalen frowned as he was not sure exactly what he was reading but it was different than anything he had ever read previously. The words, even translated as they were, flowed from the page as though trying to bring you back to the very moment the author was recording. Yet, he felt it was even more than that, as the words seemed to suggest something completely contrary to the current understanding of magic's existence! He felt a shiver of excitement at the thought and his discovery, and yet, it was not what he was searching for and so he read on.

"As the years passed a deeper understanding of the power within Eoch was garnered, the new peoples tutoring all other races in its use, until it truly permeated the everyday life of its users. Not only were spells crafted but items that would harness the power into easily usable forms and without realizing all began to depend on it. As with many other things, that dependance would be part of their downfall, with magic being accessible by all there was little advancement in other fields. After all, why learn how to make new medicine if you can simply use magic to kill the infection and heal the wound within seconds, why learn how best to grow a crop when you can simply force the crop to grow. This dependance caused the magic within the world to stretch and grow becoming stronger similar to exercising a muscle, however, even with this overuse things were well with many people flourishing in every way. Yet, this was not meant to last as power always attracts those with ill intent. After the end of it happened the end of it years several..."

Thalen reread the section several times confused until he realized he had mistranslated, grumbling to himself he fixed his error and carried on.

"After several decades had passed the beings that had arrived through the rift declared the use of magic must be curbed. They said our world would become a battleground if the current path

was continued on, implying that they were not the only species that had discovered how to traverse the realms. The people and leaders of the world heard but disregarded their warnings, something that they would come to regret. It was described as though the world was ending, suddenly crackles of lightning flew throughout the now cloudy and darkened sky, as they felt the ground shake beneath their feet as a sickly line appeared within thin air slowly lengthening before exploding open to reveal a pale white light beyond. To all observing it was immediately apparent that this was far different from those who had come before, as though the feeling of ill intent poured through the breach in their world. It was told that within moments, creatures of evil and malice poured from the breach, as though a dam had broken, several figures clad in dark armor, their skin pale came to the forefront and within a mere moment slaughtered all in the immediate area. At least that is as the stories were passed, what is known to be true is that slowly these invaders expanded their influence, the places they stood changed and seemed to be drained of life and vigor and over time that plague spread across the Northern most continent turning it into nothing but a wasteland of death. Eventually, these monsters clashed with the visitors from another realm and were contained though not driven back, the might of those that came to be known as the Dear Ones held the Dead Ones, those who sought this worlds destruction...or perhaps consumption, at bay.

As the fight between them came to a standstill these Dead ones seemed to have created those Evil races that now exist within the world. Creatures of brutish strength and color unnatural to this world, it is unclear if these monstrosities were created by corrupting that which already was or were created. These being, what we now call Orks tipped the scales, and the cycle of destruction began again..."

Thalen paused his reading somewhat astonished by what the book contained, he had never investigated the origin of the orks, or even the world itself for that matter. Then again, he mused to himself, it isn't like there was ever a reason for him to look into any of this in the first place. He picked up the tome again intent on continuing before his mind wandered further and took him from his task, he read on, finding nothing of interest for several paragraphs before the words picked up again.

"...as the war dragged on the Dead Ones seemed to gain an upper hand, with their new pets pushing the ever-shrinking forces of those that opposed them and their all-consuming desire. Yet, during this time the Dear Ones were not still and with the help of the greatest of the Dwarvish smiths crafted weapons of great power these items came in many forms. They were not like those of some fable or child's tale, they were not merely a few crafted for the hands of heroes but hundreds crafted and imbued with what seemed to be the power of the Dear Ones themselves.

Something I feel I must clarify at this point is

why the Dead Ones appear to be of much greater power than the Dear Ones. As the saying goes "It is far easier to destroy than it is to create" and this is true of the Dead vs Dear Ones question. The power of the Dead ones or rather how they employed their power was in the form of pure destruction and due to this they had a far greater personal effect on the battlefield and though some Dear ones did employ such methods they were less suited. They spent most of their time healing those injured during the fighting or crafting and creating great bastions and defenses to help delay and slow the enemy. The creation of these weapons could have been taken as a last-ditch effort, as they had never before put items of such power within the hands of other races, though the exact number was lost long ago.

Though a last effort it may have been, that it was enough to turn the tides yet again, yet this time it was in favor of the Dear Ones and the goodly folk of the world. It was said those warriors that received the Dear Ones creations found themselves able to control and channel magic better as well as channel power into the weapons themselves. Thus, any whom held these weapons became known as Salal'yantir as it was said they sang as they fought and their weapon seemed to respond with song of its own, or perhaps instead, the mortal wielding it felt compelled to sing in response to its song..."

Thalen stopped reading his excitement threatening to overwhelm him, as he could not help but think he had finally found a true lead in his search for answers. Yet, as he read on, he found his hope was a false one as the rest of the book contained only cursory mentions of these powerful weapons between the passages describing the ending of the war which culminated in the expelling of the Carthan'Oness, translated to *"Dead Ones"*, from the world as well as the scattering of their orkish armies. Yet, this also meant the exodus of the Solan'Oness, translating to *"Dear Ones"*, leaving the realm and with the approval of all goodly races sealing the latent magic of the world. It was reasoned that if they and the world's magic remained the Carthan'Oness would return to the realm intent on finishing what they had started.

Thalen closed the book, its hard cover snapping shut as he pushed it away with some disgust, just when he thought he would have answers he found nothing but disappointment. The search was not in vain, though he did not find mention of his sword itself, it very well could be one of these now fabled weapons. This being a prospect he found exciting and yet the feeling was tempered with the frustration of a story half finished, the feeling of coming so close to the answers he sought but it was snatched away. He determined he would search for more information or at least tales of these song mages, as perhaps their stories could further point him towards the story of his weapon and if he was truly fortunate how to make use of its power.

Though a look at the water clock told him the hunt would not continue that day, as he returned the book and set off from the library, his mind afire with new possibilities.

CHAPTER EIGHTEEN

Thalen continued his search over the next several days, but to no avail and as days turned into a week he simply could not justify continuing. Especially not with the advancement tests, that so affected his future, approaching ever faster. With the tests so close at hand Thalen chose to spend the remainder of his waning days practicing and studying with the aid of his friends. Once the last few weeks were up the day finally came and the tests awaited him, whether he was ready or not.

Thalen stepped out of his room into the busy hallway, going over in his mind what he had been studying the evening before. He tried, likely in vain, to absorb every small detail of it, trying to imprint in his mind the best way to imbue magic with extra power for a stronger spell. He was so absorbed in his thoughts that he did not have time to notice the change in general attitude that the day brought. An air of festivity soaked the atmosphere around him though his mind drowned out the low murmur and buzz of discussion the day had seemed to bring. It appeared as though all members of the college had thoughts about the day, whether they be higher circle members recalling their own ascension, professors wondering aloud at the skills that would be on display or the grumble of a soon to be testee. Yet, none of that made a difference to Thalen as he focused on what was before him, this was a mission just as the others he carried out in the past and he had no intentions of failing. The day was meticulously planned out, he would begin with breakfast, take some time for further practice and then eat lunch all before the opening ceremony just past noon. He could not help but think it was strange they would conduct a ceremony for something like tests, yet he would not complain as he knew deep down it would give him more time to steel his nerves for what lay ahead.

As Thalen collected his preferred breakfast of eggs, bread, and cheese he thought of the two tests that would come this day, expecting them to be difficult to overcome, given how short his time to learn and advance had been. He felt reasonably confident he could deal with the second test, it involving creativity and thinking on his feet, as he had spent time expanding his vocabulary and testing word combinations. It was by far the first test that he thought would be the more challenging. He knew his control of power was not even close to where he needed it to be, it was far too inconsistent, it was almost like a scale to one hundred. Essentially feeling he could increment his power in terms of twenties on a bad day and tens on a good day, while others that had practiced the arts far longer than he, incremented consistently in fives. *"Hell, I would even take just being able to increment in tens with consistency."* he thought to himself grumbling. *"Oh well, no point in worrying about it at this point, that is the whole point of practice. I just don't have enough time to gain such consistency…well I hope today is a good day."* washing down the last piece of bread with cool water he stood and made his way to the nearest practice room for his last chance at perfection…or at least consistency.

CHAPTER NINETEEN

Thalen tried to not move too much as he stood stock still with the other testers in the courtyard of the College Keep, the group was before a well-constructed stage that Headmaster Pelorin seemed to dominate. Standing at a lectern, he gave a speech that Thalen had stopped paying attention to several words in as his mind wandered to the tests before him. Though distracted he scanned the surroundings with a deep-seated practice that had become second nature. He did his best to take in everything as the festive appearance of the courtyard was nearly overwhelming with streamers, food stalls and townsfolk staying around the edges cordoned off from the main area by a heavy rope. Each of them jostled as politely as they could in the hopes of getting the best possible spot to view the days entertainment. Even though the spectators were good natured, here and there Thalen saw the armored forms of the keeps garrison moving about the crowd ensuring that the jockeying for position would stay polite at all times. After a few moments a shadow passed over him and he instinctively looked up spotting the elegant bodies of Winsetti patrolling the skies, if nothing else he felt confident security was of the utmost importance and relaxed back into the numbing thoughts of breaking glass panes.

Thalen dove deeper into his mind as the speech and murmur of the crowd became nothing more than white noise, this allowing him to better wrack his brain for what just might work best for the level of skill he knew he possessed. He knew the most painful and challenging part of the first test was the matching of the panes, obviously this was the point, yet it was difficult to envision the best way to set them. *"Well..."* he thought to himself *"obviously the best way would be to have them all lined in descending order, but that is not an option. Would it be best to have them alternating starting with the strongest...no no I am not concerned about the toughest or weakest pairings."* he let out a soft breath and checked in on the progress of Pelorin's speech. At this point he was thanking someone named Bayline Kanterport for allowing the use of her land, not that he had any idea who that was. He shrugged slightly before diving back into planning. *"Where was I... right I am not concerned about the pairing of weakest and strongest, if I alternate the weakest and strongest leaving one at the end and starting with seven should be enough to get me through most of them. Perhaps if I go 7, 4, 8, 3, 9, 2, 10, 1, 6, 5...but at that point I am just pairing them all down the line that isn't necessarily bad and would keep my potential losses to a minimum. No, I can't even guarantee I have enough control for seven or possibly even eight. I have to figure out how to take advantage of the stronger panes without running the risk that I will fail on the weaker...after all if I can't break it I won't be able to move forward anyway."* he mulled over the question for a few more minutes until he noticed a change in tempo of the Headmaster's words and drew himself out of his own mind. "...as we move forward with the tests, do recall that tomorrow is something equally, if not more, important than the exams this day. As we all know, we are at war and with war we all can expect combat as with the power we possess and the skills we instill in all mages. We are some of the Alliance's greatest strength and so a great weight is put onto your performance tomorrow during the battle tournament. However, do not think you can slip through the challenges that stand just before you, though tomorrow may have greater weight, failure in the coming tasks will stop you from advancing your circle. Now, let us begin."

Suddenly, the courtyard began to glow with bright white and yellow light, and before any of the group could react the world seemed to go dark and with what seemed to Thalen like an audible pop it became bright again. Thalen looked about, finding that he had gone into a low crouch by instinct, his hand at his hip ready to pull the sword that was not there. From what he could tell he had appeared in a field, along with every other participant as well as multiple instructors and staff members of the College, who seemed far less concerned than his peers about the sudden change in scenery, as though they knew this would happen all along. In fact, he expected they did, standing up he took a better look around getting his bearings in the new space. He expected a large building or some type of range to be in the area, yet to his surprise it really did appear to just be an empty field holding nothing but those around him. No keep, shooting range, or even a simple shack was within view. Just as he was about to speak up the Headmaster's voice spoke out *"Welcome! I am sure you are all somewhat confused by what has just happened. You have been teleported around twenty miles from the College and the surrounding area, this is to ensure there are no issues with..."* Thalen felt something was strange about the Headmaster's voice, but he could not determine exactly what. *"...misfires and keeps any danger from overall observers. The tests themselves will be conducted by the proctors on site, while those that score watch from a remote location via magic we have set up beforehand..."* suddenly he understood what was bugging him, the voice was not one traversing through the air to his ears but instead was directly within his mind. Looking about he realized that only some of the others had understood this, easily recognizable by their glassy-eyed look as if they were staring into an abyss.

Thalen felt that was an overreaction by the others, though it was hardly comfortable, it was not the first strange thing he had experienced since the awakening of his abilities. He closed his eyes and tried to adjust to the voice in his mind, as he listened to the end of what Pelorin was saying. *"...with this we are now ready to begin the exams, Instructor Luminaris will be the proctor of this test and should be listened to and respected as if he were myself. They and the other proctors have the full authority of my office and may remove you from the testing if they deem fit. Thank you and remember we are watching."* Once the last word was uttered, Thalen found his mind completely silent before his own thoughts took back over, to some degree it was almost stranger to hear only his own voice in his mind again. He let out a sigh of relief as he felt the unnoticed tension leave his shoulders, feeling more relaxed, he opened his eyes, prepared for the challenges ahead.

"Alright you lot, eyes up here!" a commanding voice yelled out from Thalen's left "Come on faster, we don't have all day, dammit!" Thalen's life of military training kicked in, snapping to attention as his eyes found the speaker. Proctor Luminaris was a very unassuming elvish man, his pointed ears framed by long and straight brown hair that cascaded down his shoulders. His angular face was dominated by a thin-lipped mouth and almond eyes, common features among his kinsman, his cascading robes, which were adorned with the emblem of the order had three stars below the palm showing that he was a mage of the second circle. Once the entire group turned to him, he spoke loudly not to admonish but to ensure all could hear him. "So, thus begins the exams you all know what is expected of you so let's not waste any further time." biting off the final word he clapped his hands together and as if on cue the earth beneath their feet began to shake. Fortunately, before any panic could set in, walls began to tear out from beneath the group as they pushed up from the quickly separating ground. This continued until a large warehouse-like building appeared where an empty field had once stood. Thalen was sure that anyone looking at the group would describe their wide-eyed expressions as surprised to say the least, he knew for sure that he was. *Then again perhaps I shouldn't be surprised about anything at this point.* he thought to himself as he and everyone else filtered through the large open doors of the building. The structure itself was not overly impressive, a very simple utilitarian design was present throughout with no designs upon the wall beyond an occasional order symbol, what most impressed Thalen about the space was the large five-person range crafted in a way that suggested safety was paramount. Each range was more like a bunker, as opposed to the normal range one would use for archery, with thick stone walls lining the sides of each range each of them likely enchanted to ward off any spell misfires. *"What am I doing, I don't have time to marvel at architecture I still need to figure out how I am going to get through this trial!"* Thalen admonished himself for his lack of discipline, he knew better than to get distracted by something so trivial, as he stood upon the knives edge, the question of his return to a more normal life hanging in the balance.

As the last of the group filed in, the doors closed, leaving them briefly in pure darkness before lights of varying hues came to life lighting up their surroundings. Once more, the main proctor stood before them as he looked over the gathered crowd to ensure all eyes were on him. "Now that all is prepared, we are going to determine who will be taking the test at what point. As can be seen the range can accommodate five at a time, this of course meaning that turns will be taken in the attempt to break the glass and complete the challenge. With this we have predetermined the order, and it will appear before you now." Thalen saw

Luminaris make a small gesture and then suddenly found a piece of paper appear before his very eyes. The paper's sudden appearance caused him to take an involuntary step back in surprise with barely enough time to catch it as it floated towards the floor. Snatching the paper out of the air Thalen checked his number it being twenty-five. *"Not a bad number, it will give me plenty of time to come up with something or at least I'll be able to see what others do first."* he thought to himself, yet as though reading his mind Proctor Luminaris spoke, his light voice containing some degree of mockery "I am sure some of you are looking at your slot and find yourself quite pleased with it, likely you are thinking you will get to see how others take up the challenge ahead." He paused as a sly smile crept onto his thin lips. "Yet, I have some news for you all that might just remove that happiness..." he paused again, ensuring all eyes were on him before he continued "Some might see it as unfair that they have to go before others, they don't have the benefit of seeing what others have done. So, to balance this those in the first group will have three panes forgiven, the second group two panes and the third group one pane. Of course, those in the final groups will not be forgiven any failed attempts." he stopped, seemingly to allow his words to sink into their minds. When he seemed satisfied that all understood, or perhaps when he saw enough frustration in their eyes, the proctor continued with a clap of his hands "Now! Here is where the fun begins, you may trade your number with any of the other participants. Thus, allowing you to either move further back or further forward in the order, but that is up to you. The first group will begin in ten minutes and then each will be ten minutes after that until all have gone. Make your plans now as time passes quicker than you think." As he finished an evil smile sat on his lips and with a wave of his hand a large hourglass appeared, suspended in midair, its grains of sand slowly slipping between the chambers.

For not the first time since he awakened his powers, Thalen completely unsure of what to do, his first instinct was to go deep into his own mind to solve the riddle that lay before him, yet he knew if he had not come up with an answer by now he was unlikely to at all, especially with the new wrinkle. His second instinct was to consult with his companions and that was the action he decided to take, searching out Dolgrath, Keela and Elara amongst the small crowd. As Thalen searched, he spotted them one by one as they too seemed to have a similar plan, they all met together in an open space near the center of the large structure and as was normally the case Dolgrath spoke first. "Well, this be a fine bit oh trickery now ain't it. They be tellin' us this be normal…er well as normal as a mage's test can be and yet they be changin the rules o' the game."

he said his gruff voice filled with annoyance. "Dolgrath I would think no less should be expected by now at the hands of the order. They do like their tricks" responded Keela her voice calm and light as always. *"How in all the realms does she never seem disturbed, I can't help but be jealous."* Thalen thought to himself as he looked at the hourglass noticing the sand appeared to already be nearly a quarter gone. "Alright, enough of that we hardly have time for the usual back and forth my friends. What numbers do we all have? I have twenty-five." Thalen said his tone containing the hint of command he had learned to use with junior officers. As Thalen had hoped they responded to the subtle push in his tone, each responding in kind starting with Elara and ending with his surly dwarfish friend. "So, to recap, Elara has nine, Keela has twenty-two and Dolgrath has four. That does make us rather spread out now doesn't it, I suppose the first question is does anyone wish to switch? Of course, the only ones, worth switching with are Elara or Dolgrath as both Keela and I are in the same group." he paused for a moment allow the others to digest what he had said. Stealing a glance at the timepiece Thalen found that half of the sand had rushed into the lower chamber, leaving only scant time before Dolgrath's group was up.

As if on cue his friend spoke "I think I be okay with me position. I know how I be plannin on breakin the glass as I be thinkin me control is well and good enough to do only what I be wishin. Then I can be helpin the rest o' ya figure out yer own if ye be needing." he finished throwing a look Thalen's way. "You don't have to spare my feelings friend I believe that both Elara and Keela will pass without issue. And as long as you don't get too excited over the idea of blowing things up, I'm sure you'll be fine too." Thalen said with a laugh. "If I am to be truthful, I am concerned and have been thinking perhaps it would be in my best interest to see if anyone would wish to trade for an earlier slot. The forgiveness may be the difference between success and failure in this challenge." Probing his fingers at the back of his neck he attempted to release some of the tension he felt building. "I cannot afford to go in the first group as I have yet to determine how best to break the glass, though I feel most secure at the higher ratings. Though, if I hold back even subconsciously I may be stuck without breaking any." Thalen dug his fingers deeper into the base of his neck now trying desperately to loosen the tightened tendons and muscle but to no avail. He felt a hint of panic set in, causing a fluttering of his heart, he felt the spiral that he had only experienced two other times in his life. Those being when his home was destroyed when he was young and when his dear friend was slain just scant months ago. He told himself he was being foolish, he had faced down monstrous orks and their dragon masters while this was nothing more than a test, a task for him to complete. However, he felt the pressure of what failure meant, it looming unhidden behind the challenge threatening to crush him. Then as suddenly as it began, he felt the spell break as soft hands found their way to his broad shoulders before moving up to the base of his skull aiding in relieving the tension he could not remove himself. "Relax Thalen, I am sure this will work out fine. You are far stronger than you think, and you'll just have to figure out how to tone it down a little!" Thalen turned finding that the rich and calming voice had belonged to Elara, a smile brightening her beautiful face even more, as his eyes met hers he felt heat rise in his cheeks. Breathing deep he felt the last of his stress leave his shoulders, his frayed nerves calm and to his relief his skin was tanned just enough to hide most of his embarrassment. Feeling far better than before he flashed her a smile "Thank you Elara I appreciate your words, they have helped bolster my heart." she smiled warmly at him, as they locked eyes, neither seeming willing to break the moment. Fortunately, it was broken for them from a surprising source as Keela cleared her throat with a clear indication that she had seen quite enough.

The two of them turned red as they tore their eyes from each other looking instead to the interrupting elf, who Thalen thought had a very satisfied look on her face. "Now that our two lovebirds have returned to us, perhaps we should consider Thalen's circumstances." she said with undisguised amusement. "After all we only have perhaps a quarter of the time remaining and I agree with Thalen's assertion that we three will pass without issue, but he may struggle." she steepled her fingers in thought, which seemed like a signal to Thalen that they should return to the task at hand.

The group grew silent, each absorbed in their own thoughts as they tried to determine the best way for Thalen to attack the first test. As Thalen began to feel his patience waning, Elara's eyes seemed to light up but as she opened her mouth the proctor's strong voice rang out above the general murmur. "Alright, first group up!" the main proctor yelled, making it obvious that the time had passed far quicker than they expected, as all of the proctors began yelling the same rehearsed phrase. "First group up! Numbers one through five go to the range now" the drone of the voices yelling at the top of their lungs shocked most of the first group into action, though Dolgrath had already begun moving towards the range as soon as his group was called. "We must be quick friends time is running out, if we are to come up with a plan we must do so soon" said Keela as the first sounds of shattering glass could be heard, though they were accompanied by the occasional curse. "Do we have any thoughts?" His mind nearly blank, Thalen continued to weigh his options but could not come to any easy conclusion, his greatest fear with starting with the hardest was potentially not being able to produce enough power to break the glass. His second greatest fear was incorrectly breaking the most closely matched panes, being five and six and four and seven. As Thalen continued thinking, an audible gasp ripped from Elara followed by "I think I have it! You should switch with me, it's so simple we were ignoring the answer." Thalen could feel her excitement as though the pulses of her emotions traversed through him like a sweet song. He took a moment to bask in the glory of it before opening his mouth to speak, but as usual he found himself interrupted. "I am not sure I truly follow you Elara, what is it we are missing?" asked Keela, her melodic voice feeling in stark contrast to the slightly deeper timber of the human woman. She turned to Keela her eyes seeming to shine in triumph "It truly is so simple Keela, if Thalen switches with me, he will be forgiven some of panes of glass, to put it simply it should be enough to cover any mistakes he makes. Instead of using it for the purpose they designed it for, being to provide advantage to those considering how best to break the panes, we use it instead to compensate for Thalen's lack of skill!" Thalen felt his eyes widen a little involuntarily, it was such a simple solution and one that should help him get through the first challenge, he did regret that they did not come up with this before Dolgrath's group was called. *"That one extra pane may be the difference, yet this should hopefully be enough. If I arrange the panes as one, three, two, eight, nine, ten to start I should have eight panes broken with the two forgiven."* Thalen smiled at Elara "That is perfect Elara! Yes let's switch." With the decision made they switched their numbers just as Dolgrath returned to them, having fully completed the challenge before the last grain of the refreshed hourglass fell into the lower chamber.

They brought their dwarfish friend up to speed with the plan as the voice of a proctor rang out above the crowd "Alright, time is up! Those remaining from group one remove yourself from the range any who attempt to break another pane at this time will be failed immediately! Second group prepare to step up to the range on our signal." As suddenly as the speech began it ended, bringing everything into a brief silence which was only broken by the frustrated groans of two members of Dolgrath's group. Looking down their lanes, Thalen found that only those two had not cleared the challenge fully as each failed to break all of the panes, one leaving five and the other seven unbroken. *"As long as I do better than those two, I will feel better about myself. I appreciate their sacrifice."* he chucked a little, the dark humor easing some of his tension just as their failure boosted his confidence. Once the signal for the second group was given, Thalen took a deep, steadying breath before moving to his assigned position as the ninth student.

Though it appeared unimpressive from the outside, as the plain stone of the walls were without any ornamentation, as was present throughout the school, Thalen still found them to be extremely impressive. Upon the rocky surface, stones and glyphs of power lined the wall pulsing with latent magic giving the range the familiarity of the college's many practice rooms. Embedded within the left wall was a tablet with the numbers one through ten listed out, runes of power seated below each number and above them sat instructions which Thalen prepared to read before something caught his eye. Turning to the right an hourglass came into view, its grains of sand traveling steadily downward, the base reading eight minutes of ten remaining. He swore at himself for wasting time in wonder before returning to the instructions, reading as swiftly as he could. *"Pulse magic into the runes below the pane number that you wish to appear, the glass will materialize within the range at varying distances. You can only select one pane at a time and if a pane is destroyed poorly the connecting pane will not be available. Note that the distances the panes appear are at random, so no two experiences are the same."* Reading this, Thalen felt his temper flare slightly *"Damn, well at least I didn't ask Dolgrath his experience...and once again they managed to add another twist."* He took a steadying breath intent on following through with his original plan even if another obstacle was placed before him. Raising his hand to the rune below the number one he pulsed magic into it, as the power released from him the rune pulsed green then yellow before pulsing a harsh red and producing a small puff of smoke revealing a crack across its face.

CHAPTER TWENTY

It took Thalen a moment to fully comprehend what had just happened as his mind finally processed what his eyes had just seen. "What in all the realms just happened?!" he yelled before he could stop himself, as anger and frustration threatened to overwhelm him once more. It took a few seconds to remaster his emotions and, once he was back in control of them, began to examine the rune that had shattered. *"Cracked directly across the face, it reacted poorly as soon as I began to release power into it...wait don't tell me."* A thought broke in midstream as he pulsed only a little power into the tenth rune but it did not react. *"Damnit, there is another twist to this bullshit test. I don't have time to think too deeply into it, but I would guess the runes also measure the amount of power channeled into it. I'll have to adjust my approach."* He checked the time remaining seeing that he only had about seven minutes remaining. With no time to waste, he focused his mind as he placed his hand over the ninth rune, the logic was simple if he could not depend on summoning the lower ones with ease it would be best to start with the higher ones, as they left him with more room for error. Transferring power into the rune he found that, unlike the previous, it pulsed green then yellow and then back to a more solid green color, looking down the range he saw a glass pane marked with a nine in the corner suspended about four meters away from him.

Breathing a sigh of relief Thalen started to feel a little more confident in his new system but it was short lived as he caught sight of the hourglass, its sand telling him he was running out of time. Without a moment to lose he began channeling power; he took his time as he knew from experience that rushing would cause him more problems than not and once he felt he had enough power collected he sighted his target. As he had many times before he pushed out his hand and he exclaimed the words of power "Col'Fir Tole!" that power turned to heat within his palm as a ball of flame fired forward. The attack flew through the air before striking the pane with an audible crack, as it shattered its broken pieces fell to the ground. Thalen felt a surge of relief at his success but quickly quashed it as he knew he had more work to do, having destroyed nine he felt the best decision would be to try number two as he could not pick eight and with nine already destroyed a mistake would only cost him one instead of two panes. He relaxed his shoulders and began to infuse himself with power, but he tempered it to the best of his ability trying to pull in and then transfer into the rune only what was required. He raised his hand before it and pulsed power in, much as the others it pulsed green, then yellow, and then, much to Thalen's relief, a solid green. At the same moment a new pane of glass appeared about two meters from him, without a second thought he channeled what he believed, was the same amount of power and shot a fire bolt once more. As it made impact unlike his last shot the glass pane seemed to explode sending shards out in all directions some shooting in his direction faster than he could react, fortunately, they stopped in mid-air blocked by a shield before falling to the ground. *"That may have been a bit too much power, it's hard to say if that one will count...it doesn't matter if I am to have any hope I must reign it in a little."* Though he may have failed that pane he felt his confidence grow as he better understood the design of the challenge, even though they were forced to produce the same amount of power twice, the fact they had to pulse into the gem beforehand gave them a test run. It was reasonable to assume that if they failed in the summoning they would have failed to break the glass correctly, but if they did not all they had to do was repeat what they already had done. It certainly added danger, but it also produced opportunity for correction as the gem seemed more forgiving than the glass pane itself.

Moving onto the eighth pane it went without a hitch, as he easily destroyed it while avoiding the fantastic explosion of the last. *"Three down, five left."* Feeling a need for speed he destroyed both panes six and four in quick succession, four was a close thing as he almost failed to even summon it, fortunately he succeeded, though it had pulsed yellow far longer than the others. *"Three minutes remaining, three left, just have to manage one per minute."* he thought to himself as sweat began to bead upon his forehead, the focus required for the fine control beginning to take its toll. Yet, he pushed through destroying five without a hitch, finally the end was in sight only two remained between him and the tasks completion. With one final exertion Thalen summoned number three barely managing to push enough power into it as his concentration was beginning to wane, he had been in battle and commanded in the most dire of situations, yet in the moment, nothing felt more difficult than maintaining control! As he gathered up energy intent on destroying the pane that had appeared six meters away, he felt a bead of sweat roll down his neck...and that was it. That one small bead broke his concentration on the spell and upon its release a giant bolt of fire, far stronger than what was required, flew from his palm and struck the pane, causing it to explode, it's shards burying

themselves deep within the stone walls on either side. Thalen cursed himself as he looked at the runes and to his utter dismay the panes matching number, seven, was glowing a steady red.

Thalen let his head hang, a mixture of relief and frustration washing over him as the challenge had ended, though he did not feel satisfied with his performance. *"Damnit...I don't know if that performance was good enough with the two panes forgiven, I would be marked as destroying eight of the ten. Yet, they made the scoring so obscure it is impossible to know what is good or not."* A few scant moments later Thalen heard the signal for the group to halt, those that had not destroyed all of their panes could be heard swearing just loud enough for all to hear. Thalen looked at his progress once more, the panes of glass appearing down the range, three were yellow, four were red, and the remainder green. He suspected that may indicate how well he had done...yet he found this both surprising and confusing as when he looked at the lanes of his group mates he saw only white panes. *"Magic...it must be yet another trick or I suppose a safeguard of the proctors to ensure no hint of what the true challenges are. The bastards even lied about the panes of glass requiring a pre decided order by the participant you could make your decisions as you went much as I did."* rejoining the general crowd he found his friends and relayed his feelings on the experience he had as a whole. He felt good but couldn't keep away the nagging suspicion that it would only get harder from here.

Thalen waited as the final attendees attempted the trial set before the group, though now knew he could not trust his senses to tell him how well they had done, he instead could only take queues from how they acted after their completion. In his estimation he was not the only one taken in by the tricks the test had played, though he hoped he was one of the few that had adjusted to it well. Unsurprisingly, his friends had all managed to make it through without much of an issue, each reporting their varying levels of success, Dolgrath and Keela both managing to destroy them all while Elara managed nine of the ten due to a misstep on the fifth pane. Nonetheless all they could do was wait for the judgment from the proctors on their success or failure, though they were not sure if failure would bar them from taking the remaining tests or if only total failure would.

As the last of the participants reassembled, the voice of the head proctor called them all to silence, killing the murmur of the gathering "Attention all, the first test has been completed, please leave the building and begin your preparations for the next test." As those words were said the doors suddenly opened allowing sunlight to pour into the once dimly lit room, as he basked in the newfound light Thalen couldn't help but think that although the magic lights were useful, they were nothing compared to the shine of the sun itself. Upon leaving the cool interior of the stone building, he allowed himself a moment to stretch and enjoy the relative warmth of the day. The warmth helped him relax and release the tension from his shoulders, which he greatly appreciated. Feeling recovered thanks to his bask in the sun he let his mind begin to think of the next test, it was one of wits or creativity, or perhaps a combination of both, yet much like the one he had just taken, there was nothing guaranteed, nor was it certain that any part of what they were told was accurate. *"There is not a shadow of doubt that these bastards told us something different on purpose. Perhaps this is part of the test itself, maybe they are trying to see how well we think on our feet."* Letting out a sigh he closed his eyes for a moment centering himself before opening them again. As he opened them they were filled with a very pleasant, as it was no longer the throng of people before him, instead it was Elara's shining smile. Thalen felt himself jump at her sudden closeness, the action earning him a small laugh from the young woman. Hearing that chuckle, Thalen gave her an annoyed look, but couldn't keep a small smile from coming unbidden to his lips. As though on queue he truly came to realize that he was growing more and more fond of the shy but spirited woman. As he thought of this his eyes unintentionally sought out and locked onto hers, their smiles never fading. Elara's eyes did not leave his while a redness causing her normally tanned skin to take on a coppery hue, as a smile grew upon her lips. They seemed to be locked in this staring contest for hours, until it was broken by the sound of a throat clearing and a distinctly dwarvish voice calling his name. "Thalen, do ye plan to start lookin at me like that too?" Dolgrath said with a chuckle. Hearing this, Thalen felt his face go warm as a flush came to his cheeks, and Elara's face did the same, before breaking eye contact, embarrassment surging up within him due to his open display. And yet, even with all that, he still near unconsciously said "Only if you were that beautiful my bearded friend." Realizing what he had just said he felt eyes widen slightly, as his heart began thundering in his chest. He felt like a complete fool, though it was lessened somewhat when he saw that Elara's blush had shaded even deeper, and as best he could tell, she did not seem upset at his words.

Thalen tried to change the subject in a vain hope that it would draw attention from his earlier words "That test was certainly something to behold, it was not as described in almost any way." Elara, seeming to take the given chance to move on, voice her agreement "No, it was not as described in the least, yet I do not know if we can now speak of it in detail" she fell silent, her desire to speak more seeming to war slightly with her concern over being penalized. "No, my dear, we can speak of it now, though you were unaware of the world around you." She threw both Thalen and Elara a sly smile before she continued "They released us from our silence, although we must not speak of it to anyone outside of those that have taken it with us." Keela said her tone friendly, though she wore a sly smirk, easily recognizing the intentional subject change. Her small smile slowly grew as Elara blushed, though it was accompanied by an annoyed glance at the elf. Not that it seemed to have any effect on the member of the elder race as she stood unfazed, instead seeming a little amused. After a moment more Keela placed a hand on the shoulder of her human counterpart and gave a small squeeze seemingly in an attempt to alleviate the sting from her words before she continued the conversation. "I must agree that the test itself was not as expected, though I did not fall victim to it, the potential destruction caused by the summoning of the panes, and even more so the need to summon the targets at all was a dirty trick. It causes me some concern over the test that stands before us now." She finished throwing a side eyed glance at the head proctor. "I cannot help but wonder if the changes are at the discretion of the proctors or if they are pre-prepared...no they must be to some point, I doubt they would allow the proctors such leeway and these were far too intense and advanced of alterations to have been anything but pre-decided." she stroked her angular chin in thought, as silence enveloped the group. All of them seemed lost in their own thoughts, Thalen allowed himself to be swept into the murmur of those around him, listening to no one yet hearing everything. As he sunk further into the relaxing hum of the world he found a calm center point he had not felt before the trials had begun, while he had not felt he had done anything truly astounding, he felt that his performance was beyond his original expectations and it gave him confidence that he may complete the final two tests.

He was forced from his meditation as the sounds of crumbling stone filled the air, opening his eyes he saw the test building had been completely broken down as it crumbled into nothing, this happening in time with the main proctor's approach. "Alright you lot, gather round between all us proctors." he said, motioning to where he wanted for the examinees to go. "We are going to teleport back to the campus itself, the second test will be held on the college grounds themselves and will not require the same level of caution in terms of the use of power." Thalen and the rest shuffled into position the head proctor scanning the crowd and his subordinates as they moved to their positions, once everything seemed well he signaled to them with a wave of his hand. In the blink of an eye Thalen found himself back within the confines of the walled courtyard of the College, the sudden return disorientated him as the general levity and fanfare filled the once silent air, the sounds quickly overwhelming his senses. It was apparent he was not the only one suffering from this as a quick glance about showed those around him also grappling with the sudden change. Taking a moment, he closed his eyes and allowed the sounds to wash around and through him, trying as best he could to adjust through the forced exposure. Once he felt the worst of his vertigo disappear he opened his eyes and looked around the space intent on finding the source of his next hurdle. Thalen found that many of those watchers that were milling around the area had moved away from the outskirts of the teleportation area, where Thalen and the rest stood once more. The crowds had moved on to the many stalls, games, and entertainment which had been set up a few hundred meters away in between the boundary of the courtyard and the road beyond that lead to the town itself. Taking a deep breath, he couldn't help but catch the smell of cooking meat that danced upon the light breeze wafting gently past the enormous stone walls of the keep. As if it was waiting for the cue he felt his stomach rumble, as he realized it had likely been hours since he had last eaten. *"Damnit Thalen, you have spent far too many years on this earth to allow yourself to fall into the trap of hunger. I have spent too long here in luxury I am getting soft without the rigors of campaign."* He felt some frustration boil in him as he fought down the hunger, and though he could not completely overcome it, he was able to quash it to the point where it was nothing more than an easily ignorable ache.

"Patience Thalen, getting worked up will do yourself no good in reaching your goal. I just hope they start the next test soon…or at least call a break for food and drink. It is likely past mid-afternoon as best as I can judge and seeing as how we began in the late morning, time has passed far faster than I noticed. I suppose that is what happens when you spend so long within windowless walls." Shaking his head Thalen turned to his friends, all seemingly in their own thoughts as they took in the world around them. Even so, he could not help but notice Elara occasionally looking in his direction. He still was not sure what to make of her, though he was not upset at the attention, he knew that he had neither the time nor focus to devote his full attention to that puzzle as opposed to the one that was upcoming. Realizing that his friends intended to remain silent, each in their own thoughts, he did his best to maintain his tenuous hold on relaxation, ensuring his mind remained clear as he worked to push any thoughts of Elara from his mind for the time being. He only managed some success,

yet he got lucky as he did not have to wait too long, as without preamble what felt like a thunderclap overtook the comparable silence. Thalen's eyes snapped open, and he whirled locking them on the stage and the wisp of a figure which had suddenly appeared upon it, smoke still billowing out from his fiery appearance. Headmaster Pelorin had a smile on his face as he waved his hand in front of himself to clear the air, he coughed lightly to clear his throat as though waiting for them to acknowledge his arrival, not that it took very long given the manner of his appearance. "Hello all, I hope the shock and awe of the last test was not too overwhelming! Though I am sure it wasn't even close to what you imagined, yet it was certainly more fun that way." he said, cracking a smile. "Either way we are onto the next test, this test will take place within the college itself, the first part of this test however... starts now. We will not tell you where the test itself will be held, however, we do have a riddle for you, if you can solve it, then you will have taken a step in the right direction." Pausing for a moment he cleared his throat again, as he did he scanned the crowd before looking into the air and raising his arms, his lips silently shaping words. Thalen felt the telltale gathering of power, the now familiar pressure building in the front of his head, until it seemed to pop and disappear like wine draining from a punctured skin.

With a flash, words appeared in mid-air, pulsing with magic as rainbow colors played across the script, these colors being of all hues, making them both easy to read in the still bright sky yet hard to focus on. Thalen guessed this was likely on purpose to further test and frustrate them, though he could still not tell to what end. Throwing the thoughts away, he worked to focus on the iridescent lettering in an attempt to commit them to memory.

"The way is shown by the light of the hand, finger to thumb being only of one. Lights of power flow through the wood, with tapestries of past and present that line the world. The door does not show the true way, but is just the star to guide, along the path, find where all powers intersect, speak the name of the arrived, and enter."

The words hung in the air for several minutes before fading away, leaving nothing but the blue sky above with the high towers of the Winsetti acting as a backdrop. Once the words were no longer in view, Pelorin's voice rang out, its raspy quality reminding Thalen and all that could hear of his advanced age. "Now that you have your riddle, I will now provide further information for this particular challenge. You may consult with your fellow students, communication is not off limits, however, you may find it less helpful than you would normally imagine." He paused grinning as he seemed to savor some inside joke before continuing. "The second piece of information is that this journey requires two solutions which must be solved in order, the first is the location described, the second...well I will only say it is to answer the riddle itself. Lastly, there is a time limit, you have four hours to complete this. With that I leave you to it and best of luck." With a flourish of his hands, Pelorin disappeared in a flash of light and smoke, it being a display of showmanship that Thalen began to suspect all mages were guilty of.

With the headmasters exit, Thalen turned to his companions, intent on solving the first part of the riddle quickly "Alright, we must pool our minds and understanding of the riddle. Are we agreed?" Once all had nodded their approval, he recited the words as he had seen, yet the more he spoke the more confusion appeared within the group. "What? Did I misremember it?" he asked his concern apparent. Keela spoke up first "That is not what it said..." she paused seeming to recall the words as she remembered. "The tallest peak is too far high, below the ground is too far low. Find the peak with which to see the stars and whence fullest moon light rests upon the peak, speak the name of the arrived and enter." she fell silent briefly before continuing. "I fear we all may have differing riddles to solve. This must be what the headmaster meant when he said we may speak to one another, but it would be less than helpful. Elara, Dolgrath, what of your own?" Dolgrath responded to her first "Well, ye be onto somethin missie, mine be different too." he said as he stroked his beard seeming to be in thought before turning to Elara "Ye seein the same? Yers differ?" she nodded her confirmation, the realization causing them all to lapse into silence. As the silence between them stretched Thalen let his eyes wander, as he looked about the area scanning without thought. He saw a few of his fellow testers speaking in groups while others began to leave the yard with obvious purpose in their strides. This sight forcing him to action as he rounded on his friends his mouth moving before he had fully decided what to say "Do we have any options? We have less than four hours, if we worked together perhaps, we could solve them together? Combine our knowledge perhaps then we can answer these riddles in short order?" The others seemed to consider this, with Keela being the first to respond "That is not a poor idea, though I cannot trust us to discover and go to each location within only a few hours' worth of time..." she lapsed into silence, but Elara picked up right where she had left off. "What if instead of us all working together, we instead work in pairs. That will at least mean that two minds are working on only two riddles, while giving us two hours for each one...I could go with Thalen..." she said the confidence in her voice draining away into bashfulness. Yet Thalen barely noticed as he could already see the benefits of the plan and that was what mattered most to him in the moment. "Yes, let's do that. We have already wasted enough time, and I cannot think of anything better. I wish you both the best of luck." He said to the elf and dwarf before signaling for Elara to follow him as he began the march to his still unknown destination.

CHAPTER
TWENTY-ONE

Once they left the gathering point, Thalen stopped short as he turned towards Elara intent on beginning their brainstorming session. However, he found that she was closer than he expected, his sudden stop giving her no time to react, she managed to avoid him partially, but her booted foot clipped his leg. He reacted his hand shooting out to grab her arm before pulling her back into him just as she started to fall. For a moment Thalen felt her back pressed against him and within moments felt arousal build but suppressed it as best he could as he spun her about locking eyes on her flushed face. Though he once again felt conflicting emotions rising up, he surged forward, dislodging his desire with pure force of will. "Elara what was the riddle you saw? The one I had seen is a bit too broad as of yet, perhaps yours will be easier." She pulled away from him recomposing herself as she spoke "Upon the shores of water near, water cold so ice would appear. One was saved while death was near, beneath the waves yet earth threw clear. The name of the saved will draw you there." Once Elara finished reciting her riddle she fell silent, seeming deep in thought, this allowing Thalen to take a few moments and consider what he had just heard. "That is somewhat unclear now isn't it, does it mean anything to you at all?" he asked her. After a moments she replied "No...not fully, though the part where it talks about water near. The best assumption I could make is it is speaking of the lake the town sits upon, yet there are multiple areas that it could be speaking of. It has several shores frequented by people, with most of them being more than an hour's walk, yet I cannot think of anything better or clearer." Thalen nodded, agreeing with her interpretation "Yes...yes I think you are right, it could only be talking about Vorinth...in that case we should make our way to the closest beach. Do you know the way?" Elara nodded her confirmation and turned towards the way out of the courtyard, Thalen following on her heels, within a few moments they found themselves well past the portcullis as they made their way deeper into the town.

As they traveled in silence Thalen stole a few glances at the woman, noticing for the first time the shine in her eyes and the smile set on her full lips. Thalen allowed himself a moment to think of what it would be like to kiss those lips, before letting the thought pass. As they traveled the silence between them grew, though it was not uncomfortable, it began to grate on him as he realized how ill at ease he could be with the fairer sex. As they made their way between the rows of buildings in the quickly busying street, he thought about the attraction he felt towards Elara, it was as tangible in that moment as the clothes on his very body. While he knew he could not afford the distraction, his mind could not help it, as his eyes wandered towards the curve of her neck which led inevitably to her shoulders and eventually her full-bodied figure. As he had many times before he was forced to admit that he was attracted to her, that feeling only growing stronger the more time he spent alone with her, though he honestly felt that nothing could be gained from pursuing her. No matter what he told himself, he knew it was not because he was too old or she too young, nor because he felt it was not his time to find someone to share his life with, but instead it was how fleeting the moments felt and the thought of life after his ascension. The amount of uncertainty before him made it feel as though nothing could ever be planned in his life, at least not for now.

He knew that he should be focusing on the task at hand as well as seeking out an answer to his riddle or hers, yet instead he thought only of the curve of her body. He could not help but think that even in the loose-fitting robes it was only slightly diminished. As they traveled deeper into the town, Thalen found that no matter how hard he tried he found himself only wishing to bask in her glow. His feelings as a whole had been supercharged by her occasional hints of interest and the unintentional contact their bodies had made earlier. Thalen wanted nothing more than to bask in her aura, one that came from far more than her appearance as that was elevated further by the constant positive energy that seemed to radiate from her. The more he thought about her, the more he realized that Elara had shown, and continued to show, that she was far more than just a pretty face, she was intelligent, kind and friendly to all and in some ways, he found her similar to Sarah. As much like Sarah, she held deep reserves of strength that could not be discerned from a simple glance at the surface that one could steal. He began to feel uncomfortable with his infatuation and thoughts, deciding that for now he had to place them into a box, locking that box and throwing away the key to finally return to the task at hand. To his best guess they had been traveling for ten minutes or so and had only really made it deeper into the bustling streets of the town. Elara, showed grace, as she narrowly avoided members of community with precision, at one point where the crowd had become too dense she absentmindedly grabbed his hand, the feeling of Elara's soft, smooth skin threatening to break the box back open, but he persevered.

Once they had passed through the majority of the crowd, she slowed allowing Thalen to walk at her side instead following behind her. "Apologies, I wanted us to get out of the crowds. With us having so little time, speed is our ally." she said her voice reflecting far more confidence than she normally showed, at least not amongst the group. He couldn't help but wonder where this sudden confidence was coming from, perhaps she simply felt lesser in the presence of, what was in human terms, an ancient and mystical being such as Keela. If he was being honest with himself he liked this side of her, yet there was no time to explore that thought further. "Agreed, now that we are clear of the crowds. What do you think of your riddle? We seem to understand the first portion, being the location...perhaps not with enough detail, but if we are lucky the second part of the riddle may tell us more about the first." Lapsing into silence he recalled her riddle, working not to forget any piece or mix it with his own. He was about to ask her to repeat it, but she seemed to have read his mind "Upon the shores of water near, water cold so ice would appear. One was saved while death was near, beneath the waves yet earth threw clear. The name of the saved will draw you there." she paused in thought before she continued "Maybe there is more to these riddles than something at random, if they were different for everyone...then maybe they were specific to the one who read it." They lapsed into silence again as they moved past the gate guards and through the walls of the town itself, the silence deepened as they walked another few minutes, Thalen noticed they appeared to be approaching one of the shore lines of the large lake that stood just beyond the loosely packed trees. From what he could see buildings and docks seemed to litter the shore with boats of all sizes launching from and returning to them. Only now that they neared the shore did he truly appreciate the sheer size of the body of water. It was truly massive, easily hundreds of miles across from shore to shore, and yet unlike the section they were making their way towards, a majority of it was green with trees and underbrush alike, all tightly packed together.

As they made their way further down the road Elara's voice broke the silence "I think I know what mine is related to...years ago when I was younger, perhaps fourteen, though the years have passed by as a blur, I saved someone on this very lake. What you may not know is that I am native to this town, my father was a fisherman on these very shores." she paused for a moment seeming to travel back in time, Thalen waited patiently as they walked wanting to give her all the time she needed. When she seemed ready she continued "It was my brother, Edward, he is who I saved...it was when my power first awoke within me. It was early winter, and frost had settled in early that year. My brother...he was maybe seven or eight at the time, was out playing in the snow, he seemed to have lost his place and ended up on the ice of the lake. I was outside too, grabbing firewood from the storage shed and one moment he was there and the next a squeak broke the snowy silence, and he was gone." emotion seemed to overcome her, and she stopped both her story and, catching Thalen by surprise, her movement. He turned to look at her and saw not the raw emotion he expected but instead the glazed eyes of someone remembering something almost painful, before long she continued her voice filled with emotion. "I ran through snow...it was up to my knees, even though it was so early in the season. Once I made it to the ice, I felt I could do nothing, the snow hid where he fell through, and I could not risk that I wouldn't fall in as well. My frustration, love, adrenaline, maybe a mix of them.... or maybe something else entirely must have unleashed the power within me. I felt a great pressure build within my head and suddenly I felt it course through me...as though I called it without knowing that I had." Seeming to master her emotions she started walking again, Thalen choosing to follow behind her silently, and waited for her to continue.

As they drew even closer to the shoreline, she turned from the main path to a smaller one that branched off to the left, the trees began to thicken slightly and as they did Elara continued her story "When I unleashed the built up power I threw my hands out in front of me, it was a primal...almost animalistic action. Before I knew it the earth began to rumble, ice suddenly started to crack, and the roar of water being disturbed met my ears. Without any warning the ice split and on the piece of land that appeared from beneath the sheet of ice was my brother, drenched and shivering, but very much alive. I ran, grabbed him, and brought him back in... fortunately he survived...but at that moment my life changed completely. Ah...we are here." she said as she pointed at a clearing within the already thinning trees. As they approached it he found that it was not empty instead seeing a house that seemed to be in disuse though not disrepair, a small jetty reached out into the water and not far from it a fifteen foot strip of land, so out of place and clearly not natural, reached out like a finger into the water.

Elara, leading the way, walked them out to the very edge of that earthen finger, as they did Thalen couldn't help but think of his own story. Memories of the battle, the death of Sarah and how his own life too had changed forever flooded his mind. Though his tales ending was more of a sad and bittersweet one, he could see the parallels in their experiences and for some reason found it comforting that hers had a much happier ending. Bringing his mind back to the present he spoke "So you believe this to be the place? Here at what I must assume was once your childhood home?" he said as he motioned towards the building behind them. She nodded in response, her blue eyes looking out over the lake, whether her gaze was fixed on the lake before her, earth she stood upon, or perhaps the past he could not tell. "I lived here until the end of that winter, after that I was inducted into the order itself. Eventually my parents and brother moved away when the war drew closer, though we are still far away they did not wish to take their chances. Though they did leave me the house and the land surrounding… I keep it in good condition though I rarely return here." her voice grew quiet as though her thoughts were hundreds of miles away. Thalen stayed quiet allowing Elara the time she needed and after only a scant few moments whatever emotions she were feeling had passed, as she set her shoulders and turned to him delivering a sweet smile. "I think it is time, let us finish my task so we can begin to consider yours." she put her hand on his arm still smiling and surprised him with a peck on the cheek before striding confidently to the very tip of the earth she had summoned. As she did Thalen raised his hand involuntarily to where she had kissed him and allowed a smile to creep onto his face, for the first time he allowed himself to be happy and consider a future he thought he had lost.

Even though her plan to be alone together was obvious, and even though he knew that this was probably not what she had expected when they began this little journey together...he hoped she had enjoyed it.

When she reached the end of the earthen rampart Elara paused, taking a deep breath in and saying "Edward" and with a flash disappeared before his very eyes.

CHAPTER TWENTY-TWO

Thalen was frozen staring at the spot where Elara was just moments before, his mind slow in catching up to what he knew for a fact...she was gone. He felt a moment of panic well up, before pushing it down and allowing his analytical mind to take over... *"Damnit, she must have been teleported away...they tricked us again. They altered or did not tell us about other things involving the tests and this must be another one...I don't have time for this, time to figure out my own riddle. Enough time has already been wasted...no not wasted but enough time has passed that I cannot afford to dally."* He checked the position of the sun, guessing that just under two hours had passed since the start of this challenge. He made a quick decision, choosing to go back towards Moon Shade Keep or at least he started to before pausing as he hadn't yet fully considered where his destination was. After all Elara's hadn't been within the grounds of the keep let alone the Keep itself, instead being out of the entire town. *"Nothing is ever simple...by the Gods this entire trial has been nothing like what we were told by the professor...Alright, if anything was learned from Elara's riddle it seems that the first part specifically is about the location...The way is shown by the light of the hand, finger to thumb being only of one. Lights of power flow through the wood, with tapestries of past and present and line the world...those must be the words that have to do with the location."* Thalen felt he could not delay and began trekking toward the Keep once more, though he wasn't positive about his destination, he knew it was certainly not the same place as his friend's had been.

As he made his way through the woods his brain continued firing as he knew if he could not identify where he had to go then the challenge would be over before it even began. *"The way is shown by the light of the hand...finger to thumb being only of one...Light of power flow through the wood, with tapestries of past and line the world... this is somewhat nonsensical yet overall, it does make sense. The light of the hand must be referring to the symbol of the order which suggests it must be within the Keep...that is nice enough by itself. Light of power flows through the wood, narrows it down a little further, there are only a few areas within the college that has wood so deeply ingrained with power and yet, even that does not give me much more to think on."* Breaking through the tree line he made his way down the main road all the while he mentally eliminated possibilities that made little sense. The minutes passed as he grew closer to the outer wall of the town and eventually past those walls moving forward into its densely packed streets. As the gates of the keep finally came into site he removed the final place that seemed unlikely, leaving him with only the library. The libraries large shelves, banisters and more all thrummed with power, whether from the books that sat upon them or the wood itself. Power coursed through everything within the structure, as the spells to preserver books, learning and all else kept everything safe from external threat all the way to something as simple as humidity. On top of that there were the tapestries of past and present that lined the walls of the library with some even hanging from the rafters, all coursing with power as they weaved their illusionary tales that had been spun within the material. Having decided this was his most likely destination he quickened his pace in an attempt to regain some of the lost time from his earlier misadventure. To his best guess it took him another twenty minutes to finally breach the doors that led into the college itself and another ten to reach the library. As so many times before Thalen was greeted by the smell of paper and the musk of old parchment, it was a surprisingly liberating experience to him, yet he did not have the time to bask in it further. He looked around finding a suitable space on the second floor, up close to the water clock. The clock telling him in no uncertain terms that just over three hours had passed leaving him with just over fifty minutes. Taking a breath to steady himself he recentered his thoughts and began to examine the second part of the riddle. *"The door does not show the true way, but is just the star to guide, along the path find where all powers intersect, speak the name of the arrivals and enter...wait...door?"* Thalen looked about the library from his vantage point, he had enough clearance to see throughout the room. Within seconds he realized his mistake, this could not be the place as there was no door beyond those of the entrance, hitting the banister in frustration he tried to calm himself. He still only had forty-five minutes to find the location, yet there was still more to do even if he discovered the destination, he still needed to determine what the name of the arrivals meant. Forcing down the panic he had begun to feel, he considered the issue before him as logically as he could. *"What other location could it mean...it must be somewhere that has some meaning to me. If I was to think of where I had first awakened my power as Elara had...no that would be too far away for a single day's travel. The next most likely place could be the entrance as that is where I first came to the college...yet even that cannot be correct. Where is it..."*

Thalen continued to roll the riddle through

his mind, understanding that this would likely be his last chance to get it right, now knowing he was in the wrong place he immediately left the library, throwing one final glance at the clock suspended high above finding he only had about forty minutes left. As he made his way through the crowded hallways, he found his entire being directed inwards, as he wracked his brain for an answer to the question, what place here was important enough to warrant the riddle? Realizing he had been essentially running in circles, his thoughts playing in a loop as he went over again and again the same dead-end ideas. With some difficulty he released himself from his self-imposed mental imprisonment. As he emerged from his proverbial shell, he naturally began to listen to conversations around him, those throughout the hall talking about many different things, their classes, what they wanted to eat for lunch, the weather, and so on. Once he felt he could consider the riddle again with fresh eyes he caught the wisps of a conversation, nothing truly important but making all the difference as he heard a woman's voice say. "...Have you ever been to the headmaster's office?..." Then as though struck by lightning he knew where he had to go. Before his conscious mind fully understood his actions he began moving down a little used but familiar path directly to the hallways that lead to the headmasters office and administrative section of the school. *"How foolish of me...how could I have possibly forgotten tapestries, a door with the sigil of the order upon it...everything. The location is the headmaster's office now it's just a question of getting there."* Having broken the code Thalen quickened his pace as a new sense of purpose filled him, as he knew his deduction was the only thing that could possibly answer the first part of the riddle.

After what seemed like an eternity Thalen made it to the administrative hallway, and once again saw the door to the headmaster's office. It was as grand as he had remembered it, from the inlaid symbol of the order to the lines of power which seemed to pulse within the wood, he knew immediately that this was the place. Recalling the riddle for what felt like the hundredth time Thalen determined the door itself was not exactly where he had to provide his answer, it said so directly within the riddle. No, it was not the portal but instead the northern star that would guide him to the true location...a place where all powers intersect.

Letting his eyes rove the area Thalen placed trust in his instincts, believing they would reveal to him that which, to this point, his conscious mind had failed to find. First he started with the area directly around the door itself, but quickly dismissed it as there was nothing there except for the door, and though stars sat below the palm in the orders symbol, the riddle had specifically excluded the door itself. Letting his eyes continue moving first to the right wall and then the left eyes he looked at every tapestry, disfigurement on the walls, and break in the stone. Yet, none spoke to him, the one thing he felt he was not understanding was where all powers intersect, it made so little sense to him as he searched in vain. *"Nothing, nothing, nothing dammit! Is this the fate to have come so far and yet fail once again forcing me to remain here even longer. Keeping me from that which matters most to me."* Thalen took a moment considering what he meant by that thought...what really was so important to him. He never truly thought about why he continued to move towards this goal of "graduation". At one point, he felt it must have been revenge that pushed him forward, that deep animal desire to hurt those that had harmed him and his own, yet that did not feel like it was the case any longer. Perhaps, at some point revenge had dropped away, it no longer being the primary reason for his desire to continue on, no instead it may have been something less perceptible something invisible to him right now. *"Wait...invisible...that must be it!"* as soon as the thought crossed his mind he understood what he had to do. Taking a steadying breath, he began collecting power and once he had enough released it imbuing it into words, "Zien Nazeehn", and with the release of power Thalen's world changed or more correctly his eyes adjusted. At first it only appeared as a wisp, like strands of blue yarn floating delicately in the air, but when following it from the bare thread to where more substance could be seen he found many different colors, red, green, white, and so on each representing a strand of mana. All these strands lead him to a tapestry...one he was familiar with as he had seen it before. All the strands intertwined slowly as they came to a single point where a sword stood within the hand of a hero of old...without thought, Thalen answered the riddle, not understanding how or why but just knowing that it felt right. "Solan'Oness", once the words had left his mouth he felt as though he was drawn into the tapestry and suddenly the world went dark.

As suddenly as the darkness had swallowed him it became light once more, a dimly lit room revealing itself to him. Dotted throughout the area were lights their glow unlike that of the typical magical orbs, but instead as though they were stars in the night sky. As his eyes began to adjust to the low light the glowing orbs seemed to increase in strength revealing more and more of the room around him, it appearing to be not much more than the inside of a wooden box. Yet as his eyes were still under the effect of the spell, he could see that there were strands of power mixed together, moving and appearing almost knotted at times throughout the room. After a few more moments lettering similar to the delivered riddle begin to write themselves with a flourish, the still dark ceiling acting as parchment for it to be written on.

"The way was found, riddle resolved, yet the way is still not clear. Unravel the ropes of power, find the hand and push in the power asked."

As soon as Thalen had affixed the new riddle in his mind, it began to fade from the world much as the one before; once it was fully gone Thalen went about unraveling the proverbial ball of string in front of him. Though some part of him wanted to lament the riddle after a riddle that was put before him, he felt that at this point there was no reason to allow the surprises that the tests threw his way to affect his state of mind. It took him several minutes to even begin to understand the scene before him, though it appeared nothing but a knot of strings, Thalen was able to identify twenty different ones that stretched away from the mass itself, all reaching out seemingly at random toward every section of the room. With no better idea, Thalen first looked at the spot where all twenty met, there he found nothing of note except what appeared to be a hole that they all disappeared into. Allowing a sigh to escape his lips, he selected a random string and followed it to its ultimate destination, nothing, its length ending in a random dark corner. Trying not to let the situation get to him, he did the only thing that he could, go back to the center and start all over again.

CHAPTER TWENTY-THREE

From Thalen's perspective it felt like it had taken him hours to find the correct string, though, it could not have be more than a few minutes. Yet, he knew that every lost moment could be the last not knowing if another twist or turn awaited him, he felt like he had picked the correct one at random, selecting a near translucent white string that ran its way out from the mass before slowly reaching out to a single stone within the wall. As he approached it there seemed to suddenly be a burst of multi-colored hue, those colors matching those of the knot of twisting mana veins that sat suspended in the center of the room. Unsure of what else to do he approached the light and when he was within arm's length he grabbed at its rolling hues as thought it was corporeal and, to his surprise, the near blinding light gave way to a lever, that sat suspended in the air seeming to be attached to nothingness. When Thalen pulled it a grating noise suddenly filled the air, the deep sound of stone being dragged across a floor. Without warning light appeared, not the light of magic but like that of the sun began to fill the room blinding him for a moment, as a portal began to open in one of the seemingly solid stone walls. Taking a breath that was filled with hope, Thalen prayed that the trial was finally coming to an end as he stepped through the revealed door and into the light beyond.

Thalen shielded his eyes as he adjusted to the brightness of the outside world and once they had he found a truly confusing sight as he found himself once more in the courtyard of the College surrounded by many of his fellow examinees. After taking a moment to reorientate himself he searched for his companions, hoping that they had overcome their own challenges, he found that he was not disappointed as a gruff voice spoke up behind him. "I see ye made it laddie. Ye sure prefer to be keeping it close don't ya." Turning toward the speaker he found Dolgrath standing before him, Elara and Keela close behind. "Thalen! I am so happy you made it, when I was whisked away to a dark room I feared for you. With our being so far removed from the town and keep, as well as our not answering your riddle before it all happened. I thought you may fall short of the task." Elara's voice grew quiet as she paused before allowing a bashful smile to reach her lips. "I am happy that is not the case." He returned the smile and nodded to her before addressing them all "Agreed, I must say they have once again played a great many tricks on us. I am almost of a mind that even now the test has not been completed and I am speaking to illusions as opposed to friends." Barking a laugh at the absurdity of it all he shifted his eyes to the stage which still stood erect as it overlooked the courtyard. A few members of the testing staff stood upon it, some seeming to keep time with smaller versions of the large water clock within the library, while others looked through small portals intently. Thalen's best guess was they were likely watching the rest of the cohort as they went through their own trials. This getting confirmed when one of them dismissed the portal in front of them and almost in tandem a door appeared in thin air barely fifteen feet from where he now stood. It opened inward and out stepped a young man looking quite confused over the scene before him, Thalen felt a little embarrassed as he suspected he had looked much the same when he first emerged.

He let his feelings drain out of him before turning back to the group, who he found were deep in conversation about the test and what may be coming next, but he did not join in as he knew he had nothing to add and instead let himself get swept away in their words and tones. He spent the next few minutes half listening to them talking about where their locations were and their thoughts on why they were of enough importance to be selected as their gateway, he found it to be a nice distraction especially after all the conflicting emotions of the day. Lost in thought he was surprised, much as all the others, when the sound of a horn called out a single deep note, its sound interrupting all ongoing conversations forcing them to end. Thalen looked to the stage, noticing the staff that had been monitoring testees through the portals closed them, some shaking their heads, whether it was in disappointment, disgust, or sympathy, Thalen could not tell and in all honestly did not care. However, he suspected that no matter the reason those expressions likely all meant the same things, whoever they had been watching had failed the second trial. After several more minutes one of the proctors on the stage moved towards the podium and in a booming voice called out to those gathered. "Congratulations, you have all made it through the second trial in your journey to become members of a higher circle. I am sure you have many questions, and I will answer some of them at this time." He paused stroking his bearded face before continuing. "Once more your adaptiveness, magical abilities, and most importantly critical thinking skills have been put to the test. Every part of the test, including the lack of information you were given was all for your betterment."

He gave them a moment, seeming to allow them all to digest what he had said before clearing his throat, his gaze steely as he looked upon the gathered throng. "I will not belittle you all by explaining every item in detail, as I am sure you can understand how the riddle was designed in a way to make you consider your time at the college as well as the moment you truly became a member of the order. However, we will explain why once solved you would appear within another room with a challenge of some type before you. This was for two reasons, one for any who chose to work together it would cause surprise in the ones left behind, this was desirable as it caused many to panic which needed to be fought down. As a mage that panics becomes easy prey for those that wish to harm them, though the challenges are friendly and in some ways the surprises only pranks pulled by us higher order members, in the end we are at war and must ensure those that grow within the order can recover from surprise. Secondarily, for those that were transported away it required the ability to consider the situation before them and resolve it in the most effective manner they could." He took a few moments allowing his words to hang in the air before finishing. "Though not all your questions may have been answered, it is your task and job to continue to think and learn from the situations without being guided by those that came before you. With this the second test has concluded, tomorrow will be the final test and the battle rounds. Rest, eat, and prepare for the final challenge and once more well done in passing test two." his speech complete he left without preamble walking from the stage, followed close behind by all the proctors who had remained. Thalen couldn't help but feel somewhat disappointed at the anticlimactic ending of the second test, after the stress and effort of the day, it all came to an end within a second. He knew that in the end none of it mattered, it just meant he was one step closer to returning to where he belonged. He rolled his shoulders hoping to loosen the sudden tenseness he was feeling before turning towards the others, their conversation renewed after its brief interruption. Deciding to slip away while they were distracted, Thalen headed towards his room, waving a farewell as he returned to the keep.

Walking once more through the halls of what had quickly become his entire world, he let his mind wander to everything, from how he felt about the tests that had passed and those to come. He felt tired and worn, his mind stretched beyond imagination from the trials of the day and those same trials had managed to plant a seed of doubt and fear in his mind. Though they referred to it without fail as Battle Day he did not know if it was best to believe it would be battles or instead some macabre display of skill that was a mockery to true combat. He was confident in his sense for battle, and he knew he was good in a fight and had even been slowly improving his skill in combat magic. Yet, many twists or turns to the plot could appear in an event administered by the Circle and those could easily drive him from the long shot chance he had straight to a path of total ruin. He groaned to himself at the frustration and stress that was building up, those feelings going far beyond any that he had experienced to this point, even when commanding troops in battle. He chuckled a little and wondered silently to himself if he was simply getting soft or if this was truly as difficult as it felt, yet whatever the answer was all he knew was he now needed to take a bath and nap to remove the fatigue of the day and hopefully the doubts in his mind. After a few minutes of walking he reached his room, closed the door and began his much-needed rest.

A knock at his door jolted Thalen awake from his slumber and to his surprise he found the room far darker than he expected, the last rays of the sun lighting the room softly as it dipped below the horizon. Rubbing the sleep from his eyes he realized that he had slept far longer than he had intended, but before he could think about it more, another rap on the door drew his attention. "One moment!" He called out as he made his way to the door pulling a discarded shirt over his bare chest before he opened the door revealing Elara just beyond the threshold. "Oh! Thalen, I was not sure if you were awake, and no one had seen you for several hours. I wanted to check on you and make sure all was well." Elara said, flashing him a brilliant smile. Thalen felt his heart pound just a little faster at that smile while his still groggy mind groped for an answer "Elara, I am well yes. Just far more tired than I imagined I was." he coughed a bit, clearing his unexpectedly parched throat. Taking a breath to speak he found himself instead coughing into the back of his hand, his body producing a vain attempt to alleviate his discomfort. As his fit subsided, he heard Elara laughing quietly, he had no doubt that he was making a spectacle of himself, yet before he could fully recover and apologize, she spoke. "Have you eaten? Or drank anything today?" she said, her eyes sparking as though she knew the answer already, which he readily admitted she likely did.

Though he knew he was falling into her trap he answered the only way he could once shaking his head no. "Then shall we go together? It is time for the evening meal, and I have yet to eat as well." he noticed her face redden slightly as she asked and to his own surprise, he found his own face getting a little warm. "Yes, that would be nice. Just wait here a moment, I must finish dressing, I won't be long" he finished, putting a finger up in case his words were not clear, before gently closing the door. For not the first time since meeting her Thalen berated himself for acting like a young buck in heat, but he did not have the time or energy to continue the train of thought as he did not want to keep her waiting on his account. Dressing as quickly as he could Thalen finally pulled on his boots before adding his sword and belt to the ensemble, if he was to be honest with himself he had felt somewhat naked without it earlier and did not wish to have that feeling any longer, especially not with his female companion. Opening the door once more he looked about the hall until he spotted her just a little way down the hall. Striding up to her he gestured down the hall asking, "Shall we?" She answered with a small nod before taking the lead, though it also, intentionally or not, gave him a chance to admire her figure before his better senses took back control.

As they walked down the crowded hall they fell into a companionable silence, only broken by the occasional discussion about something they would notice in passing or about how the weather had been turning. Even so Thalen couldn't help but feel a little unsettled in the situation, though he also found he did not wish to break from current course. He also knew they would talk more upon reaching the great hall itself. Though it would likely be crowded they had fortunately learned how to cast a bubble of silence around them, these allowing conversations to be both private and to block out the noise of the world around them. Thalen had found little opportunity to make use of it, however, he could see plenty of uses for the spells and may have understood how useful it would be in real scenarios far better than every other student in the College. After walking for another handful of minutes they finally reached the hall where they quickly found the food they wished and sat at a somewhat unused table. Thalen thought there were less people than usual within the hall, silently wondering to himself if this was due to the tests that were taken or if it was because of the late hour. He swiftly discarded the thought as it was hardly the most important thing he could be doing at the moment.

Once they were both comfortable Elara looked at him and gave him a small nod, silently signaling him to silence their area, he nodded in return before gathering power and casting the spell "Nazeewan Kalak", and within an instant the once loud murmur of the dining hall went silent. "Can you hear me?" Thalen asked and once Elara nodded, he smiled, happy that his spell found success, before turning to his full plate. As they ate they continued with some small talk, speaking a little about the first exam but somewhat ignoring and not truly touching on the second one, Thalen assumed this was how it would continue but as they came closer to the end of their meal Elara surprised him by asking a question. "Thalen, why did you join the order?"

Spluttering a in surprise Thalen grabbed his mug of watered wine to help clear his throat and hopefully hide his surprise. He found quickly he was not successful as she saw right through his attempt "I am sorry if you do not wish to share I understand. I was simply thinking of the second test and how I had revealed my own reasons and how I obtained my powers, so thought I would ask." Elara said with a gesture indicating for him to not worry. He nodded acknowledging the gesture, yet he did wish to share his story with her, especially since she had trusted him with hers.

Having made up his mind he steeled himself for the feelings he knew would accompany it before turning to Elara, "No, I am more than willing to tell my tale to you. It is long if you truly have the time and desire to listen" she nodded her head open curiosity on her face. "I have told this but a few times before and to be honest the feelings are still somewhat raw and present even as far removed as I am now from what had occurred. I much as yourself was not born with powers befitting a mage of the order and instead gained them through an ordeal much as you did yourself..." he broke off his sentence as his own curiosity got the better of him and asked a question he had not intended to. "Elara, have you ever thought about how you were before you received your powers?" Elara did seem taken by surprise but after it faded she pursed her lips in what Thalen thought might be confusion, realizing what he said did not make all that much sense and decided to ask again in a different way. "What I mean is, looking back since I gained access to magic I realized that I had always possessed the ability to somewhat predict what was going to happen before it did. Not like telling the future but almost like an extreme amount of focus and forethought into issues and situations that occurred." he did not feel confident that he explained himself well enough, however, Elara seemed to have a decent enough understanding of his meaning to respond. "No, no I can't say I ever had something of that nature occur...why do you ask?" she tilted her head a bit, her curious expression returning even stronger.

He sighed a little all the while screaming internally at how attractive he found her inability to mask her expressions, before putting his thoughts away in the small box in the corner of his mind with everything else. "To be truthful I came to realize that I was experiencing things exactly as I described...yet I do not know is if that in a normal experience for others to have. Yet, it appears it may be more unusual than I originally thought...then again, I did have powers that had lain dormant far longer than any other." He lapsed into silence and after a few seconds shook himself of his sudden melancholy before deciding to continue his story for her. "Apologies, I had not meant to stray far from the question. Let us continue..." within moments he began to fully recount the tale of the day he gained his powers, and the catalyst of his entire change of course, Sarah's death. The pain was still there but had lessened over time.

He couldn't help but think to himself that time and retellings really did aid in healing these wounds, but he let the thought slip and continued before Elara questioned his momentary pause. He told of his meeting with Cameral in the field hospital, and finally of their travel to the point where they now stood, Moon Shade Keep. "This is all why I wish to be done with this, why I wish to seemingly rush through the teaching and to be able to control these powers adequately. There is a journey that is yet to be finished, it is at the end of this conflict and once our enemies have been removed from this world. Every day, every moment spent here is a day spent in waste as it is a day where I cannot avenge those that have been lost before us, both those known personally and impersonally. However, I am rambling on now. As you have asked Elara there is my story and how I ended up a ward of the Order much as you, Keela or Dolgrath are." he fell silent once he was finished, he found relief in retelling, yet for some reason he also felt some level of concern and angst as he awaited her response. He found himself quickly becoming tired and worn from the random yet predictable emotions he kept experiencing when dealing with Elara. There was too much to do for these gateways to romance to be so ever present in his mind, no matter how much he may have wished for it. *"Maybe in the future Thalen, now is hardly the time…yet no matter how many times I tell myself this they just won't go away."* he sighed a little and wondered what was taking her so long to reply. Looking at her, his eyes found hers and he realized this was the first he had looked at her since the he started the tale. If he had earlier, he would have realized why she was yet to respond, as her eyes were filled with empathy and wet with tears. Even further he realized he had not looked to her directly while retelling, his eyes somewhere in center space as he remembered and retold. Perhaps, he did not wish to see her recognize the emotions that may have crept into his voice or the barely concealed pain he knew must still be within his own eyes.

Thalen gave Elara time to collect herself and once finished she spoke "That is a very sad tale Thalen, thank you for sharing it with me I can't imagine it was easy." she paused to sniffle and grabbed a nearby napkin to wipe away the trails her tears had left upon her blushed pale skin. "I am sorry to hear about the loss of your friend and I promise to do what I can to help you with your goal." she said, flashing him a sweet and supportive smile. His heart warmed as he appreciated the gesture, yet he did not wish to bring her into his troubles. "You do not have to promise such as thing Elara I do not wish to put you out and would never expect to hold you to it. Though the gesture is appreciated." he tried to soften his words with a smile, but that did not seem to placate the young woman. "No Thalen, we are friends, and I am sure there is plenty I can aid you with while we remain here." she said with a strength and determination that she had rarely shown in the past. "In fact, the final day of testing is tomorrow is it not? Let us spar some now that we are finished with our meal!" an edge of excitement crept into her voice, for what reason Thalen could not begin to guess, yet before he knew it she grabbed him by the hand and nearly dragged him from the bench and out of the hall. Thalen, being pulled along by this small woman, could not help but crack a smile at her enthusiasm...and at her hand holding his.

CHAPTER TWENTY-FOUR

Thalen yawned as he approached the dining hall, Elara and he had been up until late honing their skills in preparation for the final advancement test and he found he was paying for it. Fortunately, they were informed through a magical message, it arriving via a construct much like the one he had seen in Pelorin's office all those months ago, that the final test would not be starting until after breakfast, at eleven as measured by the water clock. He planned on taking advantage of the extra time, running over the attack spells that had been drilled into him, though they were normally drilled by being on the receiving end of them, but first came food to fill his empty stomach. As he entered the great hall, he thought further about the tests eventually settling on the question of where they would be held, but after several minutes he realized that one crucial detail had been left out of the message *"No wait that can't possibly be right, how could they have overlooked such a crucial detail in the message they sent... they wouldn't, would they?"* Thalen couldn't help but be suspicious of Pelorin and whatever group determined how the tests would be conducted. If he was to be honest with himself given their current record, he felt he had every right to be. He sighed and rubbed his temples to try and dissolve the sudden headache he had, coming to accept that he would simply have to overcome again whatever they decided to throw at him, tricks and all. Once Thalen entered the hall, he quickly obtained his morning fare and sat to eat in solitude, taking the opportunity he began reviewing his tactics and the spells he would most likely use in the battles that had been promised today.

As he took a mouthful of bread, he savored it's softness and taste, finding that it unexpectedly helped him relax, some of the tensed muscles that had gone unnoticed relaxing. Closing his eyes he let himself fall into a type of meditation allowing his body to mechanically consume his morning repast as he freed his mind from distraction *"How is it best to approach the battles before me...I suppose it can't truly plan things out in detail. But, instead let's take stock in what I can count on and where I will likely lack. Better to start on the positive, I will have more pure combat experience than nearly anyone and I should take advantage of that. It should allow me to be more aggressive and perhaps surprise a few of my less skilled opponents, I'll use fear of that aggression against them. I can also depend on most of my base attack spells, I shouldn't stray into anything too advanced otherwise I may find myself on the back foot while attempting a harder incantation."* He paused his thoughts just long enough to take a sip of watered wine before tucking into some chicken from last evening's meal. *"Maybe the chicken wasn't the best idea it is pretty dry. Oh well, back to the matter at hand. Now specifically my weaknesses, one is definitely my knowledge of advanced spells. Most of my opponents will have a better spell repertoire than I will, though they will be of varying skill levels. I will simply have to hope I can avoid them. As this goes into my second issue, my barriers still leave enough to be desired. I will likely need to spend most of my time and energy during the match avoiding direct hits from my opponent."* he continued with his planning and reviewing until he was finished with breakfast. *"So, to summarize, use my combat experience against my opponents, don't get hit and keep things basic...this is certainly not the first time in my life that was the entire plan. Oh well..."* he chuckled a little before leaving to finish his preparations for the day ahead.

Thalen suddenly found himself in a pitch-black room, not a single shred of light could be seen and he had to fight to keep panic from welling up in his chest. Mere moments before he had been in one of the practice rooms, sharpening his basic attacks and counters and now he found himself, with no explanation, in pure blackness. Ignoring his useless eyes he leveraged his other senses, hearing what sounded like boots scraping stone, yet it was not as though they were walking it sounding like the random movement of someone equally uncomfortable in this situation. With this in mind it was obvious that there were others in the room, they were not threats, instead they likely also could not see anything. Without warning light poured through his closed eyelids, which he silently thanked, as he knew if he had opened them even a second before he would have been temporarily blinded. Using his hand to shield his eyes he opened them slowly adjusting to the sudden transition from pitch black to bright light and as his eyes cleared he found himself surrounded by people. He recognized them almost immediately as other participants in the tests and before long looked beyond them to see that they were in what appeared to be a large stadium, the stone walls climbing up into grandstands. His eyes widened in astonishment as he found each of those seats filled with people, this creating a sea of blurry faces, all details lost in the mass of the crowd. The crowd seemed to sense that the participants were more aware and within moments a roar of excitement and desire shot forth from them creating a deafening noise, Thalen nearly had to cover his ears as the sudden transition threatened to take his hearing from him. He was both annoyed and impressed with the antics of the Order, Pelorin and all the other damned mages involved in this had once again left out, what could be considered, crucial information of how the tests would be held. Thankfully the roaring died down as Pelorin's voice overtook the crowd seeming to begin the day's festivities.

"Hello competitors, and welcome to the third and final test! This is a special test, as this is the test of combat, do not be fooled by the fanfare you see around you as this is truly the most dangerous of tasks set before you. As I am sure you can imagine, there is not much to do here for grandiose levels of entertainment and so this moment now will be performed and done before all of the citizens of Talisar and the denizens of the Keep itself!" he paused and as though prompted the stands erupted in cheers before dying down after a minute or so. "Though this may seem annoying or purposeless to some of you, you would be wrong, the presence of this crowd should also subject you all to further stress beyond that of if you were simply sparring with your classmates...in fact to make this even more interesting there will be a prize to be revealed later." he paused allowing the crowd to help build suspense with scattered sounds of interest. Thalen narrowed his eyes, he suspected the entire thing was rehearsed, yet in the end that held very little importance. In fact, the spectacle of it all barely gave him pause as he had felt true fear, adrenaline and shock on the front lines in true battle, such trifles as these would do little to take him from his concentration. Though as he looked at those around him, he could see that other members of the class were certainly being affected by it, seeing this boosted his confidence a little as he felt he could count this as one of his few advantages. Pelorin cleared his throat, the noise silencing everyone as it boomed throughout the chamber, once silence reigned again the disembodied voice continued. "Now to get to the details, you may not have counted, but thirty of you have managed to make it to this point, that is far too many and must be whittled down. Due to this the final test is held as a tournament and will have two stages over two days, in the first stage each of you will battle it out with four other participants and will be ranked by mainly wins and losses. However, as always creativity, tactics and general skill will be awarded by proctors that will be watching from the crowd and though it won't allow you to win it still may aid you in advancement." his voice paused for a moment, likely to allow what they were being told to fully sink in. "Now that we have that out of the way it is time for the first match to begin!" suddenly, as though on queue, two names appeared in the center space above the arena *"Thalen Melodyr vs. Seraph Alimaric"*

Pelorin's voice announced the names before providing a few last parting words "Good luck to both of you, may your magic be strong and present. All other participants, please leave the arena floor and move to the section in the stands that the nearby proctors guide you too. I will now allow our main presenter Boriqon Dalantor to take over. Again, good luck to all, I hope you make a good showing." his rasping voice suddenly cut out and near silence covered the arena, all holding their collective breath as they waited for the first match to begin.

The other twenty-eight participants were ushered away by the nearby proctors moving the group from the floor and out towards a terrace that sat lower than the stands, but well above the floor of the field. Taking a few moments to examine his surroundings, the thing Thalen noticed the most was the sheer size of the area, the arena easily being two hundred meters in length and another one hundred meters wide. He could not imagine they would make use of all the space at their disposal, but it gave him options during the fight ahead. Looking at the stands and the wall the crowd sat upon he estimated they were around twenty meters high. Those high walls loomed over the dueling area likely guaranteeing the safety of those not involved in the combat. Running his booted feet along the floor he found it was easy to identify, it being made of stone though it seemed unblemished, though it was not polished it was completely smooth. What surprised him the most was that through some magical means it seemed to have grip despite its appearance and allowed for good traction. He felt cautiously optimistic for the fight ahead as he knew that he would be underestimated in general due to how new of an order member he was, coupled with the fact that the stage was so big, and the pressure would be heightened by the onlookers. In truth he hoped that his opponents would be distracted, and he could win one, or if he was lucky two, rounds before they fully adjusted. Thalen rolled his head feeling his neck crack as he moved about to loosen his muscles, all the while stealing glances at his opponent, studying them the best he could before the match began. They were a human male of average height and build; their sandy brown hair was cropped short to their head, and he honestly felt that in every way they could be called ordinary. He knew that didn't mean much when it came to mages, but he figured he could outlast them if he drew the fight out. He certainly couldn't guess their magical power, but he could tell easily that he was in better physical condition, having maintained his soldierly habit of exercising at least once a day. Before he had the chance to strategize how to unbalance and attack his opponent the booming voice of the announcer rang throughout the arena. "Hello everyone, this is your announcer

Boriqon Dalantor joining you for this exciting first match of the Fourth Circle advancement tournament! Without further ado let us begin, first let's establish the rules of this match and all matches going forward. First these matches are set to last until either competitor can no longer participate, this will be determined either through one competitor rendering the other unconscious or, if determined by the proctors watching, to be incapable of defending themselves. Once one of the conditions have been met, each competitor will have a clear purple box placed around them. Secondarily, high level spells are forbidden as well as nothing that can kill instantly or will ignore your opponent's defenses completely. Lastly, a competitor may surrender at any time, this can be done by placing both hands in the air and yelling out that they yield." he paused, likely to allow all the participants, and possibly the spectators, to commit the rules to memory as best they could.

Having allowed a minute or so to pass the announcer continued "With that out of the way competitors, please go to the side matching your color." The announcement of colors took Thalen by surprise, *"Color...what color? By the Gods what do they mean by this?"* Thalen looked about, yet nothing obvious presented itself, that is until he looked up. Floating above his head was the sigil of the order, hand showing one star below the hand to represent his being of the fourth circle. It was a deep crimson color and matched a sigil standing firm above the south side of the arena. Taking a guess at their meaning he walked towards the sigil until it went from its deep crimson to a yellow and then finally to green before disappearing completely, he assumed that was a sign to turn to face his opponent, they also just reaching their predetermined destination. Seeming to have been waiting for them the announcer's booming voice filled the air. "Competitors ready?" Thalen got into a typical fighting stance, mind already planning his first move when the much-expected word came. "Begin!"

Thalen knew that the one to act first would have the upper hand, running to his right he pulled energy into himself deftly crafting it into a shield with a whispered spell. He had decided earlier that he would not yell out his workings to both save his breath as well as keep his opponents off balance. If he did not call them out loud, he might catch them with a lucky attack. However, he did not think he actually get that lucky as though his opponent was certainly off balance from Thalen's sudden movement he had still managed to raise his defenses. Thalen sucked his teeth in annoyance, his hope for an easy victory seeming to slip from him, yet he still felt he had the upper hand as he gathered further power and quickly formed the image of fire in his mind. He slid himself to a stop a palm out and spoke the command "Col'Fir Tole Dorint" a ball of flame shooting forth from his outstretched hand. He couldn't see if it hit its target as he began moving again, but this time to his left in an attempt to keep his opponent off balance or keeping them from having an easy time launching their own attack at him. It partially worked as Thalen felt the heat of flame pass him by, it likely targeted at where he was just standing. Coming to a stop again Thalen let off three quick blasts of fire at his opponent, this time allowing himself to watch them streak towards their target and trusting that his opponent would be forced to respond. He found himself unsurprised, if not a little disappointed, when his bolts essentially bounced off the other mage's defense, none of them even causing a crack in the glass-like surface that briefly appeared on impact. *"Damnit, this isn't going to work I'm barely making a dent and am just tiring myself out while he stands there."* He felt an impact on his shield that brought him back to reality, as it was the first hit he had taken it barely affected his defenses, but he admonished himself for losing his focus as he did not want to give his enemies free chances. He made the decision to change his defensive strategy and watched his opponent closely as he listened to them call out the spells they planned on using. This allowed him to react in a smaller area as he dodged bolts of fire coupled with the occasional jet or orb of water as he considered his next move. *"What can I do? This is a battle, real combat I am spending too much time on the defense, yet I cannot break their defense...maybe I need to get them to break it for me. I need to get them to lose concentration. What is that spell again..."* he worked his mind hard pulling words out of what felt like thin air, but once he had what he needed he called them out conjuring the image in his mind into being. "Quarz Riole Bel'ar" as the last word left his mouth he kneeled to the ground and placed his hands upon the floor. As he had hoped, the ground before him began to roll like a wave forward towards his opponent, almost as if the stonework that made up the floor was sitting atop ocean water, swelling upward slightly before plunging back down.

It wasn't as grand as he would have liked but he hoped it would be enough to throw his enemy off balance. *"Nothing wagered, nothing gained"* he thought to himself as he broke into a sprint just behind the ground swell. He wasn't sure why he had made that choice but the voice in the back of his head told him it was the right move to make. As the ripple moved forward, Thalen could see the moment of hesitation in the eyes of his opponent, seeming unsure how to react but a baser instinct seemed to take over. They shot a bolt of flame at Thalen, just as he had hoped, it deflected off his shield and sensing the shift in momentum Thalen threw a bolt of his own taking his opponents concentration even further from the floor rolling only a few feet away from him. His bolt outpaced the flow of the floor easily, but it was timed just well enough, the shield shimmering briefly upon being struck, seconds after the rolling floor reached their feet it bucking them slightly. In that moment Thalen saw the telltale shimmer of his foes shield breaking as the flow of power seemed to be lost as his opponent's concentration waned. It was in that moment that he struck, instead of fire he chose instead water as he called out "Wantari Tor Tole Dorint" and a bolt or beam of water shot forth from his hand striking his opponent in the head. His defenses having been lowered, the man was lifted from his feet and flung backward, his brief flight ending as he struck the ground, Thalen hoped they would not rise again. Several seconds later this hope was confirmed when the announcer's voice suddenly filled the room "The first match has concluded! The victor is Thalen Melodyr!"

CHAPTER TWENTY-FIVE

Thalen steadied his breathing as the adrenaline drained from him, though the match was short it had still been long enough to sap him of all his energy. Once he centered himself he looked around for any hint of where he should go, though the crowd was still cheering he did not wish to feed them further with acknowledgment. He wanted nothing more than to get off the stage so the next match could begin, he could not help but feel that the sooner this was done the better off he would be. This wasn't entertainment in his opinion; it was just a shoddy duplicate of the war and battles he had fought in the past. Though he could not stop himself from feeling some pride in his victory, he knew that it was nothing like the real thing and the ultimate gamble was never in play.

Shaking off those useless thoughts he noticed that one of the proctors was motioning for him to come over. Once reaching them, he was directed towards one of several cylindrical cutouts in the stone wall that sat beneath the participant viewing area. Thalen was unsure what they were supposed to be, he thought that like everything else in the College they most likely were not what they seemed. Accepting this he shrugged, stepping into one of them as directed. After a moment, Thalen suddenly felt himself floating as he slowly rose up to the balcony that the other test takers were upon. Once he was brought in line with the floor of the viewing area the magic slowly moved him forward until he stood upon the stone floor. Thalen could not help but think about how much material was used in the creation of this place, between the Keep, its courtyard, the curtain walls and now this arena, there was just so much stone. He couldn't tell if it was to display the opulence by the College and Order or if there was some tangible reason for it. Perhaps it had to do with the workings of magic itself, hell maybe it was just easier to work with if the building was created with magic. Regardless of the reason, he soon put it from his mind in the hopes of stealing a few relaxing moments before his next match.

After taking a few steps away from the groove he found himself greeted by Dolgrath, Keela and Elara as they approached him from the seating area. "Well done laddy, that be a good bit o' work makin' the floor move as ye did. Makin' use of water at the end to finish yer opponent was good too." Dolgrath said the pride of a teacher filling his voice. "Thank you, my friend, it came to me rather suddenly but seemed appropriate. I needed to catch them off balance so they might drop their defense. I imagine this is why you drove into my mind the importance of maintaining concentration for so many different reasons." Thalen replied, the dwarf chuckled and nodded his agreement. Thalen chuckled in turn but quickly came down from the moment of mirth "I was sloppy and got lucky. My thoughts and strategy were too conventional, far too similar to when I had no powers all I did was tire myself running around. It may have saved me a hit or two, but it was far too much wasted movement." he scowled slightly, he knew he was openly displaying his frustration, yet he did not care. He rolled his neck in an attempt to relax and slowly let himself take the fight as a learning experience to help him adjust his plans for the battles ahead. Before he dropped himself fully into his thoughts, they were interrupted by Keela's light voice "Come my friends, let us move towards some seats so we can look upon the next match." Emphasizing with her hand she led the way over to some empty seats, they seemed to be carved out of the stone itself with thick cushions upon them. Thalen thought they looked comfortable enough and found his thoughts confirmed as he settled into their ruby red fabric. "I thought you did well Thalen, I am sorry you are frustrated with your performance. But it was a good start and having no time to truly prepare did not help your case." Thalen looked to the speaker seeing Elara settling herself into the seat to his right, he felt a smile creep upon his face at the sight of her. "You are not wrong, the best way to say it is I am pleased with the victory but hardly with my performance. There is much to take from that match and improve on it...damn I thirst is there anything to drink?" Elara smiled before putting a hand on the arm of his chair, he sensed her pulse magic through it and suddenly at the very front a cup appeared filled with a deep amber liquid. Thalen was surprised for a moment before looking to her for approval, which she gave, taking up the goblet he took a sip and then a deep draught of the slightly sweet, honeyed wine.

The deep amber liquid was wonderful in taste and aroma making him want nothing more than to drink more of it, however, he knew he needed water. He suspected he knew how Elara had accomplished the summoning, though she had a somewhat devilish look as she gave him no hint as to the process. He chuckled at this, which drew a smile from her, before he put his hand on the other chair arm, thinking of cold water he pulsed power into it. Just as he had hoped, a goblet with crystal clear water appeared and he drank it greedily before summoning more of it into the goblet again. Once he had quenched his thirst he turned from the water back to the sweet drink upon the other arm, sipping it slowly as he sank deeper into the chair. Making an effort he slowed his breathing and attempted to relax further, hoping to help prepare his body for the next fight. At some point during his relaxation the next match had been called out and two more members of the participants made their way into the arena. Thalen could not see clearly from his vantage point, but they appeared to be two humans, of truly average height and build, yet he knew at this point that it told him nothing about their skill. The announcer signaled the start of the battle, and the two competitors immediately went at it, neither moved far from their spot and simply spent time hurling spells into the others shield with seemingly little effect. To Thalen's eyes it appeared as though neither of them had much experience in battle. Though, if he was honest, he could easily see that their control and defense surpassed his. Their shields deflected and received hits that would have already shattered his own, even though hardly more than a minute had passed. Yet even the strongest of defenses can only take so much, as suddenly, one of the men let out a wail of surprise as his shield shattered around him. Within seconds his opponent launched two quick attacks, he dodged one, but not the other, a bolt of flame, rammed into his chest briefly setting his bearded face alight before slowly smoldering out. At that point he raised his arms in the air and the match was called to completion, much to the enjoyment of those in attendance as they let out a cheer just as they had at the end of Thalen's own fight.

He could not help but be somewhat disappointed, whether it was with the unsatisfying way the bout was fought or if it was how much wasted effort he had put into his own, he could not decide. Whatever the case, dissatisfaction must have been plain on his features as Keela's melodic voice interrupted his thoughts. "Is all well Thalen? You seem to be disturbed in some way, is something not to your liking?" there was a moment of silence between them as he considered his feelings once again. "Truthfully, I could not say. It may just be the stark difference between this match and my own, I cannot decide if I wasted effort in my strategy for my own fights..." he trailed off as he could see her shaking her head. "Something you need not fear is wasted effort in these matches. If the mage you had faced was more powerful, standing in place and throwing spells back and forth would have been at best foolish. You would have been defeated or possibly killed near instantly. This may be because magic is so new to you in concept, Thalen tell me if you were in melee with an enemy much stronger than yourself would you fight them head on and take all of their blows or attempt to avoid them?" Thalen didn't know how to respond; he couldn't help but be dumbstruck by what she had just said. Yet, as he felt a wave of what he could only describe as relief wash over him he chuckled, words coming out between them. "It would be truly foolish to take the strikes from a stronger opponent and would be far better to avoid them. Thank you Keela, you have cleared my mind of a fog I did not realize was there." she smiled at him in return before taking a sip from a crystalline cup upon her chair's arm before settling further into the luxurious cushions. Taking a breath Thalen settled in once more, as with sixty matches in total, and only two done to this point, he thought it may be some time before his next match.

It turned out he was very correct, twelve more matches passed in which he studied his potential opponents carefully, one included Dolgrath handily defeating another dwarf. He knew he was not good enough to truly judge the prowess or power of someone's magic just yet, however, he could not help but draw comparisons between those in the matches with not himself but his friends. Dolgrath had easily defeated his opponent, and though Keela and Elara had yet to have a match he had fought with them enough during practice to have a good idea of their abilities. They all had seemed to stand head and shoulders above most of those that had fought before them. It seemed many of them were clumsy with their incantations and spells or they were weak in either offense or defense. Those that were close to being well rounded, at least to his eyes, seemed slow in their decision making and perhaps simply lacked the seasoning of combat. Of his three companions he thought Elara fell mostly in this category, he thought she was well rounded, but he could take two of every five matches from her, she lacked experience. Yet, this was something that could only come from time and though his own background was not in mage combat, he knew how and when to be aggressive and lacked the fear of being harmed or harming an opponent. Yet, when it came to Keela and Dolgrath he could not truly determine who was a stronger opponent, but he had yet to beat either of them in a match. Although, he felt excitement bubbling up in him over having another chance to try again today. He had known the whole time he would likely go up against one if not all three of them during this "tournament" the order had concocted, yet he did not know how he would overcome the hurdle they represented.

Once more the fire-like lettering appeared within the sky displaying the next competitors *"Keela Belhorn vs. Elara Skylark"* and as the lettering began to fade away the voice of the announcer boomed calling for the two competitors to approach the arena. Thalen heard a sigh come from his left as Elara massaged the bridge of her nose with closed eyes. Upon opening them he could not help but be struck by the steel he saw in her normally soft and friendly expression. She stood sharply and turned to Keela, who herself was just standing from her seat, "Come Keela, let us see how far I have come." a note of challenge was in her voice. The elven woman just smiled back a fierce expression masking any other thoughts she might have before walking with Elara out towards the entrance to the arena. As he ripped his eyes from their retreating forms he turned to see Dolgrath standing near him also looking at their two companions. After a moment he looked at Thalen "Come lad, let's be getting closer to the edge, we'll be wantin' to see this. Don't worry bout yer seat it'll stay yers as long as yer cup be on the arm." He gave Thalen a moment to stand before the pair went over to the wall separating them from the drop down into the arena. "Who do you think will be the victor?" he asked the dwarf who responded without hesitation "Keela, Elara be good, but Keela be far far better. The years o' the elfkin canny be ignored. But it should be a good ol' fight to be watchin'." He couldn't help but agree with his friend's assessment, yet he looked forward to seeing what the two could do when they were outside of a practice room and instead in a true arena of battle.

The two women walked to their designated ends of the arena, though there was still a great distance from where he and Dolgrath stood it was easy to distinguish between their two companions, as the more lithe and unearthly form of their elvish friend spun to face the left. This happened near simultaneously as the fuller figure of Elara turned about to face Keela, though Thalen could not see either of them in true detail he could easily imagine their expressions set with determination. He shook his head slightly, almost embarrassed at how poetic he was making this in his mind before settling into a comfortable position leaning against the small wall preparing to congratulate the victor and console the loser. Once it was clear they were both set and ready the voice of the announcer filled the space "Combatants ready? Begin!"

The signal given, Elara and Keela immediately began to cast spells one after another, seeming to feel each other out as they stuck mostly to spells of fire which easily dissipated off of the other's shield. Slowly, Keela began to weave in spells of pure arcane energy appearing as bolts of green with silvery streaks pulsing with light through the air before impacting into the crystalline shield of the human woman. From the best Thalen could tell those bolts made greater impact than many of those he had seen before and for a moment was unsure why, until he remembered he was once told, by Cameral, that the elves are more attuned with the abstract and pure power itself of the world, as opposed to the more elemental magics. And that strength was certainly on display as Elara almost seemed to jump at the first strike of the power, it appearing to affect her shield greater than all the previous attacks had. Elara started to move about, dodging as many of the spells as she could, she seemed to consider her next move before quickly acting. Course decided she became more aggressive with her posture, closing the distance between herself and Keela while increasing the strength of her attacks, though they came less frequently more power appeared to pour into them as they were larger and seemed to engulf Keela's form with gouts of flame. When she seemed to feel she was close enough she stopped and threw both of her hands upon the ground, then much as Thalen had done, she pulsed power through the earth causing a wave to appear from within it, it starting in front of her, though unlike his own attempt hers appeared to hold more power and crested at a greater speed, the wave quickly turning the ground beneath Keela into that of a bucking bronco. Yet, it did not seem to take Keela off guard, as she seemed to glide over the ripples within the ground with little issue. Once the floor had settled, she shot forth a gout of water from between outstretched hands, washing a surprised Elara backwards. Though she was thrown to the ground, she recovered quickly just in time to avoid another blast of arcane energy from the elvish woman. However, that momentary loss of balance was enough for

Keela to take the initiative as with a few quick words and a point beneath the floor where Elara stood a geyser of water shot forth lifting her high into the air.

With a quick word Keela turned the jet of water into pure ice, the conversion causing it to slowly crack and then break Elara's shield. Once it broke, Keela waited a moment possibly to see if Elara would surrender, yet all that greeted her was another bolt of flame which deflected off of her shield. Though they were so far away Thalen could swear he saw a smile split Keela's pale face before she shot forth a bolt of water directly into Elara's stomach, it knocked the breath from her quickly rendering the woman unconscious. In that moment she fell from the ice tower, while near simultaneously Keela formed a spell that caused air to gather round the falling woman it slowing her fall enough for Keela to position herself to catch Elara from the remainder of her fall.

Several moments passed before a voice rang out over the crowd "The bout has been decided, the winner Keela Balhorn! Give a cheer for both her victory and great sportsmanship!" Within a scant second the crowd came to life cheering on both the effort of the fallen Elara and that of the victor Keela. Thalen looked over at his dwarvish friend who seemed to have a conflicted look upon his face, one that Thalen was sure he also shared. He wanted to support Keela and yet he did not wish to do so at the expense of Elara, yet that was a problem for another time. As Keela, who still carried Elara, vanished from site as they approached the participant stands, Thalen turned to his dwarfish friend "Come friend let us return to our seats, I cannot help but feel conflicted over the situation as it stands. I am pleased for one friend and sad for another." Dolgrath grunted in agreement before leading the way through the small crowd to their destination, as he seated himself Thalen took up his cup and drank deep, trying to give himself a moment to consider what to say to Keela and Elara once they appeared.

He found he had less time than he hoped as Keela and Elara returned to them within a few minutes, seemingly once Elara had been healed as she now stood on her own two feet a rueful smile upon her lips. From what Thalen could tell Keela was also trying to be a graceful victor, and likely had plenty of practice with it as she kept a mostly neutral expression on her face only allowing a small sparkle to creep into her eyes. After a few moments of awkward silence between them it was of course Dolgrath who broke it, "Great show girlies! Ye were havin' a good ol' fight and it ain't gonna be yer last. Elara, ye better get yerself wins in yer last three fights. And Keela ye best be keepin' yerself sharp for your last few." The dwarves' surly tone elicited a small laugh and chuckle from the two women as it seemed to lift Elara and dampen Keela at least slightly. Thalen could not help but think that though Keela was of the long-lived race she deeply understood that the dwarf had seen more of the world than she had. At least that is how he read it seeing as how much she seemed to defer to him when it came to things like this. The dwarf kept up with his near sermon and after several minutes Thalen noticed Elara begin to droop where she stood, he could tell that she may have been healed but she was not recovered yet and with this in mind he interrupted his friend. "Dolgrath, I think they get the point and you may have yet to notice but it seems our dear Elara is wilting beneath your strong words." he said pointing at the younger woman "Perhaps, we should allow them to sit after all the day is hardly over." the dwarf stopped short before a bashful look came to his face as he nodded his agreement. Thalen took his queue and offered the tired woman his arm "My lady, may I offer you aid to your seat?" She took it gratefully as she leaned into him. He found himself strangely happy that she did, however, he ignored that for now making sure that she safely arrived to her chair.

As she sat she seemed to melt into the comforting cushions of the chair as he summoned her fresh cool water to sip at while she recovered from her fight. "Thank you Thalen, I likely could have made it here, but it was good to have someone to lean on." she said her voice's normal brightness dulled with held back emotion. "That was a disappointing loss, I thought I was going to top Keela, yet it seems I have fallen short yet again." falling silent she put her hands up covering her face, whether to hide tears or due to weariness he could not tell. Yet, he was intimately familiar with this disappointment and frustration, he had experienced it many times before in his thirty years of life. Placing what he hoped was a comforting hand on her shoulder he spoke "Be at ease my friend, there are plenty of times in life where a wall that seems insurmountable will appear before you. Though they may seem impassable at the time, a day will come when they were simply another bump upon the road to your success." he cringed a bit at his words, he sounded like some ancient sage delivering wisdom, yet it seemed to strike home as she appeared to straighten a little, though her hands remained on her face.

Another minute or so passed before Thalen decided it would be best to let her finish working through this herself, as he felt it was all he could offer. Turning from her he walked over to where Keela and Dolgrath now sat talking in relatively low tones, likely to keep too much of the conversation from Elara's ears. Of course, the first words he heard were those of the gruff voice of the dwarf "...ye were showin' off I be tellin ye, ye coulda just stepped out da way o' the floor movin' instead o' ridin' it..." he continued even in the face of Keela's withering and dry look before her face lit up brightly at the possibility of escape. "Thalen, tis good that you have joined us. Dolgrath was just telling me about what I could do better..." she stopped to give him another withering glance. "Er...I just want ye to be as good as ye can." he said somewhat lamely. Though this time he seemed to get the hint and even had just enough tact to look a little abashed. At that Thalen could not help but laugh, drawing some surprised looks from the other people around them, once he was able to get his amusement back under control, he put a hand on Keela's shoulder and congratulated her on the win. Before he could speak further he was interrupted by the voice of the announcer "Come friends, let us keep the action rolling our next fighters are Thalen Melodyr and Katyani Veloranti" Taking a fortifying breath he turned to his friends and gave them each nods in turn before moving towards the entrance to the arena readying himself for the newest challenge ahead.

CHAPTER TWENTY-SIX

It took several hours for most of the matches to be completed and rather quickly an obvious order was established with members such as Dolgrath, Keela and even that racist bastard Doryan Telmasar firmly established the top five participants. To round out the group there was a human woman who seemed a bit older than the others, not yet as old as Thalen himself was, but it seemed as though it was not her first attempt at advancement, as well as one of the few raital by the name of Velaria Sevelinus. None of the top five had suffered a loss yet each having three wins without a loss, next came those in the top ten Elara stood amongst that group as they all held a record of two wins and a single loss. Lastly was where he himself stood just barely within the top fifteen members of the competitors, the ones he considered to be here either only had one win or their two wins were less than convincing. He fell under the latter group, his first one was relatively clean as all could see, he was creative and clever with his attack patterns, but the second win he all but fell into. He was on the back foot the entire time to an elvish woman; however, they became overconfident, and he landed a lucky strike with a decently timed ball of water. By lucky strike he of course meant the water caused them to slip and gave me the chance to hit them with another ball of water that crashed them to the ground. However, in his third match he was completely overpowered by the Raital he considered in the top five, truthfully the next match could be the difference between moving forward and the journey being over before it began.

In the end all this meant to him was he would simply have to overcome the next challenger or if necessary, make the best showing he could in a loss. He was sure that even if he lost a second time a good show would keep him in the top half of the contestants, and if that was the case, he could at least move on to the next round. However, he felt it would be best to leave thoughts of tomorrow for tomorrow and focus solely on the final match of the day. He had a vague idea of when he would go next, it seemed that the organizers had planned it out in such a way where one half of the fighters always went in the same order. He personally had the unlucky benefit of going first in every set of fifteen matches, though on the plus side he knew how long he had to rest before his next fight. In this case he was fortunate enough to have one last match before his own, allowing him to relax a little longer and work through some final preparations. He took a breath to ease himself, eating the last morsel of bread from the meal that had been provided to them about halfway through the number of matches. It had not been anything too special but the beef stew they had been provided was filling and took the edge of hunger that had begun to distract him. His stomach completely full and mind relaxed he began to consider his next fight and whom he could possibly be against. Unfortunately for him, it was near impossible to guess, though he did know who it would not be and that concerned him greatly. He was not sure if it was blind luck or if it was planned by the Order, but those Thalen felt were in the middle of the thirty in terms of strength, were those that appeared to have a fixed order. This meant he would not be facing Elara, as she was part of that group, nor anyone who was immediately stronger or weaker than himself, this leaving only the outliers as his potential opponents.

Of those that remained only one of them was blatantly less skilled in combat, but he had already fought them in the first round. Luckily, he had also already fought the strongest Raital, who was easily in the top group, however, he did not know whether they considered his second opponent stronger or weaker. So, either he was looking at a mostly even chance or one weighted towards a superior opponent, making it very difficult to determine strategy. Sighing to himself, he quickly decided to discard the notion of coming up with any specific battle plan, as he realized such thinking would lead nowhere and decided to simply take things as they came. Fortunately, such things would come soon, as the current match ended, an elvish man defeating one of the humans that were easily the least skilled of those there.

Thalen stood, stretching his arms and legs, he knew it would be his turn soon and wanted to make sure his body wasn't tight after the long rest since his last match. He could feel his heart beating surprisingly fast, he had hoped at this point that he was used to these moments before battle, yet perhaps this was less about this match and more knowing that a poor showing could keep him from a true battle again. Shaking his head to try and dislodge the thoughts from his mind, he knew he didn't have time for them. The next match was likely to be his most difficult yet, whether it be due to his own inexperience, the difficulty of the opponent or perhaps both, remained to be seen. As though his thoughts were the catalyst the flame lined lettering wrote itself out, hanging in the sky for all to see. *"Thalen Melodyr vs. Dolgrath Boardolin"* Upon seeing this he felt his heart drop slightly, this was, to his mind, easily the worst matchup he could have received. Dolgrath was powerful, strong, and familiar with Thalen and his tactics and though Thalen knew Dolgrath nearly as well in turn, the dwarf had far more tricks about him and many, many more options.

While his mind was occupied with various thoughts and strategies, he was taken out of his spiral by a strong hand that backhanded his arm companionably, with Dolgrath's voice following soon behind. "Ye durned fool I be talkin' to ye 'nd ye be ignorin' meself!" Thalen turned to him as he tried in vain to collect himself from his internal monologue. His mind was still half in mist when he replied, "Apologies my friend, I was so focused I did not hear you." The dwarf seemed decently sated with that answer before nodding and motioning that they should move towards one of the elevators which lead to the arena floor. Thalen had found it to be an interesting name for the magical construction, as it did more than just bring someone to the area above, yet he threw the thought away as the dwarf began to speak. "Well laddie, I be sayin' best a luck to ye, I be undefeated and don't plan on makin' it easy on ye." As he finished the dwarf chuckled evilly. Thalen found this somewhat feigned threat put him at ease and he could not help but respond in kind. "I would be careful my friend, do not drop your guard or I may set that beard of yours alight. I don't plan on losing to you today." he threw the dwarf a sly wink and halfcocked grin.

They shared a few more jabs before reaching the trench elevators that sat carved within the wall. "I hope your luck is good my friend, but not that good." Thalen said to the dwarf, to which he received a rude gesture before they each burst into laughter. Several moments later they were both on the floor of the arena, where they each gave the other one last nod before going to their indicated position.

As Thalen neared his position the announcer began the typical speech, which he promptly ignored, his mind far too busy trying to create some plan or strategy to use against the dwarf. Yet, nothing impressive or innovative came to his mind, forcing him to accepted that he would just have to be aggressive in his attacks while trying to keep a tight defense, in other words keep it simple. He could feel something in the corner of his mind, some previous thought or idea trying to come to the forefront, but before it could the announcer gave the signal to begin. Thalen reacted immediately, yet it apparently was still slower than Dolgrath as the dwarf sent a bolt of arcane energy before even erecting his own shield. Thalen had no other choice but to dive to the right, using his training and practice to transition into a shoulder roll. Once he made it back to his feet he erected his shield, the words and actions second nature to him, while near simultaneously launching a bolt of flame at his foe. It struck true on Dolgrath's shield the crystalline structure showing opaque for just a moment before deflecting a majority of the blast off to the side in a spray of embers. Thalen did not wish to let up preparing to launch another attack but once more the dwarf was quicker, he had in fact closed the distance and with palms outstretched yelled out "Col'Fir Tor Cocle Dorint" Calling from nothingness a spray of fire that surged forth from his broad palms engulfing Thalen and his shield in flames. Though Thalen's shield held well enough he could still feel the heat and was temporarily blinded by the sudden light that glowed brightly in his face, it forcing him to nearly cover his eyes completely in the hope of protecting his remaining vision. Once the gout of flame had run its course Thalen allowed some of his own creativity to flow, gathering an image within his mind he yelled out "Wantorin Sa'guin Bel'ar" and stomped one foot towards the dwarf. Suddenly, as though called by winter itself, shards of ice surged forth from the ground making solid contact with the dwarf's shield, though, to his disappointment, the dwarf managed to avoid most of the damage with a quick move to the side. The glancing blow added extra momentum as Dolgrath jumped easily clear of the affected area and threw another bolt of flame in Thalen's direction, it glancing off his shield much as the others, yet he could feel the strength and stability of his construct begin to wane.

Gritting his teeth, Thalen felt frustration beginning to boil up, it seemed nothing he had attempted thus far had been truly effective and that did not bode well for him. To give himself time to think, Thalen began to launch multiple spells shooting forth bolts of pure arcane, the spells mindless and requiring little effort, as he prayed it would keep his opponent on the defensive. Sadly, he was not so lucky as Dolgrath called out some quick words Thalen could not hear clearly, but he could very much see the rise of a stone wall before Dolgrath completely hiding him from site. With the unexpected break in action Thalen was unsure what to do next, he could not approach at either side easily as the dwarf could simply appear from the other or worse yet could have lain a trap for such a move. So, Thalen did the only thing he could think of, he waited, taking the opportunity to regain his breath and somewhat reshape and strengthen his shield where it had gotten weak or malformed.

Though he was grateful for the respite he found himself concerned as the seconds stretched to a minute with no sign of his foe. *"I have truly no choice but to move forward with the attack...the question is how. I can't go to either side and going above would be foolish and leave me vulnerable. I suppose there is only one choice then..."* decidedly he began to pull in power, picking the appropriate words from thin air as he pictured the desired shape. Calling out the words "Col'Fir Shamusal Tor Sai'ale Dorint" he hoped that though the structure of his words were clumsy the picture of his desire would be clear enough to make up the gap. As he felt the power surge he pointed out a singular finger towards the wall, a beam of molten earth shooting forth, it being not much more than three fingers in width. Even so, its intensity and the energy poured into it was more than enough for it to serve his purpose. As it struck the wall it began to melt through the stone causing chunks of it to fall as they went from solid earth to something akin to molasses. Thalen felt elation at the success of the spell, but that soon fell away as he realized even with the defense slowly being etched away his opponent had yet to make a move to counter his attack. Confusion gave way to concern, and Thalen made the decision to cut off his current attack halting the flow of power into it. Thalen felt himself grow weary, having used two large scale attacks within such a short amount of time had taken a lot of effort and the lack of payoff made it, so it was more than just his body feeling the effects. Needing to finish the battle quickly Thalen decided to take a wide angle to keep as much distance between himself and what remained of the wall as possible. Strafing off to the left he kept his eyes trained on the few areas left that Dolgrath could be hiding behind, yet even as he came near perpendicular he still could not see the dwarf. "What...where the hell is he?" Thalen blurted out in confusion and as though to answer the question the ground beneath him started to swell. Surprise overtook him as he stumbled back losing his shield as his concentration broke. Before him, rising out of the earth itself Dolgrath appeared, his palm outstretched as power thrummed within, Thalen felt an impact to his chest, felt himself briefly leave the ground, and then unceremoniously return to it as he felt the hard stone come up to meet him, it knocking the breath from his lungs. He tried to collect himself, but the dwarf loomed over him and fired a ball of solid rock into Thalen's stomach, gasping for breath that would not come Thalen's vision turned from blurred to black.

Thalen found himself waking sometime later upon a cot that sat within a room of stone, it took him a moment to recognize the room as he looked about. With the realization he felt at ease as the medical area of the arena was exactly where he wanted to be at this moment, especially now that he had regained consciousness, and his body decided to protest his efforts at the damage he had received. "I see ye be awake laddie." Thalen, shoulders protesting, turned his head expecting to find Dolgrath but instead found a different dwarf, also burly and well-muscled much as his friend was, but with a longer beard and seeming more wizened. "Ye took a hard hit out there me boy. Are ye feelin well? Nothin' broken to best ye can tell?" he asked, his stubby fingers probing the areas Thalen had taken the strongest hits. Grunting at the rough touch he managed to gasp out "No, I don't believe anything broke, simply sore and apparently very bruised" the dwarf began nodding, not yet letting up his examination before making a sound of satisfaction. "Ye, be right from what I can be tellin' ye only be hurtin' on the outside. Ye can stay another few minutes but ye best be gettin' up to the viewin' area again." The dwarf didn't wait any longer moving forward to administer aid to the more damaged members of the testing class. Alone once more, Thalen allowed himself a few further minutes to relax his stiff muscles and spare himself a moment of pain from the mottled bruising that he knew was slowly growing across him. He wished healing was worth the time and effort, yet he knew how limited that vein of magic was and more precisely how quickly the effort required for the healing of a few large but minor bruises would greatly outweigh the benefits of it. It took him another few minutes to gather the willpower to get up from the hard, but in that moment, comfortable cot. A groan escaped his lips as he moved, his abused muscles protesting the effort as they nearly overcame his will and forced him back to the bed below. If he was honest with himself he wanted to grant his body its wish, but one glance by the surly dwarf medic told him that wasn't an option. He sucked in a breath and quickly went from lying to seated and then to standing, his body screaming at him every step of the way. In some ways he lamented the fact that this was his last match, as between matches he had received healing to ensure that he would be ready for the next fight, yet it seemed they cared far less the second you were done for the day, As he walked from the chamber Thalen looked about examining the other members of the group that were not forced to give up their cot, some had injuries just worse than his own while others had bones quite obviously broken, and in some cases protruding from skin. Strangely he did not find himself concerned, as he knew that unlike, him, these people would receive healing to bring them to the point where their body could take over and finish the process of knitting the bone.

He chucked a little at himself, realizing his thoughts were only a little bitter but he allowed them to play out a little longer before discarding them as he left the chamber. Turning left he made his way to the elevator room coming to the stone room with the many elevator grooves lining the walls. Reaching one of the trenches he jumped into it and willed himself to rise and as expected the magic responded quickly elevating him up to the viewing platform. It took him several minutes to find his friends, the small press of people making it difficult to navigate to their reserved area. As he making his way through the group, he found it odd that the normally intense crowd in the stands seemed somewhat subdued. It seemed that the din of the crowd was not that of energized excitement but rather relative boredom and perhaps some level of discontent. Finally spotting his companions he walked towards them and looked out into the arena itself, curious about the current match and what exactly was sowing so much disinterest and frustration. Standing within the center of the arena was what Thalen thought was an elf, but it was hard to tell as they just stood in the middle of the floor sparks of magic flying off of their near visible shield. Though Thalen thought they must be hard pressed; he could not help but notice that they appeared to be completely calm and unaffected by the offensive that had been launched against them. Their opponent was a human woman, and even from this distance he could see her blond hair was plastered to her forehead with sweat from her efforts. Even to his inexperienced eyes she did not seem weak or unskilled, yet against the power of her foe she seemed completely outmatched. In fact, if Thalen did not know better he would think that their elvish opponent was almost toying with them. It was almost as though they were not taking the match seriously and with that thought fixed in his mind it became very clear why the crowd was unamused.

As the match continued with no change, Thalen believed his earlier suspicion was confirmed as he found his own emotions welling up in the pit of his stomach, though he did his best to keep his usual calm. He could not help but think that this was no battle, match or anything that could be called a friendly competition or otherwise, this was no better than a slaughter on a battlefield with one superior force knowing that they could easily defeat the other at any time. He shook his head in frustration as he knew this would not provide any information on his potential opponent and tore himself away from the spectacle.

He was so absorbed in the spectacle that he had stopped walking towards his friends. However, as he realized the elf intended to embarrass his opponent and there would be no sudden change in the flow of battle he continued moving on. Keela was the first to see his approach as she raised a hand to both signal where they were and to ask him to approach her specifically. Upon reaching her she motioned towards the chair next to her in which he sat thankfully, the walk and movement though light had caused his injuries to flare and renew the pain. After a few minutes of viewing the still one-sided match Thalen was caught by surprise as his elvish companion let out a disgusted sound. Looking over at her he found her normally soft and elegant features set hard by anger, the expression was almost frightening on the normally calm and serene woman. As though reading his mind, she looked at him through the corner of her eye and blushed slightly before leaning back and closing her eyes. "I apologize for that outburst; I just cannot stand to see this disgraceful act by one of my people. They are simply toying with that poor woman; they could have ended this farce at any point since the match itself had begun." she lapsed into silence as the crowd seemed to gasp all in unison. They both looked out into the arena and found the source of the sudden change in mood; the woman lay upon the ground her legs and arms jutting out in very unnatural directions. The elf still stood in the same position as before, but their body language almost seemed to sneer in disgust at the display, their entire being seemed to seep superior arrogance. In that moment the announcer spoke, though with less bluster and fanfare, and Thalen felt anger rise in the pit of his stomach at what was said "The winner is Doryan Telmasar..."

CHAPTER TWENTY-SEVEN

After the elf left the arena a group of medical aids came to take away the maimed woman, but from what Thalen could tell, it would be best to do some healing immediately after seeing the state she was in. He knew how easily a broken bone could lead to death, or how an improper set could leave someone disfigured permanently he had seen more than enough on the battlefield or in the camps after one. Something he did not expect though was to see someone so completely broken during a supposed test hosted by the magical order he was now part of, in fact it was even harder to tell if the behavior that caused this would even be reprimanded let alone punished. Though Thalen could appreciate the reason for these matches, to determine who was prepared for true battle, this seemed to go far beyond preparation and was more so the sadistic nature of what he felt was an evil person. It only took a single glance at Keela to tell he was not the only one who thought this, or at least something along the same lines. For the first time Thalen could not help but feel her emotions were plain upon her face, sympathy for the woman, anger at the person who caused this, yet also a certain sadness in her almond eyes though the source of that specifically was unclear.

Without prompting she began to speak "I am sorry that such a spectacle was made of that poor woman. I feel somehow responsible for the acts of my people, especially those that are as cruel as this." she said apologetically. Silence overtook her and Thalen could tell that her thoughts had turned somewhat inward again, possibly turning her frustration inward towards herself. He did not enjoy that thought, "It was not you who caused this my friend, and the acts of your kindred are not the acts of yourself." He tried to keep his voice as soothing as possible. He did not wish to upset her further by allowing his own emotions to color his words or unintentionally influence the perceived intent of them. She gave him a small smile before sighing in what seemed to be a mix of relief and frustration, "I appreciate your words, perhaps it is simply because it is happening before me and for all the influence my family has it is nothing but a candle before that of someone such as Doryan's." a sad smile creased her lips "We were once friends you know, when we were younger. He was not always this way. There was a time when he was open-minded and almost charming. Yet some thirty years ago it all changed, and he became as he is now...and I could not say as to why." she gave a near imperceptible shrug before taking a sip of water. They lapsed into silence once again as a smattering of applause arose as the woman was taken out on a stretcher appearing to not be fully aware but at least awake and alive. Thalen mimicked the rest, clapping at the good fortune that the woman was at least alive, if not well in her current state. Once the arena floor was empty the announcer's voice took up the general quietness and began to announce the next match. Thalen unexpectedly felt a hand on his forearm and at the same time he turned to see Keela's hand on him as she gave it a gentle squeeze. "Thank you for hearing my lamenting, let us move forward towards finer things." he smiled at her gently which she returned before turning back towards the arena and the next two combatants preparing for battle.

The remainder of the matches took about another hour, none of them as brutal or one sided as the dismantling of the woman had been. However, there were certainly times when they were not as competitive, however, Thalen thought it was more based off the remaining skilled competitors taking it as an opportunity to learn and enhance their lesser abilities. This included his friends, who each won their matches which left Thalen feeling just a little annoyed with his even record. As each of his friends ended with more wins than losses and each had made a strong showing in comparison to his own, at least in his opinion. After several minutes he allowed himself a whimsical smile and laughed at himself and his unnecessary thoughts. Reflecting on his own matches, he felt he had done well, though he had lost embarrassingly in one. Thankfully, he felt good about his match against Dolgrath and believed it made up for that blunder. Though in the end it was not his opinion that mattered but instead that of all the proctors and those that scored the matches themselves.

Once the final match had ended the announcer spoke for the last time "Thank you all for your participation and you, our lovely audience, for being with us through this event! Competitors, please stay in your seats a bit longer to discover if you have managed to be in the top fifteen of the group! If you are then you will return tomorrow for the final stage of the tournament!" as suddenly as the voice rang out, it stopped, leaving only the general murmur of the crowd as a backdrop to the world around them. Unsure of what else to do Thalen leaned back in the chair and closed his eyes, the soreness of his aching muscles and the moments of sharp pain from his bruised body had slowly dulled. Nonetheless, he still knew it would require sleep and many hours before the worst of it healed and for the soreness to be eased. In fact, he knew if he was correct that he was set to be involved in the further spectacle of the tests he would not be fully healed in time. His mood darkened a bit at that as he realized this was likely planned out as had been the other twists, the only thing that kept him from becoming truly angered was the fact that some, if not all, of the other competitors would also be dealing with the fatigue and injury of today's fights.

Shrugging off the annoyance Thalen waited for word of the top fifteen, he did not have to wait long thankfully as fiery words suddenly flowed from nothingness in the sky, this being accompanied by an announcement "Before you will be the names and rankings of those that will be moving forward to the next portion of the tournament. For those that have fallen short, consider what you can do to improve for the future and best of luck to those that advance." Once the disembodied voice had quieted, Thalen could feel a tangible excitement and the trepidation that filled most of those within the small crowd of competitors and the few spectators that had remained. Going from the top Thalen, found himself generally unsurprised, but somewhat disappointed seeing that ranked first was the elf Doryan. Thalen had hoped to see that bastard no higher than five in the hopes that there would be some level of justice within the fabric of the universe, yet that did not seem to be the case.

As his eyes traveled down the list he found Dolgrath had managed to snag third with Keela's name not far behind in the fifth position. Seeing two of his friends in the top five positions made him feel some level of pride at the strength and skill of his companions. It was a few names further before he found Elara, though not within the top five, she was ranked a respectable eighth. As his eyes continued to scan the names, he felt a lump form in the pit of his stomach as it grew bigger and bigger by the moment, before it suddenly disappeared. His eyes resting at his name located in fifteenth place, at the very end of the list but at least on the list. The wave of relief that overcame him was as though some unseen weight that rested upon his chest was removed and he felt physical relief. *"Thank the gods, for a moment I thought I wasn't able to break into the top fifteen...I can't say I am pleased with my placing on the list but being on the list is better than the alternative."* he thought to himself his eyes closing as the weight of the moment took the last bits of energy from him. He found his moment of mental relaxation interrupted by the gruff voice of his dwarvish friend "Well laddie, ye did it, ye kept yerself alive even longer." opening his eyes he saw his three friends each showing their pleasure in different ways, ways that only those that truly knew them could recognize and understand. He gave them all a wry smile, his own elation returning as excitement overcame him. "You are right, friend Dolgrath, yet it is not just I that can claim a victory this day. You all have managed to move on...in fact all of you have managed to move on in a far more impressive way than I have." he finished with a good-natured laugh, to keep his words light. Fortunately, it seemed to be taken as he desired as he saw a smile or at least a smirk split the lips of each of his companions. After a moment Elara spoke out, stretching her arms above her head with a small wince "We have indeed managed to move ourselves forward haven't we, though I must admit I am very sore. The last battle has certainly left me somewhat bruised." Thalen grunted in agreement as his own injuries throbbed, almost as if to keep themselves fresh in his mind. "I believe it may be for the best if we depart and part ways for the remainder of today, it has been many hours since the tournament started. I believe sleep is what will be best for us all." Keela said her voice sweet and honeyed. Thalen could not help but agree with her words, he wished for nothing more than sleep and perhaps a bit of cheese and meat to fill his near empty stomach, though as he stood, he felt the softness of his bed call him.

Thalen stood and turned towards the elevator room, when suddenly he was knocked off balance, upon regaining it he saw the disgusted face of Doryan brushing his shoulder as though removing something foul from it. "Be careful where you are standing filth, you should make way for your betters." the words were cutting in contrast to the elf's melodic voice. Before Thalen could respond the haughty elf continued "Then again you may be too stupid to understand just how lowly you are, is that the case?" Thalen felt his face darken as his anger welled within him, but before he could explode the calm yet firm voice of Keela spoke "That is enough Doryan, you are embarrassing our kindred and making a fool of yourself." her normally kind eyes were piercing, yet they did not seem to dissuade the elf from his current course. "Who are you to speak to me as such Keelatharia, you who spend your time amongst these lesser beings. All of the kindred agree deep within them, agree with what I say and have said, this is why I speak for so many, and my family has great power within our people's dominion." Keela did not deign to respond but maintained her even and unamused gaze, the only hint given that she even heard his words was a raised eyebrow upon her fay and angular face. He held her gaze for a few moments more before turning from her, disgust evident in his expression "Have it your way Keelatharia, I will ignore your pet human for today. But, be warned that I will crush him if we are to meet tomorrow." Without another word he turned and made his way to the elevator, his booted feet echoing through the quickly emptying arena.

Keela seemed to shrink after the confrontation, though, to Thalen's eyes, it was not from fear or near frayed nerves but instead weariness. It was as though the conversation itself had taken whatever energy she had remaining, Thalen offered her an arm which she waved off but smiled at in appreciation. "I am alright Thalen, simply a bit tired from the matches and the emotions that Doryan inspires." Thalen cast a look at the retreating back of the elf before returning his gaze to his friend. "Lassie, I'd say he be deservin a right thrashin for how he be actin." Dolgrath said with poorly concealed anger. Keela let out a sigh but could only nod her agreement, her eyes seeming to gleam with pleasure at the thought. "Keela, why does he insist on calling you by your full first name?" Elara asked continuing as another thought came to mind "Actually...I always wondered why you wish to be called Keela instead of Keelatharia, I think your name is very pretty." the young woman lapsed into silence, seeming somewhat embarrassed, but her eyes doughy in hopes of an answer. Their elvish friend smiled "Let me answer the second question first then I can answer the first question second. Most elves prefer to take only a small part of their name and present it to the world outside of our own kind. Our full names are used for formal occasions and our society places great importance in the full length of one's name, both first and last. For most we hear it so often when we are amongst our own people that it is refreshing to have a more informal name that can be used by the other races and our friends." she stopped for a moment almost as if she was considering her own words before continuing. "That isn't exactly all of it but that should give you a general idea, when it comes to Doryan's insistence on using my whole first name...I believe it is to spite me. To remind me that no matter our standing within the order, or who we are outside of elven society, he and his family are currently the greater. It is something I care little for but our families are rivals within court politics and with them having the upper hand he likes to remind me." as she lapsed into silence, it was Elara's ever gentle voice that filled the gap "What is Doryan's full first name if I may ask?" her tone becoming a bit shy and bashful as she seemed unsure if the question was an appropriate one. However, Keela did not seem taken aback or surprised by it as she readily replied "His name is Mela'Doryan and he makes pains to ensure those he feels are below him are well aware of it...Enough of this talk though, we should be on our way." she said her typical expression masking any further thoughts and without a second guess he began to walk away. Thalen turned to Dolgrath and Elara, a grave and concerned expression seated firmly upon his face before he fell in behind.

The remainder of the day was uneventful with Thalen and his companions spending the evening meal together in conversation about what had transpired that day and of what to expect the following one. However, it became clear that they all were suffering from both mental and physical fatigue and that it would be best to go their separate ways. After one final goodbye to his fellows Thalen began the plodding journey to his chambers, the exhaustion evident in his gait as his normally fluid movements were replaced with clumsiness. As if to punctuate this, he nearly lost his footing on several occasions when a leg would not respond as quickly as was normal. This new feeling and sensation he found somewhat troubling, he knew what fatigue was and how it felt as there had been many times after pitched battle that he could find himself barely able to move. Yet, this fatigue was different, it was almost as though he felt like he had been both filled and drained completely multiple times *"Perhaps this is what it feels like to conduct a true battle with magic. I have felt this before, now that I think of it, though never to such an extreme."* He turned this thought over in his head a few times realizing this was likely the effect of overuse or full use of magical powers, before his fatigue got the better of him and he discarded it. After all, it wasn't likely something he could change or stop from happening, yet he determined it would be in his best interest to do some light research on it. He just hoped that a book in his room would have the answer instead of needing to make his way to the library, in fact he knew that it was not an option to do that as he felt another wave of fatigue wash over him. Rubbing his fingers against his eyes Thalen tried in vain to remove some of the fatigue from them, yet all he did was leave them momentarily blurry from the pressure as he finally reached his door. Sighing in relief he reached out his hand turning the handle only for it to open by itself from the inside. Thalen stepped back in surprise raising his arms in a defensive posture his earlier fatigue washed away in a moment of adrenaline, only for it all to drain away again as his arms fell to the side, and what he could only assume was a very stupid look coming to his face. As from behind the door came a familiar elven visage. "Hello Thalen, it has certainly been some time hasn't it!" came the voice of Cameral Darkweave, a mischievous smirk dominating his face.

Thalen stood in the center of his chambers dumbfounded and completely unsure how or why the unusual and near elusive First Mage had returned. He was even more astonished to find him not just in the college in general but literally in his private quarters and yet there he was sitting very comfortably in a chair he had conjured himself the same infuriating smirk very neatly directed Thalen's way.

Before he could fully collect himself, Cameral, unsurprisingly, took the initiative "I imagine I have surprised you with my appearance here have I not! I could not help myself. I do so enjoy the surprised look you make when something unexpected happens, it is quite fun..." As the First Mage continued to spout his nonsense, Thalen took the chance to regain command of his emotions, taking his shock and confusion at the unexpected visit and transforming it into neutrality. He did not wish to reveal to Cameral just how much his sudden appearance had unbalanced him though he suspected it was nothing but a useless hope. He decided instead to lean into it interrupting the continuous stream of words from the elvish man "Yes Cameral, what you say is true I did not expect to see you. It seemed when last we spoke there was no expectation that we would meet again at least not for some time. Yet it has only been a scarce few months." the elf seemed to have no issue with Thalen's interruption as his face went from a near impish appearance to one of seriousness. "What you say is true, in fact I did not expect to have any conversation with you, yet I have some news that you may find interesting to some degree. Would you like to hear it?" he paused, his almond eyes seeming to shine in the light of the fire. The moment stretched, as it took a time for Thalen to realize that the mage was actually waiting for a response. Closing eyes in frustration he let out a breath to calm himself before opening them again and nodding.

Another momentary smile popped onto the face of the elvish man "Good I was worried you had started caring not for the world outside of these walls. From what I have heard you have been getting rather close to some of your companions…" he left the rest unspoken as he threw him a sly wink before returning to a more serious manner "The established lines are breaking up, though in general we are still holding firm more breaks are appearing allowing our enemies to push deeper into once safe territory. It is likely that the forces of the Coalition will be pulling back to allow ourselves a chance to reform, however, as you know this will take time and enemies will continue to pull through the breaks and gaps. As you can imagine this poses a twofold danger, one being this place may become less safe over time and secondly even if this does remain safe it is going to be closer to the main lines. I am sure I don't have to spell out to you why this could be an issue." the elf paused looking expectantly at Thalen, seeming to wait for a response to which Thalen obliged "Yes, I could see how that would be a problem and gives me all the more reason to finish the last tests tomorrow and move forward. I suppose others have been told of this as well? Those that have more say in the defense of the College and town beyond?" Cameral nodded in response. "Very well I will keep this in mind moving forwards, if something were to happen here it would be problematic for not only my finishing and learning but also to the war effort."

Cameral steepled his fingers appearing to be deep in thought before nodding as though a decision had been made "Though I wish for you to keep this in your mind, it is not something for you to be concerned about. The only thing you should be concerned with at this point is putting on a good show tomorrow!" the First Mage's voice and mannerism took on its typical whimsicality as he said those final words. Thalen shook his head at how fast the mage's demeanor could change, wondering as he always did whether other mages were as unstable as he was, but in the end all he could do was laugh. "Very well, I appreciate your candor in telling me and rest assured I will overcome the challenge set before me tomorrow. I assume you will be going soon?" Cameral's smile grew wide at the question as though he had played a joke on Thalen, laughing the elf near yelled out in glee "Why my friend, whatever do you mean!? I was never here!" and with a snap of his fingers the slight figure of the elf, the chair and even the fire that had been lit within the hearth all disappeared leaving Thalen alone in the dark. Dumbstruck for the second time in an hour Thalen stood in the dark for a few minutes before summoning a globe of light, looking around the room he knew there was no signs of the First Mage, and it was really as though he had never been there. Shaking his head Thalen disrobed and got into his nightclothes, extinguishing the light once he had settled under the covers to rest. And yet his mind was still somewhat alight with thoughts of both what Cameral had revealed and his sudden departure. After a few more minutes of turning, it around in his mind he chuckled before saying to the darkness "I should have known he wasn't really here, the room doesn't have a hearth."

CHAPTER TWENTY-EIGHT

The first thing Thalen felt when he awoke the following morning was extreme soreness followed closely behind by a splitting headache, as though someone had been pounding his head with a hammer throughout the night. His body felt heavy, and the comfort of the bed called him stronger than it ever had before. He had experienced the fatigue of battle many times in the past and easily battled it away, yet that coupled with his head trying to burst completely undercut his typical vigor. Steeling himself he rose from the bed slowly feeling every muscle, joint and tendon scream at him and yet they were not nearly as bad as the sudden rush of vertigo he felt as he struggled to maintain his balance. Rising to his feet he steadied himself before dressing, his mind made up on trying to drown out the headache with cool water and wine in equal measure. "If it works for a hangover, I am sure it will work for this too." he chuckled to himself before letting out a groan as another spike of pain shot through his head. "Enough thinking about the remedy, I must retrieve it. I need to break this headache before we are transported for the matches today." Thalen began his search grumbling under his breath about mages, the circle and their annoying penchant for flair. Thalen stalked through the halls of the college, his body rather quickly recovered as the kinks and fatigue slowly dispersed, at least temporarily. Yet even as his body relaxed and recovered his mind, brain, or whatever was ailing him continued to throb with every step upon the solid stone floor. Before long his mind turned inward as he barely willed his feet to keep moving forward. He actively worked in a vain attempt to ignore the nausea that was slowly creeping up from the moments of vertigo that would flow through him in between his strides.

Falling further and further into himself Thalen slowly began to lose track of where he was and what he was doing, the momentary energy he felt upon awakening drained from him before long leaving him feeling like a husk. His mental awareness fell to the point where he failed to notice the soft footsteps that approached him from the side, that is until he felt a slender but strong hand grab his upper arm. He turned his head to see Keela looking him directly in the eyes a mixture of annoyance and concern in her enchanting golden orbs. "Thalen,

I was calling you did you not hear me?" she paused, seeming to look at him with a more critical eye. "By the gods, you are suffering from overdraw. Quickly, give me your hands." before he could make another move, she grabbed his hands taking him by surprise. Her actions cleared the fog in him slightly, but before he could ask what she was doing, her previously warm hands suddenly turned cool and another second later that cool feeling extended into his own. In a matter of moments, it felt as though a crisp mountain stream flowed through him traversing from his hands to his arms before going up into his head before seeming to flush down through his back, legs and finally his feet. This lasted for a minute or two before it slowly subsided, in that same moment Keela released his hands and looked into his eyes once again. "How do you feel my friend?" she asked, her melodic voice almost motherly in its tone. Thalen opened eyes he had not noticed were closed and found himself both astonished and delighted to find that his mind was clear, the offending pain seeming to have melted away in the crisp current that had flowed through him. "Keela, I feel amazing. I had been suffering from indescribable pain within my head. It took all I had just to function at the smallest of levels…did you say I was…what was it?" he found himself elated and hoped his words were sufficient for her to understand, even if a question was launched within the same few sentences. Keela leveled a sober look at him before pushing at her temples, though Thalen could not tell if it was in annoyance or due to a headache of her own. Though the answer was revealed almost immediately, "Damn that dwarf!" she exclaimed, her voice strained with thinly veiled irritation. Thalen found himself caught by surprise from both her outburst as well as the tirade that followed, her voice a near whisper but just loud enough for Thalen to catch phrases such as "Takes himself for a tutor but misses the basics..." and "By the gods I would have struck him down if this had ruined..." He allowed her apparent vexation to play out a few moments longer before interrupting her most recent tirade. "Keela, I am afraid to ask but what has so upset you? I also ask again, what is it that you said I was suffering from?" he asked, hoping his tone of deference was enough to placate the seemingly anguished elf.

She let out a small sigh in what he thought was an attempt to regain her composure before looking at him squarely again. "SalalPeloMolon, that is what it is referred to, it translates roughly to Mage pulls too much and is when a mage draws in and uses an amount of energy that they are not fully prepared to use. I will be happy to speak of it further but first let us get out of the hallway. I suspect we have made enough of a scene at this point." she said a touch of embarrassment present in her normally composed demeanor. She began walking towards one of the practice room doors, indicating to Thalen that he should follow behind. Once the door was firmly shut Keela seemed to breathe a little easier, the bit of embarrassment noticeable in her features draining away as she leveled her gaze at him. "I apologize for that display; I find your lack of education understandable but the lack of forethought from your tutor incomprehensible. How does he expect you to conduct yourself safely if he does not ensure you understand even the most basic of concepts! Dolgrath that stupid stupid dwarf..." she began to launch off into another small tirade before catching herself. She gave him a sideways glance which he just returned with a shrug and small smile, which fortunately seemed to disarm her. "Apologies again my friend." she said with her typical calm "Let us continue with answering your question. SalalPeloMolon, referred to in the common tongue as Overdraw, is what happens when a mage takes in and flushes through themselves large amount of energy. Think of a mage as a river and energy or power as the water moving through it. The power flows constantly through the mage, as water flows through the river, as they cast spells or make use of the power. Yet, what happens if the river begins to overflow? If the water flowing through the river becomes too much for its banks to hold it may begin overflowing the water breaching the bank and eventually forming pools in the area around the river. If the flow of the river does not abate back to its previous strength and amount, the pools grow larger. Now let's apply these thoughts instead to a mage, as they cast spells they pull more and more power, especially if it is done in quick succession, eventually the pull of the power becomes greater than the mages body can naturally handle, and it begins to essentially pool within them. The body cannot expel the power efficiently enough in the form of spells and when the spells suddenly stop too much power fills the wielder causing the bodily ailments. Do you follow me so far Thalen?" she paused to ensure he was grasping the concept.

He took a moment before answering, making sure that he had the chance to digest what he had just learned before nodding and indicating for her to continue. She flashed him a little smile before returning to the teacher like demeanor "Good, now I am sure you are wondering if this is such an issue, how did I remove the pooling power from within you." Though he had not a moment ago he very much so did now. "When it comes to dealing with overdrawing there are only two known ways, one is to rest until eventually the power absorbs into you and drains itself. The second is to have a specially trained mage, such as myself, push power through you using extremely fine control to almost flush the pooling power out of your body by reabsorbing it into the flow that pushes through you." She paused again, but this time her expression hinted that she felt something was missing in her explanation. When he opened his mouth to speak, however, she waved for him to stay silent "Hold Thalen, the thought has nearly come to me. Ah, I have forgotten, what did you wish to say?" she turned to him her golden almond eyes seeming to pierce him and pin him to the spot. For a half beat his breath caught as her somewhat alienlike beauty struck him, he had never truly considered her in that light, always knowing she was stunning but never allowing those intrusive thoughts to enter his mind. Yet, once the half beat was over he regained his focus. "Yes well, am I forever going to suffer these effects. It did not feel as though I did much yesterday when you would consider a battle would likely last much longer and possibly require even more power to be pulled through me." He could not help but feel a small pang of concern, but it was quickly dispelled by a shake of Keela's head. "No and now I remember, I wished to speak to this as well. Much like a river's water erodes away at the banks of a river, the power will slowly erode away at the limitations of your body's channels, so to speak. Over time your body will become more accustomed to making use of the power and you will be able to draw more and more before feeling overdraw's effects." Thalen found himself feeling somewhere between relief and annoyance, relief because the burden of power on his body would eventually ease and annoyance as it was another limitation to contend with that he would be behind on.

Keela looked at him, she seemed tired, almost as though there was more on her mind than her frustration at their dwarvish friend or the aftereffects of the previous days matches. Yet, he did not know how to ask, letting it pass for the time being as he mentally shrugged the thought away. "Thank you Keela, both for teaching me about this and treating it. Without your aid here I don't know if I would have been able to truly compete in the continuation of the tournament." He gave her a small bow, throwing her a small smirk at the same time, he admitted to himself that he wanted to make her smile though he wasn't completely sure why. Fortunately, his unexpected wish was granted as Keela shot him a small smile before nodding her head in return "Worry not Thalen, we are friends and I would be a poor one if I had allowed you to suffer and inevitably fail when I could help you." She put one of her hands on his arm and gave it a small squeeze before motioning to the door back to the hallway. "Shall we move on to the dining hall, time is moving forward, and we are coming closer to the beginning of the final tournament."

Once he nodded she moved towards the door her lithe form stirring Thalen's mind, but he shook it off as there were more important things to think about. As he followed her out his mind couldn't help but turn to distraction *"Perhaps it has been too long since the last time I...something to think about later."* he shook his head and chuckled softly as the door closed behind him.

The last few hours before the tournament passed by quickly, Thalen wasn't sure if it was the company of Keela or anxiety over the final hurdle standing between him and a return to his friends which caused it. Yet, he couldn't help but chuckle over that last thought, when was the last time he had truly thought of the Talons. When was the last time he had received news of where or how they we, it must have been months at least. His mind began to race as he couldn't help but wonder if they had moved on, if they would take him back as their leader or even if he had a reason to truly return. *"Perhaps they are all dead or they disbanded, they would have been fine without me if Sarah was still alive and with them. Yet, that can never be Sarah is dead and I am here."* He tried to shake the unwanted feelings and sudden anxiety, yet he found no matter what he thought about the doubts remained in the back of his mind. He admitted to himself that he had been so focused on the effort to get back to them that what he was returning to never came to his mind. For the first time since he was taken from the front, since he was told he had power, since Sarah died he questioned if he wished to return to Talon. He was not so blinded by doubts that he believed he would not return to the front at all, no, instead what he questioned for the first time since it all had started was what form he would return in.

Thalen was pulled from his thoughts by a soft hand suddenly gripping his forearm, he followed the hand to its source all the way to Elara's kind and concerned eyes. He smiled at her in what he hoped seemed reassurance before turning back out towards the crowd which had gathered in anticipation of the announcement. As if on cue the waiting ended, as a flash of light blinded all eyes for a moment. As though a being summoned from another world, the visage of Headmaster Pelorin appeared above them all, as if a giant staring down from above. Once the initial shock wore off, but before the crowd relaxed, the image spoke it nearly the entire audience to jump as the sudden boom. The raspy voice of the Headmaster seeming to come from everywhere and nowhere at the same time, or perhaps it spoke into their minds themselves. "Welcome back students and spectators, it is the final day of the advancement battles. Our participants will be fighting in a series of single combat battles where one will continue and the other will be eliminated. They battle with the opportunity to win ten thousand gold along with a guaranteed advancement to the third circle of the order!" The disembodied voice trailed off allowing the expected, and received, excitement that had built within the crowd. Thalen also felt his excitement mount, as this was the first time that the prize itself was announced. The idea of receiving such a grand prize was beyond anything he could have expected, even if he knew he had very little chance of earning it.

After several moments more the voice began again, still Pelorin's but it seemed to be less bombastic than it had previously and felt more like a teacher as he addressed the students. "Before we begin this tournament, I wish to congratulate the participants. Whether they are knocked out first or make it through they have shown they are strong, capable and have much to be proud of. I wish them good fortune in their battles ahead, now let us begin..." as the last word fell away into silence, the world fell to black for what Thalen hoped would be the last time. When he regained his vision he found himself in the familiar surroundings of the arena, yet there were two major differences. First, unlike before, and quite opposite of what he had expected, there was no crowd within the barren stands. While secondarily, though they stood within the center lined up as they were before the contestants were not alone as standing before them was Pelorin as well as other school officials and proctors. Thalen looked towards the others, and it was plain to see they seemed just as baffled as he was by this turn of events.

After a few moments of silence, one of the group began to actually voice the confusion they all felt, just for them to be cut off by the Headmaster's raised hand. "I know you all have questions; I am sure given the normal fan fair and festivities surrounding these this is the last thing you expected." He paused seeing some nods of agreement from the group. "I hope this impresses upon you all the gravity of the situation before you and the challenge you are going to face at this time. This series of battles is taken very seriously, the crowd is gone to eliminate both potential distraction as well as keep them from the possible danger in case of desperation and errantly thrown spells." He paused, reminding them all of the near miss that had occurred in the first round. When a spell that had created something like an avalanche was deflected and thrown high. The rocks slammed down into the stands, but thankfully the defensive spells held out, but it caused a delay as they needed to be checked and recast.

Thalen thought the timing of the reminder was somewhat unusual, yet it caused him to readdress his previous assumption of general safety during the trials. He could not help but wonder if this would be more dangerous than the previous rounds. He wondered if it was possible that others would take this more seriously and potentially try to severely injure their opponent at minimum, even if a loss appeared imminent. He knew he wouldn't be able to guess the decisions of others, deciding to let the thought slip from his mind in favor of running through the words of power he knew. His concentration on the task was soon broken though, as Pelorin's voice broke the relative silence. "I will say this once again, well done making it to this point and best of luck in your matches. Those that are ranked second and fifteenth please remain in the arena, all others head to the balcony. Let the final trial of the advancement tests begin."

CHAPTER TWENTY-NINE

Thalen took a breath to steady his both excited and somewhat frayed nerves as he looked across the combat field towards the second ranked contender, the raital woman Velaria Severlinus. He had expected he would take part in the first fight, given his highly unimpressive placement of fifteenth, but he hoped he would have a bit longer than the amount of time it took everyone to settle into their seats. He was thankful that they at least walked to the elevators leading to the spectating area instead of doing some sort of magic to just teleport there. He did his best to recall what he knew of their race, he remembered that typically they excelled with water-based magic and so it would be in his best interest to try and counter with something earth based. Yet, without knowing Velaria's tendencies or preferred methods he could hardly come up with plans to counter her or even predict how the combat may play out. He regretted his inattentiveness to the fights not involving himself or his friends, if he was to be honest he barely paid attention to his friends matches. During the first day he was so inside his own head that he had failed to scout out his potential opponents, though he supposed that was more an effect of his own weakness and naivety in the way of magic based tactics. Although he knew it may not have mattered, as those same traits would have likely dulled any benefit he could have received. Fortunately for his surprisingly weak nerves the wait was nearly over as after nearly twenty minutes the spectators finally sat and the voice of one of the proctors echoed through the shockingly empty space.

The disembodied voice was a dry one, unlike yesterday it did not try to heighten the emotions, nor was it trying to play to a crowd. Instead, it was matter of fact, quick and with very little fanfare, yet it signaled the beginning of the end of the trials, tests and day two of battle. "Once the flare spell explodes within the air you may begin. Combatants, prepare yourselves." As the last remnants of the voice drifted off what could only be described as a ball of hot white light and fire flew through the air into the middle of the arena. It took Thalen a moment to understand what he was seeing, realizing it was the flare he took his eyes off it not a moment too soon, as it exploded letting off its harsh blinding light. Even though he had managed to look away from it he still found the imprint of darkness filling part of his eyes as though he had looked at the sun for too long. However, he knew he had to set the tone of this fight, or he would fall to a disadvantage rather quickly. As seemed to always be the case though, he took a beat too long deciding between offense or defense, finding himself put on the backfoot as he narrowly avoided a jet of water no thicker than an inch. He kept his eyes on his opponent but heard the loud crack of the surprisingly powerful attack striking the wall behind him.

Thalen made a mental note to not get hit by that attack, though a moment later he barely avoided another, the attack leaving a hole in his robe and a friction burn along his right side. Grimacing a little, he finally reacted, he was annoyed that it had taken him so long too, yet he didn't have the time to labor on it. Thalen knew he needed to reset and gathered power as quickly as he could before yelling out "Quarz Tor Vahl." He knew it was crude and poorly worded, but his mind had formed a strong enough image as a wall of stone appeared before him. He knew it was done poorly, yet as he heard a boom followed by a cracking sound from the other side of the half meter thick wall, he was happy for it. Taking a breath to reforge his frayed nerves, he considered his next move as all the while he felt the vibrations of the many attacks slamming into his cover. Chunks flew off the side and top of it under the assault as his once large wall became smaller and smaller.

Thalen was unable to think of anything truly different or unique, making the choice that seemed most obvious, to use the wall, or what it left of it, as a weapon. Turning to the slowly shrinking stone he put his palms together as he pulled in energy, it took him a moment to form the thought and find the words to state his intent "Sa'guin Bel'ar Talin Felwarth". Pushing his hands forward he almost punched the stone wall in front of him, but before he made contact mana surged out of his fists demanding the stone to yield to his desires. Slowly the base of the wall began to crack and once released it flew across the space giving Thalen a fine view of the surprised black eyes of the Raital woman. Though the wall had shrunk in both height and width it was still a meter in width and just under one and half in height, that coupled with the speed it was moving the woman could only dive away to dodge. Unfortunately for her, but fortunately for Thalen, she only managed to get partially out of the way as it clipped her on the right side of her body. She was spun about, but managed to stop herself facing him, her face plainly showing the pain it had caused.

Trying to keep the momentum on his side Thalen began launching bolts of flame as quickly as he could, thankfully he had become familiar enough with it that he did not have to speak the words or think too hard about the form. Though the Raital woman was able to easily avoid them or block them with a barrier of mist it kept her on the defensive and gave him time to think about his next move. He knew that if this kept on much longer the battle would not end in his favor, as his opponents magic experience and control vastly outweighed his own. *"What is the best move...I can't outlast her I already feel myself slowing down...I can't overpower her...perhaps... that is an idea...woah!"* That internal thought nearly became external as he barely avoided a large stone she had managed to throw in his direction. One that she had not created but simply moved and threw it like he had with the wall. This was enough to break his rhythm and allow her to go on the offensive. As it became apparent to him that he would be put on the defensive again, he swore, deciding he only had one choice and only one shot at victory.

Thalen gritted his teeth, straining his mental abilities as he began to construct his desire within his mind. It didn't have to be perfect, but it needed to be just stable enough. He had never tried anything like it before and only knew the words in theory, but even as he took a few hits of pure mana he managed to keep his focus. *"Damnit, I haven't much longer to wait this will have to be good enough."* Thalen stopped suddenly, it appearing to take his opponent by surprise, it giving him a single heartbeat, just a single moment to cast his spell. Thalen crossed his arms in front of him and yelled out his carefully chosen words "Quarz Tor Kalak Un Bal'aram" releasing the power in time, rock and stone seemed to ooze from the pores on Thalen's arms. The rock formed a layer over them, almost as if thick protective shields sat over his forearms before overflowing about an inch or two to each side. While they were forming, he began running towards his opponent, at his best guess she was about fifteen meters away as he correctly guessed she would be caught off guard at both his movement and actions. Trusting his shields Thalen kept pumping forward even as he felt jets of water, thrown stone, and bolts of pure mana strike his covered arms. As he closed in the attacks became more haphazard, he guessed a bit of panic began to take hold on his opponent. He approached undeterred by the attacks, as any pain from them was dissipated by his mobile barriers.

It took less than four seconds for him to close the gap his arms acting as battering rams as he drove into smaller Raital woman the force throwing the more accomplished mage from her feet. Now within striking range, he did not let up using his stone covered arms as maces, swinging down and dealing another glancing blow as she rolled out of the way. Thalen kept after her, though he was slow, giving her enough time to yell words of power for the first time during the battle her voice like a cold winter river "Sa'guin Bel'ar Wantari Cocle", Thalen felt the power she pulled in before a cone of water blasted into his upraised arms threatening to take his feet from under him. However, it lasted only a few moments as the near geyser shooting from the woman's hands stopped, leaving him drenched and a few feet away but still standing. Before the woman could form another thought Thalen closed the gap, swinging his left arm down to deliver a crushing backhand blow across his opponent's face, her head bouncing off of the floor beneath them. The power of the blow completely disorientated her, allowing him time to strike her several more times, ensuring she would not stand again. The battle finished, Thalen allowed the stone to crumble away completely from his arms as he stood there battered and bruised but unbroken and victorious.

CHAPTER THIRTY

Once it had become obvious he had won, medics and stretcher bearers ran out into the field of the arena. The medics quickly tending to the woman focusing on the neck and head area of her using magic to reduce the swelling that had already started to occur. Thalen also guessed they were working to ensure if her skull had fractured that it healed enough to keep from becoming a greater problem. He did feel somewhat bad for the woman, but the treatment he knew she would get had allowed him to act with relative impunity and follow his chosen course of action. When he left the spectating area, he was met with looks and stares of a large variety. Some gave the impression of respect and awe while others showed some level of disgust or curiosity, to say the least he seemed to have neither gained nor lost popularity by how he had conducted himself and at the moment he considered that a win. He did not wish to create enemies within the order, at least beyond those that were part of Telmasar's entourage and faction. So, receiving a mixed response from them was not as good as he would have liked but certainly better than he had hoped for.

Shrugging off the lukewarm welcome he had received, Thalen searched out his friends, he knew that Keela or Dolgrath would be going soon as they were both in the top five. Yet, he could not recall their places with his mind feeling slow and groggy after all the adrenaline had finally drained away. Fortunately, he did not have to go far to find his friends, "Dolgrath, Keela, Elara!" he called out, his voice betraying fatigue though he did his best to keep it from shaking. They turned towards him, their expressions showing some relief at his victory, yet he felt there was a tinge of discomfort in their expressions. He honestly could not blame them; he knew what he had done was probably shocking for them all except Dolgrath as his actions came from his experience as a worrier. Thankfully Dolgrath proved he was the first to speak as usual. "Well lad, ye certainly made a spectacle." He said, his tone seeming to betray nothing though his eyes suggesting he was somewhere farther away from here or perhaps years away from here. Keela's light timbre followed soon after "Yes, it was well done...though if I am to be honest somewhat horrifying." This thought reinforced with Elara's emphatically nodding head. "You seemed less a mage and more like a...I do not know what the right word would be." The elf's voice trailed off as she seemed to think leaving a pregnant silence between the group. After what felt like an eternity it was Elara who spoke her voice quiet yet clear "Like a monster."

Thalen felt a lump grow in his stomach, he wasn't sure where this was going but he did not like the direction. Being compared to a monster in his mind could only mean he was being compared to the Orks that threatened the very peace of this world. To his knowledge there was no other monsters within the world, yet who was he to say having only spent time in his corner of it. Thalen prepared to walk away when Dolgrath seemed to exit his momentary stupor, though he was missing some of the normal fire his words left no room for misinterpretation. "No laddie, ye aint seem akin to beasts or monsters. Ye were a soldier, nay a worrier. These lassies..." he paused casting an eye to them, almost making it clear he was addressing them more than Thalen with his next words "... they don't be knowing what a true battle be lookin like. Neither do many o' the others here within the order. But we be knowin', we who spilled the blood of enemies and found ourselves drenched in the blood of a fallen ally or friend. That lassies...." He began turning fully in their direction "...that be exactly what a true fight be lookin like, the actions o' a true fighter. Ye just never saw it afore." Elara and Keela seemed to draw into themselves slightly, at least as far as Thalen could tell as they appeared to be thinking about the dwarf's words. Feeling there was no reason to continue the present conversation he found his seat amongst them. Settling into it he allowed himself to rest both mentally and physically, in preparation for the next battle to come.

The next battles after his own went uneventfully, at least to his mind with few surprises and little fanfare. At least none compared to the reactions he received for his own, as every match went as expected with those more highly rated such as Dolgrath or Keela defeating those against them with ease. The matches became more competitive as the rankings of the competitors got closer and closer together. This culminated in Elara's match where her opponent was close in skill but more highly placed. Though the battle was close it ended in Elara's unfortunate defeat, as she had hesitated, the brief pause in her attack pattern allowed her opponent to gain the upper hand as they sent a wave of pure force in her direction. Though it didn't do much in terms of damage it threw Elara further off balance allowing her opponent to finish a spell which drove stone into the young woman's midsection. The force of the blow driving the air from her lungs and the consciousness from her mind. As Elara was being tended to by the medics and healers, Thalen looked sidelong at his friends trying to read their thoughts from their expressions... or lack thereof. While he still felt some level of dejection from their, or more specifically his female companions, reaction, he tried not to take it personally as he knew it was more so due to their lack of true battle experience as Dolgrath had implied. Even so it was hard to keep it from his mind, although at this point, they seemed more concerned with Elara's condition than Thalen's actions.

He was also concerned for her, though it was not her physical condition that worries him but instead the young woman's mental and emotional state. The group could easily see that she had recovered from the match itself, though, with her proclivity for self-doubt they needed to know what was beyond skin-deep. Accepting that it was only something that would be revealed later Thalen sat back into the chair once more searching out a rest he knew wouldn't truly come until the battles and perhaps the very tests themselves were over. He shook himself of what seemed to be a near incessant melancholy, he wasn't sure why it continuously crept up on him though he also knew he hadn't truly bothered to dive into it and now was not the time. Shaking his head he turned towards the now approaching Elara, her gate suggested some soreness and fatigue but otherwise she was giving nothing away. Her eyes briefly met his and flashed a small smile which, he was embarrassed to confess, made his heart flutter..

As was always the case the first to speak was Dolgrath "Well lass, are ye alright? Ye did well..." he left the end hanging trying to make his point while giving her the chance for an out. Elara smiled warmly at him showing her appreciation "I am alright Dolgrath, the failure was mine. I allowed myself to hesitate and paid for it." She frowned, frustration sitting within her eyes. Yet, before another word was spoken she sucked in a deep breath and after a moment let it out slowly as a relaxed smile grew on her face. "I was so close wasn't I." she said her relaxed smile becoming a wistful one as she seemed to fall into thought. Keela, Dolgrath and Thalen shared a look amongst themselves each realizing in their own way Elara was upset at the moment but not nearly to the point she would have been when they had first met those many months ago. Thalen couldn't help but wonder when the young woman had grown so much and when her confidence had reached a point where she could handle the emotions that would come from such a loss. Thalen knew all she needed was time, so they left Elara to her thoughts. Elara's situation and reaction seemed to have reset the group as Keela became more open and relaxed with Thalen, she seemed to recognize that what Dolgrath had said was correct and without saying the words showed it with her actions. Thalen knew that his match was next, against who he was unsure as there was still the question of where the elf and first seed Doryan would slot in. Though he knew it would likely be his own match the elf would be placed into he did not wish to make an assumption, as things had a habit of not going as advertised. He would not have to wait much longer to find out, as after another few minutes the voice of a proctor rang out over the group.

Once they knew all attention was on them they spoke. "For those of you not counting with this last match we now have our seven victors, counting the currently ranked first seed that makes eight. This has brought us into the next stage of our little tournament, and as some of you were likely expecting there is a slight twist." A small smile tugged at the corner of her mouth as an expected grumble came from the collected group. "Easy now, I said slight twist not a complete change. Except for Doryan Telmasar who was ranked first, us proctors have rated and ranked you all once again. Listen up for the new rankings..." there were not too many surprises in Thalen's opinion about the new rankings. He had to admit to himself he was actually somewhat pleased with the outcome for both himself and his companions with Dolgrath having been ranked second, Keela fourth and himself at sixth. This ranking meant there was a real chance that they all could manage to be within the final four members, though it was far from a guarantee. Thalen grumbled to himself unhappily, as much as he disliked the pompous elvish man, he could not deny that Doryan's skill with magic would easily trounce his opponent making it to the final group of four.

Quickly losing interest in the line of thought, Thalen instead turned his mind to the person he was against and the challenge before him. He hardly remembered anything useful about the human man he was against, the man's cropped hair, soft features and rather pudgy appearance, left a lot to be desired. Even so it surprised Thalen that he had missed or could not remember any fight of the young man that stood between him and the next stage. Looking at his friends, Thalen could easily tell that both Dolgrath and Elara were deep in thought. Elara likely about the fight which had been and Dolgrath the fight to come, this leaving only Keela left for him to ask about the man. Though she was likely thinking about her own upcoming fight, it seemed that her own match was distant enough for her to be attentive to his casual glance.

She didn't speak, only locking eyes with him her almond orbs questioning his look while seeming to also ask if there was anything he needed. Nodding his head he motioned towards the railing looking over the arena floor, raising an eyebrow to accompany the unspoken question. Keela signaled her silent agreement by standing and walking towards the indicated location as he quickly fell in step. Though they did not move far away, the distance hardly being more than five meters, they chose not to speak enjoying their unspoken companionship. A relaxed feeling had returned to them after the tension from Thalen's previous match, which he was extremely grateful for. Once they reached their destination Keela leaned against the stone half wall facing him, leaning back comfortably as she waited for him to speak. Taking a second to collect his thoughts Thalen took a steadying breath, though it seemed the easiness had returned, he found himself anxious at potentially blundering with his words if not his actions. As though sensing his mood from this the attentive elf took the initiative "Thalen I wished to apologize for my earlier judgement, I allowed myself to be swayed by my emotions and at my inability to recognize acts that were appropriate to a battlefield. My thoughts on fighting have been steeped in those actions taken during dueling and anything outside of that seemed barbaric. I now realize how narrow minded that was, so please be at ease I will take the harder path and work on not passing judgement without reason or understanding."

It took him a moment to completely digest her words but once he did he asked the only question he could "What do you mean by dueling? Are duels often had between mages?" Thalen let his mind wander a little considering the implications before looking at the elf's face again, one that held a mix of confusion, indignation and amusement. "What?" he asked, "This is something I have to consider, I haven't been a mage for very long and the last thing I need is people demanding duels from me at random." She surprised him by letting out a peel of laughter, though it was sudden he still found it enchanting, as all things the elf did seem to be. He truthfully wasn't sure if he should be upset with her reaction or happy that things truly did seem to return to normalcy between them. He decided on the former and laughed at his own expense earning the pair a few side eye glances from those around them. As they both settled, the last laughs were drawn out as the final bits of tension left, allowing Thalen to repair his slightly frayed nerves. "Keela, I wished to speak with you in the hopes that you have some idea about the man that is to be my adversary. I had realized I never had the opportunity to watch them fight and know not their trends or skill set." He wanted to move the conversation along as he worried he may begin to cut into the time Keela had to prepare for her own coming match. The elf seemed to take the hint, leaving behind the frivolity to launch into a semi-detailed explanation of Thalen's his opponent. "Their name is Bartholameu, they seem to specialize in making use of arcane magic. Though neither have I seen them battle directly, instead I have simply heard talk of this from their other opponents. The only thing that I have gathered is it seems they don't just attack directly with the magic, yet beyond that I could not say..." as she fell into silence her face and eyes displayed a combination of apology and thought as though fumbling around in memory for any other bit of information no matter how small. Yet, after a few more moments her face fell the mental search obviously coming up empty. He nodded at her to show understanding before patting her gently on the shoulder hoping to indicate all was well. He gestured back towards their friends in question before moving back towards them upon her assent.

Thalen had a vague hope that the time there may be before his own may give enough time to learn more about his coming opponent. Unfortunately, that was not nearly as much time as he had hoped as the announced format was once where they would begin the matches from the middle instead of the ends. Meaning his match was the second one with Keela's being first, looking over at her he saw a grim and prepared look on her angular features, one he hoped would never be directed at him.

CHAPTER THIRTY-ONE

Thalen stood on the balcony watching the second match, his own having been much like his opponent, surprisingly forgetful. As always he knew he fell far short of being a master magician, yet he found that the man he had fought likely only experienced victory due to his somewhat unusual style. Bartholameu was a rather large and decently built man for a member of the order, that is not to say the average member of the order were rotund, but Thalen had noticed that not much effort was taken to keep up their fitness. Unconsciously he touched his own slight paunch, though he had maintained a decent regiment of exercise and sword practice the combination of fine food, comfy bed, and the seated nature of scholarly pursuits had slowly expanded his waist. Shaking off the thoughts his mind went back to the original matter, the human mage made use of primarily the arcane and as Keela had said did not attack directly with it. He had weaved it in a way that Thalen found interesting, though he would certainly need to research it more, Thalen had used the arcane to create items both big and small, yet his opponent had taken it to a new level. They used the arcane to create obstacles in Thalen's path, making it difficult to maneuver but what surprised him the most was they actually made use of the arcane during melee attacks.

This man was the only other person within he Order that Thalen had met that thought to attack physically and not just with magic itself. Though his dwarvish friend would engage in melee with an opponent the way he employed spells was rather conventional, with them being used at range to engage or defend from attacks. What this man had done was briefly coat a fist or foot during a punch or kick using it to not only protect the limb but also provide extra force as he would strike, it being like a bolt of energy. What was so impressive was the fine use of the power, it was done in such a timely and specific way that it opened some possibilities he had never considered. These possibilities giving a line for how Thalen may be able to meld his use of magic and sword in a more synchronous way. He had been trying to imitate the man's spell control with little success thus far. Putting that aside for the moment he chuckled to himself about how he had been the worst possible match for the man given Thalen's penchant for the martial arts. Though he had been put on the back foot early, having assumed his current opponent would have been like so many others, firing off spells from afar and forcing him to engage in ranged magic where he was least comfortable. Yet instead, the man ran forward, making use of the arcane to create some small caltrops around Thalen's position essentially anchoring him in place. The moment of surprise made him react slowly and was met with a pair of solid hits before he responded sending a wall of force at the man to briefly push him away, it was only a moment of time, yet it was enough before his opponent seemed to sharpen his spell and cut through the spell wall. Though it was an impressive display it was no longer a fair fight as Thalen let his martial training take over wearing his opponent down in hand to hand before throwing him to the ground and sending a solid ball of ice into his gut. With that the match had ended, in what could only be called an anticlimax, and they left the field with Thalen the victor making it into the final four competitors.

Leaving his thoughts behind he returned his attention to the combatants before him, one being Keela while the other was a dwarvish female who made good use of her strong earth affinity. Keela was pressing hard, throwing a variety of spells at her opponent and yet the natural stoutness and nature of earth magic was drawing out the match. Thalen knew that the longer this drew out the more potential there was for something to go wrong and that seemed to be the case, as his friend's attacks seemed to come less frequently. Thalen could feel the anticipation building in the crowd and heard Elara's quiet gasp, yet he suspected Keela was just putting on a show of weariness. He could not exactly explain why but it felt as though her movements were too consistent to be the effect of fatigue. If she was truly tired she would attempt to push through her weariness maybe unleashing another barrage in a desperate hope, but instead Keela simply kept up a patterned but slow attack that was varied just enough to seem random to the inexperienced eye. He found that he also wasn't the only one who noticed as a quick glance at Dolgrath let him catch the edges of a sly smile buried within his thick beard. He returned his attention to the match just in time for the dwarf woman to fall into Keela's trap as she left her defensive posture using the stone beneath her feet and a quick word to surge forward on a wave of earth. The trap sprung, Thalen held his breath waiting for Keela's reaction to the dwarf's coerced attack, when she finally did react he found he was not disappointed. The elf seemed to wait until the last possible second, drawing in her foe before the fatigue she had been feigning disappeared completely and her moves became sharp again.

The dwarf recognized this a moment too late as the momentum of the stone she was riding played out landing her directly into the path of a wall of pure ice erected by Keela. As they attempted to recover, the elf with several bounding steps came upon the dwarf as she was rising and with a quick word fired off a bolt of pure magic into their side knocking them back to the ground. After a few more moments of struggle, with the dwarf attempting to erect a meaningful defense, the woman's position and sudden gain of momentum by the elf had turned the match completely into Keela's favor. With a final flick Keela sent a disorienting wave of force into her prone opponent rendering them unconscious and ending the match.

With the fight complete Thalen turned from the field to return to the area the group had claimed for their own. Seating himself once more in a high-backed chair he started thinking about the remainder of this tournament, but that slowly turned into the deeper meaning behind the tournament. He thought about the past challenges that they had faced, and how the results of the trials would determine at least the next year of his life. Would he be allowed to move on and return to the war that was so easily forgotten while within these safe walls? He fell into contemplation thinking of everything and nothing all at once, yet that did not last long with the approach of Dolgrath and Elara, a more pressing topic came to mind. "Dolgrath, it seems that Keela and I have already passed that bar, I would be so disappointed if you failed to overcome your opponent as well" Thalen said teasingly. He saw the dwarf's bushy brows shoot up, his eyes widening in surprise before squinting them in mock anger. Letting out a harsh bark of laughter he responded "Oh I see ye decided ye were gonna return to yer usual self. Ye seem to have been inside yer own mind far more than afore. Well, that be no matter, believe me when I be saying me opponent won't know what be hittin'em" his friend capped his sentence with a slightly soft look which Thalen felt was a silent question.

He responded with a subtle nod, or at least what he hoped was a subtle one, before speaking his own piece "I look forward to seeing that my friend, after all if you do not win then I would be denied the chance to beat you myself." The dwarf laughed in return, whether it was at the idea of losing or Thalen's joke, he could not tell, but nonetheless it lifted his spirits a little and took him from the troubles he had been manufacturing. What made it even better was the soft laughs coming from Elara, who was at his side, which elevated his already mirthful mood. He smiled warmly at the woman, her eyes met his and seemed to sparkle which made him smile even further before turning away to hide the blush he felt rising in his cheeks. He heard her draw in breath to speak but was interrupted by the announcement of the coming match. After being called to the field Dolgrath bade them a farewell with each wishing him the best of luck. With the dwarf leaving and Keela yet to return Thalen found himself essentially alone with Elara, which had not happened in some time. Surprisingly, he did not feel awkward in her presence, instead it being comfortable and relaxing. As he thought about the somewhat intimate moments that had been between him, he could no longer deny the attraction that seemed to exist between them. The acceptance making him smile a little as he allowed himself a moment of revelry in thoughts of her before returning to reality. Even if something was to happen between them, he had to assume it most likely would not last. This was not even due to them lacking in chemistry but simply because pursuing her did not align with his current goals but even more so there was no guarantee they would be stationed in the same place. He suspected he would resume his duties with his previous command, while there was no telling where Elara would end up. This by itself made it feel as though it was not an option or not in their best interest to become involved in that way. He was pulled out of his spiraling thoughts by a hand on his forearm, he flinched slightly at the unexpected contact but quickly found it was just Elara's hand, she seeming startled at his reaction before breaking out into a warm grin. "You always seem so lost in thought, though that is the first time I have seen you react with such surprise." she laughed a little, likely thinking about his reaction which earned her a sly look from him. She did not wither as much as he had hoped from his gaze, and instead threw her his most dashing smile, which also didn't get the reaction he hoped for and instead earned him a soft punch.

"Oh, stop it, you are acting like a fool." Though she reproached him, Thalen thought he detected some amusement in her voice and her feigned angry expression seemed to crack allowing a smile to touch her lips. "Thalen I did not have a chance to tell you how impressed I am with your last win, though if I was to be honest I was rather surprised. Please take no offense but you are so new to the arts that I find it unreal to feel as though you surpassed me." her voice grew small, almost as though she feared to cause offense. He put a hand on her shoulder hoping to reassure her" No, you are right I was equally surprised to have made it as far as I have. Though I have full confidence in saying you are a superior mage, my benefit has only been a combination of my matchups along with my experience in combat. That is truthfully what carried me during the last fight as well and their style played directly into my strengths." She nodded seeming contemplative for a few moments before responding "I think that you may be right, though I believe you also sell yourself short, you have made many strides over the time I have known you." She smiled at him and drew a little closer, Thalen couldn't help but catch her scent and it excited him, as she went on to say more, a melodic voice interrupted her "Here you are, I thought you may have been looking in on Dolgrath's match." Keela said as she approached where they were sitting. The elf stopped an eyebrow raised in question "I hope I am not interrupting something..." her voice pregnant with implication. Thalen felt heat rise to his cheeks yet before he could speak Elara's voice poured out. "What no, nothing, what would you be interrupting? Nothing at all, isn't that right..." her words came out in a total rush her cheeks red displaying plainly the embarrassment she felt.

Keela laughed, a wicked smile appearing on her face "Oh truly, nothing at all? You seemed to be drawing very close to our dear friend was there something you wished to tell him?" the human woman at his side turned an even darker shade of red with nearly her whole face flushed. "No, no, nothing...I was just going to say how we should pay more attention to the match!" as she spoke Thalen couldn't help but notice her voice was much higher than normal. He shook off the thought and attempted to come to the flustered woman's aid. "Come now

Keela, we were but discussing our previous matches and Elara was congratulating me on my own match." Her almond eyes turned on him silencing any further protest, he couldn't help but be intimidated by the otherworldly beauty of the elvish woman before her wicked grin. That grin then proceeded to break into a fit of laughter as the normally reserved elf lost all semblance of her trademark elegance. Thalen shot daggers at her, yet it seemed to only make the elf laugh harder, this in turn caused him to groan as it was the second time in the last ten minutes that he found himself being laughed at by an attractive woman. This being something that, at the very least, was not very good for his ego. In the end he just shrugged it off and laughed along with his friend much to Elara's chagrin.

Once Keela's laughter started to die down, she spoke between small gasps for breath "I apologize, I was simply teasing you two. It is as though you forget at times that I am an elf, and my hearing is far sharper I knew what you were talking about nearly the entire time." Once the last of her giggles subsided, she resumed her normal posture and poise. After another minute Elara seemed to regain her composure making it clear by scolding Keela, who had enough sense to be abashed, gave a blatantly feigned sorrowful expression asking for forgiveness. Which Elara granted as she knew it was the best she would get. Thalen found this entire thing rather amusing as it was not often he got to see the elf be told off, even if in a good-natured way, yet he knew it was time for them to move on from it. "My friends, I think it may be time to..." he was cut off mid-sentence by the sound indicating the matches completion with Dolgrath as the victor. The trio looked at each other surprised at its seemingly quick end, though they could not be sure if it was because it had actually ended quickly or if it was related to their antics. Even so they were pleased that the final member of their foursome managed to make it through to the final four participants and looked forward to greet him in victory. With the third match done, the only one which remained involved the pompous Doryan and though Thalen hoped for his defeat he doubted it was a prayer that would be answered. Unconsciously his eyes sought out the man and after a moment of visually sifting through the crowd he found him, the same superior smirk upon his face as he moved with the casual grace of the elves to the moving platform to the arena floor. Thalen could not tell but he thought he caught a glance in his direction and a momentary sneer thrown at him but could not say for sure as it was just before Doryan's back turned to him. *"I hope that bastard gets his head knocked off. It would be nice to see him rolling around on the floor in pain."* He thought to himself, his mind already visualizing the possibility yet as he let the thought slip from his mind he questioned why he allowed his dislike of the elvish snob to consume him. *"Something to work on in the future..."* and with the thought he pushed all remnants of the elf from his mind, at least for now.

Thalen stood from his chair and looked to his friends each throwing a questioning look at his sudden movement. "I wish to watch this match; I hope to pick something out since one way or another one of us will be the victor. Join me or wait for Dolgrath the choice is yours but either way I will be over by the viewing wall." Once each had confirmed their understanding he walked over to the viewing area, he suspected that Dolgrath would be interested, yet it would take a few minutes for the dwarf to be checked for any injuries by the medics and take the elevating platform up to the viewing gallery. As the two combatants were set, Doryan faced off against another elven man, and though the pompous attitude was still showing in Doryan's stance and demeanor he lacked the open hostility he normally displayed towards those of other races. Even the thought of the elf's racist demeanor once more bothered him, but he stamped it down hoping to learn something from the fight. Whether it be a new concept or an insight on how his opponents would operate, he did not care. The signal for the match to begin given and Thalen did not know what happened, one moment the two elves were squared off and the next the other elf fell to the earth rendered unconscious. Wide eyed he could not even guess what Doryan had done as it had happened in truly the blink of an eye. He turned hoping that someone may have had an idea of what had occurred, but confusion masked all of the participant spectators faces...except...except those of the elves.

As he looked more closely Doryan's kindred instead wore expressions ranging from discomfort to actual pain, yet all non-elves were unaffected. He turned searching out for Keela only to find her crouched, with a confused, and concerned Elara down next to her, covering her ears with a grimace on her angular features. He approached and by the time he had closed the distance Keela was standing unsteadily, leaning slightly on Elara's shoulder. "Keela what happened?" he asked once he was near her, but she put up a hand appearing to silently ask for a moment to collect herself. Once she had the question was readily answered "I will ask you to not freely share this tactic and truthfully am shocked Doryan would reveal it. It's something that we elves prefer to keep hidden, he made use of the arcane to create a shockwave in the air at a volume and frequency that could only be heard by those with the strongest hearing" she paused to stand straight again, thanking Elara for the help. "As elves have strong hearing it is quiet effective against us and even more so in short distances. Normally we would have warded ourselves from this through magic or physical means, yet there was no way to know Doryan would make use of such a strategy as it is something we as a society attempt to keep out of core magic. Fortunately, though it is simple in principal it requires a deep understanding of sound as well as an understanding of how to affect it through the use of arcane and air based magics." As she ended, she appeared fully collected as though her earlier reaction had never happened. "The last thing I will say on the matter is I will likely launch a formal complaint about the use of this spell. Though perfectly legal it is something that is severely frowned upon in elvish society and to make use of it with others in the area was at best irresponsible." Her voice took on a scolding tone, as though she was saying this to the culprit themselves, but after a moment she returned to her previously relaxed state. Thalen took the chance to thank her for the information and made a mental note to not only look into the specific attack but also other uses and avenues for combining various magic in such ways as to affect ones senses in general.

After a short while Dolgrath returned and was immediately confused by the scene and announcement of Doryan's victory. "What happened here laddies and lassies? Didn't the match just start?" Elara was the one to answer, which was broken in two parts by the interruption of a proctor's voice booming out as it had many times before "The second round has been completed we are now onto the third round of the tournament. There are no tricks this time, your rank will be based off of simply where you fall when the defeated contestants were removed. The fight order will be the first rank versus the fourth rank and then the second versus the third. The matches will begin in one hour, enough time for a refreshment and rest. We expect the first two competitors to be in the field once the time is up. Thank you." The voice died out leaving near silence before the murmur of those collected picked up again. "Well lad, seems yer to be against that elvish arse. Ye best be ready to give 'im a right wallop." Dolgrath said, a bit of fire burning in his eyes. It was quickly followed by words of agreement from their other two companions each with their own reason to wish the elvish noble to be taken down a peg. Thalen could not help but laugh and feel heartened by this as he spoke words he wanted to turn into reality "I will not stop at knocking him down a peg, I won't stop until I have defeated him soundly on the field of battle." Though he said the words somewhat in jest, he could not deny the fire in his belly at the thought of destroying the elf. He was the worst of people, not seeing beyond himself and his own sense of superiority and Thalen fully intended to pull him down into the mud and break him of that. But, before any of that could be done, he needed to take the time he had to think and plan how he would compensate for the gap in skill and experience with magic. He knew his tricks wouldn't get him the edge as they had in the previous matches and resolved to honestly consider how his strengths and weaknesses measured up to the elves. His mind made up he looked at his friends and spoke the words he thought they all awaited "Let's go to lunch."

CHAPTER THIRTY-TWO

As Thalen stood on the arena floor, his eyes fixed on the mocking stance of Doryan Telmasar. The elvish man had his normal disgusted expression as though looking upon Thalen was the same as some sort of bug or even less than. As though he was something best smeared out and forgotten completely, almost as though the fact that he stood before him was beyond offensive. Trying to ignore the elf's demeanor Thalen stood waiting for the match to begin, he thought back to the last hour, it was spent preparing for the very person he was standing in front of now, strategizing in his own mind, going over things with his friends and working through the spells that might counter his opponents. That hour was both the longest shortest he had experienced since becoming a member of the order, since the day everything changed, the day that Sarah had died.

Thalen took a deep breath allowing the emotions that cropped up when thinking of

Sarah to slip away. He took the time to clear his mind and ensure his breathing was relaxed and slow, the hour had given the time to think, plan and relax. But, it also gave the time to reflect on everything and come to understand the importance of not just this very moment but the entire test itself. Those reflections tried to worm into his mind even now, but he pushed them away as the only thing that should matter was the challenge in front of him. This was an obstacle to his guarantee of advancement and in some ways release from his forced confinement to the college, the fact that it was someone he truly found himself loathing that stood in his way made the opportunity somewhat sweeter. He chuckled a little to himself, earning a confused and then infuriated look from his elvish opponent, that made him chuckle a little harder as he assumed the pompous elf thought his laugh was at him. What caused his amusement was that he was sure he had similar thoughts about the elf. He truly wasn't sure why he was unable to ignore the man's existence, to write him off...maybe he had become a symbol or avatar of Thalen's feelings of helplessness or inadequacy. Thalen started to get frustrated with himself as he seemed set on self-sabotage, though he kept trying to clear his mind he allowed himself to get distracted over and over. He started to clear his mind again, hopefully for the last time, closing his eyes and allowing all his senses to drop away except for the beating of his own heart. He allowed himself an appreciative thought towards Keela as she had helped teach him how to fully clear the mind and to allow all the worries, concerns and even excitement get washed away as though by a cool river. Once he felt ready, he opened his eyes again locking them to those of his opponent and awaited the signal to begin.

With the preparations completed the voice of not a proctor but instead the Headmaster himself echoed throughout the arena, his voice was raspy but clear "The time has come for our last two matches where those competing will make their way to the final and have a chance at the rewards earned in victory. However, something that should be remembered is this tournament was just another portion of the test to determine if you are prepared to advance within the ranks of the Order. So, keep within your mind that even in defeat if you make a good showing of yourself, it will have a positive effect. Keep this in mind and put on a good display of yourselves, best of luck and on the signal, you may begin!" Pelorin's voice cut out, but his words stayed with Thalen. With the fanfare of the tournament, it had almost felt like its own event, overtaking in his mind the other tests that had been overcome over these last few days. If he was honest with himself, he could not begin to guess how well he was doing as a whole. Though he knew that he had passed enough to make it to this point it did not necessarily mean that he managed to prove that he had the knowledge and skill to reach his goal He would even go so far as to say he began to accept, logically at least, that he may not manage to advance to the third circle and yet his heart, or perhaps his ego, would accept nothing less than total victory. He sighed softly, annoyed with how his mind always seemed to wander, it either running away in whatever direction it wished or focusing strictly and completely on one thing. He hoped this would soon be one of the latter times and tried once again to clear his mind, acting to focus on nothing but the fight before him. Mercifully he did not have to wait for long, as the call went out asking rhetorically if the participants were prepared and after just a moment more a proctor's voice rang out "Begin!"

Thalen would say many things about Doryan and none of them would be flattering, but the one thing he would not say is that he was indecisive in action. Nearly too fast for Thalen to react, the elf chanted a spell, he failed to catch the words of the spell but certainly not its effect, as the air suddenly felt viscous and dense almost as though he was moving through water. He cursed himself, having never considered making use of spells to affect an area and not directly the opponent but he didn't have time to consider that. In a split-second decision he attempted to apply the same concept but to an area just around himself yelling out the words "A'liare Sulorind Bal'aram!" With the final word he felt power pull through him before seeming to push out of his pores it coming together into something like a second skin made of air. That air whipped around him on the smallest level disrupting the force of the air directly around his body and allowed him to glide through the affected zone. That did not mean that it was easy to escape it as his opponent began a measured pattern of attack throwing spells of fire, earth, and conjured weaponry. Fortunately, it seemed Doryan had not practiced attacking a moving target through his slowing spell as much like a projectile moving through water, his attacks would slow or go slightly off target as they entered. This gave Thalen enough time and space that he was able to reach the edge and escape Doryan's trap, upon escaping the space Thalen threw a firebolt hoping to catch his aggressor by surprise to no avail as the elf threw up a hand batting the spell aside with contempt. Though it had failed to do damage the attack broke Doryan's momentum just long enough to allow Thalen to dispel his second skin and make the split decision to run towards his opponent. Thalen had no time to plan as he ran toward the snarling face of the elf, his mind whirling as he considered his next action, but instead he was stopped cold as the elf yelled out an incantation that Thalen could not clearly hear. The only words he could make out were "Quarz" and "Tor", but he was not sure what Doryan was creating with the stone he was calling, that is until he nearly ran headlong into a stone wall. Skidding to a stop Thalen made a quick decision and moved to the left edge of the wall before turning a sharp corner, upon clearing it he spotted something moving swiftly towards him. He knew he could not get completely out of the way in time but made the effort regardless, feeling a lancing pain go through his side as, what had turned out to be a dagger, cut through the fabric of his clothing opening an angry red line upon his skin.

Thalen winced slightly at the unexpected contact but allowed the sting to clear the bit of fog from his mind. He had been thinking far too much and allowed his own mind to interrupt the instincts he had always trusted, he stopped second guessing and instead allowed himself to fall into the flow of combat. Stopping his momentum Thalen allowed another conjured projectile to fly past him, it shooting directly through the path his movements were taking him. Ducking another attack Thalen threw his arm out, hand pointed towards the elf, calling out the words "Wantari Riole" sending out a wave of water towards Doryan. Though he knew it was not a powerful or elegant solution Thalen hoped that it would at least knock the elf off balance long enough for his follow up spells to make contact, as he sent a pair of fire bolts screaming behind. Thalen wasn't content with just his current attacks as he began moving forward again, beginning to form the wording of his next spell in his mind.

Seemingly without much effort the elvish mage used waves of pure arcane force to bash aside Thalen's attacks, "You mongrel, do you think your pathetic magic could cause me any harm? Do you believe that for even a moment my superiority will not shine through? You were lucky to get this far now accept your defeat gracefully!" The elf yelled out to Thalen, his words filled to the brim with venom and mockery. Thalen briefly felt his anger rise but swallowed it back down instead allowing a spell to rise in its place, yelling out "Quarz Tor Pilol Ben'ar" as he poured power into the spell he shot up into the air a pillar of stone pushing him fifteen feet up, surprising both himself as well as his opponent. As he was lifted into the air Thalen mentally kicked himself, realizing that his intentions had been unclear during the casting, and he did not compensate well enough with the words. He had hoped at most to elevate ten feet in the air giving him a platform to jump upon the cocky elf, using the momentum to knock him off balance before using conjured weapons to fight directly. Now, he had to think fast as he saw a smirk come to his opponent's lips as they found Thalen less mobile and so a far easier target to hit. With no alternative available to him Thalen kept to his original plan calling out a spell at the same time he leapt from the platform he had created. The spell cast was one to slow his fall though the incantation was imperfect, and he sped towards the ground faster than intended, as the ground came up to meet him Thalen bent his knees and used the momentum to roll over his shoulder and into a run. He noticed that Doryan had moved for the first time backing away upon seeing Thalen try to close in. As he used the combination of slowed fall, momentum, and the height of the platform, though it was unsuccessful. Where before there had been around twenty meters between them it had grown to thirty, yet that was still better than allowing the elf to throw spells his way as he ran in a straight line, at least that is what Thalen was telling himself.

In reality, Thalen knew he had been on the back foot the entire match, his opponent outclassed him when it came to spell casting ability and was a more competent mage in every way. However, he was nowhere near as versed in warcraft or battlefield awareness, Thalen decided that if he could not get to him directly his best bet would be indirectly. Doryan had been managing to keep Thalen at generally the same distance, but that meant he had been moving backward, if he could get the elf to stumble even for a moment that may give him an opening. Knowing he had to time it perfectly Thalen prepared the incantations for two spells, one to create a small bump behind the retreating elf and another to do nothing more but fire stone towards them. Thalen knew that it would not be easy to disrupt the naturally agile elf's footing, however, he hoped the mental and physical fatigue of their bout would be the difference. Thalen continued moving forward, dodging attacks of both the projectile and area of effect nature as he avoided walls of flame, stone missiles, and occasional conjured weapon, after another few moments he found his opportunity. Though his legs began to feel heavy, and lungs burned he saw a similar fatigue in the actions of the elf and knew it was time to move beyond firing the occasional return shot to keep the elf on their toes.

Gathering in power Thalen called out the first of two incantations "Quarz Bel'ar Vahl Dorint Salmelar!" his hand pointing out towards a location close behind the elf. Where he had pointed, a small wall seemed to grow from the ground, the elf noticed it, but it appeared his fatigued body did not respond perfectly to his mental commands as he stumbled over it slightly. Once Thalen saw the stumble, he cast his second spell firing out a ball of ice at the elf just as he recovered his footing. Thalen heard a satisfying crunch as it rammed into the side of the elf, the attack throwing him to the ground. Taking the initiative Thalen approached with as much caution as he could afford conjuring a sword into his hand prepared to strike. On his approach he saw the elf sit up and spit a wad of blood off to the side, as Doryan's eyes met Thalen's, all Thalen could see was the fires of outrage and hatred in them. Thalen slowed stalking forward allowing himself a bit of pride as he attempted to menace the elf, he couldn't help but feel anger welling in him as he considered the racism and sense of superiority this elf lauded over all non-elves. Yet, he should not have, as the elves mouth twisted into what could only be called an evil smile. At near the same moment Thalen felt a heavy impact onto his back, his conjured weapon dissipating as his concentration broke, he tasted copper and felt warm blood dripping from the corners of his mouth. With the last bit of his remaining strength, he looked down and found the tip of a spike protruding from his chest, it being the last thing he saw clearly before everything went black.

CHAPTER THIRTY-THREE

Thalen awoke to find himself not on the ground but instead in a bed, the last thing he remembered being the sight of himself impaled on a spike, yet obviously at least a few things had happened since his last moment of consciousness. His eyes were still blurry, and senses felt dull, but judging by the stiffness of his muscles he knew it had been at least a few days. When his senses finally returned to him fully, he began to hear the sounds of the Keep from the open windows, from what he could tell it seemed to be early afternoon. At least that was his best guess as the windows were blocked by thick curtains that blocked the natural light from outside. As he lay there, he couldn't help but feel some frustration welling up inside him, he thought he had won, that he finally overcame what he considered to be his greatest challenge as a mage and the last obstacle to advancement. Yet, he fell victim to his own hubris and emotions as he allowed himself to lose focus on his surroundings. He had tunnel visioned on Doryan, he had let his feelings overtake his better judgment, and if that had been a fight to the death he would not be waking up in a bed, instead it would be in the next life.

Taking in a deep breath Thalen slowly moved to a seated position, his muscles protesting with every move, though the change of position was needed it was far from comfortable. Ignoring the discomfort, Thalen did the best he could to look around the room, it was similar to his personal room within the Keep, although missing the personal touches. A door was set into the wall across from him, with a small desk and chair sitting by the adjacent wall, a few shelves stood across from the desk that seemed to have various medical and alchemical instruments upon it. Those instruments being the only sign that this room was for medical purposes, though he found it odd that they would just have them on hand within a patient's room. As he thought about it further, he supposed he wasn't sure how long he had been unconscious and so their presence could just be for ease since the other option would be bringing them in every time they were required. As usual he quietly laughed at his wandering mind before continuing to scan the room with his eyes, eventually they settled upon the desk and to two letters that sat on its wooden surface. Curious, he began to consider how he was going to get the letters as the desk, though no more than a meter away, they may as well have been on a different continent given his injuries. After several more minutes, he looked to the ceiling saying aloud to himself "You idiot, you're a god damned wizard." And with a small motion coupled with words of power, "A'liare Gid'oniol Talin Bal'aram.", a conjured wind swept up the letters and delivered them gently into his lap. Letting go of the power he felt himself drain completely, any energy he once had spent on that small act, slowly sliding back down into the forgiving softness of his bed. He allowed his tired body to recover and once he felt well enough propped himself up slightly before picking up the two letters from the bedspread. Opening the first letter, he began to read, feeling his heart drop somewhat with every word.

"*Thalen,*

We regret that we were not able to be there in person when you awoke, nor able to visit you when you do. You seemed to have been so close to victory and to see you fall like that had truly broke my and Elara's hearts, and though our dear dwarf did not have his heart break, he was nearly apoplectic with what Doryan tried to do to you after your defeat. The fool had attempted to finish you off completely, it seem that your efforts had embarrassed him, in his blind rage he had gotten to his feet and started kicking your unconscious body multiple times until the proctors were able to drag him away. To say the least he was reprimanded though no serious punishment happened, or it may have started an incident between our countries. The politics of the situation disgust me, but we were told you would make a full recovery and that those few cheap shots by a person far smaller than yourself were no more than footnotes to the actual damage you had sustained. Now onto the good news Elara, Dolgrath and I have all passed the exam and have advanced to the Third Circle of the Order..."

Thalen paused after reading this, he felt pride and happiness at the fact that all his friends had managed to ascend. In fact, he took even more pride in not just their success but in the strength and competence they had shown throughout even if he did not get to see Keela and Dolgrath's final matches. He just hoped that he would end up being able to say the same, his mood darkening a little at the thought, he looked back to the letter hoping it would lift his spirits.

"...With the completion of our tests we were informed that we would be sent out to aid in the war effort one week from the date of completion. Unfortunately, that was six days ago, and we are leaving tomorrow. We had hoped to have the chance to say goodbye in person but as I am sure you have guessed by now, we did not. Dolgrath, Elara and I regret not being able to wish you well in your recovery in person, we wished desperately that we could stay longer, but the needs of the Order and the

war do not give us that luxury. So, we will leave it at this for now, when you awaken feel free to reach out through the Order's communication network, we all wish to hear from you and until our next meeting, be well.

Yours in friendship, Keela, Dolgrath and Elara
P.S. Dolgrath wants you to know he won the tournament and gave Doryan a beating for you."

Thalen laughed a little as he read the last line, his mind's eye picturing the blustering dwarf moving aimlessly, as animated as ever, as he retold the tale of the glorious battle and revenge he received on behalf of his friend. Yet, as the reality of Thalen's situation settled onto him, he found himself saddening, as he did not know when, let alone if, he would next see his friends. He read again the flowing script, it's smooth and clear letters telling him clearly that the author had been Keela, as he knew the elf's handwriting almost as well as his own. He would have to know it well, especially given the number of notes she had given him over the months, each one of them instrumental to his learning and understanding of the world of sorcery he had found himself in. As he looked at the script, he became somewhat confused and slowly realized that there was no mention of Elara, beyond her success, he found that strange as he had thought she was a good friend of his, if not edging on something more. Feeling his back tighten he shifted, searching for some relief, but as he did, he felt the semi-sharp corner of the other, forgotten, letter, his curiosity overtook his discomfort as he opened the parchment unfolding it to see script written in a small and neat hand.

"Dearest Thalen,

I want to start by saying I am glad that you are okay enough to read this, I and the others were so very concerned when we saw you fall as you did. It was horrible in so many ways, it was bad enough to see the spike projecting from you, but then that bastard started kicking you even as your blood dripped down the spears shaft. To say the least I felt real anger, something I haven't felt in some time. I am sure you are wondering why I have written a letter separate from the other two and it was because I wanted to share some things with you that I would be too embarrassed to have Keela write as I dictate. If I was to be honest, I would probably be embarrassed if I was saying them to you in person or even had to see soon after you read this.

I will miss you Thalen, you were a friend, comrade and someone I had hoped to get to know better. I will not deny that I found you handsome or that I wish you had been more aware of my advances, however small they may have been. Yet, you seemed not to notice or if you had never acted on them. I could guess at thousands reasons this could be, but something I have learned from you,

Keela and Dolgrath, is that I should have more faith in myself. Being the most genuine that I can be is far better than the timid and afraid person I was before. Though you may not have seen or noticed, it was how I felt on the inside. Without you all, I think I would still be the same as I was before, and I don't think I would have succeeded in passing into the Third Circle and for that I thank you.

I hope we will meet again, and in that hope, I wonder if enough time will pass for you to no longer see me as the awkward girl that was your friend… but instead maybe a woman you could come to love. Stay safe and get well soon!

Until we meet again, Elara Skylark."

As he closed the letter, he felt a flush in his cheeks, though he was not a truly young man as he had once been he could not help but feel a little giddy at what was essentially an admission of love or at least of interest. This both lifted his heart and dampened his spirits all at the same time. Especially as he thought of those somewhat noticed advances and the times, he ignored them intentionally. He wasn't sure if he hadn't trusted his senses, wanted to allow himself to believe or had allowed his fear of loss to keep someone further away than he possibly had to, and yet it didn't matter. Without knowing if he had passed, how long it would take to get back on his feet, or where he would go if the first two were not issues, he doubted he would have the chance to search for any romance, let alone one that passed him by. Thalen slumped back down into the bed, the many emotions he was feeling draining him of what little energy he had left. He thought of everything that had happened up to this point, the loss of his closest friend, the discovery of his magical ability, the long months of training and learning to control it, the very trials he had just attempted to overcome and now the same feeling of hopelessness as he had when it all started. He was alone once more, rudderless, and unsure of what was to happen next, much as before he found himself missing the simplicity of a life that had left him long ago. With no other recourse and the dregs of energy finally spent he closed his eyes and slowly fell into a restless sleep.

Thalen was not sure how long he had been asleep, but the room felt cool meaning it likely was either night or just early morning. And yet, when opening his eyes he was not met with the expected darkness, but instead a hooded figure sitting in a high backed chair that had not been there before, a magic light hovered lazily above his shoulder it gifting him just enough light to read the book within his hands. The figure seeming to notice Thalen's slow and pained movements, looked up from his distraction, his almond eyes the only thing visible from the shadows of his cowl, that is before he flashed a whimsical smile. Thalen recognized him immediately, but as always was given no chance to speak as the figure took the initiative. "Hello, my friend, we must stop meeting like this. Though I like the symmetry of it, I was there when you first started your mystical journey, and I get to be here at the start something new. Not to mention, that you were injured in an infirmary bed and I the ever-dashing hero sat waiting for you now just as I had before." The hooded figure paused, his smile widening as he seemed to notice the shocked look on Thalen's face.

Seemingly pleased with his audience's reaction, the elf let out a small laugh "I see you weren't expecting me! I suppose I shouldn't be too surprised, but I received word of what happened and wanted to come see you in person." The figure, seeming to enjoy himself, threw Thalen a sly wink, that wink releasing him from the spell of the moment. Feeling an involuntary smile come to his face, Thalen was honestly surprised at how happy he was with the hooded elf's presence. "I...I am surprised to see you here...how..." Thalen moved to sit up as he spoke, but both his words and efforts were interrupted by a slender hand that was placed on his shoulder. "No, my friend..." the melodic voice began, as the hand pressed him back to the bed, "Please rest, all will be explained later, but for now I will answer the question that I am sure is returning to your mind." At the figure's words

Thalen's mind did immediately go to the exact question, as if the elf had cast a spell upon him placing it into his very thoughts. Did he ascend, did he pass? Fortunately, he did not have to wait long for the answer, as the elf supplied it with some excitement, "You have passed! Though barely...on my orders, you will be held here for another few months to give you a chance to finish polishing your skills and heal fully from your most recent injuries. Nonetheless rejoice as you have overcome what I am sure was a daunting task." With those words the elf gave Thalen a few moments to absorb what was said, and absorb it he did, he felt himself smile a little wider as relief and excitement washed over him. Though he had fallen short of defeating Doryan, he had succeeded in his true goal, and now it was time to move forward as his forced exile would finally come to an end. Although, once the relief and pleasure started to fade, his mind began to work again on what was now his biggest unanswered question, what next?

It seemed that his companion read his mind, as he spoke his tone reassuring, "You are probably wondering what comes next...well first you rest and then..." he paused looking around conspiratorially, almost like a child about to do something they knew they should not, once he seemed satisfied he leaned in close to Thalen and began speaking in hushed tones "Now tell me my friend..." he began before suddenly going silent, making a show of looking at the door behind him before turning back. As his gaze returned to Thalen, First Mage of the Order of Eoch's Embrace, Master Cameral Darkweave slowly reached down into a previously unseen velvet bag and pulled out a sword sheathed in scabbard. The well-recognized head of a robin, its silver gaze seeming to stare into Thalen's very soul, sat upon the end of the sword's hilt. Seeing Thalen's recognition, the First Mage motioned for him to grab that hilt, and as he did, he felt an unexpected channeling of power, and without thought unsheathed a now glowing blade from its home. As the glow came fully into view, song seemed to fill Thalen's mind nearly drowning out the next words of his elvish friend "...are you ready for another adventure?"

APPENDIX 1:
ARCANE LANGUAGE

A'liare (A-Liar-E): Air
Al'Zalar (Al-Za-Lar): Magic be sealed
Bal'aram (Bal-A-ram): Myself/Body (contextual in combination with the user's mental vision)
Bel'ar (Bell-are): Before/In front/forward
Ben'ar (Ben-are): Beneath/Under
Cocle (Coe-kill): Cone/Spray
Col'Fir (Cole-Fur): Fire
Col'tith (Kol-tith): Light
Dorint (Door-int): Come to be/Come into being
Felwarth (Fell-War-th): Touched/Felt
Gid'oniol (Ged-on-eyol): Guide
Kalak (Ka-Lack): Shield
Nazeehn (Na-ZEE-hun): Unseen/Invisible
Nazeewan (Na-ZEE-won): Quiet/Silence
Piliol (Pil-LEE-Owl): Pillar
Quarz (Qu-are-zz): Stone/Rock
Riole (REE-Owl): Roll/Wave
Sa'guin (Sa-gwin): Surge
Sai'ale (Sigh-All): Singular Line/Beam
Salmelar (S-al-melar): Small/Tiny (not used

for amount but instead for relative size measurements)
Shamusal (Sham-U-Sal): Be Earthen
Sin (Sin): Power
Sulorind (Sule-O-Rend): Surround
Talin (Ta-Lin): Object/Item
Tole (Tole): Ball/Bolt shape
Tor (Tore): Become/Form
Un (Un-a): Upon/On
Vahl (V-all): Wall/Barrier
Wantari (Want-Aree): Water
Wantorin (Want-ore-in): Ice/Cold
Zien (Z-EE-n): See/Show/Reveal

APPENDIX 2: OTHER LANGUAGES OF EOCH

<u>Elvish</u>
An (aun): Used to bridge an adjective with a reference to a noun.
Baiyat: Beautiful/Pretty/Pleasing
Carth (Kart): Dead/Death
Carthan'Oness (Kart-an-O-nez): Dead Ones
Molon (Mole-on): Much/A lot/Many
Oness (O-nez): One(s) (in context of beings/items i.e. Old One(s))
Pelo (Pe-ll-o): to pull/pulls/pulling.
Salal (Salal): Mage/Magic User
Salalan'yantir (Salal-an-Yant-ear): Mages of Song/Song Mages
Sol (Sole): Dear/Respected/Loved
Solan'Oness (Sol-an-O-nez): Dear Ones/Ones that love.
Tal (Tall): to/too
Yantir (Yant-ear): Song/Sing